# The Pinkerton Years

## The Adventures of W. W. Ronin
## Book Three

By Gregg Edwards Townsley

Two Bears Books Saint Helens, Oregon

*The Pinkerton Years*

*Cover design by Olivia Passieux*
*Cover photo by Josh Townsley*
*Video book trailer(s) by Bill Fogle*

Published by Two Bears Books
245 N. Vernonia Road
Saint Helens, Oregon 97051 U.S.A.
www.twobearsbooks.com

ISBN-13: 9780615995304
ISBN-10: 0615995306

Ordering Information:
Quantity sales. Special discounts are available on quantity purchases by corporations, associations, and others. For details, contact the publisher at the address above.
Orders by U.S. trade bookstores and wholesalers. Please contact the publisher or visit www.twobearsbooks.com
Printed in the United States of America

*To Rachel, my oldest.*
*To my youngest son, Josh.*
*And to Jared, who is still very much missed.*

# CONTENTS

*Vice may triumph for a time, crime may flaunt its victories in the face of honest toilers, but in the end the law will follow the wrong-doer to a bitter fate, and dishonor and punishment will be the portion of those who sin.*

Allan Pinkerton
1819-1884

## September 1880
# Silver City, Nevada

# Chapter 1

# SILVER CITY

W. W. Ronin sat on a large red rock at the edge of a narrow gorge, marking the boundary between Storey and Lyon counties. "Even the devil wouldn't be caught living here," he thought, shaking his head. He stood to stretch, as he'd been walking the American Ravine for a couple of hours, thinking about the two men who had left Carson City without a trace a few months ago. A bad man and a good man go into a bar. *It sounds like the beginning of a joke.* He kicked at a crushed and rusted metal meat can a miner had left some twenty years before.

An ex-Episcopal priest turned detective, Ronin had ridden the Virginia & Truckee Railroad up from Mound House and begged his way off the train as soon as he saw American Flat. "I don't need to head to Gold Hill," he yelled at the conductor, who above the track noise and steam wondered why anyone would want to end a perfectly good autumn train ride sooner than later. "The farther I ride," he explained, "the longer it's going to take to find what I'm after."

"What's that?" the engineer shouted back, before stopping to pull Jackson, Ronin's horse, from one of the cars.

"I wish I knew," he answered, taking the engineer's question literally.

He hoped he didn't sound too much like the confused Protestant cleric he sometimes was. He'd chastised more than a few pastors over the years for answering life's simpler questions as if they pointed to weightier truths. The effort was a cheap one, as most people didn't seem interested in musing about their lives, including Protestant clergymen. He couldn't stop doing so.

He'd kicked his priestly habit in 1873, the same year Samuel Colt perfected the single-action Peacemaker. When he left the mission he'd founded in Wichita, Kansas, the St. John's congregation had given him a pearl-handled revolver as a parting gift. It was perfect, though the pearl stocks were sometimes a little too white and flashy, and the length at times a little too short. He'd recently replaced the blackened buffalo bone grips he'd used in more recent years, particularly when he was riding coaches and rails as a Pinkerton Detective — the boys didn't take to anything too pretty, he'd found out — with the original custom stocks, musing that it might be time to be his own man.

He was turning 40 in a few months. Self-confidence shouldn't come any later than that.

"Pearl is as pearl does," he'd responded to a mealy-mouthed creep a month back in Carson City, before shooting him twice in the chest after he'd made disparaging comments about his "girly gun" and reached for his own side-arm. He'd caught the opinionated son of a bitch climbing out a west-side church window with a treasured silver service. Ormsby County Sheriff Lloyd Hill paid him part of a nice reward for that. The man had been wanted in two other states.

"It'll be a couple of months until I can get you the rest," the sheriff said, talking about different venues and payment systems, details about which Ronin was hardly interested. There were more important things to consider than money.

A couple hours later, he was in Silver City and, taking off his hat, perched on the edge of a hill a half-mile west of a house that was thought to contain similarly wanted felons from a capital city shooting. "There's a good chance you might find them there," the sheriff had said as he was heading out the door. Ronin had yet to determine the truth of Hill's statement.

At one time, Silver City, Nevada had been a productive little town. A few miles south of the Virginia City mines, boarding houses, hotels and saloons had hosted thousands of people over the years as men hammered a fair amount of silver out of its hills. But the Virginia & Truckee Railroad had made the town a mere through-way by first building — and then later deciding to abandon — its spur line into the city. The first action cut into the town's mill and teamster businesses. The second declared the city dead, if the *Virginia Evening Chronicle's* headline "Switching Off A City" was to be believed. It would soon be a ghost town, Ronin figured, if it wasn't already.

Silver City had exploded in the spring of 1860, Dustsucker had said, and "spread itself across the mountains like a woman's apron." The phrase had stuck with him as he doubted that the original dwellings looked like a woman's anything. The women he'd known — Emma, at the American Gospel Mission, Sally at the Lake House in Reno, or the spiritualist woman he'd trailed west as a Pinkerton Detective — were nothing like the piles of rocks and broken down buildings he was looking at. He brushed the dirt from his duster and began to peer more intently at what was left of the Comstock's silver days.

The women he knew, perhaps not the finest of females like those he'd met in Philadelphia or New York — high society types, fashion models and moneyed heiresses. Western women had a remarkable and enduring beauty all their own. He couldn't cotton to his friend's thought that the hastily-erected shanties and crude tents made of blankets, shirts and flower sacks, as Dustsucker had described Silver City's early days, looked like any woman he'd ever looked at or wanted to. His friend, an Ormsby County deputy sheriff, had a strange name, and an even stranger way of looking at things.

He kicked at a pile of red rocks around some pinyon trees and wondered if he had an hour to explore before the sun went down. It never seemed dark enough on the Virginia Mountains to be thought of as night. He'd wakened a few times on Mount Davidson during previous trips to Virginia City to see stars brighter than anywhere else he'd ever been. Still, dark or not, he needed to get another look at Devil's Gate just north of the city. Perhaps he would locate his the two men there. The Gate was widened a few years ago so as to form a reasonable wagon road, yet it was a hiding place for thieves and robbers, though the numbers were fewer, there anyway.

An avid reader, W. W. Ronin had been first attracted to Nevada through Ross Browne's serialized stories of Washoe's silver and gold mines, reading them when he was a Confederate soldier. Though he now understood the well-turned Western stories as poor reflections of real people, places and things, he was appreciative of Browne's description of Devil's Gate. There is an "unhallowed character to the place," Browne wrote. Ronin didn't disagree. He couldn't imagine anyone traveling the ravine with a full wallet or gold watch. Such a person should expect to be robbed of his or her luxuries. Silver City was spooky, especially after the sun went down.

He looked up as one of the men in the house lit a kerosene lantern to illuminate a table set before him. *Perhaps I ought to get closer.* He collapsed the spy glass A. B. Cobb had given him a few months before when leaving the Lake Side House at Tahoe. "It's said to have belonged to Captain Pray," the proprietor told him, assuring him that if he wanted he could still ask the old man who lived in a house just a few hundred yards from the hotel. Ronin had passed on the suggestion. Over the years, he'd held a few glasses more decorative, but none as powerful.

"Tell Bliss I'm sorry, too," Ronin said, before thanking him for his help in solving the murders of the two Washoe men at Lake Tahoe a few weeks prior. Bliss was the owner of the hotel, and a much appreciated figure in those parts due to his ownership of various mills and timber yards. "It would have been nice to meet him." Ronin didn't particularly cotton to the wealthy and powerful, and often found himself in opposition to their interests. But it had occurred to him that morning Bliss might someday be useful.

"You will, I'm sure," Cobb said before going inside, "if not here, maybe in Carson City," he said, "or Virginia City." He hadn't known the man's reputation carried him that far, but it was no surprise now that he was kneeling on a Comstock hillside where rich was really rich. The railroads, gold and silver mines had seen to that. And the poor, well, "the poor you'll always have with you," he remembered Jesus as saying, though he no longer believed Jesus saying so made it necessarily true.

Now a couple feet from the hovel he was watching, he heard two men talking. The windows were missing. It had once been a very pretty house, he mused, looking at what was left of the paint and trim. Parts of the house roof were gone as well.

"I'm not about to ask her about her crystal ball, you moron. Nobody believes in that stuff," one man was saying. A gentle wheeze at the end of the man's voice confirmed his identity as Mort Spinnaker, the former Ormsby County deputy sheriff, a sworn law enforcement officer before he'd left his post and taken some shots at the good guys.

"Spinnaker, I'm telling you," the other man said. "If you don't ask her, I will. There's no end to the information she might give us!"

"Smith, I'm *telling* you!" the wheezing man replied. "No man or woman knows the future. You can be sure of that. But if you keep yelling at me," Spinnaker took a deep breath, his lungs sounding like the leaking bellows of an old pump organ, "I might just be able to tell you yours."

# Chapter 2

# FORTUNE TELLERS AND MISFITS

Alison Oram Bowers was a seeress, *the* Washoe seeress some people said, generally folks who knew about such things. She wasn't a card or a palm reader, and she didn't talk to the dead. She simply gazed at her crystal egg and told people what they wanted or needed to know. And if a clear sphere wasn't present — quartz, beryl, amethyst, even leaded crystal had a habit of breaking during a long trip or hasty retreat — she could summon up the requisite vision by simply shining a coin or mirror. On occasion, Eilley Bowers was known to glimpse a much-needed truth in a simple bowl of water. Someone had said she could even look into a lake and tell the future.

"People who do that are called 'scryers,'" Dustsucker commented while loosening his gun belt a notch. Augustus Ash, the U.S. Marshal for the District of Nevada looked up. A sun-wizened man in his fifties, few things surprised him, including a fat man tightening and loosening his belt in public.

"How do you know that?" the marshal asked from the doorway, looking over at Ronin, who was sitting with his feet up on Ash's desk. "I mean, just how does a not-so-little deputy from so backward a town as Carson City know that to be true?"

"He's not little," Ronin said, chuckling.

"That's what I said," Ash replied.

Slade looked over at his friend — the only man in the room who could call him by his nickname, "Dustsucker," cruelly given but happily complied with as frequent baths didn't fit his preference or schedule — and replied without missing a beat. "We're not backward, Marshal Ash, we're simply not as *cosmopolitan* as you folks up here on the hill." Dustsucker practically sang the word.

"Oooh, did you hear that Ronin? He knows the word 'cosmopolitan' as well ..." Ash had completely missed the mocking tone Dustsucker had given the word before it had left his friend's mouth and laid on Ash's ears.

"Marshal Ash," Ronin said, sitting his chair down and leaning forward so as to make his point, "my friend Slade is not a small man, no offense meant ..."

"None taken," Dustsucker interrupted. When Ronin called him by his given name, there was often an important thought attached to it.

"... nor is Marcus an ignorant man. In fact, a couple months ago he was quoting Ralph Waldo Emerson to me. That's how *edjumicated* he is."

Dustsucker looked at Ronin and then back at Ash. He didn't know who was making fun of whom at this point, but he was upset with both men.

"I met a woman in San Francisco once," the deputy said. "Said she was a gypsy. Told me she could tell me my fortune." He paused to slather fresh butter on some bread he'd secured from Bond Rodgers, the owner of the rooming house he was staying at on Mountain Street, and to produce a jar of jam from his pocket. When he had left his room earlier that morning, Bond had given him a small loaf of raisin wheat bread and thanked him for the effort he had made with her son Gillom the night before.

"He'll not amount to much," she'd said, prior to asking him if he could help with some homework the boy had received from a Carson City teacher at Miss Clapp's School.

"I know you're not much for arithmetic, Mister Slade, but perhaps some geography?" Slade believed he had a pretty good grasp on people and places, given his work with the county and his being born in the Midwest. There was a lot of ground between here and there and he had traveled through most of it.

"I didn't believe much in fortune tellers in those days," he said, looking at their Indian friend. No offense meant, Happy Hands, your being a medicine man and all."

"None taken," replied the Washoe Indian, who was sitting quietly in a darkened corner of the Virginia City office. A genuine healer and holy man, there was little that bothered the Indian, particularly if it came from a white man.

"...but when she started telling me about my folks and such back in Eight Mile Prairie, well, this big Iowa boy changed his mind."

"Stop, would you?" Ronin exclaimed, suddenly standing. "You can't possibly mean you're taking any of this seriously?"

"I'm just saying, William. If Marshal Ash is asking you to look into something up here that seems a little 'woo-woo,' where's the hurt? A lot stranger things have been known to happen than a woman telling a man his future."

"No kidding," Happy Hands smiled, looking at his friend Ronin.

Ash cut in. "Look, Ronin. If it's a bother, that's fine. I'm just saying if you don't mind, I've got business out of town. But the way I hear it, one or two of these women are telling fortunes and insertin' themselves in them. It's come to a few important people being hurt."

"Inserting themselves in them?" Ronin asked. "You mean for the purposes of defrauding the men? Are we talking theft or robbery?"

"I mean just that," Ash said. "Look, this kind of stuff is entertainment up here. If it's not a banjo player or a bump reader, it's a ball gazer and give me a beer."

Happy Hands began laughing.

"I'm just saying, it's not a problem for me or the Virginia City police, either. A man's entitled to spend his wages the way he wants, I figure. One way or the other, it's going to be gone before Friday. I'm just asking as a favor."

Ronin tipped his hat back and sat back down with a huff. He put his feet back up on the marshal's desk. "Well then, I don't get the problem."

"The problem is when some of the lesser-known but richer men on the Comstock come to me about a flim-flam being run by a couple of ball-gazing ladies ..."

Happy Hands grabbed his sides and bent forward, letting out a loud squeal.

"Hands, do you mind?" Ash said, sternly.

"Sorry, marshal." Another couple of laughs burped out before he could sit still. Ash waited.

"I'm talking about a couple of back room ladies who are not only telling people's futures but somehow finding themselves in the midst of them. If they were simply sleeping with their clients I'd be fine, but it goes further than that."

"Okay."

Ash's predicament wasn't that interesting. It was a legal matter, an enforcement issue. It was certainly not Ronin's problem, and he had his own pain with card-reading psychics and fortune tellers. It was pain he didn't want to look at or experience again.

"Look Ronin, here's the rub. One of the men involved is a friend of ours."

"Right…" he said, waiting. "And Bowers? What's her relationship to all of this?"

Augustus Ash pushed Ronin's feet onto the floor and put his hands on the desk so that he was looking right into Ronin's eyes. There was a well-weathered wisdom about Augustus Ash, which had earned the marshal a good amount of respect. He didn't feel the same toward all lawmen. Sure, there'd been bumps in the relationship. But as far as Ronin was concerned, there wasn't a finer lawman anywhere on the Comstock, maybe even in the entire state of Nevada.

"Eilley Bowers is the salt of the earth, Ronin. She really believes in what she's doing. I don't think for a minute that she's involved. But she'll know the people involved and will likely be able to give you what you need."

"You're heading to Reno?"

"I am, but you can let Slade know if I'm needed. He'll be able to get hold of me."

"Usual rate, marshal?" Ronin asked, given that helping with the Indian murders at Lake Tahoe hadn't paid him anything and the reward money from the Carson City silver thief had been slim at least so far. He didn't want to appear greedy, but as Emma always reminded him, "A laborer is worth his hire."

"And then some, Ronin," Ash replied. "Once you meet with our friend, you'll know why I feel so strongly about this case."

# Chapter 3

# ALISON ORAM BOWERS

"Listen marshal," the Virginia City woman said while sitting at a red, three-legged table that had clearly seen better days, "I don't know what to tell you about the men you're asking about. They help out, that's all I know. If a window needs to get fixed or a door needs to get hung, people get hold of Spinnaker or Smith and they take care of it."

"It's Ronin, ma'am, and I'm not the marshal. I'm simply helping the marshal out."

"Of course you are, Mister Ronin. We're all helpers of one sort or another, I guess, you in your way, them in their way and I in mine."

"Of course, ma'am."

Over the last few months, Ronin had learned to be less abrupt when questioning subjects and sources. His previous preference — fist to face, kick to crotch, applied as often as needed — didn't seem as acceptable, "now that Nevada was becoming more mature," Dustsucker had argued, though the words sounded like Hill's and the change was something neither of them was looking forward to.

It was as if a man couldn't be a man anymore, he replied, forcing his deputy friend and the U.S. Marshal to issue him a stern warning about northern Nevada's growing intolerance of violence, even when violence served its citizens. "You'll not work in these parts," they said to underscore their point. "Violent men of any sort will no longer be tolerated," Ash said with a sternness that made Ronin wonder where the marshal had gotten his words.

"Marshal Ash said that you're a fortune teller," he said, before realizing he might have chosen kinder words to address a woman a great many people still found worthy of respect and concern. The years hadn't been kind to Eilley Bowers, he observed while waiting for her answer.

"Goodness, I hope he didn't call me that!" Bowers exclaimed, the lightness of her laughter a strong contrast to dark and piercing eyes. She poured hot tea as she spoke, without looking at the cup or teapot, and handed him a napkin.

Bowers was said to be from Scotland, though her name suggested otherwise. A farmer's daughter and one of ten children, she'd come to America, as many had, seeking a brighter future. Ash had met her in Silver City more than a few years back and remembered that she'd moved to the Comstock with her husband from Nauvoo, Illinois. Given the city and proximate year of arrival, Ronin figured she was Mormon.

"Look," Ash said sternly, "she was one of the richest women in Nevada at one point, perhaps the richest. You'll do best by not offending her."

"Mrs. Bowers ..."

"It's widow Bowers, deputy, or Eilley if you prefer."

"Call me Ronin, ma'am. I'm just working for the marshal."

He was sure he heard correctly. Married twice, divorced from her second husband when he showed interest in a younger wife, or was it wives? Bowers was a beautiful woman, in a larger, rugged yet worn sort of way.

"... Mrs. Bowers. Marshal Ash told me that you were a woman I could count on to get certain facts. I'm told that you practice certain occult arts ..."

"Goodness, Mister Ronin! Just who are you talking to? Occult? I'd hardly call what I do that. I'm a seeress, Mister Ronin. It's a gift that God has given me. And for a long time, not that I need to defend myself, I was considered a woman of *profound* faith."

"Of course, ma'am."

Truth be told, Alison Oram Bowers was a person of extraordinary faith, though not, as she liked to say, "in a church sort of way." And while her reputation had suffered over the last few years — she could be self-absorbed and ostentatious, having seen the best that the Comstock could bring, though more lately suffering its worst — there were those remembered her for the person that she was: generous, personable and determined. It was the latter quality that was her finest, but perhaps also the one that had brought her the most harm.

When her Washoe Valley mansion went into bankruptcy after the unexpected death of her husband, she discovered her hard-working man had also been a dependably helpful man, lending or giving money to anyone who needed it. Before she knew it, claimants and creditors had the estate up for auction. She sought help from similarly salted folks on the Comstock, the powerful elite that controlled the mines, machinery and riches, only to be turned away. William Sharon, the California bank baron and their friend, had been curt in his response. He was not interested, but John Mackay had been kind. Was it because of their similar stories? He was Irish, from Dublin. She was from Forfar, Scotland. Both were hard-working, simple people, seeking their fortunes from the roaring camps and dirt of the Comstock mines. And they had found their fortunes, she through her seer stone, subsequent mine ownership and marriage, he through hard work as a mining manager and investor. Both had been lucky.

"There is no money anywhere," Mackay had unfortunately offered. "All of us are in the same boat," he'd said before wishing her well. The Comstock mines were on the decline, and only God knew if they would be back again.

In the winter of '58, Eilley had operated a boarding house in Gold Hill. During one cold evening while playing a simple parlor game, Eilley Bowers told a man's fortune that would change both of their lives. Disclosing the location of a Comstock silver vein, she made a rich man of Lemuel Sanford "Sandy" Bowers and later became the Irishman's wife. Ten years later he was gone.

"I'm a 'scryer, Mister Ronin, in a rich tradition of spiritual folks that I'd expect a man of your simple background to know nothing about."

"I'm sorry, ma'am, I meant no disrespect. But I have quite an education in such matters. I'm only attempting to discern if you can be of use to Marshal Ash or myself. I was a pastor, once, you know," though it was clear she didn't know. The mere admission of his background often caused him to feel embarrassment. Folks had such different experiences with spiritual-minded people and things.

"Really, sir? How so?"

"I was an Episcopal clergyman for a handful of years, ma'am. I was trained in Pennsylvania right after the war, prior to beginning a parish in Wichita."

"Well, then you have some awareness of the Latter Day Saints, I assume."

"I do, ma'am." He remembered Emma's appreciation for the first Mormon prophet, Joseph Smith. The six-foot, 185-pound, sandy-haired detective smiled momentarily, remembering the quiet evenings he had spent at the American Gospel Mission south of Carson City, speaking of the man's teachings while he was recuperating from a broken leg. The months he had spent with Emma Nauman were among the happiest months of his life. He wondered why he didn't agree to her request that he stay on for a while. Who knows where it would have led?

"Then you know that Joseph had a number of seer stones and, in fact through a chocolate-colored stone, received his scriptures that way."

Ronin blinked his eyes a couple of times to clear his mind and changed position in the chair. The wood creaked. "Seer stones, ma'am?"

"Crystals, Mister Ronin. A seer sometimes sees images in the stone or on a shiny surface like a mirror to help with a question or decision that has to be made. The Prophet would put such a stone into his hat and, placing his face tight against it, was able to see the light that God wanted him to see."

"The light, ma'am?"

"Yes, Mister Ronin. He saw words, divine light. God's light. And it was in that fashion that he translated his scriptures. Thus it was that the *Book of Mormon* was translated by the gift and power of God, and not by the power of man."

"Eilley," Ronin said, "if I may call you that ..."

"You may ..."

"I'm not here to talk about your religion."

"I'm sorry, Mister Ronin. What was it that you wished to talk about?"

"Two women, ma'am — sisters, I believe — who are said to tell the future and fortunes of some very rich men."

"That is my religion, Mister Ronin."

"Indeed."

# Chapter 4

# MORT SPINNAKER

Mort Spinnaker found his way into the mountains south of Virginia City with the help of a singularly bad man, Timothy Edwards Smith. No relationship to the Mormon prophet — not that he was aware of, anyway — Smith had once been a well digger in Palmyra, New York. "The best thing about my boy," his mother said, after hearing of his being wanted in a series of robberies and assaults at Lake Tahoe, "was his good name. That's ruined now," the sixty-some-year-old woman said when contacted by a Pinkerton Detective looking for Smith in Philadelphia, Pennsylvania.

Having heard that the sand in Nevada was covered with gold — "acres of diamonds, you know" a man said in a Palmyra, New York bar — Smith, who was never one to doubt what was seriously said in public discourse, immediately started out for Placerville, California, where a group of brothers were putting together a gold-digging venture in Gold Hill, Nevada. The partnership evaporated before his arrival — his future business partners, "Reply to Paul Clancy, Placerville, California," the advertisement said — had abandoned him for other well diggers, he figured, after traveling at his own expense and finding no one waiting for him. The result was a few weeks of casting about until he found a job cutting trees on Lake Tahoe's north shore with the Sierra Nevada Wood and Lumber Company. Smith was sure that felling four foot split pine and fir wasn't a part of his very lucrative future, so when he could he took the first train off the mountain.

"That's how I came to know Larry and Leonard Crum." The Crums had recently been arrested in Carson City for a number of robberies and murders. Smith's partner, a smaller stoop-shouldered man named Jones, had been killed in a related shoot-out a month or so prior with a couple of marshals or deputies, he wasn't certain, and an ex-minister named W. W. Ronin.

"I believe you've mentioned that before. Is there any reason why we're talking about it again?" Mort Spinnaker, now a fugitive from Carson City justice, was wanted for attempted murder, simply because he had taken a liking to the man during an attempted jail break by Larry Crum. Faced with living or dying as a lawman, he simply decided to "go with" instead of "shoot at."

"No, not particularly," Smith said, hoping that Spinnaker wasn't mad at him. His last relationship, albeit with the Crum brothers, his employers, had resulted in a good amount of abuse, physical and otherwise. He rather liked Mort and was hoping that things wouldn't turn out the same way. *It might be nice to grow fond of someone who wouldn't beat me*, he thought as he turned to look out the window.

The afternoon sun was lingering on American Flat, as a solitary hawk circled above the mines. He'd hoped to find a job in one of them he'd told his friend Mort. There was no reason not to find honest work. Father Patrick Manogue, a former miner, had said at last week's mass, "Honest work is God's work," right before sneezing. The fall air being what it was, folks up in Virginia City were all sneezy, not that it mattered, the host being the Host and after all Christ was present in every fragment of the sacramental bread sneezed on or not.

Spinnaker had not intended to live his life this way, holed up in a Silver City cabin five miles south of Virginia City where he had intended to teach school for a living. But the hand bills and posters had made it impossible for the two of them to be seen together. And while growing their hair out or shaving it off was a possibility, it seemed they acted enough of a couple that people seemed to notice them no matter what they did.

"Mort, did you hear that?" Smith asked, thinking he had heard someone by the window earlier, but when he went outside to look he wasn't able to see or hear anyone.

"You hearing things again?" Spinnaker replied, picking up a magazine from the Daughters of Charity who operated a school and hospital on the hill. Paging past notices of fundraising fairs, raffles and thank you notes, Spinnaker hit on an article calling for helpers at an upcoming dinner. "You keep talking about getting out and doing something together. Do you want to help at a supper the sisters are holding at Saint Mary's? It's a women's event, Timothy. I don't imagine there would be much risk in going to that, given that women don't read much."

Timothy Edwards Smith didn't know what reading had to do with getting out on the town with his friend Mort, but he was all for it especially if it involved supper and the two of them having it together.

# Chapter 5

# JOURNAL, SEPTEMBER 1, 1873

*I feel like a weight has been lifted off of my shoulders. No longer employed by the Church — note the capital 'C' there, it was always the Church that felt so weighty, not the small 'c' of St. Johns and such — I've set aside my ordination to live more in concert with my own thoughts.*

*Diary you may not be aware of it, but I now believe that at no time in my employ with the Episcopal Church was I well suited for the task. My sense of sacraments was too low, my interest in the mystery and intricacy of what it means to be a common man or woman, too high. I'm glad that I figured it out when I did. The St. John's parish was great about my leaving, more or less, as I'm still a young man and anxious to experience the world, in particular the American west.*

*Since August, I've been employed by the Pinkerton Detective Agency. Allan Pinkerton, the founder of the agency, is still very much involved in the day to day business of what I'm hoping is America's most professional detective force. There's a security aspect to the business that I'm not at all familiar with. It's had some issues. But the Pinkerton's, unlike other organizations, seem to be focused on being a professional force of men. I've got plenty to live on plus expenses, and while it will likely cause me to work for folks I'd rather not work for — banks, railroads, the post office and other industries that seem to suck the unusual out of each and every man — working with the*

*Pinkertons will help me gain a better picture of what I want to do when I finally grow up. As if growing up is a destination, right?*

He turned the page, pulling the blanket up around his shoulders before relighting the candle so that he could read some more. The night was cold, but the hotel room had been a good idea, given that he could revisit the Silver City shack in the morning when his mind was clearer.

*The superintendent I was working with today will soon assign me to a geographical team. I'm hoping to head further west than Wichita. Though much seems to be happening with the railroads — some railroads, for example the Union Pacific, Denver, Santa Fe, Southern Pacific, St. Louis and San Francisco railroads, have their own police — the James-Younger gang and others seem to be a real concern. The Reno Brothers are long gone. For a lot of men, or so it seems, the war hasn't ended. It will be a real "baptism of fire," I'm afraid, and I trust that my training will serve me well.*

*Speaking of the war, the Pinkertons were most anxious they said to put my experience to the test. While I have no direct relationship to combat, having served the Confederacy as a freighter and cook, I'm pleased to think that I have some skills the Pinkertons find useful. Apparently, few Yankees can shoot a squirrel gun like yours truly. And the times it was tested — with Biffle's 19$^{th}$ Cavalry, throughout Tennessee and Alabama — it was not found wanting. Father will forgive me, I hope, for working for the Pinkertons as they caused so many Southerners great grief. Mother will, I trust, see the divine wisdom in my choice, even if it takes some time to season it.*

*The Pinks are also intrigued by my scholarship, "misused" I told them, in service to the Church which seemed offensive to some. I don't mean to say I don't believe. The God I believed in always seemed to believe more in me, than I in he, or she. It's just that I made a serious mistake thinking that what my Church was doing (there's that capital 'C' again) was the same thing God was doing. On that matter, I'm still sorting things out.*

*In any case, they're intrigued by my ability to follow a line of reasoning until its obvious and singular end point. And while it's not the best thing I do — I'm still searching for that, I may always search for that — it's at least a contribution.*

Ronin set his diary aside, wrapping it in the leather and canvas carrier Emma had given him. He took a sip of water and set it back on the nightstand beside his bed. He blew out the candle before lying back in his bed. It had been a while since he had glanced at his journal and probably an even longer time since he had contributed to them. Journal writing kept him steady in his years after leaving the church. Had he written more — as a Pinkerton and after — he might be further ahead, he thought, not that it mattered.

His life would be what it was, whether he hurried it or not.

# Chapter 6

# THOMAS E. KELLY

Sheriff Thomas Kelly's office was first on the right after passing through the front doors of the Storey County courthouse at the foot of the hill on B Street in Virginia City. "Tom," Ronin said, seeing Kelly standing just inside the doorway by a deputy's desk, "I'm so sorry to hear about your wife, my friend." While Kelly and Ronin weren't really friends, they had some experience together in rescuing the children in American Gospel Mission earlier that spring. A mutual respect had sprung up and Ronin was moved by Kelly's very profound loss.

A couple days prior, while meeting in the U.S. Marshal's office in Virginia City, Ash had remarked that by all appearances, Kelly's wife Winifred was only thirty-some years old when she passed. The entire Kelly family — now Tom and his five young children — were packed into a little house on A street. It couldn't be easy.

"It wasn't anything I was counting on," Kelly said, handing a list of inmates back to a deputy and commenting they'd have to find some additional jail space. "The weekend isn't even on us yet."

Both Kelly and his wife had grown up in New Brunswick, Canada, traveling over 3,000 miles to be a part of the California gold rush in 1857. Six years later, Kelly was working at the Gould and Curry Mine in Virginia City. A very dedicated man, he had spent considerable time in the lower levels of the mines in Virginia City. As the police chief, and later as the city's sheriff, Tom wasn't above picking up a lunch bucket and heading back there if he was short on cash.

"I've got two houses to care for now," he said, speaking of his home and the county's new jailhouse, replaced after the fire of 1875. The original structure had been lost, along with 2,000 others, costing Virginia City residents and businessmen countless millions of dollars. To the people's credit, much of what was damaged — including private homes, business and mining structures — were rebuilt within a year. It was a modern day miracle, if there were such things, Ronin thought, though he had come to believe that most of what passed as miraculous or supernatural had easier and more rational explanations.

"It's been difficult, I'm sure," the ex-priest remarked, wondering how anyone could lose someone he loved and still continue on. "How are you making it?" Ronin was a compassionate man by nature and wanted Kelly to understand that he had some feelings on the matter.

"Well," Kelly hesitated, "the church has been great." He gestured toward his office, about the size of one of the county's new cells, big enough for a desk and a couple of chairs. A rack of rifles sat on the wall. Ronin followed Kelly into the office and took a chair opposite a considerably cluttered desk. "Some of the sisters are helping out. The Daughters of Charity, you've heard of them?"

"The Daughters of Charity of Saint Vincent de Paul of San Francisco? Quite a mouthful, if you ask me," Ronin chuckled. Kelly didn't seem amused. "I'm aware of their hospital," he said, "having sent a few men there." Kelly frowned.

"They've got a school and orphanage as well, Ronin. Sister Frederica brought them out from Emmitsburg, Maryland to Baltimore, then to Philadelphia then to New York then to Jamaica, across the Isthmus of Panama, *then* to San Francisco."

He took a deep breath so as to emphasize their journey. "She's an amazing woman."

"Wow," Ronin replied, not knowing what to think but imagining that his own travels were miniscule when compared to the Sisters of Charity, as they were also known.

"No kidding, Ronin. You won't find many Irish women, even religious ones, just standing around doing nothing, reverend. These girls really help out. They're in and out of *this* place all the time," Kelly said, pointing to the cells across from his office, where a deputy was pushing two men into a single cell, one of which was having a hard time finding the latrine.

"By the door, moron. Jesus," he yelled. "You wonder how some of these guys commit a crime."

"It's not reverend anymore, Tom. It's just Ronin."

"Yeah, I know," Kelly winked. "Anyway, I'll get someone in, I suspect. There are plenty of folks up here looking for work, and a great many more women than there used to be."

"The mines as bad as they say?" Ronin asked, having heard that Virginia City's population was growing older, given the more recent transience of the area. Miners were said to be looking for work in more productive locations in California and Montana while older folks were staying put.

"Who knows? Everyone keeps a good outlook on such things ..."

"Or a stiff upper lip, I guess," Ronin interjected.

Kelly had seen better days. His still-strong shoulders were hunched forward. Sleeplessness had taken up residence under his eyes, leaving dark circles etched permanently into his cheek bones. The man's mouth, obscured by an otherwise healthy mustache, had begun to twist downward so as to suggest something bittersweet. The change in his Kelly's appearance struck Ronin as tragic.

The two were as different as night and day. Kelly had been a hard working Comstock miner and investor when Ronin was riding a desk as a minister and a stagecoach as a Pinkerton detective. Kelly had organized a miners' union in Gold Hill about the time Ronin was thinking of heading to seminary to learn enough Bible and theology to organize churches and Sunday schools and to change men "for the better," he used to say. Yet like called to like in the two men, and while Ronin had never actually been a sworn sheriff or marshal — not for any real length of time anyway — it seemed as if they had grown up together. Ronin sensed a steely inner something when looking at the ruddy, dark-eyed lawman. Whatever it was, it was something he liked.

Right and wrong were sometimes hard to distinguish when average men were hard pressed by even harder circumstances. But wrong was easier to figure, he thought. And really wrong things — the actions of men and women who committed crimes so abhorrent that normal-minded folks never even came close — well, that was *their* business. It was Kelly's, Ash's and his too.

"Heart issues, they think," Kelly said, changing the subject.

"We all have them," the ex-priest replied, caught in his own reverie.

Kelly winced.

"I'm sorry, Tom. I didn't realize you were speaking about your wife."

"That's all right," he said, uncrossing his arms and rocking backwards, "I'll not complain anymore, Ronin. What brings you up this way?"

"Don't mind your musings at all, Tom! We should do more of this. But let me tell you why I'm here." Ronin leaned forward in his chair, taking a pencil from a tin cup that sat on

Tom Kelly's desk. "Augustus and I were sitting in his office the day before yesterday and he brought up certain twin sisters in Virginia City who are telling fortunes. He mentioned maybe you'd had some experience with them and needed some help."

"From Hydesville, New York?"

"Didn't say."

"I believe I know the two women you're speaking about. Know 'em well, in fact. They're attracting a fair amount of attention. Word is William Lloyd Garrison, the abolitionist who I believe just died, had been real enthusiastic, too. The ladies are conducting a regular psychic rodeo, if you ask me."

"Well, I don't know anything about Garrison, but to be frank, what Ash says is that they've got some real talent and have gained the attention of a half-dozen locals with money. I heard too that they might have caught your eye." Ronin spoke gently, so as not to be misunderstood.

Kelly sat silently for a few moments. Tears formed at the corners of his eyes. The death of his wife just a few weeks before was fresh. He wondered if he should have spoken so personally. He waited.

"Ronin, I've not had a mind for spiritual things generally," Kelly said before pausing. "The Church is what it is, and I don't know what to think. Believe what they tell you or don't believe what they say. It's never really seemed to matter in my book. But I have to admit, now that Winnie's gone, I'm wondering a whole lot about things. I mean, for instance, what happens when a person is gone."

"Don't know that I can tell you, Tom.

"I don't know either."

"Listen Tom, not to pry, but is that the hook? I mean, you're the sheriff. You've got the jail, these prisoners, writs and notes and so on. You're not the police chief. What you do on your own time is your business. So I'm asking personally. Is there something I can do to help?" Kelly squirmed and looked about the office to see who might be listening.

"Maybe there is," he replied, lowering his voice. "I don't want to be talking to the Sisters, if I can help it, or to Father Manogue. God only knows what they'd say if someone told them the sheriff was casting about on a Ouija board or listening to a couple of slim-framed mediums."

Ronin laughed. He hadn't mentioned that the sisters were said to be pretty. "They've probably heard worse, I guess..."

Kelly looked at him hard and began to laugh as well. "There's nothing going on that I need to see a priest about, Ronin, not that if I needed to, you wouldn't do."

"Tom, I didn't mean to suggest ..."

"Sure you did, Ronin. Let's just say we ought to have this conversation in another place, okay? How about I meet you at the Washoe Club in a couple of minutes?"

"I don't believe I've ever been there, Tom."

"Don't imagine you have, Ronin. But we can talk about this, and anything else you might want to, when I see you."

# Chapter 7

# THE CRYSTAL BAR

Ronin was sitting at the first floor bar when Kelly came in. "Wouldn't let you upstairs, huh?"

"Yeah, no," Ronin barked, though he hadn't expected that the elite Washoe Club — famed throughout the west for its fine liquors, poker games and other accommodations — would allow him, a dusty cowboy by anyone's measure, to enter. "I refuse to join any club that would have me as a member," he laughed when Kelly raised his left eyebrow.

"Think I've heard that one before," Kelly said.

"It's been around."

Fact is, in any other time in Ronin's life he would have been invited to be a member. The product of a well-connected family and an Episcopal priest by trade — if the front door didn't work, as was the case in more than a few Virginia City businesses that preferred a pedigreed person or finer clientele — the back-door of the house would have opened just fine as well. He had spent a few years cooking Southern-style with the Confederacy. "Say what you want to say about the Confederates," he often told his friends, "they at least know how to eat."

"Let's get something ordered up then," Kelly said, sitting down.

W. W. Ronin wasn't unacquainted with the Washoe Club, given Dustsucker's explanation of the place last spring when they'd sat across the street in the Bucket of Blood saloon. The Washoe Club's bar, sometimes called "the Crystal" was a two-bit bar, where an evening's libations could cost a little more than the average miner or cowboy might be comfortable with. "It's no one-bit shebang to be sure," Dustsucker said, enjoying the imagery of the words. "It's more like a businessman's bar," he declared, when settling in for a two-fisted first round across the street.

"Yeah, there's something about the Bucket of Blood that tends to keep good people away," Ronin replied, laughing. Though truth be told, he preferred the one-bit bar to any other saloon in town. And oddly enough, the beer was colder.

While a chilled lager wasn't exactly a western thing — he pointed out to Kelly that it might take some time for an east coast pleasure to travel that far west, "they're at least 10 years ahead of us, you know," he teased, not believing the words to be true but knowing how westerners hated hearing such talk — he still preferred a cold-brewed German beer to a California brew that had been "sitting on someone's porch for God knows how long and waved in front of a stove until it was warm, maybe even hot." "Someday, he said, "they'll be hauling cold beer to places like this on railroad trains."

"Whatever," Kelly replied, thinking of other things. "Listen, I didn't tell you, but thanks for returning my Wesley revolver. I've carried that piece a long time."

"No kidding, Tom," Ronin replied, noticing that a Crystal Bar employee seemed to be having considerable trouble with a couple of men who wanted to see the tonier parts of the Washoe Club upstairs. "If I recall, the damned thing was made just after the war. How you'd come to carry such an old thing?" Ronin asked, looking at the leather sock Kelly was carrying it in. He'd fashioned a lanyard to the butt of the gun as well in an apparent attempt to make sure he didn't lose it again, a habit Ronin had seen among eastern lawman but never west of Wichita.

"Well, that's a story to be sure. I'll tell you sometime." Kelly watched a couple of the Crystal's barkeepers becoming distracted by the conversation in the Crystal's doorway.

"Ain't no reason to keep us from this place," a smaller man said while waving what appeared to be a handgun above his head.

"Tom?"

"I'm on it," Kelly said, standing up and heading toward the doorway. Ronin could see a pair of Virginia City policemen standing outside. They'd apparently chosen not to intervene. The smaller man was holding a bottle, not a handgun, but threw a punch at one of the men speaking with him.

"Ain't no reason at all to keep us out," he shouted as Kelly attempted to grab him. "We pay our taxes just like everyone else," the man yelled, looking around to see if he had anyone else's attention. The Crystal's customers seemed used to ignoring such interruptions. A few women were relaxing at tables with men nearby. Judging by the upscale dress of both men and women, it appeared that the usual Saturday night crowd — Virginia City's hurdy-gurdy girls and the working men that were attracted to them — weren't welcome in the establishment, or couldn't afford drinking there. It was no wonder Ronin and Dustsucker liked to do their drinking elsewhere.

"Do you need some help?" Ronin shouted, pushing his coat back to expose his 4-inch pearl-handled Colt Peacemaker. It was a rare action for the bounty hunter, who was learning to limit his professional attention to those situations in which he had a financial interest — it was cleaner that way — but Ash had been clear about his interest in Kelly's welfare. "Tom?"

"I got it," Kelly said as he caught the man's arm and swung him face-first into a wall. "Boys? You guys want to help?" The policemen waved, smiled and continued down the street. Ronin was confused.

"I don't get it, Tom," he said, jumping up so as to take hold of the man's elbow and wrist as Kelly did the same. Ronin caught the man's calf with the edge of his right foot, kicking his feet apart. "Don't even ..." he said to the man's friend, who was looking at them both wide-eyed but backing away from the Crystal's doorway in response. "What's with your police force, Tom?"

"Imagine we've offended some folks again," he answered, pulling the man's left hand down to meet his right hand and cuffing both wrists tightly.

"We?"

Ronin thought the inference was odd, given that the Washoe Club had been fashioned together by thirty or forty men a few years prior as the community's answer to swankier clubs elsewhere. Wealthier men from Virginia City, a few from Gold Hill and Carson City, but none from Reno were included on the roll that had grown to a hundred or so members, if the rumors were to be believed. All of them joined by invitation only. The Reynolds Building, as the three-story brick structure had been called prior to the club's purchasing it, had been badly damaged in the 1875 fire. But the club's members — James Fair, John Mackay, Rollin Daggett from the Territorial Enterprise, and others — had the building open again a year later: extravagant furnishings, beverages and women included. "Did I hear that correctly, Tom? Maybe I'm misunderstanding what you mean by the word, 'we?'"

Tom Kelly blushed as he spun the man out the door and into the street, kicking his bottle with him, his partner nowhere to be found. "You did *not*," he said with some emphasis, "though I'm greatly embarrassed to say so." He handed the small and still angry man to a jail deputy who was happening by. "I'm not supposed to be working outside my normal responsibilities, Ronin. The city and county folks weren't at all happy about my involvement with you and Ash in Reno, for instance. But some of the Washoe Club men are my friends, and they've got themselves in quite a pickle."

"How so?" Ronin rested his hand on Kelly's shoulder out front of a slim-framed, working man's house on B Street, olive trees blocking the wind and a few fruit trees standing stoically against the September cold. Kelly seemed genuinely troubled.

"A few of the men have gotten involved …with the women you mentioned, Ronin. And Ash, while he promised he wouldn't say anything to anyone — you might imagine this is a pretty sensitive thing — apparently thinks that you can help."

"Right," Ronin responded. "You can't talk to the police chief?"

"Exactly. And there's no real evidence of a crime at this point."

The situation was getting clearer. Rich men, not wanting their names or their businesses mentioned in an already pre-carious business environment, were concerned about extortion, fraud and theft.

"Let me see what I can do, Tom."

Kelly hesitated. "I know you don't like rich folks, Ronin."

"Not generally," Ronin replied. He removed his hand from Kelly's shoulder and pulled his duster shut. It was cold. President Rutherford B. Hayes was due on the Comstock in a couple of days, after a quick stop in Reno. If the newspapers accounts were accurate, Hayes would have with him the northern general William Tecumseh Sherman, members of his family and others in his administration. Sherman had been a practic-ing Catholic prior to the Civil War and a prick throughout, his scorched-earth policies breaking not only the backbone of the rebellion — leading to the deaths of hundreds if not thousands of innocent women and children — but becoming the policy *de rigueur* in subsequent Indian campaigns. *You'd think the men who conquered the south would be able to plan a warmer and more hospitable time to visit,* thought Ronin. If the two men met, and this was hard to admit, he would have a hard time not killing the man.

"People are who they are, I imagine," Ronin continued, trying to keep a positive outlook on the men and months that had passed since then. "Everybody ought to have a couple of friends, Tom. I imagine that you're a good one to folks I'd never meet or greet in a lifetime of adventures," he said, hoping to cement the man's trust and respect.

"That's not how I hear it, Ronin," Kelly said, looking up and smiling. "But a friend is what I need right now. With my wife's death, and the pressure I'm feeling from both the club and the county, I don't know where else to turn."

Ash had a funny way of putting people together, Ronin mused, and now the man was going to mess with his personal prejudices.

# Chapter 8

# MY PROFESSION

"Mister Ronin. I don't know what to tell you about the sisters. They're identical twins, you know."

"I didn't know that."

"Yes, not many folks do. One of them will give a good go at waking the dead ..."

"A Spiritualist, then?" Ronin interrupted.

"Yes, that's right. And the other is a clairvoyant. Both of them will keep you entertained, in more ways than you can imagine. From what I hear, some men don't need to imagine," she said, a deep laugh following her words.

Ronin shook his head, smiling. He'd spent a couple of hours with Eilley Bowers, "the Washoe Seeress" as she preferred to be called, and enjoyed her straight talk. While some folks evidently took exception to Eilley's lack of culture and learning, she seemed honest, and he liked that.

To his surprise, after asking around he had discovered that Eilley Bowers was the same Bowers who had once owned the Bowers mansion in Washoe Valley where he, Ash and Kelly had rescued the American Gospel Mission's children the spring before. She'd apparently weathered the selling of the house a few years prior to their being there, and had subsequently been making a living, more or less — and it sounded like less — proffering what was left of her energy as the Comstock's leading seeress or fortune teller.

"Mrs. Bowers, you and I have a common experience, I'm afraid," he offered, wondering how to broach the fact that he had been at the mansion a few months before, a place where thousands had partied and picnicked over the years, though in much better days.

"I'm aware of that, Mister Ronin, though I'm afraid I didn't connect the dots when we met the other day. Forgive me. I trust the house was still standing?"

Ronin smiled. He genuinely liked the woman. She seemed intent on turning her scars into stars and was certainly doing so after the massive emotional wounds she had suffered in the death of her husband, her three children and the loss of her mining investments, home and money. She was amazing. "It was. And I'm sorry."

"For bringing it up? Nonsense, our lives change, Mister Ronin. And the best thing we can do is to get on with them. There's no guarantee of living twice, you know." She winked, which struck him as funny, given that most of the men and women he'd encountered — who were pursing the generally lucrative calling of telling people's fortunes — pointed to an even richer life in the great beyond.

"I'm sorry?" he asked, wanting to make sure of her meaning.

Eilley laughed, topping off Ronin's glass of wine. He only sipped at it, not being much of a wine bibber, he explained as she was pouring. The glass was made of crystal and had a lengthy stem. Eilley Bowers was being a very gracious hostess, as folks had predicted she would be. "You already said that, Mister Ronin." He laughed, too. He could get used to this. Emma was at times way too serious to hold his affection and attention.

"I meant simply how your life had turned out, Eilley."

"Oh my, now it's I who have been misunderstood," she said, covering her mouth and smiling. Her dark eyes seemed softer than the first time he questioned her. "It's not over yet,

Mister Ronin. I still have a house in the valley, though it's a small one, in Franktown, actually. But I live up here when I can, or in Reno, wherever my business takes me."

"You've had some success, I understand, in seeing people's futures."

"I get lucky, I'm afraid. After the Great Fire of 1875, Virginia City people remembered my prediction — predictions, actually — concerns more probably, but still ..." She took a sip of wine. "So when they want an honest reading, I'm available here a couple of days a week and try to be in Reno a couple of days weekly as well. I tend to be on people's 'A' lists, not that they won't try someone else if I'm engaged elsewhere. But still, it's been hard."

"Mrs. Bowers, tell me again about the twins."

She smiled, placing both hands into her lap. "There's a sort of economy as to how my profession is run, Mister Ronin. And on the lower end of it — and these aren't just necromancers, you understand, people communicating with the dead, but perhaps also card readers and scryers like myself — there are those who would profit from a man's need to know about a mining claim or business transaction, perhaps a lottery number or how their luck is going to look at a card game or table. To be frank, most *women* want something different."

"Different?" Ronin asked, surprised that men and women's tastes were that dissimilar, "How's that?"

"They may want to know how to start a love affair ..."

"Really?" he interrupted.

"... or how to end one."

# Chapter 9

# EMMA

Emma didn't care for Spiritualists. The whole Ouija board, crystal ball thing made her nervous, despite the sincere effort by some in the Spiritualist community to witness to the possibility of life beyond the grave.

Emma had engaged at one point in a debate with a young man heading to Chicago for a convention of "sorcerers and soothsayers," she called them. The boy maintained that the spirit of man was eternal, a point about which she did not disagree. It was his argument that the two worlds were one that disturbed her most. "It is appointed unto men once to die," she said, quoting the ancient Biblical writings she lived her life by, "and after this the judgment," she said, taking exception to the thought that everyone, more or less, could enjoy a comfortable afterlife and that those who had passed "were just waiting" to speak to those that remained. Some men were going to hell for sure, she figured, and not too few men as well, she thought, remembering her husband Henry Nauman, who had left Carson City without warning, having whored away his eternal rewards and not even saying goodbye.

The fact that Ronin was in Virginia City investigating mediums who believed that the dead could be reached or seen or communicated with seemed silly to her at best and down-right dangerous at worst, if the Christian church's warnings were to be heard and heeded. A man could pick up an evil spirit by dallying too long or often with people who were talking to the dead, she said.

When Ronin protested her concerns, remarking that he didn't think he would be talking to Spiritualists as much as to "common clairvoyants, shysters more likely," it didn't keep Emma from saying "You'll be talking with demons, Ronin, and I'll not have that." The silence between the two of them afterward was palpable. It was barely broken by a perfunctory good-night kiss.

Emma Nauman, the director of the American Gospel Mission just south of Carson City, was opposed to such practices, figuring that if the scientists of the day — all intelligent men and some of them faithful — had proven the veracity of Spiritualism as newspaper reports claimed, then the devilish origin of those activities was the only possible explanation. It was clear that Ronin, who barely believed the Bible anymore despite his seminary training, had other more rational explanations, and thus his interest.

"So you don't know what's keeping him there?" she asked Dustsucker.

"Miss Emma," the deputy had grown fond of calling her that, having enjoyed their friendship while often wishing for more. "Miss Emma, if I knew where to find him, I'd go up and get him myself, your being worried and all. A man ought to be by his women in times like these …"

"Now, Marcus, I'm not his woman. You know that." Slade understood the complex relationship Ronin and Emma had, though he hoped Ronin might move on at some point, allowing him an opportunity to move in.

"I'm just saying," he said, though he really didn't know what he was saying or whether these were times to be especially thoughtful or afraid. "I'm just saying that if you need him, he ought to be here. God knows you were there for him when he needed you."

"I'll not have you take the Lord's name in vain, Marcus …"

"Of course not," he said, "I'm just saying ..." He shook his head, embarrassed that he no more understood his friend than his friend's woman, who had him tongued-tied. It was an awkward relationship at best, given that he didn't want Emma to know that he was as interested in her as she was in his friend. "Emma," he asked, "perhaps I can help?"

"No. There's nothing I need from Mister Ronin at this point, nor you, Marcus. I was just wondering when he would get back." She turned to leave.

"Dustsucker? May I call you that?"

"Well, sure," he smiled, "I've been wondering how long it would take you." Emma smiled.

"To tell you the truth, I'm concerned." She folded her arms across her chest and began tapping her foot. "I believe he's looking into powers that shouldn't be trifled with," she said, her brown eyes growing wide enough that he didn't know whether to feel more attracted or more afraid. "God shows his wrath toward those who do such things. That's what the Bible says. And God's wrath is the last thing Ronin needs right now."

He winced. It was her tone. He knew now what his friend was talking about when Ronin complained that Emma had as harsh a side to her as she had warm. It was painful.

"Miss Emma, with all respect, doesn't the Bible say that we should test all things?" he asked, digging deeply into his Catholic upbringing, the phrase having been regularly applied to the missionary efforts of Protestants in his parent's Iowa home and church. It was a rare Roman Catholic parish that trusted the pursuits of Protestants in their midst.

"Well, Dustsucker!" Emma smiled, "I didn't know you read the Bible."

He took a step back, wondering what to say. "I don't, ma'am," he stuttered, "not regularly anyway. But from time to time I remember things my parents taught me ...as they seem appropriate, of course." He smiled, knowing that respect for one's parents was a Biblical thing, maybe even a Ten Commandments thing if he remembered right.

"As we all should," she said, wondering what Ronin's deceased mother would think of his dalliance in things so devilish. "Why don't you and I get some supper?" she asked. Dustsucker grinned.

It didn't matter what Ronin did, as far as he was concerned. And it didn't matter a whole hell of a lot what Emma thought about what Ronin was doing either. Nothing mattered as much as the fact that he was going to get to sit alone with Emma for supper.

# Chapter 10

# THE BUCKET OF BLOOD

"Listen, I'm happy to meet you," he said, his mouth tight around the corners. "I just don't get what you have to do with the investigation Marshal Ash has asked me conduct." Ronin spoke impatiently. He didn't mind meeting the owner of the Bucket of Blood saloon. Hell, he'd killed a couple of men there a few months back. It was only fair to meet the man who probably paid for the dead men's funerals. Still, he wasn't one to hobnob when hobnobbing wasn't going anywhere. Given McBride's reputation as a mover and shaker on the hill, he had promised Ash a couple of times that he would try to catch up to the man. The fact that Ash and McBride met weekly to go over the week's goings-ons was one thing. Happening to be there when they were meeting was another. And dammit, it was Thursday.

Marshal Augustus Ash and the saloon's owner, Versal McBride, had breakfast together every Thursday. They had weathered the best and the worst of the Comstock's life together, scratching a few gold pieces out of the Comstock mines — an arduous task at best and one as the years went by neither man was comfortable doing much longer. There was a time that gold and silver could be picked up in the streets, or so the saying went. That time was over. People who were making money were taking money from those who were making money, and Ash and McBride liked it that way. "On a good day," McBride liked to say, "you can make money while you're sleeping."

"So mote it be," Ash would often agree.

Looking at the two of them meeting — W. W. Ronin, an angry ex-priest and bounty hunter facing Versal McBride, Ash's occasional friend and partner if easy money was to be made — the marshal began to squirm in his chair. It was unusual for McBride to refrain from barking back at someone who was speaking so brusquely. But Ronin had a point and McBride hadn't been smooth enough to make his yet.

"I'm not trying to gas you, my friend. I'm simply saying, Mister Ronin, that if you discover the names of the men these girls are extorting money from..."

"I didn't say anything about extortion, Versal."

Ash winced. He wasn't sure that the two of them were on a first name basis. Familiarity often pushed McBride over the edge. A few months back, he'd watched McBride snarl at a man as if he was going to bite him. He didn't, but the other man was so unnerved he left a pile of silver dollars on the table and a piece of pie. And he never came back.

"I believe Marshal Ash said that, Mister Ronin," he said, attempting to regain control of a conversation he hadn't yet gained control of. "I'm simply saying that the facts are already pretty clear, reverend ..."

Ash winced again.

"... Two of our very pretty Comstock women are extorting money from members of the Washoe Club. And while I don't know these women and would very much like to know these men, we have a common concern between the two of us."

"Which is?" Ronin asked, his left eyebrow raised, the right corner of his hat dipping slightly.

"Look," McBride said suddenly, punctuating the air with such force that folks a couple of tables away set their forks down and looked over. He glanced back and nodded, as if to apologize. "The Washoe Club caters to a different clientele that we do, Mister Ronin," he whispered. "But times are tough, and if business is going to continue as it should, all of us should pull together. I'd like you to do your share of pulling as well."

Ronin sat back in his chair, impressed. Most people folded when he put up a fight, not that McBride and he were fighting, but some folks took an argument as an altercation. McBride apparently did not. One of the things he liked about Nevada was people's ability to get to a point. And while some people pulled their pieces too quickly in such moments — turning a simple difference of opinion into a gun-slinging donnybrook from which sometimes no one walked away — McBride showed considerable restraint. Ronin smiled. "Mister McBride, I apologize," he said. "The Comstock has fallen on tough times, to be sure. And while I've not been a fan of mining ..."

"...or timber farms and railroads, from what I hear..." McBride said.

"Well, that's true. Listen, I understand your need to keep people fed and wives and husbands entertained. I like this place, in fact." He gestured across the saloon, where the Bucket's fledgling breakfast trade was attracting a new segment of people not used to frequenting the inside of a one-bit saloon. Seventy percent of folks on the Comstock visited restaurants and saloons for their board, the men coming in early prior to their shifts at the mines, their women and children closer to noon. He looked at his watch. It was an hour short of noon. "Do I understand a fellow can get a couple of kinds of meat, some vegetables and a dessert for just a couple of dimes?"

"A little more, but yes."

"Well then, let's have some lunch and talk about things some. I didn't mean to be so brief with you or so harsh."

McBride looked over at Ash, who looked over at Ronin and shrugged.

"Mister Ronin," the saloon owner said, "lunch is on me. And I'll be proud to get you another beer, too, if you like, if you'll just give me a couple of minutes."

"I'm happy to do that, Versal." The owner of the Bucket of Blood saloon in Virginia City pushed his chair away from the table and motioned for a server to come over before standing up. "I understand from Marshal Ash that you're a very resourceful person, reverend."

"It's not reverend, Mister McBride. It's simply Ronin. My reverend days are long behind me."

"Okay, Ronin it is then. Augustus here tells me that you've got a fire in you about certain things. Justice, injustice, things of that like."

"I do, though I've been told it sometimes gets in the way of my profession."

"Which is?" McBride asked, curious as to the words Ronin would use to describe the trail of dead men Ronin had left in Virginia City, Reno, Glenbrook and the state's otherwise quiet capital of Carson City.

"Most things said and done, I try to fix things, to make them right. And if there's a dollar or two to make along the way, I try to pick it up."

"That was my impression," McBride said, putting his left hand on the table so as to steady himself. "I want to get some paper, Mister Ronin, but not before I tell you a quick story. There's a Spanish man who frequents this establishment that our marshal here doesn't seem to have any interest in…"

"Now Versal, that's not fair…" Ash protested.

"It's completely fair, Ash, and you know it."

"I'm listening," Ronin replied, seeing that the server McBride had signaled was now finished and just a few feet away. A story shouldn't stand between a man and his meal, he figured, no matter how good the story is.

"I'm simply saying, we have a problem with a man who hasn't yet run afoul of the law up here, but seems to have found a way to keep some of our lunch customers away."

"Okay."

"He's worn out a few of our bartenders. And I haven't found a Virginia City policeman who's willing to sit with us long enough to deal with this man despite his being so small."

"Okay."

"I'm wondering ..."

"You're wondering if I might have a word with this man?"

"Yes, though it might take more than a word."

"Okay."

"Does that sound like something we could talk about?"

Ronin paused and looked over at Ash, who didn't seem bothered by McBride's proposition one way or another. He turned to the Bucket's owner. "McBride, if I can help a family sit down to a nice breakfast at the Bucket of Blood saloon, or a couple of cowboys belt out a poem or song to qualify for a free lunch" — the saloon had offered a few over the years, particularly to those whose stories were entertaining enough to qualify — "Hell, if I can a make a man happy who has spent his entire day digging dirt underground to hear a squeak or two from the piano while eating a ham steak, baked potato and green beans, I'd be happy to do so. The usual rate apply?"

"And what's that?" Versal McBride asked, happy that Ronin seemed interested.

"Let's figure that out as we're having lunch, my friend. You go get your paper. I'm going stand outside for a few minutes. And when you're ready, I think I'd like some pork chops."

# Chapter 11
# BULLWHIP

It didn't take but a minute or two before Ronin spotted the man McBride was talking about. Ronin had been standing on the boardwalk, trying to keep his boots dry as a brief shower had dampened the street, refreshing holes and ruts thousands of timber and ore wagons had made over the years, when a short Mexican-looking man jumped down from a wagon load of timber harvested from an inactive Comstock mine into a shallow puddle, dousing himself with road slime.

"Fuck!" the little man shouted. A bullwhip hung around his neck, coiled more than a couple times, perhaps six feet long, two or three feet longer than the man was, had he been laying down which of course he was not as he was striding toward the entrance of the Bucket of Blood saloon in a banker's hat of all things. "Excuse me, partner," the little man said as he passed by, touching his hat, Ronin moving an inch or so to his left so as to accommodate him, his mouth still open in seeing such a tiny man driving such a big wagon on so busy a Comstock street.

Ronin had seen "midgets" in the circus, though the term at the time struck him as pejorative as it suggested shorter people should be put on display, or worse still be pitted against each other for sport. He'd heard of General Tom Thumb's wedding, of course, his being Episcopalian and Thumb, more appropriately Charles Stratton, having married an equally short woman named Lavinia Warren in an Episcopal church atop a grand piano not too many years before. The New York city wedding wouldn't have caught his attention save for the conversation he overheard a couple of years later while attending seminary, where otherwise sensitive divinity students were deciding whether "midgets" should "be able to" marry.

Stratton had done well in P. T. Barnum's circus and elsewhere, so much so that the discussion for most people — President Lincoln included, who hosted the couple after their wedding for a reception at the White House — was a moot one. Of course short people should be able to marry. The couple had stayed at the Willard Hotel, she in white satin, sparkling with diamonds, he in a traditional tuxedo and shiny patent-leather shoes, before attending the well-publicized White House reception in their honor. All of which was moving about in Ronin's head as the tiny man walked by and winked.

"Mister Ronin!" McBride called from across the room, pointing in the ignorant way people sometimes do when they've seen or want to single out something they believe to be worth seeing. Ronin looked up, annoyed, as he generally didn't like his name being hollered about in public places. The Mexican-looking man turned to see who McBride was yelling at and then, with a smile, settled up into a seat next to the piano player.

Ronin nodded and then headed back to his table. "I'll have the ham," he said, "and perhaps a bit of your locally-raised beef stew," the latter coming from Jacks Valley, he figured, though any number of cattle ranches might have contributed. "And your local, garden-grown vegetables," he said, though he was certain they wouldn't be, as nothing grew on the Comstock without plenty of non-local dirt and water. "Mister McBride," he said, settling down into his chair, "I'd much rather you shot at me than called my name out." He hesitated, wondering if he should complete his thought. He continued, "... though both will get you an unfriendly response."

Marshal Augustus Ash, who had stayed at the table even after McBride and Ronin had gotten up, said "Now boys, we were just beginning to get along!" Ash continued his nervous refrain for a few moments when Ronin looked over at the piano and noted that the little man was now standing beside the piano player on the piano bench, and was apparently getting ready to sing.

"This is what you were talking about ..." he began to say, when an unnaturally shrill voice sang out.

"Oh, my God," the three men said in unison.

The small man — who McBride had just assured the two was Spanish and not Mexican, despite the earlier presence of Mexicans on the Comstock, though many had now inexplicably left — had begun to sing a Spanish folk song or some such thing with such timbre as to annoy nearly everyone in the saloon. Only the staff seemed unaffected, having turned toward the mirrors, smiling as if the same thing happened each and every day, though McBride had just assured them on his way back into the room that "today will be different."

"You're kidding, right?" Ronin said, looking at his host, who grinned helplessly. "And when you ask him to stop?"

"No one has thought to do that," McBride responded, "... recently, that is."

"Well, I won't have a man stand between me and a meal," Ronin said, getting up. Six feet tall, maybe a little taller, Ronin looked over at the piano, where the little man was tuning up, and shouted, "Stop that!" Being tall as he was, shouting and all, Ronin made a considerable impression. A sudden silence fell on the saloon.

"Are you talking to *me*?" the little man said, jumping down off of the piano bench so that he stood maybe three feet all if he was standing at all. The little man put his hands on his waist and appeared considerably irritated. "Mister Ronin, is it?"

"I'm sorry, I don't know your name," Ronin responded, walking toward the piano with the kind of determination that a parent might demonstrate on his way to physically disciplining a child.

"No, you don't," the man said nodding, his one hand up so as to signal the word "stop," *alto* in Spanish, Ronin remembered thinking before watching the little man twirl like a top, unfurling the whip from around his neck and lashing out toward his face with such ferocity that the crack of the whip sounded like thunder. It was disorienting.

While the man's whip didn't hit him, Ronin's knees buckled. Unable to think or to balance himself, he fell into a table of food where a young woman and her children were sitting down to say grace. His face landed in three generous portions of breakfast soufflé. He grabbed for his gun. The heated cheese, ham, egg and cayenne pepper bit at his eyes like a thousand fire ants. A second sudden snap of the man's whip stung at his right hand, causing him to drop his revolver. Ronin toppled onto the floor and hit his head.

Ash was suddenly on his feet, but not before the man ran out the front door, disappearing into the busy street. He turned to see if Ronin was stirring and saw McBride bending over Ronin, while pushing a wet table rag toward Ronin's face. He grabbed McBride's arm. "Water, Versal. What we need is water. God only knows what you're cleaning the tables with."

Ronin reached up and, grabbing the cloth from the saloon's owner, wiped his face. "What we need is a name ... the son of a bitch."

McBride grimaced. "They call him, 'Latigo,' Ronin, meaning 'whip,'" McBride said, standing back up and looking to see if anything on the table next to him needed to be replaced. "I believe he calls himself 'Toro,'" he added, smiling at the woman and her two small children, then looking away.

"Figures," Ronin growled, folding the cleaning rag into a square and placing on the floor.

"It figures?" Ash said from the door, still looking down the street. *Nothing. No one. How can a man disappear so quickly?*

"Yeah, it means 'bull,'" Ronin said, "as in 'Bull Whip.' Got enough to arrest him now, marshal?" Ronin was clearly annoyed.

"We do," Ash replied, stepping back from the door. "Though again, it's hardly a marshal's business. Ma'am, I'm sorry for this mess," he said to the woman and her children. "Mister McBride will be happy to order you some different food."

McBride frowned.

"Ash!" Ronin said.

"I'm sorry, Ronin. You were saying?"

"I was about to say, you better arrest him or find somebody who will, because if I find him first, I'll kill him."

# Chapter 12

# BOXING THE TREES

Ronin took the last train back into Carson City, arriving late enough that he walked to his Ormsby House hotel room. He was shaken by the turn of events at the Bucket of Blood saloon in Virginia City. Used to prevailing in a fight or altercation, he was surprised to find himself unprepared to deal with a much smaller man with a whip. "You'll want to be flexible," his boxing instructor told him in seminary. At the time his bishop, the Right Reverend James O'Reilly, had said, "You have heavy hands, Ronin, but heavy hands aren't the same as speed, or technique even. Once you learn everything you think you need to know, something will come along to unsettle you. That's the way life is."

The Episcopal bishop of the Diocese of Pittsburgh was a wise man. Despite his age, the esteemed Episcopal bishop seemed like a tough man as well. "Don't be surprised by how they settle things out west," he said, feigning an uppercut to Ronin's mid-section in the manner that some men do while pretending combat. "Get yourself a good hat, some good boots and a sturdy pair of gloves," he'd said, saying nothing about how to deal with a man with a faster gun or whip. He had not met the former yet, but he had definitely been schooled by the latter.

A few hours later, after checking on his room and horse, he wandered into the Chinese section of Carson City. Sitting outside the Joss house, where six-hundred or so Chinese residents of Carson City occasionally gathered and worshiped, he wondered what it would be like to meet the tiny, angry man again.

It was late. Carson City's sky was clear; the stars showed brightly. The nighttime air was filled with incense. The scent reminded him of the smell of sage after a lengthy spring or fall rain. After a while, he stood up, and engaging one of the trees, pretended it was Toro Latigo. In range, out of range — he moved, tapping the tree with his gloved hands as if punching, then right, then back again, reminding himself what it was like to fight a man so small. He was too tall to use his hands; he couldn't get low or deep enough without exposing his face. He would have to use his legs and, judging by what he had seen, his kicks would be too slow to counter the whip's intensity and distance.

"I knew a man once who thought he could get inside my lance with his speed and magic tricks," someone said, causing Ronin to startle. He looked about until he saw Happy Hands standing in the shadows beside a tree. He had assumed he was alone.

"Why aren't you at home?"

"It is a question I might ask my friend," Happy Hands replied. The Washoe shaman had befriended Ronin while helping to solve the murders of the two Washoe men at Lake Tahoe. His insights at the lake had been helpful.

"Don't be sneaking up on me, my friend. I'll be jumpy all night now. What brings you to town so late in the evening?"

Happy Hands smiled and Ronin read his mind. He hadn't noticed this about the man when they had first met in a colony of Indians sitting beside Washoe Lake. At that point, Happy Hands seemed old and frail. The next time he saw him, just prior to their taking a coach to Glenbrook, he seemed younger. Given his behavior with a couple of women in the coach, he seemed to be something of a barnyard rooster as well.

"You're in town visiting some women friends. Never mind," he said. Happy Hands grinned.

"You appear to be fighting with trees, William. What is it you are really fighting, if I may ask?"

The man had an unnerving way of getting inside people's heads, Ronin had observed. He took the question to be particularly personal, as he had been mentoring Ronin's spiritual side, "dwindled as it is," Happy Hands had said when they first talked about his no longer being "a white man's medicine man."

"Used to be," Ronin had said, laughing.

"Once was, always will be," Happy Hands had argued.

"Whatever," he'd replied.

"So what is it that you are doing, Ronin?"

Ronin grimaced. He hated being caught in his more private moments, When he was a clergyman, more often than not — and he had no explanation for this — when he was caught quietly musing or moving, those thoughts or moments were embarrassing at best. Discussing them had never come to a helpful end, and still ...

"Sit with me for a minute, Happy Hands," he said. A solitary street light at the rear of the capitol cast shadows through the trees, partially obscuring his friend's face. It was midnight and the city's noises, unlike the constant din of towns along the Comstock, were dissipated by the Chinatown trees and the Capital buildings immediately to their west. "I came face to face with my fear today, Happy Hands," he said, taking the risk that his Washoe friend might take his feelings too lightly. "I was out on my feet, reeling, spinning. All I saw was light."

"It is better to see light than darkness, my friend." He sat silently. "I thought you might need me. Funny that you should select a Chinaman's holy house to sit outside when thinking of your beating."

"How did you know?" Ronin asked.

The Indian paused. Happy Hands seemed to have a "sixth sense" about things at times, an ability to see the unseen and to know the unknown. It was spooky. His friend smiled. Ronin laughed uncomfortably. They were silent for a moment.

"Your deputy friend told me."

"Of course," Ronin said. He loved the woo-woo side of the Washoe man. He tapped his lips twice, whispering the sound. Both men laughed. Unlike many Paiute and Washoe men, Happy Hands seemed comfortable in both worlds, enough that he was sometimes considered wise in *both* worlds, brown and white. "Well," Ronin continued, "then he told you I was assaulted by a very small man."

"A midget," Happy Hands said, laughing.

"Hands, that's no more appropriate for you to call him that than for me to call you an 'Injun.'"

"I know. I am just making a white man's joke. Deputy Slade actually said it was 'mutual combat with a man much smaller than you.' The fact that you were both fighting, he said, kept him from arresting the very small man."

"That's not the way Ash saw it."

"It is not surprising that Ash saw it differently." Happy Hands paused. "How did you see it, my friend?"

Ronin was silent. He had been sitting on the bench and boxing the trees thinking about what he *could* learn from the experience instead of asking what he *should* learn, which was the path a wiser man might take. "I don't know, Hands. I was focusing on the weapon and what I needed to know or do the next time I face him."

Happy Hands smiled. "And you will, you know."

"I will." Ronin acknowledged.

"But it may be that you will not need to, if you take the lesson from your experience that you are meant to take." Ronin listened, reminding himself that life's situations seemed to repeat themselves until the people living them learned what they needed to know. Not that he believed that to be true, but he'd often observed it none the less and wondered.

"And when you face the man again, Ronin …"

"Yes?" He waited.

"… do not let the weapon steal your attention. It is always the man that you must fight."

Ronin laughed. When Hands headed in one direction, he oftentimes ended up in another. The effect was stunning. He put his hands on Happy Hands' shoulders and looked him in the eye, like a man might look at his friend if he were willing to admit his affection. "You were saying about the man who was hoping to defeat your lance with his speed and tricks? How did that play out?"

Happy Hands smiled — a full set of teeth, whiter than they used to be, gleamed in Ronin's direction. "He thought he could move inside my lance," he said, "which is what a warrior would think to do if he had no experience."

"Okay."

"When I was younger, William, I used to tie a colorful rope and feathers next to the lance's sharp end. It was disorienting and overpowering, as it was so beautiful to watch."

"Okay."

"Well, it was then that I often struck the other end of the lance onto his head or eye."

Happy Hands smiled. Ronin smiled, too, knowing the story might never have happened that way. "It could have happened," his friend had said before, when Ronin had questioned the veracity of a story. "What really happened is not the point," the Indian always reminded him, "the point is the point."

Indeed. Defeating the small man's whip shouldn't have been the focus at all. It was the fear that had to move.

# Chapter 13
# BREAKFAST AT MULLER'S

"So tell me what you've been up to," Emma asked, sitting at a quiet table at Mullers. Ronin's favorite place to eat, the 3$^{rd}$ and Carson restaurant catered to the working class and had a dependable bakery, in the sense that if his friend Dustsucker wanted a second or third roll or a croissant they were likely to have one. Because the restaurant had a well-stocked bar, Ronin met many of his clients there. Lena Mueller made a reasonable cup of coffee for a French woman and allowed his meetings the privacy they oftentimes needed.

"My apologies about not getting back to you," Ronin said. "I imagine you were busy anyway, the Lord's work and all that." Emma showed no reaction. The American Gospel Mission was expanding under Emma Nauman's leadership. Private support had suffered after the disappearance of Emma's husband in the midst of a county investigation. But monies had unexpectedly become available from the state, an awkward fact given the legislature's refusal of funds to the Daughters of Charity orphanage in Virginia City. But the money was needed and immediately put to work building structures the state couldn't tear down should they decide to withdraw their support.

A number of new vocational instructors had helped to regain trust among area Washoe, Paiute and Shoshone families. Emma's own personal gifts — practiced for years, despite her husband's reticence to allow her power or a public voice at the mission — had caught the attention of people in town, folks with money who were happy to see Indian children off the streets and in school. "It is the least we can do," one church lady had said after Emma had spoken to the gathering of women from the Presbyterian and Methodist congregations in Carson City. "The children have suffered so much."

"Indeed," Emma had responded, turning away so that her true feelings couldn't be seen. Religious hearts were too often the hardest of hearts, she'd noticed, having seen more generous and frequent opening of purses and wallets among the working girls and laborers on the Comstock. She'd spent many nights on her knees praying that church people would discover the humanity and compassion she'd so often seen among the church's non-religious neighbors and friends.

"I've been wondering how you've been, William. No amount of mission work can take the place of that," she replied. Emma's inference was clear. She had missed him and, if the truth were told, he had missed her, though he often struggled with his feelings, thinking himself more comfortable with the business at hand.

"It's been interesting, I'll tell you that," he said. "And I have to say a little bit frenetic, too," he replied, looking away. She had beautiful green eyes, brown if she was upset. He was too often lost in them. He wondered what else to say. "Ash approached me," he said, "to look into a couple of fortune tellers in Virginia City. How many, I don't know yet, though I did get to sit with ..."

"Too busy to send word?" she interrupted, her green eyes turning brown.

"I'm sorry?"

"Too busy to send word?," Emma repeated, a little more animated. "Listen, William. I know that we aren't exactly courting ..."

"Well, no, not that I wouldn't, I mean if things were different."

"Different for both of us, William. I don't exactly sit around wondering where you are, who you're with or what you're doing. But when you're conducting an investigation, when you're off for a couple of days and don't know when you will return, it might be nice to let your friends know how you're doing. We worry."

It was unclear to Ronin whether she was speaking of herself or including others so as to emphasize her point. "I'm sorry, Emma, I'm not following."

"I'm simply saying, Mister Ronin," he hated when she called him that, "that if you're going to be away for a while you might let Dustsucker or I know. It's not like we don't talk about you in your absence and wonder how things are going."

Ronin sat for a moment, remembering her initial reaction to Happy Hands' comment that his next investigation would have him working with a woman, or "a number of women," Hands had said at supper a week or so before his leaving the capital for Virginia City. "You'll not hear the end of it," he had said.

Of course, he had heard similar criticisms from his mother during the War of Northern Aggression, arguing that he might communicate more regularly. He had written as often as he could, but letter delivery had been difficult, and was particularly poor between states north and south.

"Emma, I'm sorry. I should have sent word. I wasn't in danger, much anyway." He rubbed his right cheek, thinking of Latigo's whip, which hadn't touched him but had left him so disoriented that the difference between being hit and not hit was miniscule.

"Much anyway?" she asked, putting her fork down on her plate. A second egg would have to wait until her curiosity was sated. "You were hit or shot? I don't understand." *Thank God he hadn't been kissed. There'd be no end to the questions.*

Ronin looked toward the windows onto Carson Street, hoping Dustsucker would arrive. They were supposed to meet at the Saint Charles at 8 a.m. and walk to breakfast. It was already 8:30. "Emma, I'm fine," he said. "I just got a little shook up. I offered to trade a favor for some information. It turned out the favor was larger than I imagined."

"Really!" she said, beginning to smile. "Larger, not smaller?" she said, her eyes returning to the color they usually were when she smiled, a powerful green, an Irish green he assumed, though he had never asked. She raised her napkin to her lips and giggled. Ronin took offense when he realized she had already heard.

"Really, Emma? You're going to make fun of something you didn't see? Are you and Dustsucker both going to laugh at me this morning, because the last thing I need is ..."

"I'm sorry, Ronin. I didn't mean to be so cruel. It's just that ..." She stuttered. The woman rarely stuttered, or even paused to consider what she was going to say. Her mouth was a machine. "It's just that I was ... worried about you, and hearing that you had been knocked down by a much smaller or shorter man, I was relieved."

"Relieved?"

"That you hadn't been hurt by a much larger man, of course."

"Of course," Ronin said, drumming his fingers on the table, his pride hurt by Emma's insensitivity. Dangerous men came in all shapes and sizes—dangerous women, too.

"Forgive me, William, I meant no harm. It's just that I'd never heard such a story before. I mean I've seen them in circuses, but I don't believe I've ever met one face to face." She stifled a laugh.

"Wow," he said. He would not believe there was a cruel bone in Emma's body. "Emma, I'm uncomfortable with this. You and I were going to meet with Dustsucker, who I notice is not here, just to catch up, nothing more. And somehow this has turned into my having to listen to your scolding me about my not conveying to you or anyone else for that matter, where I've been, what I've been doing and who I've been doing it with. And now I have to listen to your jokes about short people. What's next, Californians? You of all people might be more sensitive to the fact that people come in all sizes, colors, personal histories and shapes."

"I've made no jokes," Emma protested, raising her eyebrows.

"Really? You're talking about circuses? You work with people others discount because of their appearance or color." He was silent for a moment. "I just don't know what to say."

Emma and Ronin sat at a table in the corner, Ronin looking out as he always did and she by a window. It was a place where she typically did not dine, certainly never alone given the French Canadians who gathered there. Woodcutters and every one of them interested in her, it seemed. And here she sat nonetheless, with a friend who might someday be more, she hoped. And the roughest man she knew, all six-foot something of him and more, was right. She had forgotten who she was, and the people she was caring for. She was mortified. Raising a dark blue napkin to her eyes, she began to cry.

"I'm sorry, Ronin," she sniffed. "I'm behaving terribly. The truth be told, I've been too guarded about how much I'm missing you. I missed you terribly and … and … I wish you wouldn't go away so often."

Ronin looked down. He didn't know what to say. This is what he did for a living. He solved problems. He captured criminals. He was a hammer to the area's jackasses so that people like Emma, and countless others who made their homes in the West, didn't need to be. He was hoping she would understand.

"I've been meaning to talk to you about us, William, if I may. So I'm glad Marcus isn't here yet. I need some clarity. I need to know where we're going. There's such a hollow place inside of me when you are gone."

Ronin swallowed hard. He gazed at a younger couple near the door to an outside patio. *They seem happy.* He should have known as much, the awkwardness between them, her sudden anger and apparent prejudice, masking her frustration. Her hopes and intentions were on the table. He hadn't seen it coming and he didn't know what to say.

"You don't have to answer now," Emma said, breaking the silence, "but I'd like to know sooner than later if I am the woman you want me to be."

*Want me to be? What an odd phrase. But that's exactly the issue. Is she the woman I want her to be? Is that even fair?* He sat for a moment musing, wishing he was elsewhere. These were the kinds of questions a man preferred to work out in private before having to answer them at breakfast.

"Emma?" he said.

"Yes, William?"

"I don't think it is right that I ask you to be something other than what you're not."

"I don't know why I said that. I meant simply to say, I want to be the woman you've always dreamed of being with. And while I'm being quite forward in saying so, I believe you to be the kind of man I've always wanted to be with." She reached forward, her arms across the table so as to take his hands into her own. "Is it okay that we're talking like this?"

He smiled. He didn't know, and still didn't know a few moments later, when Dustsucker arrived. Just in time.

# Chapter 14

# A GOOD MORNING

"Good morning!"

Deputy Marcus T. Slade was late, not that being late was a bother for such a big man. Folks generally accepted his excuses, given that he was a deputy. In fact, it was his just-in-time arrival that people most appreciated. When the large-framed lawman entered a room, particularly those that were conflicted, everything changed — especially those situations that had gone unexpectedly sour.

In Ronin's case, sitting across the table from a woman he very much loved but couldn't seem to adequately like or please, Dustsucker's arrival meant the end of an awkward intimacy. Seeing Dustsucker, Emma withdrew her hands and managed an uncomfortable smile. "Good morning, my friend." Dustsucker watched her move her hands to her lap, leaving Ronin's still outstretched arms to flounder before he withdrew them. He couldn't help but notice that both of his friends appeared a little flushed.

"Ma'am," he said, tipping his hat. "I apologize for being late. I was visiting with folks at the St. Charles and things went a little lengthy. Are you feeling okay?" he asked, as he pulled a chair away from the table so as to sit down facing the street.

Emma glanced at Ronin and then back to her deputy friend. "I am. Mister Ronin and I were just talking about something ... very personal ... I guess."

"Have I come at a bad time?" Dustsucker looked over at Ronin, who was grinning.

"Not at all," they replied, which caused Emma and Ronin to grin even more and finally to laugh.

"We're happy you're here, Dusty. I hope it's okay that we've gone ahead and ordered breakfast."

"It is, ma'am." He looked at his friend. "Ronin, did you hear about next door?"

"The St. Charles? No. What happened?" He pushed his chair a couple of inches away from the table, so as to gain a little more room. Both the Muller and St. Charles hotels had been built by the same men, George Remington and Albert Muller, almost twenty years prior. The classier of the two hotels, the St. Charles, featured three floors of "the most desirable and commodious accommodations" in Carson City. The two-story Muller Hotel was no slouch, either.

"Well, you remember the suicide a couple of years back?" Dustsucker asked. "The *Daily Appeal* reported it, I think." Ronin nodded. The story was familiar, though he couldn't remember which hotel in town it had occurred in, there were so many. "A man ingested strychnine, as I recall."

"I think you're right," Ronin answered, "though I don't generally remember the cause of a man's death."

"No, I don't imagine you do," Dustsucker nodded, looking about for a server. He was hungry. If the day was going to get going, he would need a good helping of eggs, bacon and toast to see things through. "I mean being in the business you're in."

"I'm just saying." Ronin responded, pulling his coat closed so that it covered his guns.

"Well, a man from Virginia City was staying there last night, played poker a while, even had a telegraph going with some of his friends in Virginia City who were bankrolling his efforts."

"Give us this day our daily stranger," Ronin intoned, lifting his hands as if he were praying and shaking his head.

Emma looked confused. "One of the chaplains in the Nevada Legislature uttered those words," Ronin offered, though Emma's look remained unchanged. "Seems the capital city is the stomping ground of poker experts, Emma, not that you'd know about such things."

"And I am thankful every day for that, Mister Ronin. I have enough difficulty holding on to my money."

"Miss Emma, I didn't mean to infer anything untowardly."

"Of course not."

Dustsucker looked on, pausing mid-sentence so as to make sense of the back and forth between his friends. "Well," he said, beginning again, "it seems that this man took quite a beating, spending thousands of dollars as I hear it, though nobody seems to remember who else was at the table. And it appears as if he killed himself a couple of hours later."

"Jesus. That's unfortunate. I'll never comprehend folks getting so unbalanced over such things," Ronin remarked, cutting his toast into triangles so that he could scoop up some jam.

"It's no different than gold fever, I don't guess," Dustsucker answered. "I've never let it get to me, but hell, I'm not digging all that often or deeply! It's the same with whores or alcohol or anything else as far as I'm concerned ...I'm sorry ma'am, I don't mean to offend."

"No offense taken, Dustsucker."

The deputy pointed to items on the Muller's menu. "Eggs, three please, and some bacon, if you would, maybe a dozen strips. And sourdough please, with some coffee." He set the menu down and looked over at Ronin. "I mention this because it was the death of a fairly wealthy man."

"We're all equal in God's sight, Mister Slade," Emma interjected, "black and yellow, red and white."

"I believe it's red and yellow, black and white, Emma," Ronin said. His female friend immediately bristled.

"Whatever."

"Well ..." Dustsucker continued, still trying to make out what was going on between the two of them. "As I was saying, it would appear by the man's wager and clothes that the deceased was a well-to-do man from Virginia City and I'm wondering, just wondering you understand, if he might be one of the men our friend Ash was talking about."

"You mean, one of the men who is mixed up with the mediums and psychics in Virginia City?" Ronin said, putting his knife down and pausing. He held on to the jar of strawberry jam in his left hand as if it was a treasure, which it was as the berries were "fresh," Emma and he had been told, having "been picked yesterday morning in the Sacramento Valley."

Dustsucker pushed his cup to the edge of the table where a tall man was about to pour his coffee. "I do," he said.

"What was his name?"

"Well, that's the odd thing, Ronin. He didn't give a name, though someone said he was a member of the Washoe Club."

"Dead men don't generally talk, Slade."

"I'm saying, the hotel man said he simply sat down, mentioned something about having some coin, and tossing his bag on the table was dealt a hand. It was twenty minutes past twelve and by three o'clock this morning he was dead."

"Wow," Ronin said, wondering how a Virginia City man would play a poker game with such abandon that he was done in a little over two hours. "Sounds like he played thinking he was going to win, if you ask me."

"Yup," Dustsucker said, "every hand. And when he was done ..."

"... he must have been surprised," Ronin offered.

"As if someone had told him he couldn't fail," Dustsucker said.

"Excuse me, guys," Emma interrupted, "I really don't know much about what you're saying, never having played the game. But wouldn't a poker player play a little more tightly at the start of the game so as to see how others were playing?"

"Well, Emma, I declare ... you continue to surprise me!" Dustsucker hooted. "You do get around!"

"Mister Slade, I certainly do not!" Emma crinkled her nose at the thought that she had been so worldly.

"She's right, Dustsucker," Ronin said. "A good player isn't going to loosen up until he has a good sense of what's going on in the game!" Ronin grabbed his toast and, slathering it with jam, put it to his mouth. The morning was going to get real busy, real fast. "I don't imagine a Washoe Club man is going to be sloppy about such things."

"Exactly, my friend, especially if he has backers."

"I need to get back to Virginia City," Ronin said, chewing quickly and then swallowing. He stood up. "Telegraph me when you figure out this man's name, would you?"

"Sure will." The sandy-haired ex-preacher tipped his hat before hurrying out the door.

"Well, that was quick," Dustsucker remarked, as his server set a pound of bacon, two eggs and a stack of toast before him. He looked over at Emma, his attention torn between a beautiful lady and an even more wonderful meal.

"No kidding," she said, though neither man was listening.

# Chapter 15

# FUMING AND ALL

"So, Emma. What's new with you?" Dustsucker's voice sounded like harp strings, picking and pulling melodically at thoughts just beginning to take shape in her brain. Emma's head turned slowly, from the Carson Street doorway through which Ronin had just left — much too quickly in her mind — to her other friend seated beside her, his hands anxiously hanging in the air, fork and knife hovering as if ready to eat a hearty breakfast.

"I'm sorry?" she said. Her mind was still busy with questions she had hoped to ask Ronin regarding his week-long stay in Virginia City. It hadn't been that long — she wasn't counting the days though it might have seemed that way at times, she wasn't sure — she had simply missed her man. When two people *love* each other, she thought, or even simply *like* each other, unless there's something wrong it seemed right that they'd speak about their comings and goings. More recently, Ronin's goings had far out-weighed his comings. He rarely shared any of either.

"I'm sorry, Dusty, I'm sitting here wondering what that was all about?"

"Well, me too ma'am, the way the two of you were fuming and all."

"We weren't fighting, Dusty, we were just talking. I only wanted to know what he was doing while he was away."

"It looked more like a union miner on pay day, Miss Emma, you hoping to get something out of someone who isn't

willing to give anything more than what he's already given ..."
Emma sat quietly, not reacting to the words she knew to be
true. "... if you don't mind me sayin', that is."

"I don't mind you saying at all," she said, patting
Dustsucker's hand, which had stopped hovering and now rested
on the table so as to get permission, a nod or something that
he should go ahead with his meal. "You take good care of me
deputy, when William isn't around, always asking how I'm doing and all." Dustsucker blushed.

"Well," Dustsucker said, cutting into his bacon and dipping it into the yellow part of his eggs, "that's exactly what I
was asking. How *are* you doing?"

Emma Nauman sat back in her chair, thinking that
maybe she would have another cup of coffee if the nice waiter
came by again. She looked at her friend, *Marcus T. Slade. I wonder what the 'T' stands for.* "I'm doing fine, though I'd be doing
better if I knew what William was up to in Virginia City. I so
worry about his safety, you know."

"We both do, Miss Emma, though I don't imagine these
last few days have been all that busy or dangerous. When Ronin
came into town last night he stopped by the sheriff's office to
give us an update on the two boys he'd been following, Timothy
Smith and Mort Spinnaker. It sounds like he may have figured
out where there living, which is good. Marshal Ash or Sheriff
Tom Kelly will be by to pick them up. Ronin was too wound up
to brace the two of them himself. Said he would likely kill them
just as easily as arrest them, not that we've given him a badge.
Last thing the marshal wants is more killing in these parts, and
someone with a badge killing them, well that's just not going
to be okay, not since Reno anyway."

"That's good," Emma said, moving her cup closer to the
edge of the table where the server could reach it. The server
began pouring until Emma signaled for him to stop. The coffee

looked dark. She stared ahead, aimlessly, as a subtle stream of steam floated up from the cup between the two of them.

"Miss Emma?"

*There he is plucking again.* She'd never noticed how musical Dustsucker's voice was before. "Yes, Marcus?"

"You seemed to be elsewhere for a moment."

She smiled. Marcus loved her hazel-colored eyes. She blinked a couple of times as she turned to listen to him.

"I'm sorry, Marcus. Where were we?" She paused for a moment before asking, "Maybe you can fill me in? A girl's got to nurture her curiosity, you know." Marcus laughed, a big happy, distracted laugh.

"Well, as I was saying, he located Smith and Spinnaker somewhere south of Virginia City. But when talking to Marshal Ash about it, the Marshal asked if Ronin wouldn't mind looking into a couple of fortune tellers up that way who were toadying up to a half-dozen or so rich men in the Washoe Club. I hear Tom Kelly might be somehow involved as well."

"Toadying, Marcus? I don't believe I know that word."

"Well, you know, ingratiating themselves, flattering the fat boys into thinking that maybe they ought to spend a little bit more time and a lot more money on their spells and jells to get ahead in business or something like that. Sounds like a couple of them might have found love, if you know what I mean." Slade was shaking his hands in the air, as if he were excited, except his fork and knife took away from his intended message. The women involved had fools as clients. "They're quacks if you ask me," he continued, "but then there's not a clergyman in town who isn't toadying to some extent to someone, if you don't mind me saying."

"I do, Dusty. A real man of God is above appealing to people's feelings. Self-serving flattery is unbecoming to a godly man or woman."

"Of course, ma'am. I'm just saying." He looked at the pile of bacon on his plate and wondered if Emma would mind his picking some of it up with his fingers. "I know Ronin looked around a bit, as a kind of favor to Ash and maybe to Kelly, and had a conversation with that Washoe seer woman ..."

"Eilley Bowers?"

"Yes, I believe that's her name, the woman who supposedly saw the Comstock's possibilities before anyone else did, or so the story goes."

"The owner of the mansion where the children were found ..."

"Yes, ma'am, though she hasn't owned the mansion in quite a while. Last I heard, Myron Lake did, though I don't know that he's held on to it either. The Bowers woman pointed him in the direction of a couple of girls on D Street."

"The Red Light District?"

"Well, I guess you could call it that, though I don't know it was her inference. Ronin said it was a two-room house in the general neighborhood of assorted working men and women, though I don't believe he's been by yet. This St. Charles thing might cause him to say hello, however."

"Oh, Lord."

"Ma'am?"

"Nothing." She shook her head. Just what she wanted to hear, that Ronin was cavorting with prostitutes on D Street. *God help him.* "And what about the smaller-sized man you were talking about earlier?" Emma asked, blowing gently across her cup as the coffee was still a little hot. She liked it that way, but a little cream would do. She caught the eye of their server.

"The midget?"

"Mister Slade, I don't believe we call them 'midgets' anymore, do we?"

Dustsucker stopped eating, his mouth hanging silently open. He raised his eyebrows. He didn't remember being addressed in that tone before. "No ma'am, I guess we don't."

"Well, what about him?" she continued.

"The little man's name ... that's okay, right?"

Emma nodded.

"Well, his name is Antonio, apparently, according to a telegraph from Marshal Ash this morning. I don't know his last name. He often goes by the name of Tony or Toro, sometimes Toro Latigo.'"

"And is he dangerous?"

"Ma'am, every man is dangerous, depending on what one is afraid of or isn't expecting. I'm not sure I understand your point."

"It's probably nothing, Dusty. I'm sorry for keeping you from your meal." She poured a little cream into her coffee. "It's just a feeling. I don't believe the other night will be the last time Mister Ronin meets the man. I'm hoping for a better outcome when that day comes."

"Ronin does, too," Dustsucker said, folding a piece of bacon into his mouth with his fingers before taking a sip from his coffee. "In fact, I know he's counting on it."

# Chapter 16
# JOURNAL, NOVEMBER 21, 1873

Ronin headed back to the Ormsby House, where his bedroll was still sitting open, laid out upon a modern mattress and bed. He much appreciated the Ormsby House's accommodations, and the bedding was as good as anything he had experienced in Philadelphia or Chicago. "A clean, quality cotton top, affixed to natural fiber innards," Dustsucker said when comparing Ronin's mattress to the one provided him by the widow Rogers on Mountain Street. The whole contraption, large enough for two —not that Ronin had tried to fit anyone in bed with him — sat upon a cloth-covered base made of springs.

While he'd only recently come to appreciate sleeping indoors — the freedom of sleeping outdoors provided good therapy to the stuffier years he had spent in the church acting one way when he much preferred another — a box-spring frame kept him up off the floor, which he thought he liked given that he was beginning to feel older. Indoors also meant fewer critters to deal with than sleeping outside, even by a fire.

"This thing with Emma ... I don't know what to do," he wrote in his journal, before setting it aside to consider whether he should take the train to Virginia City or get his horse from Benton's Livery. He sat back in a red velvet easy chair overlooking Carson Street and wondered if it would be better to have Jackson with him, given the likely back and forth between Gold

Hill and Virginia City. He paged through the brown leather-covered book that had been his friend over the last many years, and turned to entries he'd made in 1873, the year he had left the Episcopal Church, and began to read.

*It's the "We Never Sleep" that appeals to me, I think. Three months in, I'm continuing to appreciate the people and opportunities the Pinkerton Detective Agency offers.*

*I met a man today in the Chicago office who lost his business a couple of years ago. Joining the Agency, and being involved for only a couple of years, the old man has assigned him to work with the Philadelphia & Reading Railroad. The rail company has significant investments in coal and such in Schuykill County, Pennsylvania, east of where I went to school. Union activities are causing the owners some considerable anxiety as the company's profits are "not the least bit dependable," Gowen argues. Labor and coal costs fluctuate so much.*

*The detective, a man named Jim McParland, appears to be a good man despite having owned a store that sells alcohol. A Chicago fire took his business. I fear he may be similarly consumed by the drama of it all, though the old man doesn't expect things in Pennsylvania to last that long. He's got other goals for the agency, including opening more offices west of Chicago, positions and responsibilities I'd likely be interested in when the time comes.*

*I generally don't like to choose between people hurting each other — I don't always know who to shoot! Squirrels are one thing, you know, people another. It seems to me it's oftentimes a matter of shooting the worst of two bad guys, though few men in such situations are so clearly set apart by their actions as to make the terminal choice easy.*

*I much prefer my own work thus far, as over against those agents who are involved with the nation's railroads. Allan and his sons have me tracking down criminals who are a part of an amazing system of record-keeping. Allan's second son, Robert — William is thought to prefer the thrill of the chase, more about him later — seems* to have perfected a system that maintains detailed descriptions of the nation's worst criminals. The Pinkerton Agency has become a massive gathering point of criminal information, with detectives and other agents sending their information to Chicago. Law enforcement people all over the nation are depending on us.

These cards and folders — with newspaper stories and pictures clipped from everywhere, including sources overseas — contain much personal information. The records remain active until the criminal is captured or killed. Simply caught isn't adequate in the old man's mind, as so many men and women seem to make a life's calling of their deviant talents or demeanors.

Speaking of that, the Pinkertons believe that career criminals have a certain pattern to their work. If one studies an individual's history and habits long enough, there's no harbor where a person can hide. For some, for instance, it's a matter of habit. Others, it's the vocabulary they choose. (Bank and train robbers have a language all their own.) Often, it's the physical appearance of an individual that tells the Pinkerton detective that someone has spent time in prison or makes his or her livelihood conducting certain criminal pursuits. I met a man recently who had sanded off his finger prints. Some detectives maintain that these prints can identify a criminal or at least help detectives eliminate suspects. In any case, it seems to me that adult behavior is constant, certainly among ne're-do-wells. .

Will Jim McParland find such identifications among unionists in Pennsylvania? I can't imagine, as Pennsylvania coal miners — be they Irish, English or German — are among the hardest working people anywhere. Still, in my black and white world, the next few months will teach me a lot. I'm still learning the importance of shades of gray, though it will likely take a while given the narrow-rimmed glasses I wore as an Episcopal clergyman.

As an aside, it's my earliest impression that these men (there are a few women, as well) are advancing the methods and ethics of policemen everywhere. So many for so long have been so much a part of *the criminal element that some law enforcement officers are indistinguishable from the individuals they are asked to arrest or restraint. The Pinkertons are changing all of that.*

*The old man has a code of sorts: no bribes, no compromise, partnership with local law enforcement and others when necessary, no reward money — we're paid quite well — a set fee for our clients and ongoing communication with everyone concerned. Few Pinkertons will take a divorce case, or other matter that might bring shame to one of their clients. And most Pinkertons will eschew tobacco and alcohol, though I've seen some imbibe, if it is possible, in a gentlemanly sort of way.*

*Though I wouldn't want it touted about, what I appreciate most in my experience thus far is the Pinkertons' appreciation for my intellectual and intuitive skills. I'm giving to the Pinkerton Agency as much as I'm getting.*

Ronin pushed a pillow aside so as to lie down for a few moments and consider what he had written seven years earlier. "My intellectual and intuitive skills. I can trust my own feelings," he read quietly to himself. The constant war that he had been taught to observe as a Christian that was within him — "I do not do what I want, but I do the very thing that I hate ... nothing good dwells within me" — words that the earliest Christians appreciated and lived by were perhaps horribly misleading. *I can do what I need to do,* he thought to himself. *And what I want to do is often who I am.*

He put his head back on the pillows, piled high against his headboard, and smiled. *What I want, right now anyway, is freedom from this confusion with Emma.* He took a deep breath and turned over onto his side, thinking he would rest a bit before beginning to pack a few things for his next trip up the mountain. He would take Jackson along, as it would facilitate his getting back and forth from Virginia City. Maybe his friends would be less upset.

He didn't think himself to be that tired he thought as he laid his journal aside, but was surprised to find himself waking up a whole day later.

# Chapter 17

# THE WASHOE CLUB

---

The drama that had enveloped a few of the Washoe Club's members offered fresh entertainment to the rest of the club's businessmen and Virginia City elite. Not since the "Big Bonanza" in 1877, when a group of Irish immigrants outmaneuvered the Bank of California to push 14 million dollars of gold and 21 million dollars of silver out of the hills, had the club had so much to look at or talk about. Important Comstock finds and fellows had suffered greatly since then, leading some to say that the great adventure in the hills was now over, that the roar of the Comstock Lode was now dead, that gold and silver reigned no more. Still, when six of the Washoe Club's members — six men that folks knew about, who knew how many others might be involved? — found themselves in the influential, not to mention pretty, hands of two Comstock mediums, a new sort of public adventure was just beginning.

Father Patrick Manogue, one of the few who knew about the situation, felt that the people probably were getting what they deserved. "Cavorting with known necromancers" were his private words, which seemed so much more lascivious than "crystal ball gazers" or "scryers," though strictly speaking, no one was really speaking with the dead. They were simply looking into the futures of the living. Still, the fact that these young women lived on D Street — a Red Light district where reputations suffered because of working men and women, mostly women if you know what I mean — suggested that Virginia City's leading residents might have better protected their own by steering clear of the women in question.

"It's a travesty," Father Manogue said to one of the Sisters of Charity, who he expected would keep her mouth shut, given that the admission had been made in a very private moment in a St. Mary's confessional booth.

"Paddy" Manogue didn't exactly want to wade into the popular discussion of whether the dead could speak or whether one's future could be ascertained in certain other ways. But he wasn't against taking a firm hand to those who should have known better. The men in question were asked not to come to Mass until they had straightened things out.

After the initial laughter disappeared, the embarrassment remained. It didn't take long for the members of the Millionaires Club, as the Washoe Club was sometimes known, to wish the whole matter would simply blow away. When it became known that the esteemed police officer Thomas Kelly had somehow become involved though no one was clear to what extent, folks in the club began to feel better not worse. Having an officer of the law caught in the middle might make it easier for everyone to save themselves.

"Ellie May Livestock and her older sister, Alvira Fae, are twins," Kelly said, after sitting down in one of the front rooms upstairs. The club's windows looked out onto C Street where much of the city's commerce was conducted and controlled.

"Twins? I thought there was only one of them," one of the older members said, leaning forward in his chair so that the top of his head showed. Long devoid of hair except for a handful which remained so that he'd have something to pull at should he get more worried than he clearly already was, he began tugging. "There are two?"

Kelly addressed the oldest of the group, a man in his sixties who had been chosen to speak to the former police chief now Virginia City sheriff because most of his business interests were out of town. He didn't give his name as he didn't want it remembered. "Yes, there are two," Kelly said, sighing because of his own personal involvement, a situation he couldn't hardly begin to make sense of, though there had been no real transgressions on his part.

"The one works while the other is sleeping, that's my guess," he said, looking at the six men of similar age gathered in front of him. "I imagine it's possible that one of you might have met both of them at some point together." The inference was clear, as sexual dalliances among some of the club's members were well known though not often talked about.

The men stuttered their continued innocence. "Mister Kelly, I am an old man," the group's spokesman said, pulling at the lapels of his vest while patting the top of his head and smiling, "and while I'll confess to some understanding of the drama of human relationships — I've been married, I've been divorced and I've been married again — I'm not sure that I understand or like your inference." The others nodded, looking at each other as if one of them had been accused of stealing or worse.

"I'm just saying, sir, that there are *two* women that have cozied up with some of your members," Kelly continued, "the six of you having been mentioned privately to me. And while I don't have any real jurisdiction in these matters ..."

The group exploded in protestations. "Well, I never ..." one said. "So this is why you've asked the six of us to meet you here," said another. Kelly hung his head. *A rich man's pride is a poor man's pain.* He looked onto the street below where the morning's activities were just beginning to show families on their way to breakfast, business and school. These were men who didn't understand that being men didn't entitle them to hurt others, intimates or otherwise. He took a deep breath and began again.

"Gentleman, I came here this morning to tell you that I'm in something of the same predicament, though I believe if the truth were found out, my reputation would remain as it is. Still, given my wife's death, I'd prefer for my consultations with these women to remain private. The men nodded, some of them expressing condolences that might have been better said at the time of her memorial Mass. "I'm saying you'll have my help in this matter, as much as it bothers me to give special considerations."

He looked at them sternly. "I have taken it upon myself to employ a certain detective, a former Pinkerton Detective, to look into this matter and to deliver us all, if it is at all possible, for the sake of kingdom to come."

The group's spokesman turned to face his compatriots. The men spoke quietly for a few moments and then nodded. The spokesman turned. A small tear showed itself in the corner of his left eye. "Mister Kelly, Sheriff Kelly if I may, we are most appreciative of your efforts on our behalf. If you would let us know the man's name, we would be happy to write a draft of say ..." he turned to his friends who nodded affirmatively though no amount had yet been mentioned... "one thousand dollars to aid in this investigation." The man straightened, his round belly wedging him firmly into a leather club chair. He waited for an answer. When none came, he said, "It's a travesty you know, these men being mentioned alongside these women. I hope you'll be able to attend to this situation quickly."

Kelly exhaled. It all seemed so dirty and sad. His own involvement had been to simply ask about his wife's disposition after her death. Was she happy? Could she see that he missed her? Was there wisdom she might lend to his living his life without the love of his life? "The man's name is Ronin, gentlemen, W. W. Ronin. I'll send for him, if you like." The men showed no recognition of Ronin's history in Virginia City, which included the killing of two angry cowboys at the Bucket of Blood saloon the year before.

"Indeed. W. W. Ronin. And what do the Ws stand for, Sheriff Kelly?"

"William Washington, I believe."

"English, then."

"I have no idea," Kelly said, shaking his head.

# Chapter 18

# GOOD MORNING

W. W. Ronin stood up with a start, his drawers falling to his knees before he could catch them and pull them back into position. He couldn't believe he had missed a whole day of his life. It was the sharp rapping on the door of his room that had stirred him from his dreams, a dark place where swarthy men and women were pulling at him, trying to make him do what he didn't want to do.

The impact of the knocking pushed at the room's door so that its ornate wooden frame and lock rattled noisily. "I'm coming!" he shouted, hoping to silence the banging that had awakened him and was now contributing to the pain and throbbing on both sides of his head. He grabbed the beaded brass oval-shaped door knob and paused. "Dusty, is that you?" He placed one hand and foot against the door so that it couldn't be pushed open. His other hand pulled the shorter of his Colt firearms from a holster draped over the footboard of his bed.

"No kidding. You don't recognize my knock?" his big friend said, stopping long enough for Ronin to replace his gun, run both hands through his hair and look for his hat. He couldn't believe he had slept an entire day and night without stirring. He grabbed at his pants hanging from the back of the flowered easy chair he had pushed over by the window so that he could gaze out toward the capitol buildings. First his right leg then his left, he pulled the braces up over a hastily-buttoned blue denim shirt Emma had brought him at breakfast. He had slept in it.

"Stop your goddamned noise," he yelled, spying his hat on the dresser across the room. Stumbling over his boots, he suddenly wondered exactly when it was that he began cursing so. "Put off all of these," the Bible said, "anger, wrath, malice, blasphemy, filthy communication." He had failed miserably. His ministerial years had been more restrained, not that his mouth didn't occasionally let go of a string of well-shaped expletives when they were particularly deserved.

For instance, when he had heard that the famed pistolero Wyatt Earp had been cut from his position as a Wichita city policeman after beating up a candidate for county marshal, he was in Chicago at the time meeting with Allan Pinkerton. He jotted Earp a note, remembering him from the St. John's parish. Ronin didn't care for the politics involved, or Earp's background as a habitual gadabout and gambler. Still, he appreciated Earp's pugilistic skills. Pinkerton simply looked up and smiled when Ronin began a string of not-so-carefully chosen words. "Enough is enough," the old man said. And Ronin, a new agent with the Pinkerton Detective Agency, quickly complied.

"This isn't a whorehouse," he hollered from the dresser, where he was putting on his hat. Guilt-struck, as if he had been shot through the second-story window, he wondered if there were women with his friend. They'd probably heard every word. He grabbed his head as a second series of stabbing pains began. "Jesus," he muttered, sitting down to grab his boots and socks.

"A whorehouse?" Dustsucker bellowed through the door. "Thank God it's not," he said, laughing, "It's the middle of the morning, time for them girls to get some sleep, and time for you to get up, my pretty!"

"Give me a minute, would you?" he barked. Ronin gazed around the room for a clock before sitting back down in the chair, crossing his legs and rolling a pair of socks into the shape of a donut so that he could unroll them onto his left leg.

He remembered breakfast with Emma. Things hadn't gone well. Emma was pressing him again and there was something else, though he couldn't remember what, that was bothering him about their conversation. And then his friend Dustsucker joined them all happy and such, talking about a poker game and a death of a Virginia City man at the St. Charles. Given the way the deceased had been spending money, someone said suggested that maybe he was a member of the Washoe Club.

Dustsucker rapped again. "You up, cowboy? I've got places to go other than to stand outside your hotel room, you know!"

"Jesus," Ronin exclaimed, "I'm almost dressed. Give me a second, would you?" And now a full day had elapsed since the man's death. "Was it a murder?" he yelled through the closed door.

"Was what a murder?

"The man at the St. Charles Hotel!"

"Well open up, that's what I want to talk to you about."

Ronin turned the inside key and opened the door. Deputy Marcus T. Slade stood there in all of his morning glory, a piece of pancake sitting on his chest just underneath his chin. "Dusty," Ronin greeted him. "How long have I been asleep?"

"I have no idea," Dustsucker said, using his sleeve to wipe his lips. "I haven't seen you since yesterday. I was downstairs eating breakfast when a boy from the telegraph office came by looking for you. I told him you had gone up to Virginia City, which is what I thought I remembered you saying when you got up from the table."

"You remember correctly, my friend."

"Well, your friend Goodwin was at the desk and he remarked that he thought you were upstairs sleeping. Someone had been by earlier with fresh towels ..."

"… and knocked on my door," Ronin said, completing the sentence.

"Exactly."

"Well, that explains the swarthy men and women wanting me to get up."

"The what?"

"Not important," he said, smiling. "Let me see the telegram." He pushed the door open, leaned a flat iron against it and motioned that his friend should come in. He took the message over to the window and sat down. It was from Tom Kelly. He read it aloud:

"Come to Virginia City at once. Washoe Club wants meeting. Your friend, Tom."

"Really?" Dustsucker said. "I thought you weren't welcome there."

"I guess it depends. Tell me about the man at the St. Charles Hotel, Dusty. Anything yet?"

"Just that the sheriff has confirmed the dead man was from Virginia City. Apparently he was a wealthy businessman, just as you thought."

"His name?"

"Alvin Hornbeck."

"Horney Hornbecker?" Ronin asked, his eyes brows raised.

"Yup."

"Well, I'll be damned."

# Chapter 19
# TWINS

"Alvin was a good man, sheriff. A church-going man, I believe, though I'm not sure why you're asking."

"I'm simply hoping to get a better handle on what's going on, Ellie May." Tom Kelly had hoped to hear from Ronin sooner, but when Alvin Hornbecker's death became known in Virginia City he jumped at the opportunity to interview the twins. "Look, I'm sure sooner or later, one of the city detectives will be heading your way. A secret doesn't stay a secret forever. And while others at the Washoe Club are only waking up to the thought that you and your sister may be involved with *others* in the club, I know because Alvin told me you *were* involved with *him*."

"Sheriff, he was a wonderful and giving man. If either of us had feelings beyond our professional services as mediums and confidants, I wouldn't know about it," Ellie May said. A small, attractive, slender woman in her thirties with dark brown hair, Kelly always thought it was odd that the sisters had located their parlor on D Street among working folks and whores.

"You wouldn't know about *his* being involved with *you*?" Kelly said, smiling.

"I didn't mean to say it that way," the Virginia City scryer said.

"No, of course not, and his having quite a reputation for being a lady's man is not something you're aware of either, is it?"

"Of course not," she said, pulling at her jacket collar so that her blouse, a beautiful red chemise lacy thing, was adequately covered and closed.

"So you're saying, Miss Livestock, that even as a medium and confidant skilled at knowing things about the future," he wiggled his voice as if testifying in front of a jury or preaching from a country pulpit, "having parted many a cloud for many a client," he continued feeling quite pleased with the effect, "you wouldn't know anything about that?"

Ellie May Livestock smiled. She and her identical twin sister, Alvira Fae, knew a great many things about people on the Comstock. But their lips were generally sealed. Like a Catholic priest with a mouthful of secrets fresh from the confessional booth, there had to be some compelling reason to reveal what a client said, particularly a good customer like Alvin Hornbecker.

"A promoter of everything that is good or wonderful," Hornbecker liked to say when describing himself. The otherwise handsome man in his thirties could be a real huckster when it came to spending time with one or both of them. "It will cost you twice as much, Horney," the sisters would remind him. Not an unlikeable man, Horney always had a pocketful of cash, and stories of an angle or scam, mining stocks or shares in a local business.

"Mister Kelly, you and I have spent some time together after your wife Winnie's death. And I was happy to tell you what I could about her eternal resting place." She folded her hands and looked up toward the ceiling. The D Street house had no second story and from her living room she could not see the sky.

"Oh, please ..." Kelly interrupted.

"I'm only saying that you know I'm an honorable woman, as is my sister. If you are insinuating that I'm operating a brothel instead of a haven of..." she paused, "...heavenly wisdom, I don't know what to say. And to be frank, I didn't see it coming."

"No, I don't imagine you did," Kelly said, laughing. "Look, here's my bottom line. I'm aware that you are cohabitating with a half-dozen members of the Washoe Club, my dears and I say that to include your sister, who is no doubt listening from the bedroom. While others may not know that there are two of you, or that you're huckstering earthly delights along with your so-called spiritual pearls of wisdom, I do. And I shall not remain silent about it."

Ellie May smiled, a single gold tooth gleaming in her otherwise perfect smile. She looked down at her hands, folded as if posed on top of a well-worn, brown King James Bible. She moved her fingers into the shape of a steeple and seemed to think for a moment, pausing long enough that Kelly — former Virginia City police chief, Storey County sheriff and a someday a U.S. marshal, some folks said — thought he heard someone in the back room just as he suspected he would. "Ma'am?" he said.

"Give me a moment, Tom. How shall I say this?" She tapped her thumbs together, then opened them like church doors so that she could see inside, her fingers wiggling. The popular nursery rhyme ran through her head — *Here is the church. Here is the steeple. Open the doors and see all the people.* She gathered her thoughts and then looked up.

"Tom, I don't know that you want to do that, running our names down, I mean, as if we were common women." Her eyes grew wide and intense before they grew dark and squinted. "Some people might get hurt."

"Really?" Kelly said. A former *two-term* city police chief in Nevada's, arguably, toughest city, he had been threatened by smarter folks and better.

"Really," she said, her sister peering through the curtain that separated their D Street sitting room from their boudoir. He looked over. Alvira Fae's grin was perfect and unnerving.

# Chapter 20

# THE LATE ALVIN HORNBECKER

---

Ronin didn't know Alvin Hornbecker personally, but as a single man who was regularly in and out of Nevada's bars and cat houses looking for wanted men, he had heard his name mentioned. "Horney," as he was known by his friends rich and poor, was a man who liked his card games slow and his women fast, which made the incident at the St. Charles Hotel all the more bizarre.

"Wow," Ronin said, grabbing his coat and pulling his door closed behind him. "I always wanted to meet that man." He looked down the long hallway before moving toward the Ormsby House steps. "I never figured it would be after he was dead. Did he die of syphilis or gonorrhea?" he said, grinning.

"What's the difference?" Dustsucker asked, slow to realize that Ronin was teasing. "It's not funny."

"Not funny? Really? Okay, how about this: Did he die with one woman in the room or two?"

"Ronin, I'm serious. The man was well thought of in business circles. I don't guess that his death is any laughing matter to the St. Charles Hotel or to his family."

"God save his family," he replied, shaking his head. As a clergyman, he had less concern for how folks were living their lives than most priests and preachers thought he should. People did what people did, and most people did a great many things they didn't want their preacher to know about. In recent years his attitude had changed.

"Catch 'em now or catch 'em later," the older of the two Pinkerton sons used to say. "Everyone sins," Ronin would respond, though he wasn't sure William understood the reference. Son of the Pinkerton Detective Agency's founder, William had as a 16 year-old boy worked the streets of the nation's capital during the War Between the States. His boyish face and demeanor enabled him to wander nearly anywhere unobserved. In time, William Pinkerton had a peculiar way of looking at people, particularly Southern sympathizers, "right through them," some of the detectives said. Though their politics were different, Ronin thought some of William's skill and attitudes had rubbed off. The older boy had been his first mentor in the Pinkerton Agency.

"Look. Hornbecker was a cad. I don't know what he did with his money or his mines — or his mother, for that matter. But he was popular enough with the ladies that even I heard about it. To be frank, his wife notwithstanding, I don't know that he cared where he parked his paraphernalia."

"Really, Ronin? That's how you're going to speak about the dead?" Dustsucker hadn't grown up religious, though the Roman Catholic Church had cast a heavy shadow in Iowa in those early years, the first Mass being said in that state in 1833 by a priest out of Illinois. But he understood the term "respect." Living or dead, good or bad, thin or fat for that matter, he didn't like to make fun of folks. "You don't mind me hearing you talk this way?" he asked.

Ronin ran his hands over a new brown tweed frock coat he had ordered from a northeastern clothier. The jacket was well suited for wearing about town, where the presence of his handguns was sometimes pointed to and depreciated. The coat looked good with striped tan trousers and a club collar shirt. The only shirt he had brought with him was the blue denim shirt he was wearing and had already slept in. "It's the rage," Emma said at breakfast the day before, noting that the same heavy cotton material, but with the rivets, was being worn by workmen everywhere. "And it hardly ever needs to be washed," she said.

"I've noticed it among miners," he replied, his comment immediately being misunderstood by Emma as negative and unappreciative. He'd seen the distinctive cloth in pants and overalls. He'd never seen denim used in a shirt before. He wasn't sure it was toney enough.

"My head's spinning, Dusty. Please excuse my attempts at humor. I'm sure Horney Hornbecker was a fine man," he said, brushing the wrinkles out of his pants as they walked down the steps and into the Ormsby House lobby.

"Mister Ronin," Victor Goodwin shouted from behind the desk — his voice, bald head and hooked nose towered over everyone in the room. "You've got a second telegram this morning, Mister Ronin. Do you wish it now?" he asked. Ronin nodded, taking it from his hands.

"Eaten yet?" he asked Dustsucker, before remembering his friend had been in the middle of breakfast when he came knocking on his door. Dustsucker looked at him. Ronin shifted his weight to one leg and leaned up against the front desk. He glanced twice at Goodwin suggesting that the telegram was perhaps private and that he should step back.

"Tom Kelly, again," he said to his friend. He raised his eyebrows. "'Come quickly,' it says. Dusty, what would make a man like Tom Kelly send me two telegrams in one day, both of them asking me to get to Virginia City as quickly as possible?"

Dustsucker sat down at a table to the right of the front desk, lifted his fork and began picking at food he had left on his plate. "I don't know, Ronin. Maybe he misses your particular brand of humor."

Ronin let his arms drop to his waist, his elbows up against his guns hidden by his coat. The telegram was still in his hands. "Dusty, I'm sorry if I offended you," he said. "It seems like I'm bothering everyone right now." The dark, swarthy men and women in his dreams came immediately to mind. "But I can only be who I am my friend. And right now ..." he waited until Dustsucker looked up "... I'm a man on the way to Virginia City. You want to come?"

Dustsucker shook his head, then looked back at his plate, reaching for a piece of rye toast. He pushed a small pile of cold eggs onto it before placing it carefully into his mouth. He chewed for a moment, looking across the restaurant. The tables were full. A bright, sunny day showed through the windows. The street looked busy. He looked up. "Might join you later. Got people I need to see today. Okay?"

Ronin nodded and headed out the door on his way to the bank. He would need some new clothes when he got to Virginia City. Something nice, he figured. Tom Kelly was waiting, and there were some important women and men waiting for him there, too.

# Chapter 21
# TORO LATIGO

"Look, maybe you have work for me, maybe you don't," the small man with a whip said, standing outside Ellie May and Alvira Fae Livestock's residence on D Street. "I don't care, but don't talk to me like I'm some sort of freak." Antonio Latigo, or "Toro" as he was sometimes known, had left the Bucket of Blood saloon in a huff when a tall stranger from Carson City had taken exception to his singing. Sensing trouble, and not wanting to be pursued by the saloon owner or the U. S. marshal — both men having witnessed the whipping he had given the stranger — Latigo had slipped out onto the street, leaving his wagon behind, and disappeared into the usual press of people at lunch time in Virginia City. He was knocking on the twins' door in the midst of a series of business calls before picking up his wagon and heading back to Wells, Nevada, the place he called home.

"We've got nothing, Mister Latigo. That is your name, right? I meant no disrespect by my laughter, but unless you've got a fortune that needs telling, we don't have goods or money to give you, that's how tight things are."

"Your laughter is painful, but so is my whip," he said, placing his hand on the plaited leather bullwhip handle at the end of a six-foot coil wrapped around his neck. The dark brown leather seemed well-used and well-oiled, signaling it was a much appreciated tool. Small pieces of bone were attached to one end, where strips of leather promised pain. Ellie May winced.

"Mister Latigo, perhaps there is something we *can* offer you before your lengthy trip back."

Latigo had explained that while he hadn't been born in Nevada, he was "as western as any sage rat or other desert beast." He'd arrived in Humboldt Wells, as Wells used to be called, before the Central Pacific Railroad constructed a water tower and box car, interrupting the stream of Shoshone, mountain men and wagon trains that had enjoyed the bubbling brook as long as anyone could remember. And while he hadn't traveled the high desert trail to California like other pioneers — when hundreds of thousands of people during the 1840s and 1850s had followed "the elephant" to Sutters Mill and other gold-rich California environs — he made good use of it now as a trader, plying his wares across 300 miles of rabbit weed and sage brush each month. He preferred horse and wagon to the relative speed and ease of travel that the railroad offered. And how could he carry his wares with him, he asked, if he was on a train?

The twins weren't interested in buying anything, they'd explained, which was fortunate given that his wagon was still tied to a post on C Street outside the Bucket of Blood Saloon. Virginia City offered as fine a shopping experience, thank you, as Sacramento or San Francisco.

"You'll not insult me with such nonsense," he said, his voice sounding shrill and childish. "Look at you!" he screamed. "You clearly have means. You're dressed as nice as any bawdy girl on D Street. You have money," he said, looking around the house nervously. "You should buy something!"

"Mister Latigo, if that is your name! We are seers, mediums, crystal ball gazers ..." none of the words seem to be understood. "We tell people's futures, Mister Latigo."

"You are gypsies, then?" he asked.

"We are not gypsies! This house is not a Barbary Coast dive. It is not a crib. Nor am I a common sporting girl. You are insulting me," Ellie May said, aware that her sister had retrieved the heavy revolver from the table beside their bed and had it pointed toward the little man's head. "Alvira Fae?" she shouted. Her sister parted the curtains, grinning. She walked forward until she stood beside her sister, who was pointing an old Colt Paterson revolver at their unwelcome guest. Five .36 caliber lead balls to further make their point.

Alvira steadied her finger on the trigger, the hammer at full-cock, the handgun sitting in her left palm, ready to rumble. Ellie May had argued that compared to newer Colt revolvers the early Paterson model was unsafe and difficult to operate. Alvira had responded that she was comfortable with how it sat in her hand. "There is artistry to holding a gun," she said, picking it up with her right hand. "It points well." Toro Latigo was clearly not happy.

"Now as I said, sir," Ellie May continued, "there is something that we may be able to offer you before you head back to your deserted, little hole-in-the-ground rest stop, and I mean *all* the disrespect that I can muster when I say that. But you'll have to calm down for us to talk about it."

Toro Latigo, "Tony" to his friends, the name "Antonio" spilling from his father's lips when he left Salt Lake City so as to discover the West when Nevada was just becoming a state, stood shaking at the door to their front room. "Ma'am, I will not have a gun pointed toward me, if you don't mind," he said, fingering the heavily braided knob at the end of the whip's handle. "I don't want to hurt anyone."

The girls held their gaze.

"I simply want to do some business before heading back to my home. This being my first time in Virginia City, I feel unwelcome and am unimpressed." He thought of his home behind the Bulls Head Saloon, the first permanent building in Wells, built from discarded railroad ties he had hauled to the building site himself. He remembered the other teamsters, rail-roaders and cowboys who were his friends. He waited for their response.

Alvira Fae looked at her sister, who had begun wiggling the gold cap from her front teeth until it sat in the palm of her right hand. "Mister Latigo," Ellie May said, looking down at the man who was now seated at her table, in the very same chair that the 9 year-old boy next door had sat in that morning so as to get a warm breakfast cereal before school. "I believe I have a business proposition for you."

"Really?" Toro Latigo said, wiggling like a child who had heard there were presents to be had under the Christmas tree. "How may I be of service?" he giggled, looking at the gold cap. A perfectly normal tooth sat in Ellie May's mouth where a gleaming gold tooth had been moments before.

"It is your service that we'd like to purchase, sir." Her sister nodded, as they were agreed. "A certain young man, perhaps two young men, need to be taught a lesson at the end of your whip, sir, or any other tool you may be carrying. I'm wondering if you're …"

"… willing?" Latigo interrupted, smiling. "I am," he laughed, "always willing."

# Chapter 22

# CHARITY SUPPER

Timothy Edwards Smith wasn't adverse to helping out at the fundraising supper being held by the Daughters of Charity. He had simply hoped for something better, something more intimate where the two of them — his roommate, Mort Spinnaker, more recently a deputy sheriff in Carson City and he — could set aside their more immediate concerns to make plans that might last the rest of their lives.

"We'll not always live on the Comstock," Smith had said at breakfast earlier that morning, Spinnaker having noticed that the run-down residence they were staying in had begun to attract the attention and curiosity of Gold Hill folk looking for a cheaper place to stay. "We might choose to open a bookstore in San Francisco," Smith continued, oblivious to his partner's concerns but attempting to pander to Spinnaker's fondness for books and learning. "Or Philadelphia even," he added, trying to get his friend to look up from the wobbly three-legged table where Smith had just carefully set two perfectly boiled eggs and a stack of buttered sour dough toast.

Born and raised in Palmyra, New York, Timothy Edwards Smith didn't yet understand that he was wanted in Philadelphia by the Pinkertons, America's premiere detective and law enforcement agency. He hadn't written his mother in years. Had he, he might have learned that Benjamin Franklin himself — not the colonial statesman and philosopher, but an equally driven individual named after him, the superintendent of the Pinkerton's Philadelphia office — had already spoken to his mother about his whereabouts.

"I don't know where he is," his mother had said, surprised that he was wanted for the murder of two Washoe Indian men at Lake Tahoe. "I didn't think he liked water," she said, holding out hope that he'd return to the east coast when his west coast ways wore out. "The only people getting rich on gold," she once told her son, a good Catholic when he hired onto a wagon train full of Presbyterians heading to Sacramento, "are people looking to sell ideas to idiots." She had, and her parents before that, made her money in merchandising clothes and equipment to working men. "But Tim chose to be a working man himself," she said. "He wanted to be a well digger of all things. And now, he's finding out he can't be a gold digger, either," she told the Pinkerton detective who said he'd received a "Be On The Lookout" alert, or BOLO, implicating her son in the murder of the Washoe Indian men earlier that morning. The Pinkerton Agency had sent a handbill to detectives and lawmen everywhere. "He can't be much of a Christian now," she said, shaking her head. "Not if he's killing Indians."

"Ma'am?" Franklin asked, making sure that he understood.

"I mean, he wasn't raised to hurt people, Mister Franklin. He was raised to take their money."

"Of course," the Pinkerton man replied. A Christian man himself, the Pinkerton detective nodded.

Spinnaker looked up and smiled. "There was no way we could stay at the party, you know. I thought you understood that."

"Of course," Smith said, "I'm just saying." He washed his hands with soap from a chipped blue enamel dish pan, dried them on his pants and sat down.

Smith and Spinnaker had set out to go to the supper, when they heard that it was a Ladies Fair and not just

a simple meal. The event was the result of careful planning by the sisters, a Virginia City religious community that had merged with the French-based Daughters of Charity, founded by Vincent de Paul and Louise de Marillac in 1633. It was a part of a much larger series of charity events held by the Daughters of Charity throughout the West, where success depended on the number and status of the women involved. In Virginia City, a serious effort had been made to include the most successful mine owners and managers, as well as local politicians.

"What the hell have you gotten us into?" Spinnaker said when he spotted certain well-known citizens among the fair's attendees. "That's Fair and Mackay in the corner with their wives, and William Sharon from the Bank of California standing by the punch bowl. We don't want to be here," he said, shaking his head and ducking from sight. But Timothy Edwards Smith, an enthusiastic young man with his own mind despite the sometimes controlling influence of others, was already moving among the tables of crafts and other wares the Virginia City elite had assembled for the event. He particularly liked the more colorful tables showing clothes and blankets.

The order's sixteen sisters were a fund-raising machine, hoping to secure enough cash to care for more than 400 boarders, orphans and day students in their school and orphanage. Donations were also needed to operate the Saint Mary Louise Hospital, which provided medical care and convalescence for 60 or more individuals. The need was great and well-understood, evidenced by town's attendance. The place was packed.

"I thought it would be helpful," Smith said, reminding Spinnaker that it had been a couple of days since the event, that nothing negative had come from their being there and that he didn't understand why his partner was still so unhappy.

"Look. I like being with you. I don't know that I like being with you as much as you like being with me," Spinnaker said, "but being out in public at this point is a big-ass mistake."

Smith pulled a chair from the table where they were eating over to the window that looked up toward American Flat. He pushed at his hair, which had fallen down to cover his right eye. He didn't like conflict, and particularly didn't like arguments with his friend, who thus far had been the first man in his life who didn't hit him regularly. "Mort, I want to spend the rest of my life with you, in whatever way you're comfortable," Timothy Edwards Smith said, folding his hands together. He sat silently by the window for a moment, rocking and thinking of what their life together could be like and what was necessary for them to be safe and happy. "So," he said, motioning toward the hills, "if we can't do that, going here or there, or can't spend time in Virginia City, Dayton or what have you, maybe it's time for us to make another big-ass mistake."

Spinnaker was silent. "Like what?" he asked. While he wasn't sure what it would feel like to live with a man, he was certain it wouldn't feel any better to live with a woman, so why not stay with the one you're with? They were comfortable enough together.

"Like killing us a lawman," Smith said, tentatively, "and maybe a certain mean-spirited ex-preacher, too."

An owl blew its morning greeting through the window Smith was gazing through as Spinnaker's chair creaked a morning hello. He put his hands on his seat and sat on them.

"You think that would help?" he asked, remembering the encounters he had had with the former Reverend W. W. Ronin when he had been an Ormsby County deputy. Ronin hadn't been kind to him. It *was* true. There would be no rest from their running until Ronin was dead.

"I don't think it would hurt," Smith said. "We'd have to leave the Comstock, of course, maybe head to Hangtown or Sacramento," he mused. "You'd like Sacramento, Mort. If the Nevada marshal and sheriffs can't find us, and Ronin is no longer looking, I don't see why we can't make our lives literally sing in a modern American city." Smith wondered if Sacramento had a symphony or a chorus.

"Sacramento isn't bad," Spinnaker said. "I went to the library there once. There are plenty of schools there, too."

"Exactly."

"Then I think it's something you and I should think about," Spinnaker said, "as soon as I get back from talking to Paddy Manogue."

"The priest? Why would you want to see the priest, Mort?"

"To give a donation, of course. And to ask for God's blessing."

# Chapter 23
# KOPPEL AND PLATT'S

"I'm thinking I need something blue or maybe even black," Ronin said to one of the owners at Koppel and Platt's clothing store, a few stores down from the Ormsby House, next to John Fox's bookstore on Carson Street. "Say, why are you people always Jewish?" Having never shopped in Carson City for anything other than a saddle repair, Koppel and Platt's store at Third and Carson Streets carried an "immense stock of clothing and furnishing goods," or so the ad said in that morning's *Alpine Miner News*, a newspaper from Monitor, California, the only paper he could find at breakfast.

"Excuse me?" Joseph Platt said. "I'm not sure I understood your question." Koppel and Platt had been retailers in the capitol city as long as anyone could remember. And while many of town's merchants were Jewish — Platt, a trustee of the new Carson Lodge, the Independent Order of B'nai B'rith — the question of his religion hadn't been asked in a long, long time.

"Jewish," Ronin said, "as in followers of Abraham, Moses and so on."

"My good man," Joseph Platt replied, "I can assure you we do not follow any man named Abraham or Moses. We are followers of the One True God, the God of Israel, the *God* of Abraham and Moses. Why do you ask?" Platt pulled at a tape measure he had placed around Ronin's waist. "Sir, I really need to ask again, isn't it possible for you to take off your gun belt for this? Or should we simply try on a few pairs of slacks?"

Ronin looked toward the window, where an attractive display of dress coats and pants framed the doorway. He'd generally ignored the capitol city's Jewish populations, the B'nai B'rith lodge he had been told only numbered a dozen or two individuals and did not include a rabbi. "No," he said after some consideration, "if I'm going to spend money on an additional pair of pants, I'd like them to fit just right." His last pair had been given to him by Emma Nauman, who he was surprised to learn had significant sewing skills and had applied them to a striped tan cloth of unknown fiber that went well with his brown frock coat. The few months he stayed at the American Gospel Mission just south of the city, he had not seen her use a sewing machine, despite the classes that were offered to the school's Washoe, Paiute and Shoshone students. "I did them by hand," she said when he expressed surprise. "They'll go nicely with your new coat. The color is a nice contrast to your hair and eyes." Ronin couldn't get past his feelings of surprise to sufficiently express his gratitude. And they were, by his reckoning anyway, a little large. He was hoping that Platt or his partner had the skill and time to take them in a bit.

"I know you want them right," Platt said, looking for his tin of straight pins. "You did say you wanted these today, right?"

"Yes," Ronin replied, wondering if was being too curious in asking the question. He'd been surprised to discover there was a Hebrew cemetery in Carson City and, when inquiring about Platt and Koppel's business, had discovered that Platt was a trustee of the benevolent society that owned it. Concluding that Platt was an honest man who had been in Nevada since the beginning of the gold and silver rushes, Ronin regarded the morning advertisement as more likely true than false. He'd not intended to suggest anything untowardly.

"Sir, if you refuse to let me measure you correctly — I need a waist, hip and inseam measurement and, to be frank, it would be helpful if I could measure your thighs as well — the pants are not going to fit nearly as good as you seem to want them too."

Ronin grimaced. "You're not going to measure my thigh, Mister Platt. It's just not ... not ..."

"Manly?" Platt suggested, finishing his sentence. "For a hotel guest, you sure seem to have some odd prejudices, sir." Platt eyed the bounty hunter intently. "Have we met before? Melvina and I pretty much know everybody in town?"

"We have not, Mister Platt, or may I call you Joseph?"

"You can call me anything you like, sir, but if you're not going to let me measure you so that I can make a few adjustments while you wait, you might as well buy a pair of slacks off the rack and call me helpful. I have a nice variety set out and a few more pants in the back."

"I didn't mean to suggest anything inappropriate," Ronin replied, looking over toward the door again. "I was an Episcopal priest for a few years in Kansas, Joseph. So I'm curious about your religious affiliation."

"So you were," Platt said, tugging at the tongue of Ronin's gun belt, hoping to slip the black leather belt and holsters onto the stool beside him so as to measure more exactly.

"Let me get those," Ronin said, removing his guns from his holsters and letting his hands and guns drape down to his sides.

"You'll need to stand evenly," the store owner continued, trying to get an inseam measurement on both legs. "Everybody's legs are a different length, sir. I wouldn't want you to leave here with one pant leg shorter than another, unless it's absolutely correct." Ronin winced as if he was in pain. He hated standing there with another man touching him.

"Is it possible that you might set your guns aside, sir? I don't measure many men holding two handguns. I'm afraid it will throw off my measurements."

Ronin turned to gaze at the pile of pants, hanging upside down on the turnstiles by the front door, when he saw Emma Nauman peering through the front window. Emma smiled, raising two gloved fingers on her right hand to say hello. She paused, as if deciding to come in. He stepped down off the mirrored platform to place his guns on the tall wooden stool to the side of the mirror where Platt was working. "Joseph, if you'd allow me a minute, please."

"But of course, sir."

He walked to the front door, touching a charcoal gray pair of woolen pants, set in the window as part of a display labeled "A Well Dressed Gentleman Always Wears Wool." He remembered the feel of the clerical shirt and cassock he wore as an Episcopal priest, particularly when celebrating Mass. Episcopal Church ordinances insisted that the priest wear "suitable clerical clothing," according to the norms and customs of the city or parish. He'd not observed anyone dressing similarly in Wichita, except for the Roman Catholic priests, who even when chopping wood understood their clothing habits to be a reflection of their spiritual obedience. It was nice now to not have to bother with such things. He pushed the double doors open the door to greet his friend.

"Emma! How are you?" he asked, pulling his braces back up over his blue shirt. Pratt had asked that he loosen his suspenders so as to see where his pants "sat naturally." The man's prattle was unending. "I've been thinking of you," he said, immediately wishing he'd chosen other words. It was not his desire to mislead the woman. He had hoped to clarify his intentions before Dustsucker interrupted their breakfast. "I mean, you've been on my mind."

"And you on mine, William," Emma said, adjusting the waist of her dress, moving her sun shade from one side to the other. She looked beautiful, as always, particularly when wearing a hoop and skirt. The delicate lavender lace gloves and umbrella made her dress sparkle even more.

"Where are you headed?" he asked.

"The question is where are *you* headed, William? I don't know that I've ever seen you in a clothing store before."

"No," he responded, looking back at Platt, who was trying not to listen. Ronin noticed his guns unattended on the tailor's stool. He couldn't remember ever leaving them like that before. "I'm headed to Virginia City, of course, to continue Kelly's investigation. It seemed good to take along some extra clothes, so as to blend in," he replied, wondering if he should break off the conversation to secure his firearms or if they'd be safe there some ten or twelve feet away.

"In addition to your new brown frock coat and pants?" Emma asked, her left eyebrow raised. "Surely one pair of pants and a coat should suffice a couple of days' business or stay."

"A good point, Emma," he stumbled, hoping that she hadn't noticed. "I guess I was thinking that a dark gray, navy or black outfit would better suffice when meeting with the men at the Washoe Club, their being financial folks and all that." He smiled quickly, still debating whether he should grab his guns or trust Platt not to knock them to the floor. "Upper crust, you know," he said, impatient to return to the morning's business.

"Yes, I heard," Emma replied.

The Washoe Club, having been organized a few years before, originally hoped to cater to men who had great wealth, suggesting to some that it was a millionaires' club. The charter members, some sixty in number, raised $9,000 among themselves to get things going. But after the fire, the club began allowing more colorful characters to become members, even some who were not so colorful but were cash-ready. The club's more private areas — a half-dozen apartments, a billiard parlor, reading and telegraph rooms, as well as a wine area boasting the finest spirits and cigars — were a target for Virginia City's always-hopeful entrepreneurs.

"Are you sure you're going to need to dress so extravagantly, William? Or is it your desire to impress someone?" Emma's conversations could be painful, in a needlessly Victorian sort of way. He thought briefly of Henry Nauman, Emma's estranged husband, whom he had recently decided had not died but simply fled to avoid the complexities of the relationship, not to speak of criminal prosecution. He was barely keeping his head above water in Emma's sea of interrogatives and inferences.

"I'm not following, Emma," he replied. It was a lie, but some things ought not to be asked about, even when understood between friends.

"The women, William. I'm speaking about the women you're investigating," she pressed. "Will you be blending in with them as well?"

"Ah," he said, smiling and looking again toward the store owner, who had finished policing the area of pins and papers and was now, without disguise, waiting for their conversation to finish.

Ronin stood silently in the doorway, his hand holding back the wooden door and windows that served to announce the store's wares and, at other times, simply acted as a sentry against the city's inclement winds and weather. His conversation, which had started out exciting, had turned into a something far less friendly and interesting.

"I don't know, Emma," he replied. "I don't imagine I'll be doing anything a clergyman wouldn't do." He paused. "Or even an ex-clergyman. Is that satisfactory?" he asked. Why he asked, he didn't know.

"You know what I mean, William."

"Do I, Emma? More importantly, do you?" He smiled as she left and shut the door, he hoped not on the relationship, though he didn't care much at that moment. He had work to do, and whatever feelings he was having were his feelings, and feelings only. And if he decided to share them — which he wasn't sure he would as he turned to face Platt, his Jewish tailor — it would be a long day in September before he would express any warmth again to a woman so intent on controlling him that he didn't have a place to breathe.

"Mister Ronin is it?" Joseph Platt asked, with new found curiosity. "I apologize, I didn't recognize you. Asking about a man's religion shouldn't be a crime, sir! Having it in your power to do the right thing and not doing so, well, that's my sense of what real religion is!"

Platt picked up Ronin's firearms and returned them to his hands, allowing them to fall naturally by Ronin's side. "I've followed your exploits for a long time, Mister Ronin. You're a good man, and I shall not detain you from your business. Let's get these pants measured so that you can be on your way." He took a final measurement, pinning the hems of both pant legs so that they draped naturally but were not too long. Pratt looked up, with a half-dozen pins still perched between his lips. "People are depending on you, Mister Ronin, and some of them are my clients."

The former Reverend William Washington Ronin smiled. Goodness has some edge to it, he believed, and he was going to cut himself some in just a few days.

# Chapter 24

# IN THE MONEY

Ellie sliced a piece of apple and handed it to her sister, who took it, wrapped it in a thin slice of yellow cheese and smiled. "For me?" Alvira asked, grinning. She pushed the "cheese and apple sandwich," as she liked to call it, into her mouth, a crumbling piece of cheddar lingering on her lower lip until she caught it with her fingers. Smiling, she turned to her sister. "Do you want to play today?"

Ellie shook her head firmly. There were no clients coming to visit. Alvira's favorite activity — moving trumpets and chalk boards in the darkness that was necessary "to get a good read on what the spirits are saying to us," she often explained — would have to wait. There was cleaning to do. The day's spiritual possibilities needed to be put aside so that the sheets were washed and the rooms dusted for potential overnight guests or friends. No man liked to smell another man's rhubarb when laying down with one of the Livestock twins, and Ellie made every effort to make sure that would never be the case.

"We've got work to do, Alvira Fae," Ellie, the older of the two twins explained.

To the natural eye, illumined by candle light or lantern in the simple house they knew as home, Ellie's sister was as normal as the Nevada day was long. But having been born second in what had been called "a difficult pregnancy and an even more trying delivery," it was thought that Alvira Fae may have been damaged by doctors and nurses. It was possible she had not been able to breathe for a time, her mother had said, lamenting her choice of practitioners in Iowa City. Subsequent appointments, many years later, with a young physician in Nevada's capital suggested that Alvira Fae's difficulties were no one's fault, really. "It's just what it is," Amos Quinn had said. The girls had enjoyed their consultation with the young doctor and thought he had a future as a medical man, given his caring ways. Whatever the case, the two sisters were making the best of Alvira Fae's condition, and life on the Comstock as a medium, fortune-teller and occasional overnight friend — despite the Comstock's economic changes and subtle decline — wasn't bad at all.

"Mister Leighman said he might come by this evening," Ellie continued, "and if not him, then someone else very special." Ellie watched her sister frown. "Come on. It'll be fun," she said, grabbing one end of the bed spread and throwing it toward her sister, who caught it awkwardly and giggled.

Alvira didn't appreciate Ellie's nighttime guests. It meant that she had to stay next door with friends. While she liked the neighbors well enough — their youngest child seemed like a much younger brother, at times —s he preferred to stay at home, play with her sister's crystal balls or the instruments they kept locked in a small desk behind the drapes

Sometimes, when Ellie's daytime clients wanted "a testimony" of spiritual power or desired to summon a particular presence — a loved one from the past, or certain Comstock miners were always favorites —s he would use a heel off of an old pair of shoes, tacked to the bottom of the desk, to make the sound of feet passing by. Occasionally, she was allowed to embrace a small set of cymbals she concealed in her bodice, or a tambourine that sat high up in a large brass chandelier, so as to signal that a spirit had come or was attempting to speak.

Once, when attending Father Manogue's church —s he was sure he would someday be a bishop — she witnessed the priest swing a pot-shaped silver bell to let everyone know that the sacred bread had changed into Christ's body. She asked her sister about that. "He shouldn't do it so that everyone can see," she responded, when Ellie explained that the bell was used to help people focus on the Mass. "It would be more mysterious that way."

Alvira Fae much preferred her sister's daytime guests to those that came at night. On occasion, and only when she wanted to, Alvira Fae was asked to share a bed with her sister and her guest, which left her feeling hollow, sometimes dirty and unimpressed.

Alvira Fae grabbed the other end of the flowered bed-spread and pulled it up toward the pillows, hers to the left, her sister Ellie's to the right, and tucked it underneath so that only the pillows and their red satin pillowslips showed. She was not to lay her head on the satin cases, she'd been told, as they were more difficult to clean. Other pillows were for sleeping. When the satin pillows came off the shelf, she knew that visitors were on their way.

"What's for supper?" Alvira Fae asked, a second slice of apple in her hands, sitting in an upholstered chair next to the window with a coffee cup full of locally made cheese sitting in her lap.

"What would you like?" Ellie asked, smiling, as she fluffed the bed cushions so that they stood up against the maple headboard, a gift from their parents when the girls moved west from Iowa City. Looking back, their parents seemed happy to see the twins go but, in retrospect, Ellie wondered if they weren't worried about their well-being. The twins had never married, and Alvira Fae, now in her thirties, would likely never couple at all.

"Can we have beets?" Alvira asked, pointing to the bed bolsters, red being her favorite color and the swirling wood patterns of the headboard something she could trace with her index finger all day long. Ellie checked the empty flour tin she kept in the other room above the stove, where religious offerings and wages gained from more intimate work were deposited without discrimination or scrutiny. The gold and silver coins in the can jingled, like the ringing of the Sanctus Bell during the Mass at Saint Mary's in the Mountains Church on E Street.

"We're in the money," Ellie said, laughing. Beets it would be.

# Chapter 25

# FORTUNE TELLING AND MORE

Ellie and Alvira were living the good life in Virginia City, as good as it got for fortune tellers anyway. While not privileged enough to live among the city's finer families — situated in homes higher up the mountain above C Street — the girls' single-story D Street cottage offered certain comfort to two women who were making the best of their circumstances, no matter what other people thought. And it wasn't like folks were judging.

German immigrant John Piper owned opera houses in three cities, sat on the city council, had been the mayor and even served as a state senator. But like many other Comstock businessmen, he held properties on D Street where women offered sexual services to those who could afford them. "Middle class girls," he liked to say, aware that some of the women living there called their D Street home address as "Piper's Row." It was fine with him.

The way most people saw it, working women needed a place to lay their heads and conduct their business. The houses on D Street were a better place for women to proffer their wares than the grander houses on A or B Street. Doggery continued along "the Barbary Coast," south on C Street, but Ellie and Alvira didn't participate in anything that crude. And it wasn't like the sisters were entertaining men full-time, the girls said.

Nor was sex the focus when they did, when "diddling" was good. Evening friendships were formed as an offshoot of the Livestock twins' more spiritual business, and were born out of a client's interest or the sisters' necessity.

In the end, the Livestock twins' evening business provided companionship, when "the perfect customer sought out their perfect talents," Ellie said, "both of which spring from heaven above." And if their physical contribution helped a client probe life's more difficult moments or profundities, then the resulting confidence clients gained about themselves or their loved ones was a good thing. "Loving someone physically isn't all that different from sharing one's more intimate thoughts or feelings, not in my experience," Ellie had whispered to a Washoe Club guest the other night. "I want to do whatever helps you think more clearly, dear" she'd said, while smoothing the front of his pants until a large bump appeared and then playing with his suspenders. The older gentleman who was thinking about divorce, having discovered his wife in the arms of a stranger, moved his lips from her right breast long enough to mumble breathlessly, "I agree."

The girls knew there were at least four other houses on D Street where men might spend their money and time. There had been more, but the city's economy was changing. With girls charging $10 or $20 per intimacy — more if their men stayed all night — an evening's entertainment presented a tough choice for many, as some men preferred poker to poking. For many girls, the work could be grueling. But the twins took only what they needed. And that helped keep their lives in perspective.

The Livestock twins hadn't always proffered what some church folks considered to be less-godly pursuits. Ellie had tried nursing at the St. Mary's Hospital. But neither Ellie nor Alivra had much of a fondness for faith beyond the pageantry of it all.

The traditional garb of the sisters — blue and white, whether they worked in the asylum, school or hospital — offered even less appeal. But the hospital's thirty-six patient rooms, five patient wards and a dozen private rooms as well seemed an easy fix for their housing dilemma. Still, after a few months helping the sisters care for the brokenhearted and broken-down, Ellie's mind began to change. Alvira had suffered, with Ellie being so busy about the Lord's business. Thoughts that the girls might find room and board among the Daughters of Charity — the hospital had hot and cold running water, gas lighting, steam heat, attractive fixtures and furniture — disappeared when the sisters made it clear that there was no place for Alvira, saying she would be better suited as a patient than a provider. "There's something wrong with that girl," they said to Ellie, which wasn't a pleasing thought at all, given that it had been uttered by someone who had considered herself "Christ's best friend and bride."

When the pope proclaimed his infallibility in a special Vatican council, *infallibility of all things,* Ellie closed the door on living and working with the Daughters of Charity. She'd never met a perfect man or woman and that included her father, who had suffered sinlessly caring for her aging mother and demented sister. Her mind made up to leave, Ellie didn't know what to do until a local newspaperman pointed the way.

"There's a plethora of men on the Comstock," said Alfred Doten, a local journalist and friend to the Spiritualist movement in Virginia City. "They need what you do," he said, "and you won't find as many critical people outside of the church as you do in." Ellie May didn't know if Doten's comments were meant to be taken generally or as a compliment. But they were life-giving. As soon as she separated from the sisters and the church they served, her life seemed happier. "Listen," Alf said, "Virginia City is coarse, but it's also cosmopolitan. It can easily host another fortuneteller, particularly an attractive one like you." Doten, the owner of the *Gold Hill Daily News,* had a way of making women smile, and Ellie May enjoyed every bit of his effort.

The girls' parents had been Spiritualists in Iowa, and "were fierce defenders of the thought that the spirits of the dead, residing in some other place, had both the ability and desire to communicate with those they had left behind," Ellie said at a meeting of the Virginia City Spiritualist Society one night, in their hall located underneath the office of a dentist on B Street, between Taylor and Union. When her father sent her copies of the books, *Poems of the Inner Life* and *Poems of Progress,* by Lizzie Doten, Alf Doten's sister, it was if the "we'd received a sign," she testified to a group of women and men who had particular status in business or mining.

"It won't be long," her father wrote in the letter attached to the paper-covered parcel that arrived on a Sunday, though no postal delivery was made on that day. "It won't be long before people begin to regard you as they do Lizzie," he said, the sheer coincidence of Alf and Lizzie Doten's relationship and the unexpected invitation to attend the society seeming like proof positive that the Spirit was moving. She would do what she could to help the hopeless, to befriend the faithless and to inform the sinner that there were better days ahead for everyone, the living and the dead.

Lizzie Doten was a popular lecturer on spiritual phenomena who often concluded her performances by channeling poems by Edgar Allan Poe, Shakespeare and other writers who had gone on to the great beyond. "She really knows her stuff," her father said, "and what she's been through, she can teach you to go through," he wrote in a missive that must have taken him hours to write, an even more impressive feat given that he had rarely written over the years. "It will come in time," he said, "the gifts and the goings-on. Do what you need to do to build people's faiths, bending their perceptions and realities, if you must, with misdirection and magic. In time you won't need to do that," he advised. *"Real practice,"* he underlined, "will be as surely yours as it is others' in the Spiritualist movement. And I will be your proud fan and follower."

The letter had made Ellie May smile, and the choice — to leave the Sisters of Charity, not that she could ever become a nun, or even a devout Catholic — had been a good one. Ten years later, in a little house on D Street, "the magic" was no longer necessary, other than to build her sister's self-esteem and purpose. Ask anyone, Ellie May's presence as a full-grown female was magic enough.

# Chapter 26
# BENTON'S LIVERY

"I thought you had left, Ronin!" Dustsucker said, pushing past a boardwalk full of "lunch and go" folks looking for a brief excursion around Washoe Lake before supper. "Excuse me," he said to one particularly anxious man who seemed set on not losing his place in line. Dustsucker glanced at the counter clock through the window at Benton's Livery. "It's not like they're not going to take your money," he frowned, catching the man's forearm so that he wouldn't fall against the plate glass window. A series of carriages were lined up underneath the Lake Tahoe Stage sign on Carson Street, waiting their passengers and drivers.

Ronin looked over and laughed. He'd rarely seen his friend in such a hurry.

"Looks like a goddamned Sunday School convention," Dustsucker exclaimed, before realizing his tongue was wagging while his badge was hanging out for everyone to see. "Excuse me, ma'am," he apologized to the woman accompanying the anxious man in the hopsack suit, whom he had poked in the hip, hinging him in half like a dollar bill on its way to a gentleman's money clip.

"Slade! Hold your tongue," Ronin said, while glancing around at the dozen or so people gathered outside the Carson City stage office. "These folks are out for an afternoon ride. They're not asking to be ridden," he laughed. Ronin hadn't heard his friend curse before, not that he had anything against a healthy string of expletives, particularly if they were artistically linked, which his friend's were not. Even when a bullet folded Dustsucker onto a wooden sidewalk outside a saloon in Reno while attempting to arrest the Clancy and Crestwell brothers, he hadn't heard Dustsucker curse.

"I hate this!" his friend wheezed, grabbing the side of the building to stabilize himself. "Why anyone would hope to make a dollar from a two-hour horse and buggy ride when they could make a bunch of dollars taking someone somewhere useful? Doesn't Benton have enough business than to be catering to tourists?"

"Excuse me?" a baritone voice yelled from inside the building.

"I have no idea, Dusty," Ronin whispered. "I just lodge my horse here, and from what I can tell, Jackson's not much interested in seeing the sights, not for money anyway." He stood staring at his friend, who had apparently finished his morning business in a hurry so as to accompany him on his trip to Virginia City. "Coming with?" he asked, smiling, noticing that a bedroll was attached to the deputy's saddle.

Dustsucker nodded, pulling a red handkerchief from the back pocket of his blue jeans to pat at the sweat on his forehead. He pushed one sleeve of his long underwear up underneath a plaid cotton shirt that had seen better days. A threadbare vest hung on his bear-sized shoulders. He appeared irritated. "Feels like summer, don't it?" Dustsucker said, wiping the sweat from his nose.

"It does," Ronin said, pulling back his jacket lapels with his thumbs and hooking them into his new, four-pocket vest. A fresh white shirt and a gold-colored cravat punctuated the outfit, recently purchased from Koppel Platt's clothing store.

"Whooee! You sure look good!" The deputy looked his six-foot friend up and down. A black almost-a-derby except for its wider brim hat sat on Ronin's head. Dark gray pinstripes ran throughout the rich, black wool cloth that matched jacket with trousers with vest, the pinstripe's color picked up in the design of Ronin's new tie. Braided leather braces, with tiny brass buckles, held everything together. "Emma said you'd made a purchase!"

The corners of Ronin's mouth suddenly turned downward, his countenance expressing concern and surprise. "She actually told you I was buying a suit? Seriously?"

"Well sure, Ronin, we're friends." Dustsucker shuffled his feet.

"Listen, Dusty. I'm not upset about the two of you talking to each other. I don't care about that. I know you're friends. And maybe you'd like to be more — that doesn't matter to me, either," he said, though he wasn't sure he meant all of what came tumbling out of his mouth. "I'm just surprised she sought you out to tell you what I was doing."

"What you were doing?"

"I was buying a suit." The former priest clenched his hands and then relaxed them, while shaking his head and looking at the dry mud outside Benton's livery doors. He picked up his feet to inspect the soles of his favorite boots

"She just happened to see me, Ronin. She didn't go looking for me, not that I'm aware of, anyway. What's *really* going on, my friend?"

Ronin looked up. "What's *really* going on? I should ask you. You're the one pushing people around on Carson Street!"

"We're talking about you, Ronin, not me."

Ronin shrugged. "Maybe I'm just upset. You know Emma and I aren't getting along, exactly."

"Of course I do, but I'm not asking about that." He placed his hands on Ronin's shoulders. Closer to the front of the line, a man in an ill-fitting brown hopsack suit wearing a black bowler pointed to his own index finger with his left hand, then rubbed his hip and looked Dustsucker's way. Ronin momentarily lifted his chin to signal the man to stop staring and to go about his business. The man's wife took the hint and pulled her husband's attention toward the counter. "I'm just saying, why are you so sensitive about what Emma's thinking or not thinking, Ronin? It's not like you."

Ronin shook his head and smiled and returned his gaze toward his friend. He paused for a moment. "I think I'm about to fall in love again, Dusty. Things with Emma — an otherwise wonderful woman — are just not right."

"You're falling in love with Emma, and things aren't right?" Dustsucker asked, a sinking feeling in the pit of his stomach. His friend had finally made up his mind.

"No," Ronin laughed. "That's not going to happen, not with any regularity anyway, until she and I work a few things out."

"Right," Dustsucker replied, relieved. "Then, what are you talking about?" Dustsucker pulled at both of Ronin's lapels, so that his coat closed, concealing his firearms so that they'd be less apparent to the tourists and travelers on Carson Street. Ronin hadn't spoken of falling in love before, not he could remember save for a woman he'd met in the midst of a Pinkerton investigation years ago. That had ended badly for everyone concerned. Ronin had lost his job because of the relationship.

"I wish I knew," Ronin continued, buttoning his coat. He turned and looked toward the lake, where snow clouds seemed to be forming. *It isn't cold enough. Hell, it's hardly fall.* "It just feels like springtime, Dusty," he looked up at a clear sky. "Do you know what I mean? It's springtime, and I know I'm going to fall in love because it's springtime."

"It's September, Ronin," Dustsucker said, noting his friend was sporting a new grin as well as a new suit. "It's an extended summer at best," he argued. "It's not spring."

"So it is," Ronin replied. *What was there about heading to Virginia City this time that made things feel so different?*

# Chapter 27

# VIRGINIA CITY

Versal McBride was standing outside the Bucket of Blood with a push broom in his hands when Marshal Ash stepped up onto the boards in front of his C Street saloon. "Ronin's agreed to work at the usual rate, Versal. I believe we'll see him back here today. Slade said something about trying to join him as well, given Alvin Hornbecker's death."

"Horney Hornbecker is dead?" McBride exclaimed. "What happened?"

"We'll know more about Mister Hornbecker's demise when Sheriff Kelly joins us. You had coffee yet?"

Versal shook his head in disbelief. Five-foot ten, with a mustache half as wide as each shoulder, the silver spectacled dark-haired owner of the Bucket of Blood wasn't usually caught without something to say. He wasn't usually out of the loop on such things. "I don't understand," he said. "When did this happen?"

"A couple of days ago," Ash replied, taking the broom from McBride and pushing it briskly in front of the saloon doorway so that it raised a minor dust cloud. "Don't know why I didn't hear anything about it either, though I believe they're still looking at circumstances where he died."

"Which were?" McBride asked, grabbing the broom back and clearly annoyed. It was bad enough he hadn't been told about Horney Hornbecker's death. Worse still that the marshal should be standing in front of him sweeping dirt *into* his saloon and dawdling about which part of the story he was going to tell next.

"I'm sorry, Versal." Ash stomped his feet, hoping to be invited for lunch and not wanting to track dirt into the saloon floor if McBride was buying. He pulled a black kerchief from his back pocket and began wiping one of the windows. "Mister Hornbecker was found at the St. Charles Hotel with a bullet hole in his head."

"Where in his head? Jesus, Ash, you're killing me ..."

"The side."

"Which side?"

"His right side," he said, breathing on the glass so as to loosen a bug or bird splatter, he wasn't sure which.

"Hmmm ..." McBride replied. He didn't remember which was Hornbecker's dominant hand. "Well, I guess if he was right-handed, it may well be a suicide."

"Yup," Ash said. "Played some cards somewhere in town, haven't heard where yet," he continued, "though it's said that he lost quite a lot of money." Ash swatted at the bottom of his pants to knock the dust off. "There was some talk, Slade said, that he was being bankrolled by men at the Washoe Club."

"Wouldn't be the first time," McBride interjected, handing the broom to a Paiute and flipping him a dime. The Indian nodded and smiled, attracting the interest of other Indians farther down the street. McBride waved them off.

"No, it wouldn't. Amazing what use the telegraph has come to, if you don't mind me saying."

"I do, marshal, what with work to do and the details of this man's death still for waiting me like a preacher wondering how much money is in the offering plate ..."

"I'm sorry, Versal."

"Stop with the 'I'm sorry' and get on with the story, would you?"

"Sure." Ash winced. He tolerated McBride's tone because the owner of the city's most popular drinking hole could muster a whole lot of pressure on his office. Over the years, gathering weekly for a morning repast and review, Ash had grown fond of the man and the information he brought to bear on things happening in Virginia City, sometimes Reno and Carson City as well. He wished he had something more to report. "Look, at this point, the Ormsby County sheriff is thinking the suicide is self-evident. Hornbecker was mumbling something about how he couldn't lose and all that ..."

"And everyone saw that as a little bit cocky?" McBride asked. Hornbecker wasn't a sloppy man. He was surprised.

"Well, actually not. They were curious about his confidence, Deputy Slade said, as he normally didn't talk that way. So they asked him and he said — and this is why I got here as soon as I could, Versal — he said he'd been told he couldn't lose by a pretty little girl in Virginia City during a sitting of some sort."

"A sitting?" McBride barked. "What the hell is a sitting? I'm dying here, Augustus."

"You know, Versal, one of those Spiritualist things, like the people who hold those lectures in churches and meeting halls."

"He was told this by a little girl at a lecture?"

"No, at a sitting, Versal. Sittings are held in homes. You know, people gather in a dark room, hold hands and ask for signs and such from family and friends who have gone on."

"Gone on?"

"Dead people, Versal. Spiritualists are people who talk to dead people about live people's concerns. Get it?"

"Jesus ..."

"Exactly. Someone talked this man into thinking he couldn't lose all his money. And when his money was gone — and I'm just free-wheeling here, Slade will probably have more for us when he gets to town — Hornbecker wakes up, feels stupid and figures the only thing he can do to make things right is to kill himself."

"Man ..."

"You sure seem upset about this, Versal. Were you close to the man?"

McBride looked up. "Close to Hornbecker? Nah, no one was close to Horney Hornbecker, save the women he hired or preyed on, and a few members of the Washoe Club I guess. Why do you ask?" McBride seemed lost in thought.

"Well, you seem troubled by his death."

"Troubled? No, not troubled. I'm bothered. Hornbecker's investments were crashing like everyone else's I imagine. Sooner or later, he would have met the grim reaper. No, I'm bothered because we ought to have a silver-tongued, crystal ball gazing good-looker sitting here saying the same thing to stupid men! You know, 'You can't lose, baby! Lady luck is smiling your way!'"

"Gotcha."

"I doubt it, Augustus," McBride smirked. "Listen, how are Slade and Ronin getting here?"

"By stage, I think."

"Well, soon as it comes in, you make sure they come straight to my office. I want to get on top of this before more money is wasted in god-damned Carson City because of some fortune-telling tramp."

"Tramp, Versal? I'm not sure this lady was a tramp or anything like that. She might have been a perfectly normal woman, even a Methodist maybe."

"You're right, marshal. She might have been a perfectly normal religious lady, not a fortune-teller or anything like that. It's me who's sorry. I can't believe I'm calling a blood-sucking, sooth-saying seer a bad name! I mean, before long, people will figure out that it's all rubbish and go back to spending their money on beer and booze. Jesus, Augustus, you can be dim-witted ..."

"Versal, I think I've had ..."

"... enough? Really, marshal? You think you've had enough?" McBride's mouth and mustache was twitching. "Tell you what, when you find Ronin and Slade, bring them to my office. I'm not done talking about how concerned I am about the number of priests, prohibitionists, crystal ball gazers, Methodists and Mormons there are sucking up all the money in this city when a good man like myself is trying to make a living. Understand?"

Ash hadn't seen McBride explode like this since the Great Fire, when McBride and practically every other person in town had to scrape to get their businesses and buildings back together so as to make a living. A new water system had been put in place since then, and a number of new fire houses were built as well. Still, McBride hadn't relaxed.

"Listen Augustus, I'm not concerned about the tramps on B, C and D Street. I want to know why a perfectly good old man would travel to Carson City to get what he could get in Virginia City cheaper, faster and with more fun. And if either Ronin or Slade mention that wonderful gift to Virginia City tourism *told* him to play cards in Carson City, bring her here, too. I've got a fortune to tell her and it won't be pretty!"

# Chapter 28

# JOURNAL, NOVEMBER 30, 1873

Ronin grabbed his journal from his saddlebags and took it into the coach so that he would have something to read as they headed out of town. He'd been neglecting his "inner life," as Happy Hands called it, since getting back from Lake Tahoe.

The experience had reminded him that there was an important inner something to what he was doing. Maybe it wasn't a religious thing. He used to think that "serving God and enjoying God forever" was the point of it all, though he couldn't remember what scripture or creed had suggested such. He didn't think so any longer. Still, an occasional and gnawing sense of emptiness had convinced him that there was an inner quality to a man's life that needed to be tended to.

Happy Hands had told him to listen to his intuition and feelings, that each person's life was different and that the beat of a man's drum, or woman's for that matter, was akin to the rhythm his heart made. That rhythm or "inner witness," a term he thought was Quaker, was as certain a voice as could ever be heard by a man or woman. "Listen to it," he had said.

Sitting in the coach with tourists talking on each side of him, Ronin wondered if that wasn't the issue with Emma and him. She listened to a different voice than he did. Their hearts, though sometimes tempted to beat as one, preferred a different cadence. Their senses of self —forged by separate families and faiths, or lack of both over the last many years of their thirty-some year journeys — didn't reflect the same values or concerns.

Clearing the station in Carson City, the team pulled a quick pace toward Mound House, where the coach would turn left and head uphill toward Silver City, Gold Hill and Virginia City. "This is no express ride," Benton told Dustsucker, when they were paying for the ride. "I've got a pack of people in from New Jersey who want to see the Comstock and I intend to take every dollar they have showing it to them!"

Dustsucker laughed when Ronin told the livery owner that he didn't mind how long the ride took. "I've got some reading and thinking to do," Ronin explained. "It'll be nice, you'll see."

Dustsucker nodded, though it was now clear he hadn't needed to hurry his morning meetings. "You surely do," he said, thinking of Ronin's relationship with Emma, while looking for a newspaper or two to read along the way.

There had been some talk about their taking a train as Dustsucker wanted to take some additional baggage that their horses couldn't comfortably carry. But Benton had announced an additional stage on the route to Virginia City while they were standing there talking. The back and forth of the coach seemed like it would offer a nice rhythm at the time. It wouldn't "be a problem to tie their horses behind it," Benton had said. Neither of them had counted on the visitors wanting to talk so much.

Ronin pulled the leather wrapped journal from his coat pocket, and unwound the leather cord that kept his more intimate thoughts private. He took a deep breath, and opening it like it was a book of scriptures, laid it on his lap. He reached into his vest pocket, and put on a pair of rounded, gold reading glasses and tipped his hat so as to block the noise and light.

"Really, Ronin? You're wearing glasses now?"

Ronin looked up. "Always have, even when I was preaching, Dusty. Don't guess you ever saw me reading or preaching before."

"Don't guess I have. You going to read now?"

Ronin nodded.

"Well, alrighty then. A big man needs a big nap from time to time. Wake me when we get to Virginia City and not before, William."

Ronin smiled. Silver City wasn't much anymore, not since the railroad eliminated the freight business in the city. When the Virginia & Truckee Railroad was completed, the boarding houses, saloons and hotels began to close. Even the icehouse didn't seem near as important as it once was. They might not even stop there, he figured, though it would likely depend on how much fuss the folks from New Jersey made about seeing half-used buildings that in less than a hundred years wouldn't any longer be there.

They'd surely take a break in Gold Hill, or even a couple of breaks. He expected they'd disembark to see the Yellow Jacket, Crown Point or Belcher mines, or the Crown Point trestle. They'd maybe wet their whistles in Gold Hill or take a meal. Whatever the case, he'd let his friend sleep through it if he could.

He unbuttoned his duster, but kept the flaps close so as not to touch folks on either side of him and glanced out the window. It'd be a while yet. And if his professional walk had taught him anything in the years he was a practicing pastor, it had convinced him that there were clues in one's past about one's future. He didn't need to be a damned clairvoyant to know that. He settled into the annotations he'd made a few months after leaving the church and joining the Pinkerton National Detective Agency.

*The Pinkertons made their reputation by dealing with the most difficult men. Their assignments were those that others had left behind or* were unable to solve. *Thefts of property, government intrigues and certain murder investigations are still talked about as if they were yesterday.*

*The old man's writings — Allan Pinkerton has written quite a few books over the years I'm told, though I've yet to see one — talk about how Pinkerton men always get their man, or woman for that matter. I figure a Scottish barrel-maker can't be any brighter than a former clergyman, so I'm excited to get to work*

*Founded in 1850, and originally thought of as railroad detectives, the Pinkertons gained national fame by protecting President Lincoln in 1861. More often than not, however, they've served as security for railroad companies and banks. Despite having spent considerable time around both and having seen their abuse, I'm not a friend of either. I don't know what life is about anymore, but I do know it's not about money. When all is said and done and I stand at the ass-end of my life — pardon the phrase but it's quite refreshing to finally be able to talk that way — I hope that someone will stand and testify that I cared about things deeper, higher or better than the those that move so many others.*

*Still, while you can't take it with you, it's important to have enough. But if you don't have enough, then a good sit-down is necessary. And while a priest may not be of some help — their advice seems too spiritual at times to be at all useful, it seems to me — a thoughtful man or woman might do you one better. In all things, it's important to keep one's balance.*

*There's talk about my working a rail assignment. It figures, right? One of the western-most railways is losing money from its strong boxes. The boxes, I'm told, are being put on board the train by Pinkerton agents, taken a good number of miles and then taken off the train by Pinkertons as well. When unlocked — and this isn't every time of course, but often enough that thoughtful men and women are quite confounded — they've been found empty. So there's the possibility that one of the middle men, so to speak, a company guard or detective, is in on the theft.*

*Typical of many Pinkerton operations, someone is needed to work "undercover." The office in Chicago is filled with wigs and costumes; that's how strange it gets in this sort of work. Given that I'm not known by anyone in the company, or the railroad for that matter, I'm being considered for the assignment. I'm supposed to speak with the old man about it tomorrow or the next day. He keeps a busy schedule and likes to make up his mind in his own time.*

*The Pinkertons have a long memory about such things, given their daily reports, files, rap sheets and mug shots. So a similar case from 1858 is still remembered and talked about. A southern railroad, running Georgia to Alabama I believe, experienced a series of unexplained heists where as much as $50,000 went missing. The company couldn't understand how its strongboxes were turning up empty upon delivery. Suspecting a railroad employee, as no other possibilities arose during the investigation, they fired the men most responsible for the shipments.*

*It turned out that one of the employees, a man named Maroney, acted most suspiciously upon observation. The Pinkertons were able to break the case only after planting agents who ingratiated themselves with Maroney and his wife. The fast passing of dollar bills soon turned into faster lips, and a crooked trail of cash was suddenly spent in getting Mister Maroney out of jail where the old man had him situated because of suspicion.*

*Kate Warne tells me I might have to wear a mustache if I'm assigned this new case! I hope she's teasing, as a mustache I cannot currently endure. But Kate, a slender brown-haired woman and Mister Pinkerton's closest associate, is to be trusted and listened to. No one hires a woman as a detective or a policeman nowadays, though someday I suspect they might. But Mister Pinkerton does. A woman will worm out of a man, or a woman for that matter, secrets that other detectives will never hear. Men trust them, women too, which brings me to news I need to share with my parents. I have not yet met a woman that I care that much for or trust. Grandkids will be a long time waiting.*

Ronin looked up. His friend was fast asleep between two men dressed in dark rifle coats that had no doubt been purchased more as a fashion statement than a place to hide a rifle or shotgun. Chattering like love-birds, the men couldn't keep from pointing at this and that, extending their hands through the side windows. They would surely wake his friend if they continued so. There were no flowers on the Comstock to point to, not visible from the coach anyway. Sage brush and cheat grass, the occasional windblown scrub tree, brown and yellow rock and a September rain barrel's fill of mud splashed alongside the coach as it turned up the mountain toward Silver City.

He looked across the seat from him and exhaled. *I need to get my love-life in gear. Before long, no woman will want me.*

He looked at Dustsucker, whose head was resting back upon the seat, his lips trembling. He was snoring and his two seatmates seemed irritated. Slade wanted the same he guessed. A real man, sitting between two girly men, my how things were different and yet remained the same.

# Chapter 29
# TEA TIME

"Join us for tea?" Tom Kelly asked, upon finding Ronin and Slade at the International Hotel on C Street. The six-story building sat between B and C streets, with an entrance opposite Piper's Opera House. The third emanation of Isaac Bateman and Andrew Paul's, the first building was shipped 170 miles east to Austin, where it was rebuilt and re-christened the International Hotel of Austin. The second was destroyed by the Great Fire in 1875. The third — easily the most prominent building in town — had gas lighting, a French-style roof and an actual elevator operated by hydraulics. Ronin and Slade were sitting in the restaurant downstairs.

"A little out of your league, isn't it?" Kelly asked, before pulling a chair from the table, turning it around and straddling it as he would a horse. "Or is this the new W. W. Ronin I've been hearing about?"

"Jesus, Tom, seriously? Is everyone talking about this suit?"

Kelly's eyes squinted. He then looked at Slade, who was having trouble fitting underneath the table given the chairs and the proximity of other diners. Slade shrugged before pushing his way past the encumbrances. "I'm not following." Kelly shook his head but grinned when he saw the gold watch chain and fob hanging from Ronin's four-pocket, striped vest. "I didn't notice, Ronin. I'm sorry. Nice suit, Bobby."

"Bobby?"

"Just kidding around," he said, putting both hands on his thighs and springing to attention. "Listen, Marshal Ash and

I are wondering if the newest employee of the Virginia City police might want to grab a little bit of breakfast or lunch over at the Bucket of Blood? McBride's got a burr under his saddle about the dead guy in Carson City and the lady who is advising fools to sit with folks in Carson City to play poker."

"Lunch is good," Ronin replied, "though I'd caution you about thinking I'm working for anyone other than myself." Checking his watch, he discovered they'd slept late. Benton's stagecoach had taken much of the afternoon and evening touring Silver City, Gold Hill and the Six-Mile Canyon — a place he had never been — before depositing them at the top of the hill in Virginia City. "I'm afraid we didn't get in until real early this morning," he explained. "McBride owes me a great deal more than a sandwich, I'm thinking, given that I was stuck on a stagecoach all day yesterday."

"Don't know anything about that, though it sounds like you took the long way around. I do know they're hoping I'll fetch you and bring you over. Honestly, this thing with the Washoe Club is heating up, as there's now one very important guy complaining and a dead guy, not for lack of trying, also pointing the finger at a couple of loose women with crystal balls."

Slade laughed. "Now, that's funny," he said, pushing himself up and away from the table, but not before grabbing his glass of milk. "Take a short walk, Ronin?"

"God, a man can't sit for minute without someone wanting to take him somewhere? How you been, Tom?"

"It's been difficult Ronin, but no one said it wouldn't be. A day doesn't go by without my missing Winnie." He took a last sip of coffee. "Ash is over at his office beneath the Odd Fellows Building. We'll pick him up on the way."

"I've been thinking about you."

"I'm sure you have, Ronin. Hurt doesn't happen alone. We all have our share of it."

"The kids?" Kelly had six, the youngest being only four.

"They're doing okay, I guess. Lots of help. Here he is now."

"Well, Mister Ronin!" Ash shouted from the sidewalk. "Slade, good to see you boys. Wondered how long it would take you to get here."

"Quite a trip, Augustus. We took every evil twist and bend in the goddamned road, if you ask me."

"Dusty, I thought you were sleeping most of the time," Ronin said, laughing. "Man snores like a lumber mill in full swing."

"I was just resting my eyes. I was half afraid those New Jersey tourists would ask for an interview."

"New Jersey?" Ash asked.

"Truth be told."

"Well, that explains everyone asking for tomatoes at breakfast. One small, bowler-headed man got very upset when he heard there weren't any tomatoes to be had at the Bucket. Said he'd had a tomato every day for breakfast for seven years and hadn't suffered any ill effects." McBride told him it was September already, and that there weren't many fresh vegetables in Virginia City. Well, the guy gets into an argument about it being a fruit, not a vegetable ..."

"It's a fruit?" Slade asked. "I thought it was a vegetable, not that I eat them."

"It's got seeds, Dusty. That makes it a fruit," Ronin said.

"I think it has more to do with the fact that the tomato plant has flowers," Kelly said.

"Who cares," Ash interjected. "So McBride gets into an argument with this guy ..."

"Brown hopsack suit?"

"Yeah, why do you ask?"

"Met the man. He's a moron," Ronin explained.

"Not that it matters," Kelly said. "Is this going somewhere? McBride's waiting."

"Actually, he's not waiting, Tom. He got so angry at the man that he hit him, a quick short punch right into the nose. Hat falls off, the little prick goes down like he'd been hit with a tree limb. I come back into the room after taking a leak, and there he is, standing over the man, screaming at the top of his lungs with the little guy's wife yelling at him, too."

"Wow, seriously?" Ronin asked, beginning to smile.

"Got my hands on my fly, buttoning things up, I'm that serious. I take hold of McBride by the back of his vest, push the woman into a chair when the little guy wakes up, sits up and takes a punch at my belly."

"Really?" Ronin grins.

"Well, not my belly, but my point is McBride is over at the courthouse pressing charges on these two for 'tortious interference with a business' or some such thing and we need to head there right away.

"Wouldn't miss it," Ronin said. "And if the bowler-headed man is lucky, they'll keep him there. His woman didn't seem all that happy with him when we saw him in the livery in Carson City yesterday. I can't imagine what she'll be feeling now that her man has been denied his tomatoes."

# Chapter 30

# THE BIG-ASS MISTAKE

Truth be told, Timothy Edwards Smith wasn't feeling all that religious. Despite his recent return to the Roman Catholic Church, Paddy Manogue's gain hadn't really cost Smith anything. The secrets of his heart were safely tucked away from prying eyes, particularly from those who were too cruel or religious.

He had hoped to achieve something new in his life, after having suffered the loss of his friend, slain by the angry ex-preacher outside the Glenbrook House in Lake Tahoe. And he had endeavored to make a good go of it: attending Mass, contributing where he could, and attracting a goodly amount of attention for an ungodly amount of volunteer hours in a Comstock soup kitchen and clothing swap. But his efforts hadn't changed things, save to make things worse between Mort and him, his buddy being so private about the time they spent together anywhere, including Virginia City, where they had joined a church but were now regularly criticized for not showing up to weekly religious services.

The charity supper had turned out to be giant fair attended by just about everyone in town. And dumb as it was to be seen in public at this point — both he and Mort Spinnaker being wanted for robbery, attempted murder, aggravated assault and whatever else the capital city lawyers could invent or envision — Timothy Edwards Smith had a need to be with people. "I feed on it," he'd told his partner, hoping he'd understand.

Now realizing he did not, Timothy was about to do the only thing he imagined he could do to make things right for himself and his friend. "A big-ass mistake," Mort had called it, referring to their being seen in public at the well-attended event that gathered the Comstock's elite so as to raise significant money for the Roman Catholic sisters' hospital, school and orphanage.

"I thought it would be helpful," Smith had argued over the days that followed, constantly being reminded that his friend was still critical of their attending the event and the choices he had made leading up to it.

"Nothing will solve this," Spinnaker had said, "save for something really stupid, big-ass stupid, if you don't mind me saying."

Since his conversion to the Roman Catholic Church, Spinnaker had been extremely careful that the words that came out of his mouth were pleasing to the church and to God. "With it we bless our Lord and father," he'd said, if once at least a dozen times daily, reminding them to keep themselves "pure for the Lord." Not that he minded, though the repetition only underscored how different they were becoming since deciding to sit with Father Manogue weekly for confession. "It will do you good," Spinnaker had said, though he very much doubted so. Confession wasn't a practice Smith enjoyed, given that they had to take turns sitting in a lavishly decorated but dusty booth with a man he didn't particularly like.

"Why can't we just say these things privately?" he'd asked, hoping that "confessing the lies, envies, prides and spites," as Paddy put the purpose of their private time together, could be done in a more comfortable and less intimate setting. Neither Father Manogue nor his partner had said he should mention

Mort's or his intemperance or impurities — not that he was getting enough of either — so he left that out of their weekly get-togethers in the confessional closet at St. Mary's in Virginia City. "Talking to Paddy is like talking to my brother," he'd said to his friend, hoping the comparison would be construed as a compliment, since he had little else positive to say about the experience, except that the chapel was pretty and so sometimes were the stoles Paddy wore while listening to his confession.

"That's so ... so ... Protestant," Mort had replied. Though Smith didn't understand the word, it was clear that his partner didn't take it in the manner he'd hoped he would.

"I don't care what I've done," Smith had argued in a more open moment when Spinnaker was interested in hearing about his feelings. "Big sin or small sin, I just don't see the point of telling someone what I've done when he and I could be talking about the things I'm thinking of doing. That would actually help."

"Huh," was all Smith said, which was hurtful because he wanted desperately to portray himself as the positive-minded individual his mother believed him to be, "when you put your mind to it," she used to say. No matter what he did or where he did it, his mom had told him, "make me proud. You can do it. Make your mommy happy."

Timothy Edwards Smith wasn't feeling proud and had begun to believe that he wasn't going to feel happy either, unless he could figure out a way to make things right between him and his friend. So when they began to speak about the obvious — eliminating W. W. Ronin from the mix of their lives and fleeing to some state or city where law dogs weren't sniffing into their personal business — he began to feel some hope that things would work out between them and that both of them, despite what had happened in Carson City, or Lake Tahoe or the places in between, they might actually achieve their God-given dreams.

Standing out front of St. Mary's that morning, he happened to catch a glance of Ormsby County Deputy Sheriff Slade and his friend Ronin getting off of a stage. And he began to think again and to feel again. His 'what-ifs' turned into 'can-dos,' and it made him proud enough to want to tell someone that he'd figured out a way for the two of them — Slade and Ronin on the one hand, but also Spinnaker and Smith — to work out their differences and to put the past behind them.

He glanced down at his pocket, where he kept the tiny Smith and Wesson Model One revolver Spinnaker had found him, a busted-up single-action derringer that held seven .22 caliber cartridges. "The stocks are bad, but we can make you new ones," Mort had said when he gave it to him, despite not having gotten around to it yet. The gun could do some serious damage if he got close enough. Smith cocked it, closed it and cocked it again in his pocket, taking care not to snag the trigger on the inside of his pants and fire it. He debated whether now was as good a time as any. His father had always said so. But it had been late, and Slade and Ronin had begun to pull their luggage and horses away from the carriage and move up the street toward the city's saloons and hotels. Still, D Street was surprising empty.

Smith began to follow in the shadows instead. When Slade and Ronin signed in at the International Hotel between B and C streets, he decided. He would make that "big-assed mistake" they'd talk about. And maybe he would do it right there, in the lobby of the biggest and nicest hotel in Virginia City. And maybe everyone would see how determined he was to make his life right, and their relationship right, all one-hundred and sixty-some rooms of people. And then they'd know, or then Mort Spinnaker would know, how happy he was to set out in a new direction, a different direction, as long as they were together. And they would make it. Together, they'd make it, or life just wasn't worth living.

# Chapter 31
# HEART AND HAYES

"Did you hear that?" Ronin asked.

"Hear what?"

The second rifle shot slammed through the third story B Street window of the International Hotel into an ornate, white French Provincial dresser, splitting the highboy so that the top drawer's contents poured unrestrained onto the bedroom floor. A red night shirt, an extra pair of long johns, a hand-knit tan and black muffler and three pairs of socks spilled onto the rug, sending Dustsucker over the edge of his bed, scrambling for safety as much as to pick things up before anyone else could see them.

"Heard that one!" Dustsucker hollered, his arms and legs suddenly askew as the rifle's rapport — a buffalo gun, a .45-70 or bigger, Dustsucker figured — echoed off of the side of Mount Davidson into their room in Virginia City's nicest hotel.

Hardly awake, the deputy sheriff pushed his clothes into the corner and began patting around for his handgun and holster. The lamp beside their bed had shattered also, sending glass along with the bureau's white and gold splinters throughout the room. The smell of kerosene flooded their nostrils as tiny pieces of wood grabbed at their hands, knees and feet.

"Holy shit," Ronin said as they met, creeping along the floor.

Despite the staff's protestations that they not take a kerosene lamp into their room, they had anyway. "We don't permit the outside lamps to come inside, Mister Ronin, it's a fire hazard," the staff had explained before folding to the ex-priest's explanation that he had reading and writing to do and didn't want to keep his roommate awake. "He's a light sleeper," Ronin explained, before hearing a houseboy say to another, "I doubt he's a light anything."

"Excuse me?" Ronin chirped, hopping the counter and following the fear-struck teenager into a back room. "Isn't it time for you to head to bed, son?"

They'd gotten in late to be sure, dragging their luggage up from the rail station, where one of the passengers insisted on stopping, having heard about D Street's entertainment opportunities. The driver had said he would make one stop only, and given that the coach had ground to a halt already, demanded that everyone disembark despite the fact that everyone — women, men, teens and children — would have to pull their luggage uphill toward the hotel.

Ronin wasn't in the mood to disagree. Jackson was happy to take the load. And Dustsucker's mount — a horse he had yet to give a name to — was just as agreeable, though it meant a handful of people remained complaining that they'd "never again ride a Benton stage, nor any other coach line that stopped at Benton's Livery in Carson City."

Two nights later, the two of them found themselves crawling across the floor of their room at the International Hotel, wondering why they'd come to Virginia City at all.

Ronin finally stood and pressed himself into the northwest corner of the room, where he figured he couldn't be seen or shot at, and pulled on his pants. "What the hell was that?" He peeked out the window between their beds before lunging for his gun belt, hanging over the headboard spindle. He grabbed his hat and began inching toward the door.

"Hell if I know, Ronin." His friend paused, his hand on the hotel door.

"You going outside?"

"You bet," Ronin said. "I'll be back in a few moments." He shut the door so that Dustsucker wouldn't be silhouetted by the gas lights lining the hotel hallway and stairs.

"Hell you will," Dustsucker said, grabbing his gun belt, pants and shirt, and tumbling out into the hallway. "I'm with you."

They jogged down the hotel's wooden steps into the front lobby, where a surprised night watchman asked, "What's going on upstairs, Mister Ronin? Good morning, Deputy Slade."

"Good morning and good question," Ronin said as he ran out the front of the hotel and turned to sprint up Union Street. "You able to move?" he yelled to Dustsucker, who had one leg caught in his trousers, having pulled the other up to his hips where he was holding pants, gun and gun belt, feeling around for an outside handrail. "Watch the steps," he said before beginning to run. The building's south wall was still in the shadows, the moon not being full and the sun still hours before rising. Skipping upward, treating the Union Street steps like a steep Tahoe hiking path, he paused to kneel at the top and waited to catch his breath.

"Jesus, Ronin," Dustsucker wheezed as he caught up to him. "Could you run any faster?"

"I had to take it easy, Dusty," he laughed. "It's still not quite morning."

"Funny. See anything?"

"Just the usual," Ronin replied, "a couple of B Street houses with lights on. But judging from the angle of the shot into our dresser, I'm guessing he'd have to be pretty far away."

"Third floor," Dustsucker offered.

"Exactly. He'd have to be up on the mountain a ways to make that shot."

"Or she."

"Or she?"

"Or she. It's not like you don't have a handful of women upset with you," he said, pulling his braces up over his shoulders and finally kneeling beside his friend.

In that moment Ronin knew what was going on with his friend, or with the two of them. It was a springtime thing, he'd explained a couple of days before. And it had never occurred to him that Dustsucker might be having some of the same feelings. Kneeling in the early morning moonlight, but not so early that the shadows were short and Nevada's starry brightness muted, he realized the two of them were in love. Not with each other, of course — most men didn't feel that way on the Comstock, though some did or might, it didn't matter — No, Slade and Ronin happened to have feelings for a certain mission lady a few miles south of Carson City. It was all about Emma. How was it that one woman — so independent and cantankerous a woman at that — could tie the two of them up so? He surely didn't know.

"Sleepy?" he asked.

"Nah. Little chance of me catching any shut-eye now, Ronin, now that I'm up, anyway. How about you?"

"Nope. My mind's racing, my friend. And getting shot at stirs me in a way that nothing else does. Let's grab a beer and talk some," he said, still keeping to the dark side of the building as they walked back to the hotel's C Street entrance.

With no one at the desk to ask, they grabbed a couple of beers from the bar and headed up the steps to the second floor and out onto the balcony. A third story balcony, more of the French style, sat above them, protecting them against an early morning rain. "Listen to that," Ronin said, facing east toward the early morning noises on C Street.

"The rain?"

"Nah, the city. It's not even sun-up and the city is aflame."

"Careful with those words, Ronin. Nobody up here takes to joking about fire."

"Not meaning to. Just thinking how busy 'busy' has become." He pulled the cap off of both bottles and handed one to his friend.

"Not like it used to be."

"Maybe so."

He dragged a chair over to the balcony's edge. The balcony provided a grand view for parades and would be pressed into service in a few days when President Rutherford B. Hayes visited the Comstock. It was expected Hayes would be accompanied by Civil War hero General William Tecumseh Sherman and other Washington dignitaries. He'd also be accompanied by his wife.

Ronin had little use for Hayes and even less for General Sherman, who had implemented a "scorched earth" policy against the Southern states during the Civil War. Sherman's march through Georgia and the Carolinas had broken the Confederacy's ability to wage war. He'd punished the American Indian similarly as well. The resulting devastation, to both the Indian nations and the South, left Ronin wondering if America would ever be the same.

"Going to be a lot of picture taking here in a couple of days, Dusty. Speeches, parades — I'm hoping we've got our business wrapped up and that we're out of here by then."

"President Hayes?"

"Exactly. I read this morning that he'd been in Iowa, Illinois, Wyoming and Utah so far. The son of a bitch is expected to speak about free schools and the power of reconstruction. Jesus."

"Don't like him?"

"A good Southern boy? Of course not."

"I thought you were from Pennsylvania, Ronin?" Dustsucker asked, taking a beer from Ronin's right hand before tapping the two bottles together.

"Someday I'll have to explain, Dusty."

"Okay."

"One of the things I agree with, though, is Hayes' thoughts about free schools. The paper said yesterday morning, he'd said in Iowa, 'When universal suffrage prevails, there must be universal education.' What do you think about that?"

"I think it's too early to be thinking about anything, Ronin. But as a man who's had a little bit of education, I'd be happy to see free schools for free men and women everywhere. Don't see the problem with that."

"That's what he said, my friend. 'The ignorance of one section of the country is detrimental to others.'"

"Don't imagine they've talked to anyone in Tennessee about that, Ronin."

"No, I imagine not," Ronin laughed. "Some folks aren't going to have the money to attend school, black *or* white. Everyone is poor right now, Dusty, not just folks in Nevada. But that's not what I want to talk about."

"I'm headed back to bed, Ronin," Dustsucker said, standing up and taking a final swig from his bottle. "Got something that can't wait?"

"Well, somebody's shooting at us, for one. And while you and I can likely get some sleep despite that, we ought to talk about it before seeing Ash and McBride again for breakfast."

"And the other thing ... I'm assuming there's another thing."

"How your heart's been hurt, my friend. I want to apologize for my part in that. I want for you whatever you want for yourself."

"Even if it's what you want for yourself?"

"You're assuming a lot there, Dusty, but yes, even then."

# Chapter 32

# THREE O'CLOCK IN THE MORNING

Dustsucker tapped a Carson Brewery steam beer bottle against his leg. "You really want to talk about this at this time?"

"I'm just saying, it's finally come together for me, Dusty. I haven't been honest with you or with Emma about my intentions and that can't have been easy. Can we talk a bit about it?"

"Shoot."

Dustsucker looked over the brow of the building through the dark toward the Dayton Valley. A September moon threw light across the city to the busy factories and towns below already lit for the sake of laborers pulling silver out of the ground. It wouldn't be long before snow fell. He waited. Ronin took a long sip of beer and then began.

"I sometimes wonder who saw her first."

"I did, if you're really asking. You didn't meet her until she was helping Quinn patch up your leg ..."

"And you met her a few moments before that, when she was brought to the sheriff's office because she'd fainted outside," Ronin replied. "I don't know that that counts so much ..."

"It wasn't like that, William. I greeted her many times on the street over the years, not really saying anything to her, but still. She was so lovely, the first day I saw her. Five feet tall, give or take, long brown hair that she never let down. But I bet if she ever did, it would be the most beautiful hair any man has ever seen. And the darkest eyes ..." his voice trailed off. "Wow is all I can say, Ronin. I've been looking at that woman for years. And as hard as it is to tell a preacher this ..."

"... ex-preacher, Dusty, especially if you're going to tell me something randy."

"Please!" he said. "She's an inviting, passionate and provocative woman. I wouldn't ever speak about her that way."

Ronin cleared his throat. He appreciated the risks his friend was taking. He wanted to be more sensitive. "Listen," he said, "I think it's swell, the feelings you've got. I didn't know that about you. You're a passionate man, Dusty. I had no idea."

"You never asked."

"No, I didn't."

"Look, Ronin. I don't know what the deal is with you, but it seems to me that you can have any woman you want. I see you talking to this lady or that, and I just don't get it."

"You don't get what?"

"I don't get how you do it. I don't get why you do it. And I haven't figured out what it is that you're doing. As a man who has so much to offer, I don't understand why you haven't figured out a way to settle down by now. Your playing the field is killing me, and it can't be kind to the women you're playing with."

Ronin sat back in his chair. "You're talking to me about my relationships? I had hoped to talk to you about yours."

"Probably so, but listen to me. Some men, some women too, I imagine, are lucky as hell in this life. And others, like myself, are not so lucky." He tilted his head and looked directly at his friend. "So what comes easy to you isn't so easy for me, you know what I'm saying?"

"I do."

"And while you're doing so much of it — whatever it is that you're doing — I'm here, wondering if I can't just have a little. You know?"

"I do."

"So I'm asking you, if you don't have any good intentions toward Miss Emma, I'd certainly like for you to tell me so, because I do. And if you don't mind me asking …"

"I don't."

"… I'd like you to step out of the way so that I can court that woman."

Ronin felt like a big weight had been lifted off of his chest. He uncrossed his arms and legs and leaned forward. "That's what I'm apologizing about, Marcus. I've been unintentionally sitting in your way. And if you think you have a shot with her, take it. There'd be no better man in my mind than the man in front of me. Have at it, my friend."

Dustsucker smiled, and thought back to the first time he had met his friend. Ronin had asked his help in a Pinkerton National Detective Agency investigation. "Do you remember when we first met?" he asked.

"It was my first time in Nevada. I had trailed Madame Bovary to Carson City. I couldn't find her anywhere at one point, and thought she had left for Reno when you told me she was making a living in Virginia City on B Street under a different name."

"I did. You were one of three Pinkerton agents, I think, and you'd followed her through what, a half-dozen states?"

"I think so."

"And you finally brought her to justice, facing multiple counts of fraud, bigamy, prostitution and I don't know what else."

"I did."

"But not before falling in love with her. Remember?"

"I do."

"You had some strong feelings for that woman, Ronin. They were not at all the same as the feelings you have for Emma and others."

"Well, I don't know about that ..."

"Sure you do. You loved the woman, Ronin. And while it wasn't okay with the Pinks since you were investigating her, you found her so utterly fascinating that you resigned to pursue the relationship."

"Wish it were so, my friend. I was fired. And after getting fired I sort of regained my composure." Ronin took a long sip of his beer and patted his shirt, wishing he had a pipe or cigar.

Bovary had been intoxicating. He had known her a few months, more or less and it wasn't long before he was head over heels in love with her. And while he'd not resigned to have a relationship with her, his resignation was a fact. He'd barely blurted it out before his superintendent fired him. His heart still hurt over the matter. It would always hurt, he guessed.

"So let me ask you, William. What's different?"

"Different?"

"How is it you find yourself so easily giving up one woman, when what you actually want to do is to be in love with some other?"

Ronin sat silently on the second story balcony of the International House hotel wondering. Long after his friend Dustsucker had gone to bed he was still searching for an answer for the hole in his soul and why he had crammed so much, and so many, in there in an effort to fill it. In the end, he knew that Emma Nauman wasn't going to speak to his life's deepest needs. Their differences were too profound. Their emotional tone and tenor, from the day he met her to the last day he'd seen her, told him that they were cut from a different cloth. And while he could be that man, that person that Emma wanted — holy and true, moved by things beautiful, heavenly and new — he also knew his ghosts. He'd once loved a woman so much more. The only honest thing was to let her go.

Ronin returned to his room, and securing a pipe and to-bacco from his saddle bags, he took a long draw. He tasted the cherry wood, the hills of western Pennsylvania and thought of Reelfoot Lake in western Tennessee — it felt like it was spring-time. And while he knew it was September, he sat by the window, wondering. What would the next few months bring?

# Chapter 33

# THE SPRINGFIELD TRAPDOOR

The 1873 Springfield "Trapdoor" was the first breech-loading rifle adopted by the United States Army. Generally thought of as an easy firearm to operate, a new recruit could put eight rounds per minute down range. A seasoned soldier could fire as many as fifteen rounds per minute, making the rifle a highly efficient killing machine.

Toro Latigo's experience with the trapdoor rifle was minimal, having taken the gun from a man in Elko, Nevada, who no longer had any use for it given that the fact that he was dead.

Concerned that he might be wanted for questioning in the matter in Wells, Latigo had lingered in Virginia City long enough that his particular set of skills were wanted, "even needed," the pretty girl had said, though her words were difficult to understand, as if she had a mouthful of marbles or was just learning to speak.

Alvira Fae Livestock was a pretty woman, Toro concluded, after she and her sister shut the door on their D Street home. He didn't mind the single gold tooth; it sort of set off her smile. The fact she had warmed up to him after only one cup of tea suggested the two of them might have a future together, if her sister Ellie May didn't mind and if he could get this thing handled for the two of them. "A bullet in his heart," Alvira had said, before her sister corrected her.

"Or in his head," she said, even after being told not to speak that way.

"I'll speak any way I want," he thought she had said, though he couldn't be certain. Alvira's accent when speaking was unusual. He hadn't heard anything like it in Nevada or Utah, not that it mattered and not that he had traveled enough to know about such things. As long as two people were happy with each other, Toro didn't' think there were any rules at all to follow, though he wasn't sure and didn't know how things would work out between them since he hardly knew the girl and not that she was necessarily looking.

"How do I work this thing?" he'd asked the man he'd taken the rifle from and just tomahawked in the head, before fleeing to the nearby Ruby Mountains to hide. The dead man was unable to respond, though Latigo's mastery of the breech-loading concept didn't take long after that.

The little man concluded that "breech" meant bottom, as his mother had told him he'd been born that way and that perhaps that's why he was so small. The word was German or Danish or something like that. And he wasn't sure that's why he was so short except that it had made him something of a "rapscallion," a word he had come across in Reno one time when he was asked to leave a physician's office after complaining of a rash. The word was the same as saying "rascal" or "scamp," the doctor had explained before he kicked him in the knees.

"Use a word I can understand," he shouted on his way out the door.

"Disreputable person" is what the physician said as he clubbed him with one of the office chairs. Toro was a disreputable person, which he was of course proud of, though being so didn't give other people permission to call him that.

"The neighbors had a hard time getting you out," his mother used to say when she was alive, too often for it to be something he was comfortable with. "You were born ass-end first," she'd insisted, despite his raising his hands and asking her not to say such things, knowing that she'd go on to tell him other details of his birth that Toro found too intimate to experience or remember.

"Bottom," he repeated to himself, every time he used the 52-inch rifle. The long gun was longer than he was tall. He wondered about trading the full-length rifle for a shorter carbine, like those used by cavalry soldiers. But after Custer's disaster in 1876, he didn't see as many of the shorter rifles as he thought he would in his travels.

A *copper* .45-70 caliber cartridge was popular when the rifle was first introduced. But initial investigations into the slaughter of Custer's battalion of soldiers at Little Bighorn suggested that either the rifle or the cartridge was partially at fault. He didn't know the outcome of the Army's discussion, though he did have personal experience with the cartridge as it was all the Elko man had available. The two shots he'd fired at W. W. Ronin's window were a good example of why some people didn't like the rifle any-more, as it took Toro a good number of tries with his knife to get the spent cartridge unstuck so as to load another.

"Antonio, why can't you be like your brother?" his mother often said, before launching into another story about his birth. And he'd still be listening to her if it wasn't for the fact that she was dead also, the product of Toro's having to listen to the story one too many times. He much preferred the shorter version of his name, he'd told his brother before the taller and apparently more beloved son scrambled out of the window of the their Salt Lake City home, leaving for parts of the world unknown. He left the house "and all the rest of those fucking Mormons," a few hours later after cleaning up. He had never returned.

Cleaning up was what he was doing when he spied Ronin running alongside of the red hotel on B Street. He'd sat and watched them painting the building a few years ago — in November he was pretty positive, given how cold he was standing on the stone blocks outside the International Hotel on C Street. The six-story structure was wonderful, he thought. And the windows' marble caps and sills were a nice touch, though he couldn't imagine the hotel ever being the success it was, even as Ronin knelt at the end of the sidewalk boards on B Street looking his way.

There was no way the former Pinkerton detective could see him, despite the moon and starlight illumining parts of the hillside, creating a winter-like contrast on hills that would soon be covered with snow. He was firmly fitted into the corner of an old porch quite a ways up the mountain and thought about chambering a third round — 1,350 feet per second, the man at the store in Elko told him, prior to his leaving the city for parts west. One 405-grain piece of lead in just the right place would certainly cleave the man's head, though at 400 yards he wasn't sure he could manage the multiple-yard drop the bullet would make shooting that far. In the dark, it was simply way too difficult to do anything different than what he had done.

"I hit the window," he said to no one in particular, before moving further up the mountain when the house lights came on. "We'll have to take care of Mister Ronin later," he continued, wondering if he should get some sleep on the mountain or return to the city for breakfast in another hour or so. He put an unused third shell back into his belt, closed the rifle's breech — a hinged door of sorts, at the end of the rifle barrel — and set the tang sight so that it laid flat and wouldn't catch on his clothes.

"Breakfast sounds good," he concluded aloud, while walking a couple hundred yards north to reclaim his horse. "I need to tell my baby that I'm about to brand me a cowboy," he sang, putting the rifle into its pouch. "Can't wait, uh huh, can't wait," he chanted, pulling himself up onto the pony he'd borrowed from the Virginia City livery that was holding his wagon and stock because he'd failed to pay the charges. "Maybe, just maybe, she'll want to have breakfast with me," he repeated, "Uh huh, uh huh. My baby, my baby, my big, gold-toothed baby …"

# Chapter 34
# THE LATE ALFONSO JACKSON

Alfonso Jackson shuffled out of his coach and up the steps of Ellie May Livestock's D Street home. He'd met a great many people in his railroad career, in Maryland, Nevada, California and elsewhere. He'd been impressed with many of them — hard workers, honest investors and friends who had accompanied him on the way up the ladder. Railroad friends were like that. There were plenty of them. But when he arrived at the top — he owned and exploited a bundle of short lines in gold and silver fields throughout the glitter states, even up into the Northwest — it seemed like everything changed. He stepped away from the trough and found folks anxious. People who had been with him from the beginning began to look elsewhere. Once he took his hand off the spigot — selling some companies, trading others, making the sometimes unpopular decisions his friends didn't need to be a part of — the entourage declined. He was left only with his wife. And when Guinevere, so to speak, fell into the hands of a younger Lancelot, he was truly alone. Until he met Ellie May Livestock.

Ellie May turned his life around. The young, brown-eyed lady, with a figure that was different than any woman he'd ever met, seemed to dote on his every wish and whim. A simple dinner was transformed into a night of unending conversation and love. When he got to know the woman, really know her — the lights low, her body undraped, her hands eagerly seeking his and more — he realized it wasn't only the cow that he was interested in. It was the whole farm he wanted. Her effusive spirituality — something he originally considered to be nonsense — deepened his inner life, a dynamic he'd been missing in the first sixty or so years of his time on earth. When she spoke of heaven and places even more wonderful than that — where lives never died and only love lived — he imagined he might live forever, and that they might live forever together. It was all very exciting.

He knocked on the screen door, which he had helped Ellie and her sister paint red. "It's the color of divinity," she'd explained, though as a former Presbyterian he thought a divine door would be better painted purple or blue.

"Ellie," he called through the screen, leaning on an ivory-handled cane he'd bought for himself to make an impression at his wedding thirty-four years prior. "Ellie May? Are you home?" he called. He loved coming by unannounced. Typically, Ellie May and her sister were entertaining folks hoping to contact their loved ones in the Great Beyond. He didn't want to pry, but he enjoyed listening to their gatherings, though he'd never attended a larger meeting at the Spiritualist Society Hall on B Street. Big gatherings brought back memories of the days when he was surrounded by people he thought were his friends. Now certain they were not, he didn't like pretending. Most folks didn't like him, he figured, so he didn't need to like them either.

"We're enough for each other, aren't we Alfonso?" Ellie May had said the other night, while he lay in her arms, his head resting upon her breast as he might lay upon a pillow.

"We are, dear one," he'd replied, remembering how she'd lovingly unbuttoned his jacket, his vest, his shirt and finally his pants as well. The tumble of clothes sat by their bed until the early morning hours, when he woke with a start thinking he needed to check his banks and the markets. "I'll be just a few moments," he whispered, before slipping his feet onto the floor, nudging his clothes closer to the door.

Alvira was already up and in the front room, though she didn't seem to mind. He dressed quietly in a corner behind a tall chair, looking up at her at times, wondering what was running through her head. They were comfortable together, the three of them, though things were certainly more intimate between Ellie and him than with the three of them together. Still, they'd often eat breakfast when he stayed over. And occasionally, he'd take them both in his carriage to Carson City, or even aboard the train to Reno.

Caring for one meant caring for the other, he reminded himself as he pulled his suspenders up over the shirt that had been perfectly pressed the day before. He'd surely divorce his wife in the days ahead so that he could be with these two women. Ellie was the light of his life. He'd never cared for another woman the way he cared for her. And if that meant that Alvira would live with them as well, then that would be as much a part of God's plan as anything ever was or should be.

Turning around to fasten his fly, he felt a hand touch his back. Turning, he found Alvira offering him one of his shoes, smiling. He thanked her, and crossing his leg, placed his shoe on his left foot. She bent to offer him his other shoe. He shook his head. If he could be helpful to these two that is what he wanted to do. Whatever it means, for whatever reason, his wealth was their wealth. There was enough for all of them to spend freely.

He parted the drape and went back into the bedroom, where the love of his life was just beginning to stir. "Alfonso? You're leaving so soon?" she whispered, wiping the sleep from her eyes, her morning scent like the flowers he used to keep on his railroad desk.

"I've got to go, dear. Tonight?" he asked, hoping there'd be time in Ellie's busy calendar of meetings and appointments.

"Of course, my love," she said, her eyes fluttering. God, how he loved this woman! "Come around eight, would you, dear? I've got ... so much to do."

"Of course," he said, leaving the bedroom before embracing her sister, who seemed equally as sad to see him go. "I'll be back, and all three of us can have a good time, okay?" he said, touching her cheek. He'd bring the papers as well, settling the matter between him and his wife and putting "in plain English," Ellie had once asked, "how you really feel for me."

Ellie May nodded, pulling the covers up over her shoulders and turning over in bed. Alvira Fae smiled, her gold tooth gleaming. Three was better than two any day, she wanted to say. But her sister told her she needed to keep silent. Maybe not tonight, she thought. Maybe not tonight.

# Chapter 35

# HEART ATTACK

"Of course we get heart attacks up here, Ronin. People die from all kinds of things." Augustus Ash leaned back in his chair. "Squalor, infections, accidents, whatever. Generally, I'm not all that interested in people dying."

"So what's got you worked up on this one, Augustus?"

"This one was found in a woman's bed."

W. W. Ronin smiled. There were a lot of awkward places to die. But dying in a woman's bed? Well, that sounded like heaven.

"The woman in question had a problem with that," Ash continued, his head turned at an angle, wondering what Ronin had on his mind.

"Of course," Ronin said. "What was I thinking?"

"I was just considering that question, but listen, here's the reason we're still sitting here with McBride pulling what little hair he has out of his head wondering where we are. The woman was Ellie May Livestock, Ronin — the lady you're supposedly investigating."

Ronin looked at the marshal. *Supposedly? What the hell does that mean?* "I can't be responsible for the lady's actions around the clock, marshal. And I don't want to be, either. I had me a woman like that once. She was called 'church.'"

"Yeah, listen. You got a dead man in Carson City, somehow connected to her, another one in Virginia City dying in her bed, and a few points in-between where she's not killed anyone yet. Is that enough to light a fire under your ass?"

Ronin looked at his friend Dustsucker, who was looking at the ceiling. It was the first time he'd been in the marshal's office located in the Odd Fellows building on C Street.
He couldn't think of any other time when someone had offered to build a fire under his friend's derriere. "I didn't hear
that, William," he whispered, thinking it best he stay out
of things.

"Yeah," Ronin said to his friend. "Look Ash, I don't mind
doing some work for you. And you can tell McBride that the money was nice, as I sure as hell am not going to be your boy." He
waited. Dustsucker couldn't tell if he was counting. He hoped not.

Ash shifted his weight. "I'm sorry. I'm just saying …"

"I know what you're saying, and I'm happy to head over
there right this moment, marshal. But I'll be cutting you a box
if you keep talking to me like that. Agreed?"

"Agreed. How about I go with you?"

"I'll head up for a sarsaparilla, if you don't mind."

"You do that, Dusty. We'll see you and Versal in a bit."

Marshal Augustus Ash and the former Reverend W. W.
Ronin walked toward Saint Mary's and made a left on D Street,
taking a few moments to compare personal notes about the
weather — "mild, thank you"—the number of trains the V and
T was still running into Virginia City — "about twenty a day,
I think, why?" — and the price of rooms at the International
Hotel — "down to $12.50 a month now, can you believe it?
Same room used to cost $25 a month, that's how bad things
are getting." It took but a few moments to arrive at the sisters'
home. Ronin took the steps, knocking on the door.

"Well, Miss Livestock, good to see you again," he said,
looking at Ellie May, who had opened the door.

"Have we met, sir?"

"Briefly, ma'am. Tom Kelly pointed me out to you, I believe." She barely smiled. *Impressive. She didn't even blink.*

"So he did, Mister Ronin, my apologies. And Marshal Ash, how nice to see you again, also."

"Thank you, ma'am. Mind if we come in?" Ash asked, his right foot up against the door. A lawman's habit, Ronin figured, before noticing his hand was on the door as well.

"Of course, gentlemen. More about the dead man, I presume?"

Ronin looked over at Ash, who had taken to wiping his fingers on a marble table before sitting down in a red velvet chair. Ronin sat opposite him, next to the table in an identical chair. "Miss Livestock, Marshal Ash has got me to asking a few questions about the death of a couple of men from the Comstock Club, I hope you don't mind." She nodded. "Turns out we've got a few of them dead."

"A few of them, Mister Ronin? I know of only two."

*Amazing.* His misdirection had produced no visible anxiety in her face. No flinch to her neckline, no flush to her skin or anything. *Practiced.*

"Two, ma'am. You are correct. My apologies."

"No need …"

"No, I try to be exact ma'am, which is why I'm here this morning. And pardon me, I've been up for a while." *Her pupils constricted. Huh.* "You had a man die in your bed this morning, ma'am. And the marshal and I are wondering …"

"You and the marshal, sir, or just you? Which one of you is most interested in the details, gentlemen?"

They blushed. *Masterful. She's deflected my question and it's entirely appropriate that she has.* "Well, primarily me, ma'am. I have no idea what details the marshal is after, but I'm a simple man and can't imagine not wanting to know things as they are, ma'am, nothing left out, if you don't mind."

Ellie May Livestock recoiled, as a proper lady should and might, a fact that made Ronin even more curious about the woman, as a working woman might have been more brazen. Someone stirred in the back room, separated from the sitting room by a flax-colored drape, picturing roses in shades of pink, taupe and crimson with green, pink and lighter taupe leaves. Ronin leaned to his right side before asking, "Is there someone with us, ma'am?"

"My sister only," she smiled. "Alvira Fae? Come out here and meet these men," she called. Her sister appeared at the drape, parting it with her hands, grinning, a gold tooth the only blemish to an otherwise perfect smile. "Alvira is deaf, gentlemen. She can't hear us, not much anyway. You may speak as you wish. She's not listening."

"It would appear as if you've done some cleaning, Ellie May," Ash asked, "I mean, given that I was here earlier this morning."

"That we have, marshal. Alfonso was an excitable man, Mister Ash. And I'm afraid his heart couldn't stand what I was doing to him."

"Ma'am?" Ronin asked. Ellie May smiled. Other than the gold tooth, the two sisters looked like identical twins. It was amazing. They were both very beautiful women.

"I should say, 'we,' Mister Ronin, what we were doing to him."

"Ma'am?" He raised his eyebrows — he hadn't heard of anything like that before.

"Let's just say, he had a big smile on his face as he passed, gentlemen ..."

*Jesus.*

# Chapter 36

# I HAD HIM IN MY SIGHTS

"I had him in my sights, Mort. It was maybe 2 or 3 in the morning. You know how I like to go walking at night, right?"

"I do."

"So I'm standing outside of St. Mary's talking to a couple of guys I know when I see this stage roll up the street. It doesn't stop in front of the International, like most coaches — and what the hell is a stagecoach doing unloading passengers in the middle of the night, right? — no, it stops on D Street, in front of a working girl's house, and the first people I see getting off the coach are Ronin and the deputy from Carson City!"

"Slade."

"I guess so. The big guy, right?"

"Yup, that's Slade."

"Okay. So I look at them — they're not looking at me, because I'm standing in the shadows — and I've got the Smith and Wesson in my pocket and I'm cocking it and uncocking it, cocking it and uncocking it ..."

"You've got to be careful with that, Timothy. It's a tiny gun and you don't want it going off inside your coat pocket. You might get hurt."

"Right. So I'm thinking, I'm going to do it. I'm going to shoot the son of a bitch, and maybe his friend. So I line him up in my sights, Mort. You know. And all of the guys are looking at me. And I'm trying to decide what to do ..."

"There aren't any sights on that gun, Timothy. It's a belly gun, for close-up work only. I told you that."

"Yup. But the stage had a lot of people on it and I figured that what I was going to do could wait. It's not like we have to do this right away, right?

"No, we don't."

"So I followed them up to the International Hotel where they got a room, or maybe two rooms — I don't know, that's all I know — and then I came home."

Mort Spinnaker was silent. He liked Timothy Edwards Smith, probably more than he'd liked any other man, any other woman for that matter. They got along. Most of the time, Smith was quiet, though moody if he were honest. But occasionally, he sure could get wound up.

"Timothy. Let me ask you," he looked into his eyes and saw a generally kind man, a man who desperately wanted to settle down somewhere, with someone he trusted. They both wanted that. He reached toward him and put his left hand on his friend's shoulder. He seemed high-strung, as if he hadn't rested at all last night. "Did you sleep at all?"

"Sure, Mort. I slept. Why?"

"I'm just concerned," he replied, thinking his friend had a lot of energy for eleven o'clock on a Friday morning. "Listen," he said, "are you really able to do this?" he asked, thinking of his own reservations, being a renewed Catholic and wanting to live a better life. It wasn't as if murder was anything to be trifled with, spiritually speaking. It was a mortal sin. And according to the church's teachings, unless they could figure out a way to kill the two of them accidently — not that you could think that without actually planning to do so, so maybe it wasn't an accident after all — going through with their intentions could easily mean that one or both of them would spend their eternal destiny in a less than favored place. "Timothy, I'm telling you. It could cost us our souls, you know. Are you willing to risk that?"

Timothy Edwards Smith stood listening to his friend, blinking. How is it that anyone could change so quickly, he wondered? A couple of weeks ago, his friend was sitting in the Ormsby County sheriff's office, doing whatever lawmen did, when the sheriff pressed him into a gunfight he didn't want any part of. And before you knew it, the two of them — he and Smith, people who had never seen nor met each other — had skedaddled from their relative roles in the gunfight and ended up in a bar together on Carson Street planning out their futures. A Roman Catholic barkeep had set them straight. Praise God for Jack. "Unless it's in self-defense," Smith offered. "If we didn't start it, maybe it wouldn't be so wrong."

Spinnaker smiled. He guessed that might qualify. The catechism study with Father Manogue was obviously doing his friend some good. It'd be a venial sin, not a mortal one, he figured, not that he could ask the Father next time he saw him, though he might ask one of the sisters. "'The works of the flesh are manifest,' Timothy. That's what the Bible says. They are 'adultery, fornication, uncleanness, lasciviousness,'" he paused to remember, "'idolatry, witchcraft, hatred' and a bunch of other things I don't remember, except murder and heresy." He liked the *Epistle to the Galatians*, by Paul the apostle. He liked lists, and the founder of the church — judging by the book at least in his mind, though the church probably said something else — seemed to include so many lists.

"That's what I'm saying, Mort. If it's not something we *want* to do, 'in the flesh,' but it just happens … well, you know, it's not really something we did. It just happened."

Mort stood thinking for a moment. There might be wisdom in that, he mused. His friend might have stumbled on a whole new category of grace, or sin or something. Though he wasn't sure what it was, it surely wouldn't be a mortal sin if they got into it with Ronin and his lawman friends, and it just happened. He died, they died, whatever. "Timothy, you might be on to something," he said, thinking that it was getting closer to lunch time than breakfast time, so maybe they should head up the road a piece to get something to eat before the restaurants got too busy. "We should think about this, Timothy. Let's take a walk toward Gold Hill, or maybe Virginia City."

"And maybe we should pray about it too," Smith said, looking up at his friend and hoping for approval. He touched Mort's hand, which was still resting on his shoulder. "If we're going to start a new life together, Mort, I don't want to do it by putting the wrong foot forward."

"Me neither, Timothy. We'll say a quick prayer, then let's get something to eat."

# Chapter 37
# AS I SEE IT

"So here's the issue as I see it," Versal McBride said, cutting into a rib eye steak at the Bucket of Blood saloon. "The club now counts two men dead. Not a big deal, given their age and the way they lived their lives. But if the trend continues, and the Washoe Club loses a few more of its members, it will become a big deal. That's why we've asked you here."

Ronin nodded. It seemed like they'd had this conversation before, though he wasn't in the habit of critiquing his employers, no matter how repetitive or ignorant the speech's content was. He liked to remind himself that everyone had a right to say something as long as it didn't conflict too much with the norms he was used to. And after all, the man *was* paying him. "Look, Versal..."

Marshal Ash winced. He *still* wasn't sure McBride wanted to be on a first-name basis with a rowdy ex-preacher. He didn't like cowboys. He sure as hell didn't like preachers. "Mister McBride," he interrupted.

"What?" McBride replied, turning to Ash who was seated beside Slade and Ronin, neither of whom were paying any attention as they were hoping to get a server's attention instead.

"Nothing. Go ahead, Ronin."

Ronin looked at Ash and then back to the owner of the saloon. "I was about to say that I get your concern. And I understand that you want me to look into what's happening with these women that wiser, richer men are acting so stupid. But I need to point out, being stupid isn't against the law."

"Well, it sure as hell ought to be," Tom Kelly said as he lifted a glass of juice from a server's tray and pulled a chair over from another table. "Ronin, gentlemen," he said. He sat down and looked across the table at Slade and Ash, who were still looking for a server's attention. "Beating the stupid out of people is half of what we do ..."

"The other half?" Ronin asked, laughing.

"Locking up people who don't get the point."

"Well, here's what I'm thinking of doing today," Ronin continued. "I'm going to head over to the Washoe Club and talk to a few of the men there. Maybe you want to give me a list, Tom. Or perhaps you have one, Versal." McBride shook his head, indicating he did not. "I'll get a better sense of what's happening at the club, and perhaps that will put your anxiety to rest."

Ash looked at McBride. He wasn't sure that comment was going over either. Versal McBride was a self-made man. Most of the men on the Comstock were. He'd be no more likely to cop to feeling anxious than a priest would to feeling horny.

Ronin continued. "Then I think it's time to attend one of their meetings."

"Meetings?" Slade asked. "Like in church?"

"Exactly, Dusty. Spiritualists hold big gatherings, where there's a lecture or preaching, sometimes singing, poetry and such. At least that's been my experience. He thought back to Madame Bovary, whose travels had first drawn him to the Silver State, and whose wiles had kept him interested when he should have had his mind on other business. "They have small meetings as well, in their homes. It's time for me to see who's saying what and to whom."

"You mean, who's *doing* what and to whom ..." McBride argued.

"Maybe."

"And then?" Kelly asked.

"Then we'll figure out where to go from there." The ex-preacher had learned to be slow about such things. When he approached the sacred texts as a priest, he'd allowed them to speak. Old Testament. New Testament. Even the Intertestamental Writings, between the time the Hebrew scriptures were written — he didn't know, maybe 1500 years before Christ, maybe as few as three or four-hundred years before Christ, it didn't matter — and the Christian books written a hundred years or so after Jesus' death. He didn't know where the inspiration came from, but he was certain it wouldn't come if he didn't allow time for their words to sink in. An investigation, with events, witnesses, perspectives and so on, wasn't all that different. It took time.

"I hate the waiting," McBride said. "When something is wrong, you fix it or before you know, it will set a whole city on fire."

"Understood, Versal. Just give me a few days."

"The President will be here in a few days, Ronin," Ash interjected.

"I know."

"It'll be more difficult to talk to anyone is my point," Ash continued. "If you wait too long, everyone is going to be busy."

"Got it, marshal."

A tall, slender woman approached the table. "I didn't realize you'd joined Mister McBride," she said in a perfectly southern accent. Tennessee, Ronin thought, maybe Mississippi. "Forgive me," she drawled on and on … it was like heaven, Ronin imagined. And he wouldn't mind going there, he thought. It may be September, but it felt like springtime.

# Chapter 38
# CONSIDERING THEIR OPTIONS

"You're smiling, Ellie."

"I am, Alvira. Anytime I have a man in our bed — whether he's living or dead in the morning — it makes me wonder why I spend so much time with the other side of the coin." Ellie stripped two red satin pillow slips from the bed and folded them. She stood looking for a place to store them on a high shelf on the west wall of the bedroom.

"The other side?" Alivra asked, putting down the fresh stack of sheets and blankets on the bed that her sister asked her to fetch out of an ornate trunk in their front room. The two sisters smiled at each other. While they normally didn't invite a man to join in them in *their* bed — Ellie generally preferred entertaining her Washoe Club clients alone, which was fine with Alvira given that she sometimes felt "dirty" when a strange man touched her or made her touch him. And sleeping next door wasn't all that bad, when she was entertaining — the other evening hadn't been difficult at all. Alfonso Jackson had barely unbuttoned his shirt when he grabbed his chest and fell onto the pillows on their four-post bed. Alvira immediately turned him over onto his back to see if he was breathing, but not before Ellie began rifling through his pockets for money and papers.

"I'm just saying, Alfonso was a nice man and I hated to see him go. But he left us a nice gift!" Ellie said, almost singing in an ascending scale. She waved a raft of British railway shares. "There's maybe a thousand shares here, Alvira. I think that means we're rich!" Ellie grabbed her sister's hands and began dancing in a large circle around the bed that had been pulled away from the wall for cleaning.

"We're dancing! We're dancing!" Alvira Fae sang as they swished and swayed their way around the four-post yellow pine bed sitting in the center of their bedroom. Hands touching, then apart until they caught up with each other again, Alvira was delighted because her sister was happy. She didn't understand the meaning of Alfonso Jackson's gift, or the value of the stock if there was any.

"If this is genuine stock, of the preferred variety, Alvira, we're headed to San Francisco, or New York, or wherever you want to live."

The sisters often spent evenings on the front porch of their home, when they weren't involved with Spiritualist concerns or entertaining friends. They liked to imagine what it would be like to live in places more populous or successful. While Virginia City had done well over the years and they couldn't wish for better neighbors, there were days Ellie thought they could do better, particularly as folks were beginning to talk about mines closing and businesses moving away.

"Maybe ..." Alvira always said, as a sort of trigger for Ellie's imagination. And when Ellie would run out of made-up responses — we could move here, we could move there — she'd offer a quick prayer to the Universe for options she hadn't yet considered. Stare at a crystal ball long enough, or a lake or even a glass of clear water, and certain things floated into her mind. "Certain things, not uncertain things," she always said, "it isn't the same as guessing," though her afternoon clients sometimes wondered aloud when she told them about events and people in their lives or loved ones. "Pray about it, Ellie!"

Alvira would say after sitting silently for a few moments waiting on Ellie's response. "Maybe we'll go to Philadelphia or
Atlanta," she'd answer. "Atlanta would be nice," she'd sometimes shout, knowing that neither of them had ever been to
Georgia or any other southern state before waving her arms in
a silly, wild, wavy sort of way.

"We'll talk about it all, Alvira," she'd respond, touching
her sister's arms so as to calm her. They needed money first.
And she didn't see it happening anytime soon, not in her crystal
ball or imagination. That's why they'd begun to get to know
some of the men in the Washoe Club. Hell, it wasn't like everyone knew there were *two* woman working in the house on D
Street, not during their gatherings anyway. Alvira always stayed
hidden and their guests, typically well-heeled women but sometimes couples who had means, would be enamored with the
extra effort Ellie made to speak to a predicament or contact
their loved ones. Only their special guests knew that there were
two, or so it seemed anyway, as certain of the men believed
Alvira to be a Spirit creature, conjured ectoplasm or real flesh
on occasion when Alvira actually touched them. In a dimly lit
room, with flickering candles and transparent flowing gowns,
and most particularly when the two of them were partially or
completely undressed — wearing the best and most beautiful
boudoir clothing — they looked so alike that some men didn't
believe there were actually two of them.

"Were the marshal and Mister Ronin pleased with your
answers?" Alvira asked. Ellie paused for a moment to consider,
picking up a sheet from the pile of bed clothing Alvira had
placed at the bottom of the bed.

Ellie had introduced her sister, with the gold tooth in
place as one of the continuing "misdirections" she used in her
business whether she was telling fortunes or playing house.
"The central secret of all magic," her father used to say. The

deception was subtle and kept people guessing, which she figured was a good thing, especially given the marshal's interest in her Spiritualist practice and the men and women attracted to it.

"I think they were, Alvira. It was fun last night, wasn't it? She wondered if she was putting Alvira in a position she didn't want to be in, sharing her bed, participating in intimacies she'd never experienced except with her sister and another man.

"It was fun," Alvira Mae replied tentatively, "until Mister Jackson fell over and died!" She laughed. The man's death wasn't funny. But dying in their bed was so strange she didn't know what else to do or say.

"There is that," Ellie said, sitting down opposite her sister, smiling. "Alvira, I need to tell you something."

"What?" her sister intoned, in her broken sort of way.

"That man who is helping us ..."

"Antonio?" Alvira smiled. She liked him and often thought of Toro during the day, when her sister didn't have her cleaning or doing other chores, and when she wasn't so tired that she stopped wondering if she'd ever have a different life.

"... yes, Toro. That man has been shooting at Mister Ronin, Alvira. I don't believe that's what we told him to do, is it?" The word 'we' bent the question so that it appeared gentle and less accusatory.

"No," she said, "I was just teasing."

"But do you remember what you said, Alvira? 'Shoot him in the heart? Shoot him in the head?' You don't think Toro believed that's what we wanted, do you?" Ellie took a deep breath, and after holding it for a moment, began to exhale in a careful, measured sort of way. Ellie didn't know if there had been any additional conversations between the man and her sister that had led the little man to try to kill Ronin.

Alvira looked down and began to wring her hands. A tear dropped into her lap. She pulled a delicate handkerchief from her sleeve. "I don't know," she said, before looking up at her sister, tears beginning to well up in her eyes.

"I don't mean to get you upset, Alvira." She waited a moment for Alivra to finish blowing her nose. "But we can't fix anything by hurting people, dear."

"Isn't that what you said you wanted him to do?" Alivra asked, tucking the tatted handkerchief back up her sleeve.

"Yes," Ellie said, smiling. "Hurt him," I said. "But don't kill him."

# Chapter 39

# PAY ATTENTION

Ronin grabbed a notebook and laid back in the bed to rest his eyes. It had been a busy morning attempting to track the trajectory of rifle shots originating on the eastern slope of Mount Davidson. He had been unsuccessful, though the two of them felt confident it was a .45-70 slug that had winged its way into the dresser of their second-story bedroom. Given the size of the slug, it was unlikely the shot was accidental, as no one fired a cartridge that big or bruising for fun, even in Virginia City.

With Dusty lingering behind at the Bucket of Blood to relate the story, Ronin hurried back to their room at the International Hotel to grab a notebook for the afternoon's interviews. He was hoping to question some of the men at the Washoe Club before discovering when the next meeting of the Virginia City Spiritualist Society was. It struck him as funny that the fortune tellers had an office in the same building as a dentist, as sitting through either procedure would cause him a fair amount of pain. Faith was difficult enough, but faiths different than his own encouraged a greater amount of effort than he was sometimes willing to spend. He was wondering which was more trustworthy — the tooth puller or the soothsayer — when there was a sharp rapping on the room's door.

He rolled off the bed, landing on his knees with his long Colt outstretched toward the door when he heard an Indian calling his name. "William?" the voice inquired. Ronin holstered his hog leg.

"Happy Hands?" he asked, through the closed door.

"It is I," his friend answered. He could almost hear the man smiling.

"What brings you to Virginia City?" He opened the door and stood off to the side so that his friend could enter. Happy Hands was wearing his usual clothing: a dusty, brown white man's hat with a short brim and feather, an old cotton jacket, a colorful flannel shirt and darker brown pants. A handgun was tucked into the top of his trousers. He had never noticed Happy Hands carrying one before. It was an 1875 Remington single-action Army revolver.

The tall Washoe man entered the room, looking about as if it were his first time in a Virginia City hotel room, which it might have been as the city was full of Paiutes. In Ronin's experience, it was a rare Washoe man or woman who would feel comfortable in town, given the number of Paiutes who lived and gambled there. Ronin looked up and greeted his friend with a smile.

"I was hungry," he said, grinning. "And it occurred to me that you might want my advice."

"You were hungry?" Ronin peered at his friend inquisitively, tipping his hat back with his right hand before tucking his gloves into his gun belt. "So you came to Virginia City?"

"Well, yes. And I wanted to see you."

"And you wanted to see me, because you thought I needed your advice?" Ronin laughed. "I'm not following, Happy Hands. You knew I would be back in a couple of days."

"I did not know when you would come back. I only knew that you had bought a suit."

"You knew that I bought a suit?" Ronin cocked his head to the side.

"Exactly, William. Now that we're all caught up, I'm wondering if we could get something to eat …"

"I'm not sure that we're all caught up, Hands." He put his hand on the doorknob to prevent their leaving. "Emma told you that I had bought a suit?"

"Why yes, how did you know?"

Ronin began laughing. Emma hadn't told him about the suit as much as she had inferred he was heading to Virginia City *in* a new suit, and now the two of them were curious. He needed to talk to a couple of Spiritualists. Emma knew what had happened the last time he had talked to a Spiritualist — he had fallen in love. And now she was suspicious, perhaps even jealous of the time and attention.

"Listen, Hands. We'll get a quick lunch, if you like. And then I've got to head over to the Washoe Club to ask a few questions. That's a men's club if you didn't know."

"I didn't know that, but a men's club is a wonderful thing to behold. White men do not have enough of them. They spend too much time with women."

"Whatever," Ronin replied, grabbing his notebook and diary, looking again at the perfectly-blued revolver tucked into Happy Hands' waist. It had been an interesting morning — between getting shot at, talking to Dusty about the woman in their lives and sitting with Versal McBride and August Ash, both of whom seemed to want a great deal more than he was currently willing to give — he didn't want any of it to go unrecorded. He looked over at Happy Hands, who was standing by the door with his hands on his hips, practically framing the gun and smiling. "What?" he asked.

"Nothing." Happy Hands jumped.

"Nothing, Hands? What is it that woman has put you up to?"

His friend scowled. "That woman has not put me up to anything. No woman has put me up to anything, Ronin, not in a great many years."

"No, of course not." He remembered Happy Hands telling him that he used to be married to two women, not one, and that he lived with neither. He was in control of his life, or seemed to be anyway.

"I'm simply concerned."

"We've established that, Hands. What's going on?"

"I am concerned that you will not be paying attention to the women you are about to meet. And that could be a very dangerous behavior."

"Jesus," Ronin mumbled, reaching to pull the door open. *Too much time, not enough time — too much attention, not enough attention. I don't need any of this.* Pulling the door open, he stepped out into the hallway and collided with a young woman carrying a baby.

"Excuse me," he said, fumbling to get out of the way.

"Excuse yourself!" she responded, pulling a blanket over the child's head. "If you don't watch where you're going, you're going to end up there in a hurry. And you'll hurt a lot of people on your way!"

"Yes, ma'am," he said as she angrily scurried down the hallway.

Ronin looked back at Happy Hands, who was standing in the door grinning. "Exactly, what I was saying, my friend. You must pay attention."

# Chapter 40

# HIDING NO LONGER

Dustsucker sat up in the chair to make the point that if it hadn't been so dark out, the shooter might have navigated the usual arc to the heavy bullet and put one right in his head. He was pointing to the crown of his beige-colored cavalry hat when he saw a wheezing — and wanted — Mort Spinnaker standing in the doorway of the saloon. Next to him stood the also-wanted Timothy Edwards Smith. He stood to draw when Spinnaker saw him and kicked a chair into his knees, driving him back again into his chair.

Marshal Ash was on his feet but immediately found himself staring into the business end of Smith's 22 caliber revolver. McBride croaked, "What the hell ..."

Spinnaker leveled a .45 caliber Colt revolver toward the bartender and explained. "I don't know that we intended on meeting you all this way. It was simply my thought that we'd get something to eat here at the Bucket of Blood before heading out of town ..."

"... Maybe you should have left earlier, Spinnaker. You're not wanted around these parts." Ash interrupted.

"He sure is!" Slade said, rubbing his knees. Slade was considering whether he could draw a 7½ inch revolver from either of his California Hickok-style holsters when Ash replied.

"I know he's wanted, you dumb shit!" The inference was clear, and Slade did not care for its tone. "I meant he's not welcome!"

Spinnaker smiled. The *former* Ormsby County deputy didn't care whether he was wanted or welcome as long as they got a decent sandwich before retiring from the room. "How about the three of you put your hands on the table and sit down where we can see you? And Mister barkeep, whatever your name is," he waited until he had the barkeep's full attention, "how about you make my friend and me a sandwich here before we get all angry and begin shooting up your place?"

The barkeep — a young man from New Jersey who really didn't want any trouble as he'd never handled a gun until he had moved to the Comstock and McBride, Virginia City's unofficial mayor, had shoved a shotgun at him and said, "Here, use this if things get out of hand" — didn't want any trouble at all and was much happier slathering mayonnaise on a ham and cheese sandwich than splattering the insides of a couple of ne'er-do-wells on a wall he'd have to clean-up afterwards anyway. "Happy to," he said, when what he really meant was, "I'm so scared shitless right now that I'm certain I've got to clean my pants before I can attend to anything having to do with food." But he didn't. Because he needed the job and no one was interested in what he was thinking.

"Would you prefer mayonnaise on that or mustard?" he stuttered. The difference was unimportant, he gleaned from the look his employer gave him from across the room. But because he asked, Smith replied, "Mustard, please, if you have it."

A trio of surprised men sat back down in their chairs at McBride's usual table by the usual window and all three of them hoped that Ronin would be right there and would be paying attention to what was going on before Spinnaker or Smith got the drop on him. Only Slade looked out the window, wondering.

"Can I help you, deputy? You seem to be looking for someone," Spinnaker said. "Miss me?"

Slade looked over at the bar, where Spinnaker was now leaning, about sixteen feet from the front door. A piano stood quietly nearby, with a sign that said "Squeek plays here to-night." A couple of men at the end of the bar were finishing up breakfast, cutting into their hash browns and eggs, uninterested in whatever else was going on. "Like a rock on Easter morning," Slade replied. McBride peered at the deputy. *What the hell does that mean?*

"I didn't miss you much, either, Slade. Of course it's only been a couple of weeks."

Slade looked over at Ash, who at this point had Timothy Edwards Smith's tiny Smith and Wesson Number 2 revolver pointed so directly into his left ear that it was touching. Ash shook his head no, hoping Slade would get the message, "Don't even think about it."

McBride spoke, "This going to take long, I mean the two of you being here for lunch? I've got a business meeting to conduct."

Spinnaker began laughing. He'd never be able to get a job teaching in Virginia City, now that he'd been recognized by one of the men everyone knew had something to do with everything that went on in the town. And while it was the death of a long-hoped for dream, every death meant a new beginning, "a new opportunity," his dad used to say. He'd likely never have this chance again, for instance — an Ormsby County deputy, the U.S. Marshal for the State of Nevada and one of the Comstock's great businessmen — he wondered if he could get three shots off before one of them returned fire. He very much doubted it.

The man making the sandwiches brought him back to reality. "You want a pickle with that?"

Spinnaker stared at him, not believing what he was hearing. Guns about to blaze and a chicken-necked Italian-looking guy in his mid-to-late thirties was asking if he wanted pickles.

"Yeah, pickles would be nice," he said, laughing. "What do you think, Slade?" he asked, turning toward the lawmen. "Should I get pickles with that? I always did like pickles."

"I like pickles, too," Timothy Edwards Smith said, imitating the same informality about eight feet from the door, where Marcus T. Slade, the Ormsby County deputy, Augustus Ash, the U.S. Marshal and the saloon's owner, Versal McBride sat. "You boys, Catholic?" he asked. Smith, always the intimate one, who regularly preferred to focus on people rather than the task at hand, took his nickel-plated gun away from the marshal's ear and scratched his head with it while he was waiting for an answer. God knows why he even asked the question, except that in that moment, someone must have known, someone must have planted the question in his head, Spinnaker thought, because he watched the whole table shift its attention to God knows where, reaching for God knows what from their belts and pockets as the place erupted like there was a giant panda prize at an explosively popular indoor shooting range.

The sudden barrage of guns and bullets drove the New Jersey boy to the floor, sandwiches with him, pickles and bags in hand as he clawed east along the bar toward the deck out back, hoping he'd make it in time to pray a prayer of thanksgiving to his Father in Heaven who had brought him this far west that he no longer wrote his mother, remembered his father, or wondered about the sister and brother he'd left behind.

Spinnaker dropped to both knees, fanning his .45 so that it splintered the chair his former coworker was sitting on, eliminating its two back legs and dropping Dustsucker onto his back, his hands and legs clawing at the air like an upside down turtle hoping to right itself.

Ash fired from beneath the table, clipping Spinnaker in the right hand, causing him to drop his gun, but not so seriously injuring him that he couldn't pick it up again and roll toward the door where a tall Washoe Indian stood smiling. "Fuck," the Indian yelled, tumbling into the street.

"Hands!" Dustsucker shouted, seeing his Indian friend upside down on the boardwalk as Ronin appeared in the doorway, dropping to one knee and leaving a string of bullets chasing Timothy Edwards Smith across the saloon floor until the wanted man crashed through the deck window onto the street below. It was at least a 12-foot fall but Smith appeared to make it easily. Ronin rushed to the window and continued firing, but wasn't able to hit him.

When his guns clicked dry, he turned around and found Spinnaker gone, too. And the saloon — which was never one of the nicest looking places on C Street in Virginia City, but certainly one of the friendliest — looked like it had become the polling place for a conflicted union election. "Everyone okay?" Ronin shouted.

The New Jersey boy answered first, pulling himself up off the floor with two sandwiches in hand, perfectly bagged, the pickles wrapped in wax paper, just like they used to be served in Jersey City, New Jersey, founded in 1617, thank you, and still a fine place for a fried egg sandwich and coffee.

The owner of the saloon groaned. McBride had been knocked onto the floor by the marshal, who seemed at the time to be concerned for his well-being, though he now wondered if the lawman had simply taken a "free shot" at him, given that no one was watching and everyone was about to wake up dead.

Dustsucker spoke next. "Jesus, it's good to see you."

"Help you up, Dusty?" Happy Hands said, his perfectly-blued 1875 Remington single action Army revolver still tucked into his pants, unfired and nary a scratch on it.

"What the hell was that about?" Ronin asked.

"Two fellows looking for lunch, I 'spect," Ash said, laughing, but loading his six-gun nonetheless. "Don't know that I've ever seen such a shit show," Ash added, looking over at Slade, who was just beginning to get up.

"Me, neither," Ronin said, eyeing McBride. "You ever seen these guys before?"

"Sure, why?"

"Because they're the men we were talking to you about earlier!"

"Ah," he said, in about the same tone as a person hearing the end of an uninteresting story or joke. "Shame we didn't get them, then."

"Yeah, damn shame," Ronin replied, forcefully. "Second time I've nearly been killed here in your saloon, McBride. Believe I'm going to find myself a new place to pour a drink."

"... Or have breakfast," Dustsucker sat down, disgusted, wiping his hands on his vest. He'd let his friends down and ruined a perfectly good Denver omelet, all in the same morning.

# Chapter 41

# PICKLES

"Look, Marshal. This sort of thing isn't okay in my town." McBride sat back in his chair, looking to see if anyone had begun cleaning up. He was gratified to see the Jersey boy recruiting a couple of men who had been standing at the end of the bar, one of whom was still climbing out of the upright piano he had jumped into when the shooting started.

"Come on, McBride! This sort of thing doesn't usually happen in *your* town?"

"Call it what you want, Ash, I've got a business interest in Virginia City and I'm not about to permit a couple of wild ass yahoos to shoot up my saloon while you debate the crime statistics. What the fuck was that about, anyway?" The longer McBride spoke, the more upset he got. It was an observation Ash wasn't going to spend any more time testing. He was opening his mouth to respond when Slade jumped in.

"I believe I can speak to that, Versal," he said, turning his chair around so as to sit more comfortably, his previous perch still scattered about on the floor, despite a couple of saloon hands beginning to clean up the broken glass, table and chair splinters.

"Nobody wants to hear from you, Slade. I'm talking to the marshal here."

"Had you handled things better, we wouldn't have just gone through that," Ash joined in, pulling cartridges from his belt to top off his handguns and rifle.

"Are you talking to me?" Slade said, his belly firmly pressed to the back of the chair, which was now leaning into the table, causing Ash to have to push back so that he wasn't pinned into window or corner. "I don't remember you being there when we first tried to capture these damn cowboys!" he said, giving the table a shove. McBride smiled.

"He was your deputy, deputy!" Ash continued.

"Not hardly ..."

"Not hardly is right, Augustus," Ronin said, sitting down, having come from the saloon doors and not seeing Spinnaker or Smith anywhere in the street. "Fact is, Dusty didn't hire that yahoo. The sheriff did. And neither of us have ever had much of a stomach for him, I'm afraid."

"You're afraid? What the hell does that mean?" McBride said, setting his chair upright.

"I'm just saying, I can't be in two places. These sons of bitches need my attention first."

"Are you talking about us, William?" Dustsucker said, poking his thumb first toward himself and then toward Ash.

Ronin began laughing. "Not hardly, Dusty. I'm talking about a sandwich order," he said, chuckling. "I don't believe I've ever seen two men hold up a saloon for a couple of sandwiches."

"And pickles," the barkeep said, "don't forget the pickles."

Ronin, Ash, Slade and McBride looked over at the kid from New Jersey, who had kept the order together despite losing a couple of chair legs and a mirror. "No, we shouldn't forget the pickles," Ronin replied, "never the pickles."

Though cured cucumbers hadn't been a staple in Pennsylvania, he'd enjoyed them once in New York City, where cart vendors were selling them on the Lower East Side. The spicy delicacy had enabled him to have some fun as a preacher, when he'd pointed out to some of the women of the church in Wichita that pickles had been mentioned at least twice in the Bible, and that the

Egyptian queen, Cleopatra, attributed her beauty to the number of fermented cucumbers she ate. "Ew!" the church women had said.

"On a hot day, there's nothing more comforting that a finely spiced pickle brought up fish-like from the barrel below the stairs of my mother's cellar," he said to the New Jersey boy. "But we're not talking about pickles right now, son."

The boy nodded.

He turned back toward McBride. "I'm saying these men need to die, sooner than later. If we let them run around your city, there will be more shots through windows and more broken chairs, and maybe even more dead people as well."

"You're saying that you suspect that Smith and Spinnaker may have taken those shots at you and Slade earlier this morning?" Ash asked, tucking his handguns back into his holsters and propping his lever-action Winchester in the corner of the saloon, underneath the window.

"I don't know, Augustus. They don't strike me as long-distance riflemen, to be frank. But there's no reason to ignore that possibility, especially given their demonstrated interest in escaping arrest and being willing to kill in order to do it."

"Jesus," Ash said. "I don't remember anything like this up here, not in recent years, anyway."

"No, I believe you're right, marshal. How about we do this?" McBride said, practically stuttering as he watched the kid from Jersey pick-up the shattered glass from the mirror which used to sit above his bar. "Ash, you and Kelly and the rest of your bunch should focus on these spit buckets so that we can let Ronin talk to the two women and the men who love them so."

"If that's how you want it," Ronin said.

"It is."

"We're okay with that," the lawmen said.

"Then I'm off to the Washoe Club."

"Exactly."

# Chapter 42

# HEATED HEARTS

"I'm telling you everything I know," the man replied, adjusting a crimson cravat that had seen better days, if Ronin's recent jaunt to the men's shop in Carson City was any way to judge. Portly was, well, as his name suggested, quite round. September toasty in his three-piece suit, Ronin was curious why he continued to tug at his crimson cravat. They hadn't ever met and he was not in attendance, Kelly said, when he had raised the possibility of Ronin's helping the club better secure and protect the reputation of its members.

"Look, I'm not trying to put anyone on the spot," Ronin said, referencing back to Kelly's earlier conversation, "I'm just trying to get some information." A white male, at five-feet-six or seven inches, Portly appeared to have had a successful career in banking or publishing, perhaps. Still, it was clear that he was uncomfortable. Stress did that to people. Some folks heated up during questioning — touching their face and hair, grooming themselves or their surroundings in general — their bodies betrayed them. Others acted too calm and collected, which sent the same message, that there was information the individual wanted to keep hidden. Clearly, Portly wasn't saying everything. There was something he didn't want the questioner to know. "Bob, was it?"

"Yes, Robert Portly at your service, sir."

"Well, thank you. Here's what I'm thinking, Bob. I'm no marshal. I'm no sheriff. I'm just the agent of a local businessman who's trying to do a good thing here. There's obviously something bothering you and others in the club, judging by what's been said to me since I visited today. And you've been a big help in helping me to understand what's happening ..."

"That may be, but I don't believe I've told you that there's *anything* happening, Mister Ronin."

*Smooth.* "No, you haven't said anything inappropriate, of course. You're a businessman, so you've only said what you've needed to say to help your friends. I appreciate that."

"Exactly," Bob Portly said, shifting himself onto his left side, in a brown velvet club chair, a new chair recently provided the club by C. C. Pendergast, the club's secretary and treasurer. "I don't want to hurt anyone."

"Exactly," Ronin said, "and that's what makes me think that you and I can talk. You clearly want to help everyone involved."

"I do," the man said, pulling at his collar and straightening his tie. Portly gestured to a wine steward who was standing outside of the meeting room and asked for a glass of "bubbly." "Anything I can get you, Mister Ronin?" Ronin shook his head.

"Negative," Ronin replied.

He loved the back and forth of a good conversation. He thought he had grown to be pretty good at it over the years, working for the Pinkertons and then on his own. His work as a clergyman had helped as well. There was always a mystery to discovery. A good man — a person with the right skills and training — could tease meaning or material out of a person as well as he could out of an ancient paragraph or language. He was leading the man, joining him, helping him feel more comfortable talking about his friends and their concerns. *It was time to ask.*

"Is there any reason someone might have seen you with Ellie May Livestock?" he inquired. He knew the question would elicit a more honest response than "Have you ever been with that woman on D Street?" A simple "no" would be too easy.

"I've met her on occasion," Portly responded.

"Well, that's what I'm asking. She's quite well known. I would imagine you have, Robert. Now listen, I know you're a businessman and not likely to delve into the supernatural, or maybe you do, I don't know. But have you ever sat with the woman for spiritual advice?"

"My wife's into all that stuff," he said, fidgeting in his chair. He looked toward the doorway to see if the champagne was ready. "I've got a reputation to uphold," he said. "I'd never do anything inappropriate or illegal." Prostitution was illegal in Virginia City, though plenty of men participated in it. The restriction was rarely enforced.

"Of course not, Bob. I'm just asking. Have you ever sat with her for spiritual advice, I mean apart from your wife and all?"

Bob Portly, a sixty-five-year-old man who had been a member of the Washoe Club since its inception in 1875, prior to the fire when sixty-some men met at the California Building in a private office to talk about organizing a social club in the city. He'd paid $150 that night to get things going. And while he liked the thought of the club's future building having a fine library and holding the best liquors, he most appreciated the thought that members might be able to meet non-members there, privately. If he wanted to entertain a businessman, or a business woman, the inference was, he could do that in one of the club's apartments or rooms.

The Washoe Club's immediate popularity made it so that he couldn't use the club that way. And its unexpected destruction during the October 1875 fire caused him to look for meeting places in other directions. Spiritualism, and the particular popularity of Ellie May Livestock — a medium and clairvoyant who lived on D Street, allowed him a safe place to explore his needs and interests, whatever they were.

"I'm not sure what you're getting at," Portly said.

"Sure you are," Ronin replied, chuckling. "I'm not faulting anyone for wanting to talk privately with a beautiful woman about one's future and loved ones, certainly not you, Bob. Lord knows, I like talking to women, too. I'm just asking, have you ever spoken with her in that way? Privately, I mean."

"I have, though nothing untowardly should be assumed by that, Mister Ronin."

"Of course not," Ronin smiled. "So you've met with her, shared some private ... uh, thoughts ... and have some understanding of how things work with Miss Livestock. Is that right?"

"There are two of them, you know," he whispered. The admission that there were two sisters, twin sisters, surprised him. It was a fact known by very few folks in Virginia City.

"Well, I did not know that, Mister Portly, thank you." *A small lie is okay if it leads to a bigger truth.* He was "testing the scriptures," so to speak, going at a text — or in this case, a person — from a different direction. "Two women? Well, I'm surprised." He leaned back.

Portly leaned forward, "I was too, Mister Ronin. Let me tell you, there are things two women can do that one woman cannot." He sat back in his chair and held his gaze on the gunfighter, nodding his head and smiling.

"Huh," Ronin said, wanting to appear neutral. "So ... for this pleasure, Mister Portly, and I don't necessarily need to know what it is that we're talking about, unless it is important for you to say ..."

"It is not."

"Okay, so for this experience, shall we say, do you pay these women?"

"Well, of course I pay them," he said, as if agreeing to one of the lines in the Nicene Creed. *We believe in one God, the Father Almighty, Maker of heaven and earth, and of all things visible and invisible ...we acknowledge one baptism for the remission of sins ...* "The Bible says the laborer is worthy of his wages, you know. First Timothy 5:18." He clipped along at a self-assured rate.

"I imagine that goes for women, too," Ronin said, smiling.

"I imagine so."

"Well, then. You've been quite helpful, Mister Portly. I'm wondering if there's anyone else I might want to speak to while I'm here."

"Oh, I don't know, Mister Ronin. You know how men are. They don't typically want to talk about ... their business arrangements."

"No, I guess not. Well, thank you again. I'll show myself out."

"Take the back steps, would you, please? They're quite the showcase, sir. You'll want to tell people that you've seen them."

"I'm sure they're very special," Ronin remarked, as a young man set a tulip-shaped piece of crystal filled with the finest champagne in front of his friend. "Mister Portly, let me bother you with one additional question, if I may."

"Of course." Portly picked up the flute by its stem and sniffed at the glass. "I wonder if there's any salmon?" he asked.

"I'll check, sir," the young man replied.

He lifted the crystal flute to his mouth and paused. "It's very complex," he said, "the pick of the bunch. The finest vineyard in France, you know." He sipped it slowly and waited. Ronin smiled.

"There were six men who sat with Tom Kelly the other day," Ronin said, "and you say you were not one of them?"

"That is true. I was not."

"Where are those men today?"

"This is a very full-bodied wine, Mister Ronin. Are you sure you'd not like some? It has quite a lingering finish. I believe you would like it."

"I'm sure, Mister Portly. None for me, thank you."

"The six men, where are they today?" Portly repeated, twisting the long-stemmed glass between the first and second fingers of his right hand, as if considering how to answer. "Well," he said, "out of the eight of us who were originally concerned about these women, two of us are now dead. Alvin Hornbecker, of course, who died in Carson City just after a card game, and the late Alfonso Jackson, who died in the Livestock twins' bed."

"Where are the others, Mister Portly? I am concerned for their safety."

"Why yes, of course. They are concerned for their safety as well, Mister Ronin. So they are not available today."

"Not today or not ever?"

"Let's just say they're hoping this problem goes away, Mister Ronin. And that you're the man to help it go away. Can you do that?"

"A talented man can do many things," he responded.

"Good, then I'm authorized to pay you another thousand dollars."

"Thank you, Mister Portly. I'll send my man around to pick up the check."

# Chapter 43

# JOURNAL, DECEMBER 2, 1873

W. W. Ronin returned to the International Hotel and laid down for a nap prior to having dinner with his friends. It would be fun to have Happy Hands call on Mister Portly. He doubted the Indian had ever seen such opulence nor had the club members ever entertained such an interesting Indian. He chuckled to himself as put his head back onto the extra pillows the hotel staff had put out for the Dustsucker and himself, given the interruption of placing new furniture and building a new window and sill for his third-story room overlooking B Street.

Ronin had arranged for a private dining room south of the lobby, despite their being designed and equipped to accommodate children. The privacy would serve them well, and should they have visitors — Marshal Ash and his wife had mentioned they might drop by, Tom Kelly as well — Joseph Reynolds had produced an excellent kitchen, with August Portal holding forth as its chief cook. While he didn't know any of the men personally, McBride had promised the meal would be "among the finest you'll ever eat on the Comstock," boasting that the hotel's large wait staff had helped to make the hostelry known world-wide for both its quality and service.

Ronin didn't care a whole hell of a lot for service, as long as it was clean, quick and friendly, and he had grown to regard upscale establishments as more puff than pastry. But he'd give it a try he said, wanting McBride to understand that the Bucket of Blood owner's attempts to help, including the assignment of Ash and Kelly to try and locate the hazers who had been such a problem in Carson City and were now hassling folks some sixteen miles up the road, were appreciated.

How stupid could a man be to assume he could be a deputy sheriff in one town and not be noticed in another so close by? Perhaps Spinnaker was as brainless as he was bothersome. Whatever the case, he mused as he pushed the pillows into position to read a bit before sleeping, he'd see both hanged or kill them dead if he ran across either of them again.

He picked up his leather journal from the bed stand, brushed construction dust off the cover and began reading.

*It's Tuesday. It turns out that on a day the New York Times has nothing newsworthy to note other than Ulysees S. Grants' return to office as a second term President, I've found out I'm headed west. Big news, indeed.*

*The old man is opening Pinkerton offices from Kansas to California, parts north and south as well, so that whenever a Pinkerton man is needed one will be nearby. The strategy is to form a sort of net — a kind of union, so to speak, like the Yankee vision of our country — not just states (agencies) working together because it serves their separate interests, but parts of a whole doing what it needs to build its interests.*

*While I resisted the concept as it was presented during the War Between the States, I can see the Pinkertons' point. Soon, there will be no place to hide, anywhere in the United States. Bad men will find themselves caught, sooner or later — and more often sooner if Mister Pinkerton has his way — by a Pinkerton man or woman anxious to do what is right.*

*The vision is one I can buy into.*

*A good example of the Pinkerton National Detective Agency's success was the Reno Gang, "was" being the operative word. Every* one of them dead by 1868, the gang — led by three brothers, Frank, Sim and Bill, I believe — was a giant pain in the ass to people in the Midwest. Horse thieves, card-sharks, fire-bugs and deserters (according to the Union Army), the gang terrorized travelers and trains throughout Missouri, Iowa, Indiana and God knows where else until they were captured. A host of other gangs mimicked them. At the height of their criminality there were at least ten of these gangs troubling common folks.

It's said that a local vigilance committee hung the three brothers and one other in December of 1868 outside New Albany, Indiana, the only time I'm aware of that federal prisoners have ever been lynched before a trial, though I have no idea what went on during the War of Northern Aggression. The story is told that sixty-five hooded men traveled by train to New Albany, beat the sheriff and shot him in the arm because he resisted their efforts, and then strung ne'er-do-wells up on trees outside of town. The local newspaper had as its headline, "Judge Lynch has spoken!"

I'd rather see a lawful interdiction of criminality than a vigilance committee any day, but justice starts slowly at times and some folks have no patience for it. Simply said, and don't quote me here, but dead killers are better than live killers still killing. Can I get an "amen?"

An interesting note is that the boys — including another brother and sister, whose names currently escape me — were raised as Methodists. Methodists! They were made to read the Bible every Sunday without fail, not that it helped any, which is an argument the Episcopal Church might consider when it contends for the importance of weekly sacraments. It didn't seem to make much difference at St. John's Episcopal in Wichita, when I was pastor there. The redeemed acted as unredeemed as any unredeemed ever did.

Darius (Dave) Munger, one of the early stockholders in the Wichita Land and Town Company, served as justice of the peace in Kansas. Munger wasn't all that impressed with juries as I recall.

*"Too often," he said, "they're unable to reach the decisions they need to reach." Munger was a good man. He and Julia had five children. I doubt they would have been happy if their children had done as bad as the Reno boys. Their mothers incidentally shared the same first name.*

*Here's how I figure it: bad is as bad does. And while grace may sometimes redeem — I'm sure I couldn't have said such as a priest, but still — it doesn't redeem everyone. Pinkertons, it seems to me, take care of the rest, and some folks, not to sound a constant refrain, need to die sooner than others. But as I said, it'd be best if I'm not quoted saying these things as an ex-priest or Pinkerton Detective.*

Ronin laid the leather journal on the pillow between his knees, turned to his left and put his hands together underneath the pillows. He'd have himself a steak when he got up, maybe some potatoes too, though the rice had been nice the night before. Then he'd attend a special meeting of the Virginia City Spiritualist Society, underneath the dentist's office. His mother and father would be proud to hear, if they had lived, that he was attending church again.

# Chapter 44

# VIRGINIA CITY SPIRITUALIST SOCIETY

Stopping on B Street at the sign that read "Teeth Pulling by Appointment," Ronin jiggled the freshly painted door of the Virginia City Spiritualist Society, in the event it was expected that he should announce his presence rather than simply enter and take a seat. Dustsucker had remarked he could quietly stand outside the building and wait for the society's clairvoyants to "sense" that he was there, which Ronin had found humorous.

While he wasn't a disbeliever in such things, he wasn't a believer either, arguing that the clear teaching of the Christian scriptures was, "it is appointed unto men once to die, and after this the judgment." Ronin didn't much believe that statement either, though he thought the New Testament book of *Hebrews* to be a better source of thinking on such matters than a grizzled old man or lady with a crystal ball sitting in front of them. "Not that there's anything wrong with that," he said as Dustsucker made a list of excuses that would keep him from accompanying Ronin to the evening meeting.

Entering the hall, Ronin remembered why he had bought a suit. Ellie May Livestock was one good-looking lady, he thought to himself. The room — with some thirty or forty people seated within — didn't have a single shopkeeper, miner or cowhand attending without a proper business garment or dress. Ellie May was standing off to one side of the crowd as an older man Ronin didn't recognize was apparently starting the meeting off with forceful and apparently popular opening words.

"We do not need manifestations of the Spirit to know that what we're about to see and hear tonight is real. Nor do we regard the suspicions of some to be reason for proof that has already been supplied to so many."

The individual's tone and litany had a familiar cadence, reminding him of camp meetings he'd attended in Wichita and Pittsburgh. He took a seat six rows back from the front on a side aisle. "No!" the speaker shouted as people nodded in agreement. The faith and fervor of the room's inhabitants were clear, as men and women alike punctuated and propelled the rhythm of the man's words by saying "yes" or "amen," or by grunting other sounds signaling agreement. Ronin didn't think he had ever seen a meeting, even a Methodist meeting, eliciting such a display of enthusiasm.

"Now listen," the speaker, a tall, professional-looking man in a three-piece charcoal-colored suit said, smiling. "We respect all beliefs. We encourage the questioning of our faith and philosophies. We want you to doubt. We need you to investigate. How will you know the truth of these things if you do not follow in such an important endeavor?"

For a September evening, the room was hot and stifling. Ronin pulled a handkerchief from his breast pocket and patted at his forehead. He'd left his long gun at the hotel, thinking that a church meeting — even a Spiritualist Society church meeting — was no place for such a firearm.

"Use your hands and your feet," a fur trader had once told him, "whenever you can. Put a bullet in a man and you'll never recover the time that you and your intended victim will lose. Whether at the hospital or in the courtroom, you'll feel a profound loss." He'd intended to mentor the grizzled trader spiritually, as he was expected to. Instead, he'd gone on to learn the old man's very unusual fighting art, adding to the much-appreciated boxing skills he'd enjoyed during seminary. None of that was important tonight. The speaker moved closer to introducing Ms. Livestock as the evening's entertainment.

"This night, our good friend, Ellie May Livestock," he intoned musically, "will reveal personal destinies and secrets in a way that few mediums are able. A friend of our own Eilley Bowers" — Ronin strained to see four rows forward and to the right as Mrs. Bowers, "the Washoe Seeress," nodded — "and a companion to many of us on the journey, Miss Livestock will be available after our meeting to set a personal appointment with any or each of you who are moved by the meeting's events. And now, without any further delay, let me introduce one of Virginia City's finest women, and most talented prophets. A protégé of the *Gold Hill Daily News* editor and owner Alfred Doten's sister Lizzie, and a good friend of the entire Spiritualist community in the great silver state of Nevada, I present to you Miss Ellie May Livestock."

Enthusiastic applause filled the room, with few exceptions, mostly pale-faced men who, while still clapping, seemed set apart by a common distraction. Ronin smiled. *I'll bet she's slept with every one of them. And who can blame them? She's beautiful.*

"Miss Livestock, the podium is yours," the tall man at the front said, before sitting down on what appeared to be a permanent speaker's platform, draped in crimson and black velvet. No other decorations in the room seemed as fixed. The gathering hall had a small kitchen and bathroom adjacent to it, and the room's platform — or chancel he would have called it had it been a church — featured doors on both the left and the right of the performance area, forming a large open space between two small rooms that might be used for storage or support. The raised area of the room seemed similar to community stages he had seen throughout the West. All in all, especially given the lack of liturgical or seasonal decorations typical of church bodies, the Virginia City Spiritualist Society's gathering place was both inviting and uninviting at the same time. The singular and most remarkable contribution of John Calvin's influence on religion, Ronin thought to himself — a boring and unattractive room.

While not missing the politics of his ministry at Saint John's Episcopal Church — he'd come to desire something more than his denomination could offer or its religious perspective could provide — he occasionally remembered in a fond way the building's décor. Seasonal decorations, provided by the women of the church, who busied themselves throughout the months prior weaving colorful wall hangings, even "hanging the greens" during the weeks of Advent and Christmastide, made Saint John's a very special place certain times of the year. The color and smell of the church's liturgical seasons, the principal feasts, festivals, lesser festivals and commemorations, set the Episcopal Church apart from its Protestant brothers and sisters. Advent, or the four weeks that led up to the church's Christmas Day celebration, felt "almost Catholic," his mother had remarked upon visiting, an insight that had shimmered as much as any other note or teaching provided him during his years of seminary training in Pennsylvania. As old as the Spiritualist Society was in Virginia City, aside from fresh paint and the event-driven maintenance of its bulletin boards, he imagined the room looked as good lit as it did dark.

Ellie May looked out over the room and waited a moment before speaking. *Effective*, he thought. "My friends," she said, "Spiritualism is a science. It is a philosophy that helps us live our lives. It is a religion that keeps us in touch with those we miss and love most. It is the scientific proof that the traditional church does not provide, despite our wanting it, even needing it." She took a breath, and in that moment smiled at every person in the room.

"I don't mean to say that our wives are unimportant." Ronin noticed the same men squirming. "I don't intend to say that our husbands aren't essential." Some of the women laughed. "I mean to simply suggest that we love most those we miss most, and that Spiritualism — God's gift to those of us who sometimes waver in our faiths — is the answer to that dilemma. We know those we miss most. We see them, who miss us as well."

Ronin had spent a few moments speaking with Father Patrick Manogue, the Irish cleric at St. Mary's, prior to his attending the meeting. Manogue had been caught up in an earlier experience with the church, "if it is that," the cleric had said while taking supper with a number of Catholic women.

"I don't want to bother you," Ronin had said, believing a short quip from the priest would be adequate given that a half-dozen or so church ladies seemed to be enjoying his attention.

"It's been a good many years since I've paid attention to the movement," Manogue had said, remembering an event some eight years prior when his opinion of a certain young medium made national news in the *Catholic Guardian.* "I don't believe I have much to give you," he said, noting the reactions of the women he was sitting with. "Perhaps later I could say more, except to observe that it's quite easy to get caught up in things, Mister Ronin. A fourteen-year-old girl named Agnes McDonough was simply rapping on tables ..."

"Rapping?" Ronin asked, acutely aware that he was interrupting the good reverend's business.

"Exactly, rapping with her knuckles I assume, though the noise might have been provided by her feet, like the Fox sisters who claimed to be communicating with spirits in New York. You've heard of them?" he asked.

"I have."

"Well, they're the real founders of this movement, as far as I can tell. Before you know it, this fourteen-year-old is having conversations with her dead father. The newspapers — don't get me going, but the *Territorial Enterprise* was so incredibly gullible in its coverage — puffed up her visit so much that everyone in town had an opinion. I mean every businessman, miner, mother and whore."

"I see." Manogue was refreshing. Ronin had never met a Roman Catholic priest who spoke so confidently and clearly. *If he doesn't offend the wrong people, he'll be a bishop in no time at all.*

"I'm just saying, Mister Ronin, if your business is as confidential as I understand it to be — I spoke with Versal McBride this morning, and he briefed me of your calling here — you'll not want to get into a pissing match with a skunk." Manogue, a former miner, suddenly turned pale. "Excuse me, ladies. That was inappropriate. I apologize." He picked up his fork and turned, before looking over his shoulder and saying, "You know what I mean, Mister Ronin."

"I believe I do," he'd said, pushing himself out the door of the C Street restaurant where they were gathered and heading to the meeting. The last thing he wanted to do was to upset a bunch of people who were probably upset enough already.

"Mister Ronin!" Ellie May called from the front of the room. He startled. "I notice you're in attendance this evening."

"I am, ma'am. Thank you," he said, wondering what the point of it all was.

"We're glad to have you here, sir. Our town is safer with you here. And the accusations plaguing our community, our spiritual community — that we're hurting people instead of helping them, that we're drawing the drapes instead of opening the blinds — can only be helped by your investigations."

"Investigations, ma'am?" He was surprised she was speaking of things so openly.

"Why, of course, Mister Ronin. We seek the Truth in this place, do we not?" Folks nodded. A few adherents agreed aloud. "No one wants to be accused of anything less, Mister Ronin. It's the sacred we seek, not the sinister!" A roar of sudden and heartfelt applause was followed by a ripple of whispers, leading Ronin to believe that some folks weren't aware of an investigation into the Spiritualists' influence, let alone Miss Livestock and her deaf and possibly demented sister's role in it.

"Ma'am, I'm just here for the meeting."

"Do you not believe in an infinite intelligence, Mister Ronin?"

"I don't know, ma'am."

"Do you not believe that people should live in accordance with their religion, Mister Ronin?"

"I'd like to think that people would."

"Is there a chance that people's lives continue after their death, Mister Ronin, or rather, their passing?"

"I imagine there's a chance that all kinds of things we think of may be true or not be true, ma'am. I'm missing your point." Still, Ellie May continued.

"Is it possible that we might still be able to know these persons, these people that we love," she said with a well-honed cadence, "after they have transitioned? Like your wife, Mister Ronin?"

"My wife?" he asked, certain that he had never been married. *Was it deliberate?*

"Have you ever heard of people so touched by the Divine that they have unusual abilities, Mister Ronin?"

Now angry, he replied without thinking. "I have not. If a person is fast with a gun, it means he's practiced. If he's clever with truth, spiritual or otherwise, it means ..."

"Mister Ronin?"

"Yes, ma'am?" He'd spent too many summers growing up in the South. It was his habit to be polite, particularly with a lady. He waited.

"These are the things that we believe, Mister Ronin. Do ... you ... have ... issue ... with ... us?" *She was attacking, not physically, but verbally.* Ronin stood stunned and surprised.

Individuals in religious meetings are sometimes asked to testify publicly to how the Spirit is moving in their lives. It's an acceptable piece of a church service — no matter what the brand or denomination. The testimony builds other people's faiths and helps the person giving one to grow as well. At least that's the thinking, he mused. He imagined in a Spiritualist meeting, the interaction back and forth between people was the grist that their grace was built upon. No question — Is my dead wife happy? Will I ever see my diseased child again? — no answers. No answers, no offerings. Ronin smiled, a little uncertain how to reply.

"Ma'am," he said, after some consideration. "I believe I'll wait out front. I do not wish to interrupt your meeting any further. Perhaps we might speak after the meeting is over?"

"Of course, sir," Ellie May replied, looking about the room and encouraging people's enthusiasm. "Every question is welcome!" she said to enthusiastic applause. "Every individual is loved!" she shouted as people nodded and shouted out in agreement. "Every soul, not just remembered, but revered for who he or she is and who he or she is still becoming!"

"Yes!" someone shouted in the front row, as applause and "amens" filled the hall.

"Jesus," Ronin said through his teeth, as he got up, grinning.

An hour and a half passed until the meeting's end. Ronin sat opposite the dentist's window on South B Street, between Taylor and Union, trying to picture how dentistry had become a profession. He shook his head. A leather-bound book sat on the sill of the window of the dentist's office so that passerby's might stop and read from its open pages. He read the title aloud, *"The Natural History of Human Teeth,* by John Hunter." "Huh," he said, observing a series of small silver and gold-plated probes and other tools that sat above it on a glass shelf, along with a display of photographs Hunter had taken to illustrate the diseases or conditions of the teeth or mouth.

Generally speaking, Ronin was interested in everything. Yet he had no enthusiasm for dentistry. Certain dentists, he'd heard, had become professional gamblers and gunfighters rather than suffer the indignity of placing their hands in someone else's mouth day in and day out. *The profession seemed so, what?* He wondered sitting under a gas lamp on B Street. *Unprofessional, that's it, even barbaric.*

"Miss Livestock," he said, standing, after a good number of people passed his way, nodding and smiling as if they had somehow become friends during the religious meeting.

"Mister Ronin," Ellie May said, stopping to respond.

"Ma'am, I'm sorry if my presence at your meeting was distracting."

"Not at all," she said, pulling a handkerchief from her sleeve.

She was a beautiful woman to be sure. He tugged at his tie. *Hadn't Kelly said she sported a gold tooth? Maybe it's Alvira Fae who has the dental repair?*

"Ellie," he said, wondering if he was stuttering. *It's in my head.* "I heard you mention that you're taking appointments.

Very clever, if I may say: take no offering, but aim your entire presentation at getting people to pay you money later, say for other services."

"I'm not following, sir. We're happy to take an offering, every now and then. And there's hope that someday we'll be able to build our own building. Most people, Mister Ronin, are happy to lend their support to the work of individual mediums or the Society as a whole. What is it you're talking about?"

"My apologies, ma'am," he said, noting her response. "I mean no disrespect. I mean to simply offer a compliment, one spiritual practitioner to another."

"Ah, yes. I heard you had been a pastor at one time ..."

"A priest, ma'am, an Episcopal priest." The difference was important to him, though not really. He didn't know why he was saying what he was saying, and except for the cover of darkness, was certain that she would see him blushing.

"Great!" she bubbled, leaving Ronin confused about his intent and hers.

"Ma'am?"

"Then you'll want to come by and see what I do, Mister Ronin. I believe you'd be very pleased and impressed."

"Ma'am?"

"With a crystal ball, Mister Ronin."

"Of course."

"Was there something else you were thinking about?" She smiled, and then turned onto Union Street and began to walk toward her home a couple of streets down the hill. A few feet away from the ex-preacher, she turned and smiled. "Are you coming?"

# Chapter 45
# FISTICUFFS

Dustsucker got up to leave the saloon. Spending the evening there, listening to the piano player and sipping sarsaparillas had been nice. "Miss Squeek?" he said.

"Yes, Mister Slade." The slender blond-haired woman, a regular at the Bucket of Blood according to the sign above the piano, was walking toward him. She was a vision of beauty.

"Thank you so much for your music tonight," he sputtered. "I truly enjoyed myself." He stood smiling, a little uncertain, as he generally didn't talk to women he didn't know, except in a professional manner in Carson City, or when speaking with Miss Emma occasionally at the mission just outside of town.

"Well, thank you, deputy! I enjoyed your enthusiasm!" She smiled, picking up her chin. "I don't believe that anyone had a problem with it at all, or should have anyway." She cocked her head to the side. It was deliberate and only underscored how desirable he found her.

"You mean the other table?" he asked, thinking of the two cowboys sitting to his left who'd found their way to Virginia City, Nevada thinking it was some wild-ass town like Bodie, California or Butte, Montana. "I hope I didn't embarrass you ..."

"You did not, Marcus," she said, smiling. "I hope you'll come back sometime, and maybe bring your friend."

"Ronin?"

"Yes, the man you were talking about. He seems like an interesting character. I'd love to meet him."

"He's a peach, Miss Squeek, and truth be told he would have handled those cowboys without your missing a beat."

She laughed at the double entendre. "You did fine ignoring them deputy. I'm most appreciative."

He had ignored them alright. For a good twenty minutes or so, he'd let them carry on, talking about how they'd heard better piano players in Hangtown or Mormon City, which he took to mean Genoa, since neither of the men — dirty and rough and not a couth bone in their bodies — appeared to have ever spent any length of time in Salt Lake City.

He had stood at one point, towering over them like a bear does over a coyote or mountain lion, but the barkeep — in an apparent effort to keep the liquor flowing — waved him off. Despite the noise, the kid from Jersey pointed to the saloon's owner, Versal McBride, who seemed happier with the amount of liquor being served than the pianist's consternation over their behavior. He hated to see a bad deed go unpunished, and would have knocked their hat-clad heads together as suddenly as the surprise the men showed when he stood up to face them. Still, it wasn't his saloon, and what happened in Virginia City wasn't any of his business unless Marshal Ash said it was.

"That's very kind, Miss Squeek …"

"Please call me Squeek," she said, smiling. "There's no need to call me 'Miss' anything." It was a beautiful smile. A naturally blond woman in her thirties, Squeek's slender frame was unusual on the Comstock. Women worked hard on the hill. Their weight and muscles showed it. And while some folks preferred women a little bigger, Dustsucker had come to appreciate the smaller frame some women sported. Squeek reminded him of Emma.

"Ma'am, thank you. Please call me Dusty, then. All of my friends do."

"That I shall, Dusty. See you again?"

"Absolutely," he replied, watching her backside as she walked over to McBride, who handed her three coins without a smile. She was a regular for sure, and he'd be back to see her. He pushed his chair away from the table and stood up to go, pulling his gun belt tight. He was in the habit of loosening things when he sat down, but couldn't afford his gun belt slipping to the floor if he stood up and needed it. *She sure is pretty.* He smiled at McBride. Hours tallied, he'd spent the entire day there, having lunch and listening to music until nightfall. He was headed toward the front of the saloon when the louvered doors blew open and the two cowboys reentered.

"You leaving so soon, fatty?" The taller, toothless one giggled. The shorter man, clearly pleased with the words he'd just uttered, grinned as if he'd been reading a dictionary and had found his name written there under the word "stupid" or "jackass" or "fool." The small man's head bounced back and forth, touching both of his shoulders like the clapper on the inside of a broken church bell. Once clapped, the hazer rubbernecked forward, removing his hat as if inviting a response.

Dustsucker threw an overhead right into the small man's face, knocking him back through the doors and into the street. Continuing forward — "Never backward," Ronin liked to say, "always forward" — he picked the taller man up by the lapels and threw him against the front of the saloon, lifting him until his hat touched the decorative molding. "Oh, please," Slade said, "sing me that song again! You know, the one where you describe my appearance! Sing me that song again, you son of a bitch! I'm pleading with you! Open your mouth!"

The man covered his face with his arms and hands and began crying. "I didn't say nothing, mister. It was my stupid friend. He didn't mean nothin'!"

"Really?" Slade said. "He didn't mean nothin' at all ..."

"No sir. He's a good church-going man from Placerville, a Methodist I'm pretty sure. Just out for a good time, looking for jobs, sir. That's all."

"Just out for a good time and looking for jobs, that's all?"

"Yes, sir." he said, wiping at his tears. "Put me down, please. I don't believe I've ever been hefted about by a big man. Let me go!"

"A big man?"

"I don't mean how that sounds," he blubbered. "Let me get my friend and we'll just be out of here." Slade looked over at McBride. Squeek was sitting next to him, and despite their business being concluded, he watched her touch his arm. McBride didn't seem happy.

"Okay," Slade said, allowing the man's boots to touch the floor and picking up his hat. "Take your hat. Get your friend and leave."

"We left yesterday, sir! We're gone already. Thank you so much!"

Slade wiped his hands on his pants and waited a few minutes, until he was sure the walk outside of the saloon was empty, and then left. *What would it take to be a smaller man? A thinner man? A faster and fitter man?*

"Dusty!" Squeek yelled from the back of the saloon. "Have a minute?"

He turned around, quick enough that he saw Squeek smile at McBride. She hurried to the doorway, and then standing close enough that he could hear her speak but no one else could, she whispered, "A big man like you could be real handy at the Bucket of Blood."

"What?"

"I'm just saying, Dusty." She touched his shirt with her right forefinger. He'd have noticed if it had been her left. One of her knees touched as well. The moment fixed itself in time — a Friday night in September that felt like springtime. "A big man would be real welcome here at the saloon."

"Ma'am?" he said, not following until McBride smiled at him. At the saloon, he realized, not at supper, or walking to church, or sitting through the evening on Squeek's porch talking about old times.

"I'll have to think about it," he said, smiling. "Goodnight ma'am."

# Chapter 46

# MOUNT DAVIDSON

A bird in the bush was better than two in the hand, or was it the opposite of that? Dustsucker wondered, as he wandered away from the Bucket of Blood toward Virginia City's highest hill. It was easily 10 p.m., he thought, judging by the moonlight and street noise. He crossed B and A Streets on his way up the mountain and what he hoped would be a peaceful view of the International Hotel and the rest of the city. It was a good half-hour of huffing and puffing before the bear-sized deputy had the energy to think about the slender piano player at the saloon.

It seemed like they had connected, Miss Squeek and him, thought they hadn't spoken at all intimately that night, or on any other for that matter. His mother used to say, "A girl doesn't want to hear about facts and opinions, Marcus. A girl wants to know about your feelings. Facts are easy." And that was mostly what they talked about — the goings-ons in Carson City and Virginia City — not much, and nary an opinion or feeling, except for the steady stream of compliments he sent her way. They would have sprung from his mouth even if he hadn't intended them. He was that kind of man.

He sure loved her piano playing, he mused as he began humming and wheezing the 1850's tune, "Jeanie with the Light Brown Hair." Most of Squeek's repertoire was a good deal quicker than that, the old honky-tonk of a piano at the Bucket wouldn't have taken anything slower or prettier. But when he mentioned the parlor song by the Pennsylvania composer

Stephen Foster, he had her attention. She played and they sang it together — hell, everyone sang along — until Jeannie's light brown hair turned gray!

The deputy kicked at a rusted tin can as he walked a steep incline toward the mountain's peak. Mount Davidson sat at almost 8,000 feet, someone had said. He'd settle for a stoop somewhere on the east side of the mountain as the height and climb beat at his breath. The can clanked against the mountain's rugged gray rocks and settled in a patch of rabbit brush. *I sure love her music.*

There was something there, he thought, between the smiles and the crow's feet, though he'd never suggest that Squeek had any wrinkles at all — he'd never tell any woman that, except that most women did have wrinkles on the Comstock. The Nevada sun was so hot and the air so dry, who could help getting a few?

He particularly liked the way she listened to him while he was talking. It was as if she was *really* listening, like his mother listened. Squeek's eyes didn't skirt about like so many other people when new folks walked into a room — McBride's, for instance, a behavior the Bucket of Blood's owner demonstrated so consistently that it bothered his friend Ronin to the extreme. Sudden noises didn't seem to distract her, either. Someone had thrown a wine bottle against the wall over the bar where the mirror used to hang. Green glass splattered everywhere, but she didn't flinch one bit. Once her attention lit on a man, it stayed there until she was finished. *Lordy, I'm attracted to her.*

Was it possible that all she had in mind was that he'd come and work at the saloon? And how was it they needed to hire security? There were rougher places on C Street. The few incidents that had bothered the Bucket of Blood didn't seem like much, compared to the dug-outs and lean-tos he generally stayed away from. He counted a shooting a year ago by his friend, and then the most recent one where Spinnaker and Smith somehow escaped without harm. Hell, everyone got out of that scrape unharmed. And then there was the short guy with the whip. Latigo — *was that his name?*

*I already have a job*, he figured, sitting down on a stack of rocks someone had piled into a cairn, so as to mark a path or set a memorial. He stood up, but then concluded the dark, wind-blown hillside would be a terrible place for a grave site.

*I'm a deputy.* And working for the Ormsby County sheriff's office wasn't all that bad, though the part-time aspect of it kept him hungry at times. Lloyd Hill wasn't a bad boss, though he'd never measure up to Shubael Swift, not in anyone's minds. Shubael had held the office for ten years. Five terms! It'd be a long time coming before anyone beat that record.

When he wasn't sheriffing — the term made him smile, though the work was sometimes dull and dreary — he tried to spend as much time out of the courthouse as he could, given the jail's reputation. Old, new, it didn't matter. A couple of years ago, the *Nevada Tribune* in Carson City said "it was bad enough to be a criminal or to be hung by the neck, but nothing is so bad as to be confined in that damnable hole called the county jail."

*Hell, I don't care.* He was part-time, and the human stench of the place, despite efforts by county sheriffs and deputies to keep the building clean, didn't bother him nearly as much as others. He was away far more than he was at home. He had no time for an extra job, couldn't she tell? If he wasn't wondering where a prisoner went — running here or tracking there — he was looking for yellow or blue, and packing the precious metals back with him to Carson City to be assayed. A man couldn't eat on so paltry a budget as what the sheriff's office provided, couldn't eat much, anyway.

He pulled at a piece of beef jerky he had hidden in his pocket the day before, and wiped his hands on what he believed to be the cleaner side of his vest. It was salty enough that he looked about for his canteen. Finding it more by feel than sight, as the moon was hidden momentarily behind a long bluish-white cloud, he uncorked it, leaving the cork stopper to fall alongside the smooth-sided container. He wet his fingers first and dried them on the canteen's wool cover. He took a long sip and sat thinking, flicking at the tin and copper canteen's side with his finger and listening to the sound echo across the landscape.

*Three jobs is at least one too many.* And if the offer wasn't out of personal interest — how could it be, it had been extended by her employer — he didn't see the sense to it or the economics of it, for that matter. Uphill and downhill, it would be trains or horses all the way. If he didn't wear out, the liveries or tracks would. He looked about for a stick to pick at his teeth. A yellow glint flickered to his right. He reached over to claim what he suspected would be a fleck of gold only to discover that it was a discarded brass cartridge, a heavy caliber cartridge at that... perhaps a .45-70.

He looked up and located the International among the city's buildings. It wasn't hard, given how tall the building was. Counting up three floors, he found his and Ronin's window and sat there wondering. Given the cairn and the cartridge, was it possible he was sitting exactly where the rifleman had been sitting? He looked about some more, forcing his tired eyes to see more clearly in the dim moonlight. And though it was dark, he was surprised to find there a small banker's hat and whip.

# Chapter 47
# THE HOUSE ON D STREET

Ronin straightened his tie and then wondered why, given that it had been years since he felt like he needed to dress up to be entertained by a woman.

Ellie May Livestock sashayed a few yards ahead of him, tugging at his attention like a he was cow headed toward a kill chute. He didn't know what he was going to do when he got to where he was going, though one thing he did know — Ellie May and Alvira Fae's little house on D Street afforded a very small porch, with too little room for two chairs and even less privacy to visit, particularly in the late hours of the evening when their voices would carry so easily. He knew he would have to enter her house to have a conversation, and he knew he'd be uncomfortable doing so.

While he'd kept an appropriate distance from the woman every time they'd met, he wasn't certain that he'd be able to resist the woman's charms, given the evening wearing toward midnight, the woman's attractiveness, his new suit and the demonic magic that the outfit was apparently working since he bought the damn thing.

Ellie turned left and gestured a few houses up toward a small red bungalow on the west side of D Street. "Yes," he blurted out, though he didn't know why. Trailing a couple of feet behind her, he wondered what the hell he was doing. Voices from his professional past shouted at him like angry bishops. Church bells rang in his head, tolling the arrival of sinful imaginations, though he wasn't sure he believed in sin and he was doing his best to keep his thinking focused on the business at hand, whatever that was, not that it was working.

*Passing through the street near her corner, he takes the way to her house, in the twilight, in the evening, in the black and dark night. Behold the woman comes to meet him. Her feet do not stay at home. "I have spread my bed with tapestries," she says, "colorful linens and perfume. Let us take our fill of love until morning!"*

Oh God, he groaned, closing the imaginary book of *Proverbs* in his mind. Solomon's words weren't helping.

He couldn't blame her for what he was thinking. It was as much his self-control, or lack of it, as hers. And she was so pretty. The first time he'd seen her, fixed in a simple cotton, go-to-meeting dress, she appeared strikingly different than other women he had met. So alive, so capable, so powerfully engaged with the people around her. She was amazing.

Ronin shook his head, trying to clear his mind. He'd been caught up in a few embraces, intimate embraces, over the years. His Reno friend Sally, for instance, had pushed him over the edge a couple of times, and while he had regained his self-control, their relationship had been strained ever since. Strained enough that even at love's first offering, he'd warned her — as he did a couple of months ago, when she slid across a table into his lap — "I'm not that man," he'd said, though he knew that he was that man, that every man was that man if he was pushed to the extreme.

There was something to the Livestock twins that men — or some men, powerful men anyway — found irresistible. The gold tooth, switching between sisters, kept them guessing. Sometimes Ellie wore it, other times Alvira slipped it over one of her front teeth, proving to some that the women were "spirit-creatures" in the parlance of Spiritualism — dim reproductions of the real women who, when the tooth was removed, men could speak to or pray with or fondle so as to explore life's more difficult mysteries. Now's there's one, now there's two — the whole thing was likely *very* intoxicating, when the night was late and enough alcohol was had to lower one's inhibitions.

"Come in," she said, pushing her front door open, not finding it necessary to use a key. A thin paper night shade masked an ornate lantern, its light flickering on a marble table by the entryway into her bedroom. *Their* bedroom, he thought, the two of them, and if he wasn't careful, the three of them. "Would you like something to drink?" she asked, gesturing to a selection of liquors, none of which he recognized as he was a beer man, wine occasionally, never whiskey or a mixed drink. "Perhaps a brandy?" she said, turning the lamp up higher so that it cast shadows across the room, illuminating a four-post pine bed, big enough that four people could sleep in it. *What?*

There had been a Spiritualist woman as well in his life, who he would sometimes talk about when he was being honest. It just was what it was, he figured. That relationship, entered into when he should have been more professional. There had been a hidden blessing to it. He now worked independently, and liked it better that way. "No ma'am," he heard himself say, when what he was really thinking was, *Yes. Sure, of course. Would you serve it in the bedroom? I'd love to drink that ... and you.* His focus was scattered. His thinking was distorted and unclear.

"Sit, Mister Ronin," she said. "I don't want you to be uncomfortable."

*Of course not.* "I'm not uncomfortable," he said, though he knew that he was, and more so, knew that she knew that he was and that he knew that she knew that he knew that he was. *Whatever.* "It's late," he stuttered. "I'm just struggling a bit."

She laughed. "I can see that, Mister Ronin." It was a delightful laugh, like a child playing, though it had been years since he'd heard children playing.

There was the mission, of course, south of town, but they were Indian children and there was something different about that. The laughter of the Washoe, Paiute and Shoshone children staying there had been halted and careful since the kidnappings in Washoe Valley. He couldn't blame them. The events had been terribly traumatic. Ellie May's laugh had no care to it. It was simple and inviting, like a little girl experiencing a new toy for the first time.

"Really, Mister Ronin," she said. "Sit down. I'm not going to bite you."

*You're biting me is not what I'm afraid of,* he thought, pulling a chair away from a dark-stained table in the girls' living room so that it sat in front of the door, allowing passerby in the street to see in, not that there were many and not that they'd look if passing by and not that it mattered. He was no longer a pastor. Folks generally averted their eyes, respectable folks, anyway.

She walked past him toward the front door, a subtle scent of cinnamon trailing. Her gown created a slight breeze. It was refreshing. "We don't want to catch cold, do we?" she asked, as she closed the front door and fastened its lock. She smiled and touched his shoulder before returning to the couch.

"No, ma'am," he said. Such a clown — he couldn't believe how he was acting. "Ma'am, I appreciate these few moments you're willing to share," he struggled. "I've got a couple of questions, if you don't mind. They've been weighing on me."

"There's no need to hurry," she said, patting the cushion next to her on the love seat across from the bedroom entryway. He could sit on one of the two chairs in the living room or on the davenport with Ellie May. The room afforded very little else, though what furniture there was elegant enough. A pleasant wall paper — roses, if he wasn't mistaken, and a subtle green plant that appeared to be Lily of the Valley — decorated the room. The plant, and its delicate white, bell-shaped flowers were poisonous, if he remembered correctly.

"Join me," she said, patting the cushion next to her. "We can get better acquainted."

"Ma'am?"

"I don't mean to sound forward, Mister Ronin. May I call you William?"

He didn't remember telling her his first name. "I'm more comfortable with my last name, ma'am." He had gone by the name "Ronin" for as long as he remembered. Everyone called him that. The name defined him. It inferred that he was his own boss. He shook his head no, to reinforce his desire or intention, though he wasn't absolutely sure of either.

"Well, I insist that you call me by my first name, at least. It's 'Ellie,' Ronin. Practice it with me, would you? 'Ellie,'" she said, playfully. "Put your tongue up behind your teeth and touch it gently to the back of your teeth ..."

"I'm sure I can accommodate you, ma'am, I mean Ellie ..."

"I'm sure you can," she said, smiling.

"Ma'am?"

"Ellie," she repeated.

"Of course," he said, wondering if the double entendre was his or hers, but it was hard to miss. There was no way she wasn't aware of it. "Here's what I'm hoping to accomplish tonight, Ellie," he offered, pronouncing her name as if it were a drum beat, a disciplined drum beat determined to keep him out of the arms of the harlot, not that she looked like one, not that she was one. He didn't know, not for sure anyway and what did it matter? He was just there to ask her a few questions.

*With her enticing speech she caused him to yield. With her flattering lips she seduced him. Immediately he went after her, as a beast goes to the slaughter, as a fool goes to the correction of the stocks. Listen to me, my children. Pay attention to the words of my mouth ...*

The Old Testament scripture was pleading in tone, not that he was listening to it.

"I'm hoping that you'll hear me when I say that certain men in Virginia City are concerned about ..." He didn't get to finish his sentence.

"Mister Ronin. If you won't come here and sit next to me, I will come there. And I am certain that you will find it less comfortable our sitting there in one chair than our sitting here on the couch." She was shaking her finger at him, taunting him. "I am not used to shouting across my parlor to be understood," she said, "and I'm quite tired from my lecture, I can promise you. There's *very* little chance that I'm up for much else."

*Very little chance.* "Much else, ma'am?" he said, standing.

She smiled, waiting ...

"Ellie."

"Thank you," she said, smiling. She patted the red velvet cushion next to her until he came across the room and sat down next to her. "Very little chance that I'm up for anything ... how shall I say it, Mister Ronin? Too intimate..."

"Ma'am?"

She sat smiling until he seemed certain of her point. She was letting him know that he wasn't there to be flirted or philandered with. She was too tired, *actually* too tired to do anything else. Or was she? He felt foolish. It had all been in his head, every damn bit of it.

He looked down for a moment and then looked up.

"Not that I wouldn't be interested some other time, Mister Ronin. You're quite the handsome man, I mean." She reached out to touch his chin. He pulled back.

"Ellie, there's something I need you to hear. I believe you are deliberately misleading businessmen in this city, to invest in your spiritual practices and in your personal life. And I want you to know that I'm here to stop it." *There, I said it.*

"Really?" she said, laughing. She patted his leg with her left hand, pinching the woolen material of his suit as if to appreciate it or to know where the suit ended and his skin began. She then reached toward his right ear, brushing past it gently as she rested her arm on the ornate carving at the top of the couch. "You're here to stop me?" she said, playfully.

"I am."

"Fascinating," she said, "truly fascinating. Perhaps we might talk a bit about this after all, Mister Ronin. May I call you William?" She didn't wait for an answer, but placed her lips momentarily on his, and reached across the ivory side table and turned out the light.

# Chapter 48

# GOOD NIGHT

"So what happened after that?" Dustsucker asked, from atop his bed at the International Hotel. It was after midnight and the Carson City deputy was sitting up in bed. A red night shirt covered his considerable frame.

"Nothing," Ronin replied, laying a fresh shirt across the back of a chair. Rolling up the previous day's shirt, he tucked it into one of his saddle bags.

"Really?" Dustsucker said, "nothing?"

"Well, you know what I'm saying …"

"Yeah, no I don't," Dustsucker said, hoping to hear that his long-time bachelor friend — never married, at least not to his understanding — had at least been with the woman in some memorable way. It wasn't natural, he told him, not that he cared.

Ronin pulled the shorter of his Colt firearms from its holster beside the bed and opened the loading gate. He removed one cartridge and put it back into an empty belt loop. He'd loaded six not knowing what to expect at the Virginia City Spiritualist Meeting. He replaced the gun and lifted the longer Colt from its cross-draw holster, doing the same. "I can't say that I wasn't tempted," he smiled. "She's a pretty lady."

"But a thousand dollars is a thousand dollars, right?" Dustsucker laughed.

"Exactly," Ronin rubbed the outside of both guns with a towel before hanging the belt and guns at the top of his bed. "How about you? What did you do after I left?"

"Same deal, buddy. Got to talking to the piano player, figured out her name, tried not to act like too much of a horse's ass — and by the time I left she'd offered me a job."

"What are you talking about?"

"I'm saying the Bucket of Blood offered me a job. Sounds like they're getting a bit busted up about people being shot in their saloon, so McBride is angling to get a policeman or sheriff in there part-time to keep an eye on things."

"You thinking about it?" he asked, pulling his boots off and getting into bed. He grabbed the cotton bedspread and pulled it up so that it covered his chest before spying the woolen blanket on a shelf opposite him. "You going to use that?" he gestured.

"Nope, got one. That one's yours."

Ronin threw the sheet and coverlet to the bottom of the bed and spun around, placing his feet on the floor. "I mean, you're up here enough. You could probably give him an evening or two, if you really wanted to."

"Ronin, life is short and then it's over. I figure if I don't enjoy what I've got going on already, I'll lose sight of it and never have a chance of ..." Dustsucker paused, as if looking for a word. He rubbed the front of his face with his fist, thinking.

"Finding the right woman?" Ronin suggested, having grabbed the blanket and diving back into bed. For September, the weather sure seemed cool. The fact that he was sleeping buck naked didn't help.

Dustsucker smiled. "Maybe, maybe not. This lady — Squeek is her name — sure seems like a nice gal. But the nice ones are typically spoken for and we didn't do any speaking about that, so maybe. But then, there's Emma back in Carson City."

"Emma, yup." Ronin sat there on the edge of the bed, wrapped in the wool blanket so that it draped onto the floor.

"We ought to be thinking about her, I 'spect. So why is it that we aren't?"

The two men sat looking at each other, Ronin on the edge of one bed, Dustsucker in the center of his own bed, a worn-out night shirt covering his knees and feet. Finally, Ronin shrugged his shoulders. "I guess that's been the issue all along, Dusty. Not enough there to keep me captured. It's probably the same on her side as well."

"Not likely, my friend."

"How do you mean?" Ronin asked.

"More likely, too much man in the other direction, Ronin. Emma likes her men like she likes her school like she likes her children and so on. And you don't, if I may say my friend, fit her idea of what a man should be."

"Part of me, anyway." Ronin remembered the lengthy conversations the two of them had endured when he was convalescing at the American Gospel Mission. She had her opinions to be sure, but he'd always found her to be generous and kind toward those who thought differently, which didn't mean that she wasn't praying for them to change their minds. "Whatever the case, Dusty, I'm not one to think a man should change his life for a woman."

"Me neither, my friend."

"For anyone, for that matter."

"Exactly."

"Well, you keep that in mind then. Hey, speaking of friends," Ronin asked, "where's Happy Hands?"

"Oh, he's about, though I couldn't tell you where he's sleeping." Both men looked at each other and laughed. "Well, at least one of us is happy!"

# Chapter 49

# THE SON OF A BITCH

He'd left his hat and whip by a stack of rocks on the mountain's east slope, at least that's what he remembered. "I left it right here!" he shouted. The girl with him tittered. It wasn't an inappropriate laugh, she thought. It was more a nervous thing than anything else. And she surely had meant nothing cruel or maddening by it, having concluded that the little man known as Toro Latigo — "the Bull," he said — wasn't the kindest man she had ever met, though he had promised to be.

Sitting with her at Vesey's Hotel in Gold Hill — *the* Gold Hill hotel, someone had said, though a series of incidents at the hotel had caused her to wonder over time — the midget had promised to take her "somewhere she had never been." Given that she'd been pretty near everywhere on the Comstock — from the town of Empire along the Carson River, a shit hole if there ever was one, up and over the pass into the foothills leading downhill to the railroad town of Reno, a good deal better — she was entertained by the small man's promises. And not having ever been out with a man so tiny — she'd known big men and small, though never anyone this small — she thought the otherwise uneventful night at the Vesey House might turn into something better, something worth remembering or talking about.

The former Riesen House had grown with the town, though significant pieces of the structure, even by Nevada standards, had fallen down during a spring runoff in the early sixties. When Horace Vesey acquired the house a few years later, things began to look up. Smiles returned. Dinners were held. There were even dances.

But then the accident happened, the shooting as well. A giant steam engine on its way to the Yellow Jacket Mine decided to break bread with all of them one night by crashing through the hotel's north wall. Or was it the hotel's east wall? She couldn't remember. Then there was the time when a crazy man tried to settle his hotel bill by throwing lead at the hotel's proprietor. Kindly James Lowery ducked in time, not that anybody stepped in to help him. A string of events at Vesey's Hotel sort of broke the magic spell. She'd been sitting there ever since hoping that someone or something might come along to reignite it.

The woman knew that Toro Latigo wasn't the flame she was waiting for. But at forty-some years of age, there wasn't a whole lot to hope about. So when he invited her to take a walk up the mountain, she thought it meant just that, a walk up the mountain. She figured out too late that what he meant was that he was hoping she'd lay with him somewhere *up on* the mountain, something she wasn't entirely against assuming the little man had some money, but when he began yelling — yelling at her because he couldn't find his hat and his whip, his whip of all things — she was simply finished, a fact she was beginning to relay to him in the darkness when Latigo landed his first punch.

The blow broke her jaw, she figured, though no one had ever beaten her that badly and she didn't have a medical education to know about such things. And the punches and kicks he'd landed afterward, on her head and to her ribs? They'd left her badly bruised. So when the next morning came and people just out for a walk stumbled across her crumpled frame next to a rock cairn on the east side of the mountain, she'd been unable to describe what had happened to her, the son of a bitch. Her lips just hung there, trembling.

But Toro Latigo knew, and the Sisters of Mercy knew, too, given that they'd promised to get a surgeon up from Carson City who could patch her up and make her into the woman she "used to be," though being the woman she used to be wasn't much toward the woman she wanted to be. She wanted something more. She needed something more.

She was hoping the church — the goddamned Roman Catholic Church — would help her be that woman. And Latigo, that sorry son of a bitch if she ever saw him again, would pay dearly for mistreating her and a whole host of others, she figured, since the first time wasn't ever really the first time and there were always a few more times thereafter. And if she could find a rich man to tell her story to? Or a kind man who had the means? Or a murderous man who — despite his penchant or partiality toward doing evil when everybody else was trying so hard, so damn hard, to do right — might take a life because the life deserved to be taken, well, she'd tell him for sure. She'd *surely* tell him, and he would make it right.

A sour-minded woman if the Comstock had ever produced one, she was stumbling back to the Vesey Hotel when Marshal Augustus Ash called out to her, asking if she was "alright." Hell, she hadn't been alright in years, not that it was any of his business. Not that it was anybody's business. But maybe she'd tell him anyway, he and the fat man who was riding a horse way too small to survive the weight on top of him. She'd tell him.

# Chapter 50

# ALL GOD'S CREATURES

"That big of a man ought not to be on a horse, marshal!"

"That may be ma'am." Augustus Ash glanced over at the deputy who, swatting at flies around his horse's ears, seemed unaware that anyone was talking about him. "How are you doing?" he continued. "I don't mean to pry, but you seem a little swollen up." He pointed toward his own face.

"Nothing I can't handle, marshal, I mean when I find the midget who did this to me."

Both men pulled up on their reins. "Midget?" they asked, simultaneously.

"I apologize, marshal, I mean nothing by the term. It's a circus word..."

"Actually, it's a kind of fly," Ash responded, remembering that P. T. Barnum had borrowed the term to describe the popular entertainer General Tom Thumb and other smaller members of his touring group. "You said midget, ma'am. May we ask what happened?"

Slade's horse circled around so that it sat alongside the woman, preventing her from traveling any further toward Gold Hill. He nodded and smiled. She didn't return the greeting.

"The fucker took me for a walk on Mount Davidson is what he did. I'd hoped it would turn into breakfast." She shifted her weight from side to side and was clearly annoyed at having to speak to what turned out to be lawmen. Ash took it in stride. He couldn't remember a time when people were happy to see him, him being a marshal and all. "Is there any reason you're holding me here, marshal? I've got business to attend to."

"No ma'am. It's not my intent to keep you from your day. Nor the deputy's, I assume. May I ask where you are headed?"

The woman pulled her shawl tighter around her. A brief shower had left the smell of sage in the air. The hill out of Virginia City was crowded with people heading both ways and the trip up the hill to attend Mass had left her a bit winded. If she hurried, she might be able to catch a late lunch with one of her friends in Gold Hill. "I'm in a hurry, gentlemen. I have little time for the law."

"Ma'am?" Ash responded.

"Gold Hill, if you must know."

The marshal nodded.

"Thank you, ma'am," Slade said. "I'll not to keep you any longer than is necessary. I'm interested in this shorter man ..." Ash looked over. "... *We're* interested, that is. Do you have any idea where he might be?"

"I do not, sir. And you really ought to do something about your weight!"

"Excuse me, ma'am?" Dustsucker snarled.

"It's hard enough walking up and down these hills, deputy, than to be carrying someone so heavy as you. Can't you walk? Can't you find a larger, stronger horse on which to ride? Can't you take the train?"

The woman didn't stop, but continued to blather as Dustsucker looked down at the mustang he was riding. He'd had a larger horse at one point but it'd been killed in a gun fight up King's Canyon. He was still sore about it and missed the horse immensely. He pushed his hat further up on his head and smiled, despite feeling like he wanted to scold her for being so insensitive. "I'll have to think about that, ma'am." He took a moment. "You can't help us with Mister Latigo's whereabouts?"

"You know the man, deputy?"

"We both do. He's a mean son of a bitch with a whip and a gun. And if he's done this to you, he's gonna get what's coming to him sooner or later."

The woman took a step toward the lawmen and put her hands on their horses. "These are good creatures," she said, "God's creatures." She looked up, glancing first at the deputy and then the marshal. "We're all God's creatures," she said, "even Toro Latigo."

"Ma'am?" Ash asked.

"I'm just saying, marshal. I'm pretty angry about his beating me so, and I'm sure as hell going to give it back to him when I see him again. But it occurred to me this morning when I was sitting in church that all of us are doing the best we can with what we've got, deputy. Maybe Anthony is doing the best he can as well."

"Anthony?" Ash asked.

The woman nodded her head.

"Huh," he said, "Who would have guessed? The man had a mother," he said to Slade. "Look, I'll tell you this," Ash said, pulling up on the horse's reins. "I don't know you. I haven't even asked your name. But if beating you is the best that short son of a bitch can do, he ought to live somewhere else. Deputy?"

Slade leaned forward in his saddle and touched the woman's hand, which was resting on the nose of his horse. "Thank you for your concern about the horse and me," he said, "and I'm terribly sorry for your pain. When we see Mister Latigo, we'll make sure to convey some of your pain." He took a silver dollar out of his vest and pressed it into the woman's hands. "Get yourself some breakfast." The woman smiled.

"Deputy, we've got some business to attend to. Let's get moving." Ash began heading toward Gold Hill. "You coming?"

Marcus T. Slade got off of his horse and smiled at the woman, who was hefting the Carson City dollar and tossing it in the air. "I'm going to walk a bit," he said. "It'll do me some good and it'll give the horse a break." She smiled.

"Really?" Ash growled.

Slade ignored the marshal's tone and mouthed the word, "thank you." The woman grinned.

"Give me a couple of minutes to walk with this kind lady. I'll be along in a bit."

And for a few moments in Marcus T. Slade's day, it felt like springtime. The sage had left a lingering perfume in the air. And a forty-some-year-old woman was invited to sit on a horse she could neither afford nor ignore. And Augustus Ash, a normally dark-spirited marshal with too large a territory to cover and business interests that never quite hummed along as he hoped or intended, was reminded of his wife and children, their joys and concerns and the missed opportunities he'd suffered. There were busy days ahead and he knew it. He wouldn't return until he found three men: Mort Spinnaker, the former Ormsby County Deputy; Timothy Edwards Smith, a criminal if there ever was one; and a little man named Latigo, who'd worn out the kindness he typically extended to people he didn't know. They'd get what was coming to them. And only then would he relax.

# Chapter 51

# HIDING IN HIS WAGON

Toro Latigo sat over on D Street. He'd pulled up the wagon's canvas cover so as to shelter a few boxes and himself from the noon day's sun. The boxes presented to the rear, so that only someone intent on gaining control of the seat or jockey box might look in and around the wagon's contents. They might still miss the comfortable little room he had made for himself.

It wasn't like he was hiding. He was waiting. Out of sight, he was out of mind.

His taking a whip to the ex-priest hadn't been the brightest thing he'd ever done. No one had told him the man had a serious temper. Nor had it been smart to throw a couple of bullets through the window of the man's room. No one had said that a Carson City lawman was staying in the room also. He had simply heard there might be some work available for a man of his stature and skills, and as much as the women were willing to pay he assumed they wanted the priest dead. How did he know the priest might turn into a love interest? *Jesus.*

And speaking of love, what kind of crazy whore had he hooked up with in Gold Hill? He was looking for a nice place to lay down and get some nookie. It didn't seem smart to take her back to his wagon, even with the "We Make Caskets" sign hanging on it so that people wouldn't bother him as they sometimes did. Who figured that all hell would break loose if he needed first to find his whip and hat? When she began pulling at his pants, leaving them half-way down his legs so that they tied up his ankles, she'd begun laughing. *Laughing.* If there was one thing he didn't abide in a man, or a woman for that matter, it was being laughed at.

Ronin had gotten what was coming to him, he figured, and he would get a good "two-fisted dose of some more" when he saw him again. And the woman — well, smashing her in the lips seemed the right thing to do at the time. With her howling at the moon on Mount Davidson, people would surely come looking for him. Given that he was wanted, or at least he assumed so by the way Ash was looking for him as he ran out the door, her silly tittering and hollering wasn't something he could tolerate either. So he broke a few teeth, big fuckin' deal.

The girls had gone to breakfast a couple of hours earlier, promising to bring him something he was so hungry. They were headed toward the Delta when he lost sight of them and the damn stilts he was using to obscure his height. Funny thing, he had gotten them from a regular-sized man at the circus who wanted to appear even taller. They were beginning to hurt his hands and feet, so he had folded them in half and headed back to the wagon when he heard the marshal's voice.

"We ought to be checking the cemeteries," the marshal had said to the fat man he later learned to be an Ormsby County deputy. "Folks don't hang out there as easily when the weather turns cold like this."

"No, they don't." Slade had responded, though the man said he'd had little experience with the cemeteries in Virginia City. From time to time, he explained, he found himself in the Lone Mountain Cemetery in Carson City attending to vagrants or vandalism. "It's an uncomfortable place to be sure, despite it being a place of eternal rest for the pioneers and civil war veterans and all." The man said he'd lie there too someday, but that didn't make him comfortable. *Big duh.* "You think that Smith and Spinnaker could be up there?" the fat man asked.

"Hell if I know," Ash responded, before mentioning his name. The little man shuddered, hoping he hadn't made any noise. *How the hell did they find out my name?* He hated being so small and identifiable. He was so much tinier than the smaller Irish, German or English immigrants who had a few small men in the tighter places deep in the Virginia City mines.

"What are you saying, Augustus? These men are hiding in the weeds?" *City folks could be so stupid.*

"That's how some people make do," Ash had said. *No kidding.*

The fabric-covered walls of so many Virginia City homes weren't all that different than the flour-bag shacks that Nevada's early settlers had lived in. A cardboard covering wasn't uncommon at all, when people first prospected in Nevada. And some folks hadn't gotten much past that. "Yeah the weeds, Slade, and the cribs, backyards and floors of people who aren't paying attention, deputy. For some people, it's just like that."

Latigo rolled over on his side and moved closer to the edge of the wagon.

"I'm not stupid," Slade said. "I'm just saying, these guys have been up here for a couple of weeks. We should be looking in the lodges, rooming houses and so on. I'm sure the city police have a handle on everywhere else."

"Maybe," Ash said, looking at the wagon with the "We Make Caskets" sign parked on D Street. A well-used chamber pot hung alongside an empty chicken coop and water barrel. The Conestoga-like wagon was built for traveling and was quite different than the usual conveyances he'd seen. "Like this wagon, for instance. Who's to say our friends aren't living in this prairie schooner here?" He patted the canvas covering.

Latigo jumped.

"Hell, that's not a prairie schooner, Augustus. Haven't you ever seen one?"

Ash glared at him. "Not my point, deputy. These guys, these three guys and God knows how many more, are living in caves and holes in the ground. I've seen 'em, Slade. Down Six Mile Canyon, and places like it all across Nevada — it's time we flush them out."

# Chapter 52

# SMITH'S REVENGE

It didn't make any sense at all that they didn't kill them. The marshal, the Ormsby County deputy, Ronin, the whole bunch of them just sitting there — how the hell did they miss? It would have been the end of their troubles and the beginning of a whole new life together. But instead, Timothy Edwards Smith ran screaming out the back of the saloon where no back door had ever been before. Right out the window, he leapt a good 10 or 12 feet into a lady's backyard on D Street, rolling himself up into a couple of sheets before stumbling his way between houses until the shooting stopped and his heart slowed down.

Spinnaker, he found out later, simply backed out of the place, having emptied his "hog leg of every piece of lead he had" at the table, not hitting a damn one of them since he was fanning the gun instead of thumbing it like any sane felon would. It was a miracle, a goddamned for sure Roman Catholic miracle that his friend survived.

It would have been his preference to leave the saloon the same way they came in — friendly-like, his right hand in his pocket fondling the tiny gun his friend had given him and hoping only to leave a simple statement at the table of lunching lawmen: "Leave us alone. We're not hurting anybody. We're just trying to start a new life, together."

It was the together part he was least certain about, not that he had brought it up again given how Spinnaker reacted when he spoke about it last time. Had they not started shooting at the two of them, he might have gotten around to saying what he wanted to say. But when Spinnaker dropped to his knees and commenced firing, and the big guy appeared in the doorway, guns a-blazing like it was the Second Coming of Jesus Christ — Jesus, he had only one thought in mind. That was to get the hell out of there, which he did, ending up in a back yard where a slender brunette woman was hanging her wash — funny thing, the gold tooth and all, sitting there in the midst of an otherwise perfect smile. The pretty woman simply waved at him. Off down the street he went, his small gun in hand, clicking empty as if he'd fired it, which he had of course — all seven .22 cartridges, not that he'd hit anything. The whole experience had left him both sad and mad.

Spinnaker had a small red spot on his hand that he said came from the gunfight, though he'd seen worse wounds than that, especially when he'd partnered with those two desperados at Lake Tahoe. And he'd heard an Indian had been hit as well, not that anyone cared, except that Spinnaker had to bowl him over in order to get out the doorway in time to grab the back of a departing stagecoach so as to get out of town. Spinnaker didn't ride the stage for its entire route — they had no money for that — he'd hitched a ride a quarter-mile or so until he was sure the shooting had finished.

So when he and Spinnaker finally caught up with each other, in a small ravine a little ways down Six Mile Canyon, in the shadow of Sugar Loaf Mountain overlooking the abandoned Gould and Curry Mill, they had a big decision to make. Should they head back and kill the sons of bitches, this time really kill them, maybe taking their time to finish the job since they couldn't hit shit when being shot at, but who could? Or should they simply say, "fuck it," which is what the Indian said Mort said while telling the story, laughing, and maybe head somewhere nicer, like Dayton for example, or parts east from there? They were so totally screwed now, Smith figured. Spinnaker would never teach, to be sure, not in northern Nevada anyway. And if things didn't calm down between the two of them, he didn't know what he'd do, having lost his first partner in a gun fight at Lake Tahoe, and now nearly losing a second one in Virginia City.

"Mort? Does it hurt?" he asked, pointing toward the former deputy's left hand. Spinnaker was seated by a rock underneath a small cottonwood tree.

"No, it doesn't hurt!" Spinnaker barked, wiping the sweat from his head with his hat. "That bullet breezed right by me, not that you were anywhere to be found."

"Hell, Mort!" Smith said, spitting the dust from his mouth, wondering if the stream water was any good. "I had to jump out that window. There was nowhere else to go, what with that tall ex-reverend running toward me. Who runs while shooting a gun, anyway?"

"You ought to count yourself lucky, my friend. Had that mad man planted his feet on the floor and aimed, you'd be a dead man right now."

A moment of silence passed between the two men before Timothy Edwards Smith asked the obvious question that both of them knew would come, especially given what they'd been through. "You'd be missing me then, right Mort? I mean, if I wasn't here and all?"

Mort Spinnaker turned to face his partner, shoved his hat back on and smiled. "Yeah, I'd be missing you then, you old fool." The two men smiled at each other, Smith wondering how old he looked and whether Spinnaker really meant what he said. Then his friend looked away. "What was all that Catholic talk, anyway?" he asked. *Ouch.*

"I don't know, Mort. I was just wondering."

"While you held a gun in his ear?" Spinnaker smiled. "Now that was funny," he continued, though neither man really laughed. Spinnaker pulled a folded map from inside his shirt and thought for a minute while squatting a little closer to the stream. There was too little shade to be had in the canyon that started the Comstock mining craze. Mines and mills had come and gone over the years. The area now boasted a few houses, though he'd found the only accessible real shade there was in the ruins of the Gould and Curry Mill.

Smith scooted closer, not quite under the shadow cast by the tree, and asked, "What are you looking at?"

"I'm looking at our future, Timothy. We can't stay here any longer. We're going to have to move on."

"Even if we killed those men?" Spinnaker growled and threw the map down into the dirt, like a teacher or preacher might when folks weren't listening. It was embarrassing.

"Not even then?" he said, as Mort stood up and began stomping on the ground like an Indian on the warpath — a large fire, dancing, drums and all that, not that he'd ever seen one. He'd just heard about such things.

"You fucking retard ..." Spinnaker said. And that's when he knew he couldn't stay any longer with the man, not the way things were, anyway. He'd have to do something to make Spinnaker like him again, or at least tolerate him — maybe someday love him like a friend, or a son or a father. He'd have to fix things, he figured as the tirade continued. He didn't hear a single word of what was being said. He'd kill those sons of bitches if it was the last thing he did, because living alone just wasn't an option. While Mort Spinnaker might turn into someone he couldn't live with, there was no living with him if he didn't calm down. So he'd kill those sons of bitches using Mort's guns. *That's what I'll do.* That's when he took them from him.

Timothy Edwards Smith rose up from the crouch he was in, and slamming his right hand into Mort Spinnaker's head, knocked him off the rock he was sitting on right into the water.

He took two now-wet Colts he'd been admiring since the first day he met the man from Spinnaker's strong side holsters and tucked them into his pants. He'd kill those sons of bitches for sure when he found them. And then maybe Mort would understand what he had done. They could be together, as long as both of them behaved. No more yelling, no more hitting, on either of their parts, goddamnit.

The sun was hot as Timothy Edwards Smith tightened the laces on his boots and began trudging up the canyon toward the school and church in Virginia City. He'd get this done by lunch, or dinner if it took a while, or maybe a day or two looking for the men who nearly ruined things between the two of them. And then, if his friend Mort would take him back, they'd look for a new town to live in and start again there.

# Chapter 53

# AN UNINTENDED MEETING

Ronin came around the corner of St. Mary's Church at about the same time that Smith — a man he'd met only twice, both times briefly and under the duress of gunfire — marched by him on D Street, pulling at his collar and mumbling something about needing to find a new place to live. Smith apparently didn't recognize him, Ronin concluded, briefly touching his gun through the pocket in his duster. Taking his hands out of his pocket, he smiled. It wasn't hard to imagine why. He'd thrown a dozen pieces of lead at the man's backside the night before, as he blew through the back window of the Bucket of Blood attempting to escape the hell storm that had erupted inside. He thought about stopping him, but had decided instead to follow him when a female voice called to him from behind.

"William," the voice cooed.

He hesitated and then turned around.

"Emma!" he exclaimed, looking back to see if Smith was still in sight. *He was.* How someone could shoot up a saloon one day and hope to hide out in town the next was beyond him. "Emma, how nice to see you!" he said, not knowing what to else to say or do.

"I was hoping to run into you before I left," Emma said.

"Left? Walk with me, would you?" he asked, taking hold of her arm and speeding her up Union toward C Street. But Smith wasn't stopping. He was continuing up toward the better houses on B Street, and past it toward Mount Davidson. "I didn't know you were here."

"I know," she said, smiling. He loved her smile. "I've been meeting with some church ladies the last couple of days, and hoped that I might see you."

"Trying to raise support for the mission, I imagine."

"The Lord's work never stops, does it, William?"

"No ma'am, I suppose not," he said quickly, pushing both the walk and the conversation along. "I've got to keep this man in sight," he said. "I hope that's okay. He shot up a saloon the other night."

"Is he dangerous?" Emma asked, her eyes suddenly wide.

"Actually, he is," Ronin said, before realizing he was putting Emma in danger by walking with her up the hill.

"Should I be doing this?" she asked, pulling away.

A hundred snide remarks floated into his mind as he pushed her into a doorway and stopped. "Jesus will protect you," he might have said, had he not cared so much. "Not to worry, when it's your time it's your time," he could have said, but thought the sentiment no wiser or sensitive than the previous thought. "No one would shoot a girl as pretty as you," he imagined. *I should have taken him when I had the chance.* He looked over his left shoulder and saw Smith climb the steps onto B Street and turn left. *Damn.*

"Emma, where are you staying?" he called out as he began to run up the hill, leaving her in the narrow alcove between two breweries.

"The International Hotel," she replied, smiling.

"Stay another night," he shouted, before taking the Union Street steps in stride. "I'll meet you tonight for dinner!"

And with that, he was full speed forward. The gentle sound of a woman's voice calling his name had caused him to pause. But a storm couldn't stop him now. He'd have his man before the evening meal, and then meet one of his favorite women for the dessert.

# Chapter 54

# AMBUSH

Smith opened the gate, pulled the Colt's hammer back two clicks and rolled the cylinder across his sleeve to see if the gun was loaded. He did the same for the second gun he had lifted off of his friend, after striking him soundly on the side of the head with an open palm and leaving him lying there streamside, hoping he'd understand. If that was Ronin on D Street — the man who had chased him across the barroom floor the night before — he'd surely be coming his way in just a moment or two. There was little time to waste.

He'd first met the man when an Indian called out across the lobby of the Glenbrook Hotel at Lake Tahoe. It didn't appear as if he wanted to be identified, neither he nor the marshal, given how they looked at the Indian afterward. He'd heard of him, of course, having read that he'd rescued a dozen Indian children from the grasp of two gangs now shot-up, dead and gone, for the most part anyway. When Leonard Crum told him the ex-reverend was heading toward the lake to look into the murders of two Washoe men the Crum brothers had been involved with, he knew it was the same man. He told his friend Jones that, moments before his hot-headed companion drew down on the cowboy outside the hotel in full view of God and everyone else. God took sides that day as Jones died in the street, his head blown open by one of the reverend's .45s. What a moron his friend was, and still he loved him, especially after he died.

The second time he met the man he was shooting at him with his Winchester rifle, when fleeing Carson City with Spinnaker, who mentioned later that the man he was shooting at used to be a reverend, whatever that meant given the fact that the ex-reverend's bullets seemed to work just as well as anyone else's that day. "It means you shoot to wound," Spinnaker had said. It was about the biggest load of bullshit anyone had ever handed him and called it sweet.

"Who shoots to wound?" he said back, not waiting to hear a response from Spinnaker, who obviously needed to leave the Ormsby County Sheriff's Office or any other law enforcement agency if he thought like that.

Now, seeing him on the street, he'd pretended not to recognize him. There was no room to maneuver. Best case of all the worst scenarios, he figured, would have been to turn in surprise and hope to get off a lucky shot. But the preacher was rumored to be quicker than he was. He was glad Ronin also thought better than provoking a gun battle mid-day on D Street, what with all the whores and clergymen around.

He laughed as he loaded an extra cartridge into both guns, bringing the total up to 12, the same number of shells he figured Ronin fired at him the night before clicking empty. He stepped back into a narrow alley between two buildings and waited. The ex-priest was about to meet his maker. Lucky he was a Protestant priest. He couldn't imagine killing a Catholic one.

Ronin stopped by the north wall of a red house on B Street and peeked around it — head out, head in, as little of the head as he could move or show. His bishop in Pennsylvania had told him to do the same thing when boxing. "Shoulder up!" he said. "Don't do what everyone else does! You wanna get your block knocked off?" Funny words for a clergyman — of course the man was as much a fighter as he was a fisher of men, having more than once threatened to punch a man's heart out for stirring up disagreement within a church. "It's the anti-Christ," he said, when seminarians in tow looked his way, surprised.

Ronin quieted his breathing and waited out of sight. Smith had turned left to be sure. He was either hiding or had walked on toward higher ground. Either way, it wasn't safe to move quickly. And if he'd been recognized — there was always the chance that Smith had seen him and ignored him for his own safety — then he'd be waiting for him to step onto the boardwalk or walk out between two houses.

Ronin had been in this place many times before. The first Indian killed by a white man had been shot at Lake Tahoe forty-some years prior by not waiting, he remembered someone writing. And it had been hell for Indians and white men ever since.

"Fast isn't necessarily smart," the bishop had said one day when sparring. He had been dancing all over the place, *duck, evade, jab and fake* — the bishop "cutting the circle" with a straight line and side-kicking him out of the crude ring they had drawn in his Pittsburgh church basement. "You want to look pretty? Buy a dress!" he'd said. Ronin's ribs still ached when he thought about it.

"What the hell was that?" he'd exclaimed, holding his side.

"That was nothing," he said. "Now, if you're asking about what I did, that's something you'll half to learn from someone else," which, of course he did when he found an old French trapper in Wichita. Years later, he still preferred fighting with his hands and feet than killing a man with a piece of steel.

"Ronin?" someone shouted. The voice seemed to be coming from between a couple of homes south of him.

"Smith?"

"Yeah. What do you want?"

"You know what I want, Timmy. How about you throw your gun out onto the street and we talk about it, man to man?"

A couple of moments went by before Timothy Edwards Smith broke the silence. "Sure," he said, tossing his gun into the middle of B Street and stepping from a narrow space between two buildings.

# Chapter 55

# A BROKEN PELVIS

Two men facing each other in the street — their hands jittery by their sides, waiting for the other one to draw and fire — it never really happened in the American West. Sure, there may have been some exceptions, quiet burps in the history of women and men hoping to best a political rival, friend or foe. But this narrator knows of none and will not propagate the dangerous myth of angels sitting on the shoulders of good men standing out in the open while bad men fire indiscriminately away.

As it turned out, Ronin rounded the corner onto Virginia City's B Street and immediately saw the glint of steel at Smith's side. Reading his intent, he drew his own firearm.

It wasn't as if Timothy Edwards Smith was a virgin about violent matters. He'd participated in the sort of crimes that communities couldn't stomach anymore, assuming they ever could on their way to becoming real-life western cities and states. Smith had coupled with men who were willing to see their names written in the nation's history as criminals, miscreants, murderers and thieves. He hadn't ever been a Sunday school boy, not by any means or mention, though this writer wonders if there wasn't at one point a mother's love or father's cool intention that wanted something different, something better for their boy than the desperate life he had chosen.

Ronin didn't wait for permission or fair play. He didn't stop to examine the shine at Smith's side or to ask Smith if he was serious or to warn him. "Put your hands up or I'll shoot." At the core of his being he knew what Smith was up to, so he dumped his 4-inch Colt out of his horse-hide holster with nary a sound or word and with absolutely no hesitation at all, thumbing a .45 caliber slug Smith's way. He then rolled over a fence into someone's front yard where a tall, two-story white and black Victorian house stood guard over his now prostrate frame, and laid behind a hedge in a rock garden where winter pansies and purple snapdragons were his only cover.

Smith did the same of course, except in his excitement at seeing the ex-priest so close, he blew three bullets Ronin's way, all of them similarly fanned into the dirt — spraying loose stones and soil at the detective's well-worn boots, scratching deeply into the silver and gold-flecked Comstock dirt and damaging an old woman's flowers.

The gunfighter knew that in all likelihood his first shot was a throw-away. He knew it would startle his opponent, like a boxer's quick left jab or back-fist propelled toward an unsuspecting nose or chin. He took better aim with his second shot — his short-barreled side-arm as it was, wishing he had laid it down in the street instead of his longer barreled gun — and hammered a second shot toward the man who should have known better than to be standing in the middle of the street with his mouth agape, waiting for a storybook showdown.

The 200-grain .45 caliber bullet exploded into Smith's hip at a little over 900 miles per hour, tearing the iliofemoral ligament and splintering the top of the femur, causing him to twirl around and cry out. Not wanting to shoot his quarry in the back — nor desiring to attend to the requisite but still bothersome curiosities of lawmen doing their duty — he held his third, fourth and fifth shots as he watched Timothy Edwards Smith fall into a small rut in the middle of B Street.

Smith's partner, a man named Jones, had simply sat down when Ronin shot him at Lake Tahoe. The single bullet, out of the same gun, hit Smith's friend squarely in the forehead as Jones was beating his Washoe friend, Happy Hands, in front of an historic Glenbrook Hotel. Ronin watched the light fade from Jones' eyes as Smith, and an even more desperate man he learned later to be Leonard Crum, ran off into the Sierra woods for safer ground. Had Jones any good intentions at the time — any desire to be a different man, a better man, a kinder man, a more religious man — they perished with him. His final thoughts were never shared or known.

Smith was awake, however, squirming like a fish out of water on a rutted residential street. Hardly erect, his hands propping him up like the lengthy fore flippers of a sand-covered sea lion, alternately sitting on one ass cheek and then the other, Smith appeared to be in horrible pain. He began crawling to the side of the road where a splintered wooden walkway offered summer entry into a single-story home. Seeing he was unable to move quickly, he thumbed the hammer back one more time on his handgun but heard only a "click."

His friend Mort Spinnaker hadn't been kidding about needing to find a job to buy food and ammunition, damn it. Smith might have checked to see if Spinnaker's two guns were loaded with live ammunition rather than empty shells after he threw the palm of his hand against the side of his friend's head, hoping to do short-term harm on the way toward a long-term favor. Seeing no more cartridges in his gun or belt, and having no ability to even crawl away, he began to beg. "I'm hit!" he cried.

"No kidding."

"Come on, Ronin. I want to give up."

The ex-minister took a deep breath. He'd forgiven others many times in the midst of their misspent lives only to see them take to the same path again. Grace offered no guarantee, no matter what the Bible said. And he was not interested in being anyone's priest.

He squinted toward the path he'd been surveying to get a better shot at Smith if needed — up and back over the fence he had hopped and then a quick run toward the blue house to his right — when he'd decided to take an additional shot instead from where he was. If he could place it right, it would hit the other side of his hip and make Smith's escape impossible.

He'd been lucky with his first. At 15 feet or less, he rarely missed with a handgun, even the double-action ones. At 21 feet, it didn't matter what he was shooting. He hit only sixty-some percent of the time. At thirty yards, with a 4-inch barrel? He didn't see much hope, unless the gods were in his favor. The odds were surely not and the man certainly did need shooting.

He thought for a moment. "Tell you what I'm willing to do," he said, sitting up behind the hedge and pushing the brim of his hat up with his handgun. "Turn over on to your stomach. Put your hands and feet straight out, away from your body. And we'll decide when I get there."

"Decide what?"

"Decide whether you live, son."

# Chapter 56

# EVERYTHING ELSE IS EXTRA

---

"Everything else in life is extra," Ronin used to say, when he served the St. John's Episcopal Church in Wichita, Kansas. Folks used to come to him as their priest and pastor and tell him their troubles. And he listened, as much as he was able to, never having been trained to be a nurse maid or counselor. More often than not, he didn't know what to say, except to point to the sections of the Christian scriptures he thought to be "more honest than others" and hope that those selections expressed some useful and profound truth or wisdom.

The phrase that came out of his mouth more often than not came from the book of *Ecclesiastes*: "A live dog is better than a dead lion." The fact that it came from the Old Testament portion of his Bible — making it more Jewish than Christian and arguably more secular than sacred — was irrelevant to him. They were the most helpful words Ronin had ever read. And more to the point, they were among the most gainful words his dad had ever said to him.

His father, who had grown old working the bituminous coal fields in Pennsylvania, told his brothers and sisters one day that he hoped to better the family's future by returning to his father's farm in Obion County, Tennessee. His mother, being pretty much a city girl, couldn't see leaving Pennsylvania for lands that were not that long ago considered "Indian in nature," not immediately anyway. One year turned into two years, and two into three and before anyone knew it — despite protestations by *both* parents that the family's separate times would someday end — William Washington Ronin was a young man wanting to be with his father in a little railroad town named Union City, having spent most of his years with his mother in Pennsylvania.

"Everything else in life is extra," his father often said, when questioned about being raised in two different homes. Ronin understood his father's words to mean, "Be satisfied with where you are ... it certainly could be worse." Living with his mother, Ronin learned generosity and compassion. Living with his father, Ronin learned to endure difficulty. The arrangement was as good as it might be.

During the Civil War, Union City suffered a painful back and forth between Confederate troops — Obion County providing more soldiers to the Confederacy than it had registered voters and Union forces who valued the same tracks from which the town's railroad name sprung. In time, and much in conflict with his father's Confederate affinities, the town was held by Union troops, having suffered extensive damage as the result of the struggle between the two. Union City's dreams of becoming a hub of north-south transportation were decimated.

"It's better to be a live dog than a dead lion," his father said about their family's experience before and after the war. It was wisdom he had learned to offer as well, when parishioners unwrapped their life's burdens hoping for something different, something more. "Everything else is extra," he would say, eager to see his church members value the moments in-between.

Growing up quickly, as a young man living in two families and then later as a young soldier surviving sometimes multiple or conflicting loyalties, Ronin concluded that nobody knew the future. Those who traded on knowing what the future would bring — politicians, priests, doctors and generals — were more often interested in building their own certainties than helping others to do the same. He assumed Virginia City's criminals and clairvoyants to be no different.

Ronin dried his hands on his pants and shirt, and wrapped the hammer straps around his guns to prevent them from slipping from his holsters. The only thing certain in life was uncertainty, and pain — heart felt, or pounding like a gunshot wound to the hip, Timothy Edwards Smith's current situation — only cemented that perspective. Life involves suffering, and those who would live their lives with any real wisdom or honesty must face the fact sooner than later.

He picked up the tall, balding bad man and threw the 180-pound man over his right shoulder. There was no other way he could move him, given the wound. He carried him, despite having to listen to his whining cries for understanding and mercy, toward the Saint Mary Louise Hospital run by the Daughters of Charity. He picked him up, despite thinking that a bad life ought to end sooner than later, and that adult behavior was constant, more or less. He carried him on his shoulders, despite a strong preference to see the world's pain put to an end, or Smith's part in it, anyway. There was always "the possibility of redemption," the church taught. Let God sort it out, but still. He turned onto Union Street, with the whimpering mouth-breather slung over his shoulders, wondering which way to go, when he spotted his friends coming toward him.

"Well, lookee here," he called out. "Were we making too much noise?" he laughed, stopping to fold God's most recent petitioner for forgiveness and faith up against the north wall of Piper's Opera House. Dustsucker, who was carefully navigating Union Street's incline, paused to lean up against the International Hotel. Ash looked on, amused.

"I don't imagine there are any others that need shooting, William?" Dustsucker twisted his lips into the kind of smile a man might make when trying to catch his breath, but not wanting to purse his lips so much as to give his breathlessness away.

"There are not," Ronin said, grinning, "none that I could see anyway."

"Then what do you say you leave the dead man on the Opera House doorstep and we'll send a couple of coroners his way?"

"Dead man?"

"Well, I just assumed ..."

"You assumed wrong." Smith whined, pushing himself up and away by grabbing the back of Ronin's gun belt. "I'm in pain, but I'm not dead yet," he wheezed.

Ronin looked over his shoulder so that he could catch Smith's attention. "There's still time," he whispered. "I don't have dinner plans until seven or so, and we haven't had our talk."

*Things could certainly get worse*, Timothy Edwards Smith thought, holding on to Ronin's hip pockets so as to keep from slipping over the ex-preacher's backside. But right now, he wasn't feeling anything other than pain and gratitude.

# Chapter 57

# SO CATCH ME UP

"So catch me up," Emma said, seated at a two-person table in the dining room of the International Hotel. She raised a chilled water glass Ronin's way and waited for him to do the same. Their glasses kissed each other briefly with the tiny bell-like ring of fine crystal. "It feels like weeks since I've seen you," she said, smiling. "I've missed you."

"Well, I've missed you, too, Emma. It has been ..." Ronin was struggling to select a word describing his feelings when he was interrupted.

"I know," Emma said, holding the menu up so that it hid the corners of her mouth, which he was certain, if he could see them, would confirm Emma's disappointment in their not talking since he had left Carson City a couple of weeks ago wearing a new suit.

Understanding a person's facial cues, he had learned — or an individual's gestures and other mannerisms — took a number of readings. A one-time action or smile didn't mean anything unless it was accompanied by multiple supporting observations. The science wasn't certain, but it was a lot better than feeling the bumps on top of a person's head. Emma was anxious or angry, as awkward seeing him as he was seeing her.

"It's been intense, Emma. I'm working," he said, wondering why he had to explain himself to a friend. Their relationship was already too conflicted. "It's what I do, Emma. I've explained this before, and it's not as if we have an understanding ..."

"No, we do not." Her face softened. "I was simply hoping to see you before I left."

His heart stirred. There was something about the director of the American Gospel Mission in Carson City that consistently caused him to wonder if there wasn't a future between the two of them, even when he had set those thoughts aside. While their lives were quite different at times — he roaming the rural hills and havens of northern Nevada, looking for criminals who had escaped the full treatment of the law, she sheltering those who had been most harmed in Nevada's quick expansion to become one of America's newest states — they were alike in their best intentions. Emma Nauman wanted to find the good in people, particularly in the Paiute, Washoe, Shoshone and other tribal children she served. He, more often than not, saw the good still in the people he was killing or arresting.

Like Timothy Edwards Smith, for example, who might be on the edge of deciding to do something good with his life. Or Ellie May Livestock, who seemed at her core to be a fiercely friendly and independent woman, the kind of woman the West was made of. Or perhaps neither — he was occasionally too kind in his considerations of others, and dangerously naïve.

"Still looking after the Livestock twins?" Emma asked, her smirk unconcealed.

"Twins?" Ronin was surprised to hear the detail.

"Happy Hands told me."

"Happy Hands?"

"Yes, he told me yesterday that he was up here to deliver a warning to you."

"A warning, ah ..." he said, letting his thoughts trail off. "Well, good to know he found his way back to Carson City, I guess."

"I imagine so," she said smiling, as if there was more to talk about, not that either was saying, and not that he would admit given Nauman's experience with an ex-husband who had made himself quite a reputation running around with Carson City courtesans, bar maids and entertainers. "Tell me about the last couple of days," she said, relaxing into her chair before taking another sip of water. He wondered what she would be like if she drank a little wine.

"I'd be happy to," he replied, looking again at the menu and then ordering. "We'll have the pheasant, I believe." The attendant nodded, glancing at Emma to see if she agreed. She nodded.

"Can I bring you some wine?" he asked.

"No," Ronin replied, for the two of them. He preferred beer and Emma didn't drink. "We're good." The server left the dining room and crossed the hotel lobby on his way into the kitchen as Ronin returned his gaze and continued. "It's been interesting. The Spiritualists aside for the moment, I had an opportunity to kill or capture Timothy Edwards Smith today. You might remember him from the jail escape in Carson City?"

"I do, actually," she said. "He had something to do with the Crum brothers, didn't he? And the deputy who fled town as well, Spinnaker wasn't it?"

"Yes. Smith and Spinnaker arrived here a few months ago, together in fact. I spotted them in Gold Hill a week ago and just happened to come across him today on Union Street when I ran into you. By the time I followed him up to B Street, he was gunning for me."

"Did you kill him?" Emma's voice stuttered. Her eyes grew wide.

She had struggled with the amount of violence that was necessary to rescue the mission children last spring, but had come to rest, however uncomfortably, on the thought that killing was sometimes necessary when bad men turned worse. It was a prickly point of view with her board of directors, whose members were having difficulty keeping the funds flowing after the event that left nearly a half-dozen men dead and one in prison. She was no pacifist, she had decided, but peace was almost always preferred, unless the criminals were crawling in one's windows and threatening one's children.

Ronin smiled. "I did not, though I apparently did a great job of shattering his pelvis." He laughed. It wasn't funny, but somehow it seemed so.

"Where is he now?" she asked, taking a bread basket from the waiter and placing it on the table between them. She looked for a moment, before selecting a whole wheat roll and placing it on her butter plate. "I'm sorry, perhaps ..."

"No, that's fine. I don't feel like bread tonight." Their hands touched as he offered her the butter tray. She took it, and sliced a small pat of butter off of the tray before putting it on the plate beside her roll. "He's at the hospital, with the sisters. Hopefully, he'll get the care that he needs before being locked up God knows how long."

"And Spinnaker?"

"Well, good that you ask, as I haven't seen him in a couple of days. The last time anyone saw him, he and Smith were shooting at the three of us at the Bucket of Blood saloon."

"Three of you?"

"Dustsucker, Marshal Ash and myself."

"I'm sorry. I didn't know they were involved in your investigation, William." She looked chastened, as if her jealously was misplaced, which of course it wasn't. It wasn't as if the subject of his investigation was your average Montgomery Ward woman sent west on approval. Ellie May was interesting and pretty. He rather enjoyed her company. But business was business. He hoped they would stay uninvolved.

"They are not, but they were looking for Smith and Spinnaker when I came across them. I'm supposed to meet with them tonight after we're done here, to effect a transfer of sorts."

"A transfer? As in moving Smith from the hospital?"

"Exactly. A city policeman is sitting with him now."

"So tell me about the Livestock twins," she said, in a sing-song sort of way.

"I've made some headway," he said, wondering about her intent. "I attended one of their meetings, but I haven't gotten real involved yet."

"Involved yet?"

*Wrong choice of words.* "I should have said, I haven't come to any real understanding of what's going on yet."

"What's going on? That's easy, William," she said. "It's the same everywhere with fortune tellers and their kind. The dead live. The dead live and speak and the people who are entertained by that give lots of money. Do you believe the dead live again, Ronin?"

Emma's cheeks were flushed. He noted the change in tone. "I do not," he said.

"Exactly, except for the resurrection. It's a flimflam game, William, and while there may not be a law against gullible people believing what they want about their departed loved ones, there ought to be about folks taking gullible people's money."

Their server came into the dining room and presented two entrees: a small mound of meat surrounded by oranges, thyme and wild rice. A "Whisky Cumberland Sauce," according to the menu, complemented the pheasant breasts that had been heated to 160 degrees and set on a sizzling hot plate. "It looks wonderful," Ronin said, hoping to redirect Emma's attention.

"Everything looks good, William, until you strip away the tidiness of what you're looking at and see the crazy for what it is. A few minutes ago, this was a filthy field bird, cut in half so as to lie on your plate."

"Emma!" he exclaimed.

"I'm just saying ..."

# Chapter 58
# HOME MEETING

Ellie May pulled a foldable wooden chair out of the shed beside their house as Alvira gazed out of the living room window watching. They would have guests for the night, Ellie had said, though not overnight, not in the sense that they sometimes did. These people would spend similar amounts of money in an effort to speak with dead family members about all kinds of things. And if needed, Alvira would be there, in the booth they constructed between the living and sleeping areas of their small D Street home so as to convince the meeting's participants that their loved ones had in fact shown up.

The ruse was a simple one — sometimes a bugle, blown when needed, or a chalkboard to write on, or a lengthy piece of silk to wave around in the air — and if she dressed just right, her body and face wrapped in black most typically, no one would see her moving in the thin place between "the real and the not so real," her sister often said.

When they had moved west to spread the Spiritualist Gospel, so to speak, their father had told them that a little bit of trickery went a long way in introducing people to the other world. And while it wasn't the usual way, not for "women of character," he said, it was a good way for people to get started in their spiritual walk. It pushed them through the doubt into the darkness where the Other lived. "Indescribable and only able to be perceived through the eyes of faith," their work was important, he said. "Be good girls," he said, and when they couldn't be good girls, he counseled them to be at least careful.

Alvira Fae didn't know a whole lot about the other world save what her sister had taught her, or about being good or careful. But she knew that her sister knew, and most nights that was enough. "It's like what they say in church," Ellie said when they first moved to Virginia City and began attending the Catholic cathedral, St. Mary's on the Mountain just up the street from their home. "The real stuff isn't as real as they make it. Nobody's mother remains a virgin, and being a virgin isn't all that special anyhow. And Jesus wasn't all that exceptional a man, except that he didn't lay with any women, not that we know of anyway. But the Virgin Mary and Jesus are to be venerated nonetheless," she said. "Doing these things, believing these things is what makes religion spiritual," she said. "There's a truth hidden in all that language and practice, not that I can always tell you what it is."

She had asked, of course, because she wondered about all kinds of things.

Ellie had taught her to spell, and to read, more or less, and had told her the history of their religion — how there were these sisters living in New York, not the city but nearby, and that they were having trouble sleeping at night because they heard rapping in the house. "In time," she said, "the girls began to regard the rappings as coming from a dead man who was buried underneath the house."

It was a scary tale at first. But when Ellie told her that the sisters were named Kate and Margaret and were just like the two of them — seekers of truth and love, and friends forever — she felt more comfortable with the story. "From that moment on," her sister said, "people knew that those that had passed over were not lost to all of us, but could communicate with the living just as if they were living still."

It was a beautiful thought, she figured, and it appealed to her as her grandparents were no longer living. She had loved them dearly. "They're not gone," Ellie May said, correcting her, "they've simply transitioned to another place." While Alvira didn't know much about the other place, she knew it had to be a better place, where there was no pain, hunger or humiliation. Alvira had experienced all of these feelings growing up, and didn't want anyone to feel them as deeply as she had or sometimes still did.

Someday they might attempt to talk to their grandparents, Ellie said, but for now they needed to be busy helping other people with their problems. "They need us," she often counseled. "We're a medium to which spirits can come and grow — Spiritualists," she said, "who are able to sometimes pass along the messages that our loved ones give us for hope and healing."

Alvira loved how her sister's words sounded when she spoke that way. Her words were like poetry, she thought. She'd never heard words prettier than the ones her sister said. *Her* job, Ellie said, was to provide the music, the voices, sometimes the actual touches and apparitions so that people could believe what Ellie was telling them. And when she did it correctly, sometimes there were tears in her eyes because other people had tears in their eyes.

Ellie pushed at the front door with her feet, dragging four blond-colored wooden chairs behind her. They'd start with some trance work, she thought, maybe see who wanted to speak with whom. She'd do her usual shake, rock and roll until someone asked something. And if there was anyone there they knew anything about — Alvira kept a large book in the bedroom, noting their regular clients' personal details and dates, the kinds of things people were impressed hearing during their séance sessions — then maybe they'd be able to schedule some private meetings as well and really pick up some money. "It is a simple upsell," her father had said, "and an experience that most people need before they can progress on their spiritual path."

She put the chairs down in the living room, propping them up against the wall for her sister to unfold, and returned to the shed for five or six more. It had gotten too difficult to see clients at the Washoe Club, to lunch or to visit with men even in the Crystal Bar below. Those wealthy men, who had used their services in the past — to locate precious metals, or lost objects and pets, to speak with departed loved ones or to discern how to live with their still-living girlfriends and wives — were too skittish to do so now given the investigation by Misters Kelly and Ronin. Sooner or later, the police would figure things out, and there'd be arrests or attempts at arrests. No matter the outcome — and there was lots to be decided yet — the exposure would be damaging and they'd have to move. While that meant abandoning their house on D Street, it also meant that a new future was just around the corner for the two of them.

"We'll need money to travel," she'd told Alvira the night before, and maybe help as well. Do you think that short little man with the wagon would be willing to move our stuff somewhere?" she'd asked, thinking of Latigo, who had taken to doing them a favor but thus far had been unable to stop Ronin's investigation.

Alvira nodded. "Perhaps he could be useful to us in other ways?" she replied, thinking the small man pretty in a manly sort of way. Ellie smiled. There was no reason her sister shouldn't have a normal life. Perhaps she had been too restrictive.

"Maybe so, Alvira," she said. "After the meeting tonight, why don't you go looking for him? I'll stay home and pack."

"I'd like that," Alvira said.

The two of them pulled the wooden folding chairs away from the wall and set them in a semi-circle facing the special closet they had made. "We're going to be okay, you know," she said to Alvira, as she set the last chair in place.

"I know, Ellie," Alvira said. "If we can't take care of our business, maybe Mister Latigo can."

Ellie May sat down on the red velvet couch, behind the chairs they had set up facing their bedroom. She patted the cushions until Alvira sat down beside her and smiled. "I believe in God," she said, "even when God doesn't seem to believe in me."

"In us, Ellie, in us," Alvira said.

"Together always, sis," Ellie said, "We'll see it through."

# Chapter 59

# WHERE IS MY PARTNER?

Mort Spinnaker woke up with a start. Crumpled by the back door of their home in Gold Hill, he wondered about the puddle of blood around his pants and boots. A pounding headache lived where the side of his head usually was, and when he touched it — hoping to relieve some of the pain by pressing on it or by pulling gently but firmly at his hair — he began to remember what had happened: his friend's meaty palm slamming up against his head, his staggering across the floor, his laying on the floor next to the small table they had bought together at a fair held by the Daughters of Charity, his partner taking his guns from his holsters, and kneeling silently by his side as if to pray or to apologize for hitting him.

He shook his head hoping to jog his memory, but the pain and the fog continued.

Rolling over onto his side to reach the embroidered dish towel hanging from the back of a kitchen chair, he sat up slowly to review his options. He didn't recall the conversation that led up to his being hit. Patting his chest pocket where he kept his wallet and coins, it didn't appear that his Smith had robbed him. Had they argued? Where was his friend?

He pulled the pitcher from the table, which had scooted up against the north wall of their home and wetted the towel. There was blood everywhere. From the bullet wound in his hand, he guessed and maybe from the side of his head that had kissed the table as he fell onto to the floor. He felt a long slice above his opposite ear. His hair was wet and matted — he found the major wound and began dabbing at the cut with the wet corner of the towel. He'd have to figure things out before he went looking for a doctor to stitch him up. It wasn't like Timothy to leave him without telling him where he was going. But then it wasn't like him to strike him, either. And why was he so wet and dirty?

*Wait a minute. I wasn't at home when he hit me.* After the shootout at the Bucket of Blood, they'd fled down Six Mile Canyon to the creek below the old Gould and Curry Mill. And Smith had asked him twice, maybe — when he was already good and riled up — if things could change if they killed "those sons of bitches." And he had probably lost his temper and yelled the words, "you fucking retard." Yes, those were the horrible words he'd said, right before Smith him on the left side of his head with a big open-palm strike that had knocked him horizontal before catapulting him into the creek. *No wonder I'm wet and dirty and bleeding.*

*But how did I end up at home?* Smith had carried him, that's right, head over ass, his feet pointing the way uphill, a good twenty minutes or more before he pushed open the door to their home and knelt down beside him to see if he was okay. *Jesus.*

Spinnaker pulled himself up by the back of the chair and looked into what was left of a kitchen mirror, hanging where a cabinet door used to be. He brushed his hair with his hands and looked around for his hat. Where was that son of a bitch? Smith would get himself in trouble if he didn't catch up to him soon. He picked his hat up off the porch and pulled the door behind him so that it closed.

It was clearer now. They'd shot up the Bucket of Blood, hoping to kill the marshal and deputy sitting there with the saloon owner, who had proven to be an otherwise nice guy save for getting a little bit mouthy. They had been such piss poor shots when all that lead came flying back toward them. Smith had jumped out the window when Ronin appeared. He had collided with that stupid Indian as he was backing out the door onto C Street. Bullets flying, bad words, too, not that it could be prevented, God help them. *I mean, when you're doing evil, there's a lot of evil that gets done while you're doing it. Bad words can't always be prevented.*

He stood on the porch for a few moments, putting the towel to his face and rubbing at his teeth and chin. If Timothy Edwards Smith was hunting those boys down alone — he looked around again for his guns — he'd likely end up dead before anyone could find him. *Fuck!*

They'd had a little bit of history, before coming to words. You'd think another man wouldn't mind that, given the experiences they'd shared in Carson City and now 17 miles up the road on the Comstock. Relationships survived much, good ones anyway. And they had one, he was pretty sure, not that it was anything like what a man or woman might feel for each other, not exactly anyway. But they enjoyed each other. Smith kept house, what there was of it, while he worked here and there, sometimes finding time to plan what they might do or where they might go when they got out of the hell hole they had created. Good relationships survived this kind of stuff. And he wasn't going to hold the thumping he took against him, not this time anyway. If they could keep their hands off each other, and their voices down to a dull roar — beneath the sound of the mines, and the mills, and the riff-raff around them — they might make a life together. But not like this. Not with his running off with a couple of guns to finish their business. *That's what he said, "finish our business!"* He was looking for those clowns. And there'd be no protecting him if he couldn't find him before he found them. *But first, there's the matter of this head wound.*

He dabbed at the wound above his left ear. It was still bleeding — maybe the sisters would take a look at it? — and with his memory finally intact, Mort Spinnaker stepped off the corner of his porch and walked resolutely into God's good future.

# Chapter 60

# LAST COACH OUT OF TOWN

Emma Nauman took the last coach out of town in order to get back to the capitol city before midnight. Happy Hands had agreed to meet her at the depot on Telegraph Street in Carson City and accompany her to the mission site a few miles south of town. Given the hour, he'd stay overnight in one of the ranch buildings. Perhaps they'd have breakfast together the following morning.

It wasn't as if she needed her Washoe friend there when the coach came in. Rather, she felt safer with him there. So much had occurred over the last few years. Despite improvements to what many people were calling "America's littlest and most modern capital city," she liked the way Carson City used to be. She enjoyed the buzz the Comstock silver strikes had brought to the Eagle Valley — the frequent in and out of people associated with the mines, the businesses that had grown, too — but she remembered an earlier time, when city folk knew everyone in town, and those out of town were greeted by name as well. Life felt more predictable, more stable, safer.

Her husband, Henry, had been a complex man when it came to his affinities and affections, so freely and inordinately spent on the city's prostitutes rather than the children or his home. But Henry's willingness to pick up a rifle or handle a handgun when times seemed rough frankly made up for some of that. It wasn't a godly act on his part, stepping into the void to protect life and limb. But it was a good act, and despite the increasing friction over the care and curriculum of the mission's children, she'd come to a place of forgiveness. What was there to life, if compassion couldn't bloom when faith was broken? It had taken her a good many months to get to that point, but she had gotten to the place where she *practiced* thinking fondly of him. She was grateful for the contributions Henry had made to her life, even if he was a shit.

Once gone, Paiute and Washoe wranglers stepped into the void created by Henry's death or disappearance — she still didn't know which, and didn't know if it really mattered, he was simply not there. And when the men weren't available to help, she marshaled her own assets and "took care of business," she liked to say, when business needed to be taken care of, no matter what it was. She didn't much tolerate the hooligans who more regularly and recently pushed their way past the corral fence to knock on the front door of her mission home.

"Jesus will protect us," she sometimes said, but what she really meant was, if Jesus didn't protect her family, Jesus would just as surely raise up men and women who would help. That was the God's way, she was certain, remembering the Bible's stories of the first frontier judges: Deborah, Gideon and Samson. She thought too of Israel's first kings: Saul and David, and others who followed, who fought off brigands and pulled together kingdoms in the face of dark and perilous times. She could do that, she concluded. Nevada could do that, as well, with the help of women and men like her. Even Jesus was remembered to have occasionally carried a sword.

As the coach began to creak, she sat back on the leather-covered seat in the beautifully dark wood and leather-paneled cabin to remember the conversation she'd had with Ronin over dinner. He'd looked happy. *Maybe clothes do make the man*, she mused as she looked about the cabin. It seemed spacious without the usual passengers and luggage. It was kind of Benton's driver to make the run just for her.

*Ronin is such a kind man.* And while it didn't always make sense that she had feelings for the ex-preacher — he was so different than her, their values and work so disparate, his movements at times so dangerous, even desperate — still, feelings were what they were and didn't want to judge them. When she faced the facts, she knew that she loved him in the same way a wife loves a husband. But only God would determine whether they'd ever be together. And maybe being together wasn't all that important anyway. She had her work. There were the children to care for, and the future of Nevada to think about as well.

She lit a lamp on the cabin's wall and took out her Bible. "We have this treasure in earthen vessels," she read, from Paul's *Second Letter to the Corinthians*. "We are hard-pressed on every side, yet not crushed. We are perplexed but not in despair. Persecuted, but not forsaken. Struck down, but not destroyed." She wondered about the words.

Ronin's life seemed so difficult — with men trying to kill him and wily women waiting in the wings to do whatever — did Ronin trust God in such things? And did trusting God matter if God had dispatched Ronin in the same fashion as he had the men of valor so many years ago? Maybe God would do what God would do, and Ronin's choices — to be faithful, not to be faithful — would matter very little.

She returned to her reading, before falling asleep to the gentle rocking of the wheels and the sounds of the horses breathing, pulling their weight and hers down the mountain on their way to Carson City below. Happy Hands would understand, she thought as she drifted into her dreams. It was good to have a friend with whom she could discuss such things.

# Chapter 61
# LATIGO IN LOVE

Toro Latigo pulled the old wool blanket back from his shoulders, having rested underneath it in his wagon since sun-up. Rubbing the sleep from his eyes and pulling a shirt over his body, he noticed that it was evening. It was time to get up and to get moving.

Dozing during the day never seemed natural to Latigo in his trips back and forth across the California Trail along the Humboldt River, and the Central Overland Trail a few miles south. His family had moved people and freight between Utah and Nevada since the mid-fifties. But when the Transcontinental Railroad was completed in 1869, everything changed.

The heroic effort by the Union Pacific and Central Pacific Railroads produced the nation's first across-the-continent railway and set the United States on a path to prosperity. Its completion fulfilled a decades-long dream begun in 1832 when Dr. Harwell Carver — the great grandson of the first governor of the Plymouth Colony — published an article in the *New York Courier & Enquirer* advocating the building of a transcontinental railroad from Lake Michigan to Oregon. But the 1907-mile rail route caused great pain as well, replacing wagon trains, Pony Express and stagecoach lines. The subsequent explosion of train travel ruined the Latigo family's freight business and set Toro on his criminal path.

Despite efforts to revive the six-hundred mile wagon route between Salt Lake, Utah and Carson City, Nevada — "take more time," "see more scenery," "visit sacred desert sites along the way" and so on — Latigo moved cargo along the century old roads only occasionally now, catering only to people who squatted in old stage and telegraph stops.

No one wanted to follow the "Hellboldt River," as it had become known, or travel the historic pioneer trail that ran 300 miles alongside of it before turning into a dreaded, dry forty-mile desert. No one needed to view the graves of hope-filled lawyers and politicians, doctors, ministers, blacksmiths, storekeepers, farmers and laborers who were seeking adventure, hoping to build new homes or desirous of finding places to better themselves, their occupations and faiths. "What mean these graves so fresh and new?" an early traveler wrote of the river trail that had caused so many to expire because of accidents, Indians or the mischief and murder of family and friends. "I'd rather be in happier hands than longer live upon your shore." Latigo understood the sentiment, and years later still mourned the loss of his family's business.

The change accounted for his sometimes lingering here and there for months at a time. And with train travel being what it was — faster, cheaper, better in pretty much every way — Toro Latigo had come to a place where he didn't know what he was going to do and where he was going to live.

Sleeping in his wagon during the day and creeping through people's businesses and houses at night didn't bring in the kind of money his family was used to. And now, with lesser mouths to feed — having killed his father during an argument a couple of years ago, his mother too — he protected his privacy. Keeping his mouth shut was the only way of keeping his secrets.

Landing as he had in Virginia City for the last couple of weeks, he'd come to appreciate "the lovely Livestock twins," he called them, though they didn't know his name and almost always shushed him when he spoke of them in the plural.

Occasionally, they threw work his way. While others thought his short stature a hindrance, the Livestock girls did not. Alvira, the dimmer of the two lights, seemed to take a liking to him. He was thinking of her as he hopped out of the wagon around 9 p.m. and was surprised to see her standing there.

"Alvira! What are you doing here?" he asked, surprised that she even knew where he lived.

"My sister says we're moving. She wonders if you'd be willing to help?"

"You're moving?" he replied, remembering that he had business with the twins. "I don't understand?"

"She says Mister Ronin will soon tell stories about us that will cause us to lose our friends and money. We're holding meetings in our home this week and next, hoping to raise enough money to move to San Francisco, or Reno. I don't know where."

"Now there, dear," he said, patting her shoulder. He loved the twins, or the way they looked anyway. Smaller than most women on the Comstock, the girls hadn't packed on the weight like some women. Bigger women scared him. Barely four-feet tall, Toro Latigo had a height problem that larger women and men accentuated. He climbed back up into the wagon so that he could hold her against his chest. Her bosom pressed up against him causing him to feel happy. "Alvira, dear. Can I ask you a question?"

Alvira nodded. Toro Latigo was the only man who ever embraced her and never asked for anything more.

"Would you like me to solve your sister's problem so that you don't have to move?" Alivra nodded again, smiling. "And would it make you happy if I did?"

Alvira pulled away for a moment and then spoke her heart, which she had never done before, not to her sister or her parents, or the Daughters of Charity who first cared for them when they first moved to Nevada. "It would make me happy if I stayed," she said, "and it would make me happy if I moved." She smiled, and in that moment seemed indistinguishable from her sister. "As long as I was with you."

Toro Latigo didn't know what to say. But he knew this — no woman had ever said such a thing to him before. He jumped down from the wagon and grabbed his friend around her legs, squeezing with all his might. "I love you," he said as the girl giggled, lifting him up by his elbows and placing him on the wagon's tongue.

"I love you, too."

# Chapter 62

# ONE DOWN, TWO TO GO

---

"So you've got one in custody?"

"That's right. Tom Kelly has him on the 4th floor at Saint Mary's, in the event he tries to flop his broken hip down the steps on his way out of the hospital."

"And you've got three more to go?" Ash asked Ronin, who had pulled up a chair at the Bucket of Blood saloon, hoping to grab a beer before turning in.

"Me? That's your job, my friend! I'm after the woman," he said, laughing. He'd never pictured his life that way, focusing on the worst of the worst or "the finally forgotten," a sort of lost case file of felons and other miscreants that had escaped the grasp of the Pinkertons and other law enforcement.

As a pastor, he'd fished the bottom of the barrel as well. "How is it you never bring in normal folk?" one of his vestrymen had asked after he'd recruited a new members class consisting of a drunk, a whore-hauler and an underwear thief, all of them hoping to experience what he had promised, the grace of the Lord Jesus Christ.

"Luke 19:10," the then-reverend had replied, not that he expected the members of his church board to remember their Bibles, let alone read them. "The Son of Man came to seek and to save the lost." The recitation of scripture didn't crack a smile on the vestryman from Saint Johns, who was simply looking out for the health of his church. Folks on the seamier side of the social scale wouldn't contribute nearly as much to the church's budget as those employed in more socially acceptable positions.

"I've got money paid me to follow the woman," Ronin said.

"Someone's got to be focusing on the women," Dustsucker echoed. Ronin grinned. He'd watched Dusty look around earlier in the evening for Squeek, the Bucket of Blood's piano player. Too embarrassed to ask where she was, he had all but given up when he spied her climbing onto the piano stool against the saloon's south wall. "Hey, honey!" he yelled. Ronin and Ash shook their heads. Some men didn't get it. Dustsucker wasn't on her "A list" at all. McBride was simply hoping to fill a position, and Squeek — a comely-looking blond-headed female with a small frame and big eyes — was the best hook he could put out there. What was there about a little woman and a big man, Ronin wondered? It wasn't the first time he'd seen a grown man look so stupid.

He turned to the marshal and began lining out an understanding about the next couple of days when Versal McBride approached the table. "You still up?" he asked. Ronin turned, thinking it was an odd question, when he saw that McBride had brought him another beer.

"One's enough for me, Versal."

McBride winced. "I'm just saying, there's still a lot of work to do before I start seeing the Washoe Club men out and about."

"Versal, I'm on it, okay? I was just telling Marshal Ash here that I had caught one of the men he was looking for."

"That right?" McBride looked at the marshal for confirmation.

"He was," Ash replied, "Timothy Edwards Smith, in fact. Sitting all safe and sound over at the Saint Mary Louise Hospital," he said, enunciating the name "Louise" as if it was funny, despite the fact that doing so showed Ash to be a stranger to the city, as locals always omitted the second name preferring to call it simply "Saint Mary's."

"Uh-huh," McBride said. "Then you'll explain to me why I just saw Mort Spinnaker walking in the front door of St. Mary's with a towel wrapped around his head so as to protect his identity. The dumb shit even looked straight at me, all confident and such, as if he was headed to the fourth floor himself with the 1st Nevada Cavalry right behind him."

"Hell, Mister McBride! That unit was disbanded in 1866. That couldn't have been the cavalry behind him," Dustsucker said, obviously distracted as he watched Squeek turn around to face the piano and begin to play.

"Shut up, Slade!" McBride barked, "I'm not talking about the cavalry. I'm talking about two wanted felons about to meet up at the Daughters of Charity hospital, and the three of you are sitting over here like it was Tuesday night at the church and we were all waiting for ice cream. Hell is about to break loose on the hill, gentlemen! And if you tell me you've got only one guard on that man — I don't care what condition you left him in, Ronin, one guard isn't going to be enough — I'm going to sit down here at your table, and after I finish pounding it with my fists I'm going to put my hands to my face and cry. Seriously, guys?" he shouted. "What does it take for the three of you to get something done about the riff-raff shooting up my town?"

Ronin didn't respond, as he didn't hear the last couple of words, nor did Marshal Augustus Ash either. They tipped their table over on its side, crushing McBride's newly shined go-to-meeting shoes, and rolling through the door like the Virginia and Truckee Railroad a dozen miles away, were half-way up C Street when McBride began bleeding and screaming. Slade wasn't all that far behind, either, having stopped to grab his 10-gauge shotgun, filled with dimes in the event that Mister

McBride offered him that job — after all, he figured, it'd be nice to work alongside of Squeek even if it didn't mean that he was her boyfriend.

Ronin was a block ahead of the others when he turned to see if Ash was keeping up and noticed a city policeman standing on the corner of Union and K Street, still a short distance away from the hospital on R Street. "Hurry, man!" he shouted, before catching up to him and pulling at his sleeve. "There's a whale of a fight about to happen! Come on!"

The policeman, an Irishman "didn't know nothing" about a fight brewing at Saint Mary's or his own personal future, which would be shortly determined by an errant bullet fired at the man who was now tugging at his sleeve. But being Irish, and not wanting to miss out on a fist fight and the opportunity to hoist a few and boast about it afterward, he hurried along as well. And all four men were about to meet their fate, not that a Washoe Seeress or an especially good-looking brunette wannabe could have told them about it even if she'd wanted to. Sometimes, the future simply is what it is. It isn't what we want it to be. A step in this direction or a couple of steps in that, and suddenly everything changes.

# Chapter 63

# HIGHWAY TO HEAVEN

Mort Spinnaker had wrapped a dirty dish towel around his head to stop the bleeding from the wound above his left ear. But given the difficulty of keeping so short a towel tight, he'd had to knot a small stick into it on the opposite side of his head, which he kept twisted with his right hand, which ordinarily would not have been a problem.

Skipping up the steps like he was on his way to a Sunday School picnic, which of course he wasn't, having never been to Sunday School and only recently darkening the door of a church, albeit Catholic — he hoped to find one of the sisters to help him with a proper bandage. The Daughters of Charity's distinctive dress made spotting one easy: a dark blue habit, accentuated by — if it's appropriate to use such a word when describing a nun's traditional religious garb — a white, high-necked blouse or "guimpe" and a similarly shining white "cornette" or hat. The large folded piece of starched white broad cloth looked something like a sail, and no doubt acted like one in the sometimes-brisk northern Nevada winds. The whole ensemble created a not-so-humble-looking reminder that the Roman Catholic sisterhood, while not hosting a regular Sunday School like Protestant churches on the Comstock, did at least bear witness to a holy God who didn't always understand the foibles of men — but chastened by the blood of Jesus might be counted on to give grace where grace was due, if grace was needed.

Spinnaker was of the recent opinion, given Father Manogue's preaching at Saint Mary's, that all men and women needed the grace of God, and that some men — while struggling with what it meant to be good Christian men — might still merit God's kindness if they at least *wanted* to live their lives that way, which of course he and his partner did, though they were not always successful. Being hit in the ear by a ham-sized hand was good evidence that grace hadn't yet worked its full measure in Mister Smith. But still, the forgiveness that Spinnaker was feeling toward his male friend, while not merited — Smith could be a real jackass at times, he was certain — was at least heart-felt and freely offered. That was evidence that God was at work somewhere between the two of them, Spinnaker believed, and hopefully that would be enough.

The ex-Ormsby County deputy-turned-felon ploughed through the doors, and although wheezing because of the walk from Gold Hill to Virginia City, shouted to one of the sisters on the first floor who was standing with a pail of water by a patient's room. He pointed to his head and asked, "Can you help me?"

The sister smiled, slid the bucket down the hall by nudg-ing it with her right foot, and said, "of course" at about the same moment that Ronin slid through the doors on his left side with his gun drawn.

"Spinnaker!" he yelled. The sister gasped, but recog-nizing the piece of iron in his hand did not argue and dove onto a first floor bed as Spinnaker grabbed for his gun with his right hand only to have the head bandage, soiled badly with blood and dirt, slide to the bridge of his nose and rest there. As Spinnaker's gun was still pointed toward him, Ronin thumbed the hammer back on his 4-inch Colt Peacemaker, but waited.

Spinnaker slipped.

Pushing his well-worn boot into the bucket and sliding onto his ass and back, Spinnaker's gun ripped a round into the hall ceiling. He tore at the towel with his left hand, but ended up kicking helplessly on the shiny linoleum floor with his right bucket-bound boot unable to get traction. He began to cry.

Now here's where it gets weird.

Hearing him, albeit from three floors away, his friend Timothy Edwards Smith began crawling — off of a bed, sliding down the fourth floor steps and landing on the third floor steps, the second floor and so on until he shimmied up to his friend who was laying on his back, a bucket on his boot, sobbing.

Ronin, moved by whole scene and not wanting to shoot a man who was not shooting at him, remained vigilant but held his fire until the two of them lay next to each other on the first floor of the Saint Mary Louise Hospital, offering solace and for-giveness to each other but gazing at the ex-priest in such a way as to wait for a word of wisdom.

All Ronin could think of saying was, "What?" And then he began laughing. He didn't know why. How two men could find themselves in so profound a mess in their lives was, simply said, moving to him. And while he would have won-dered — in a more fervent and faithful time — if God had his hand on the lives of Mort Spinnaker and Timothy Edwards Smith, he was satisfied enough to simply raise his own hand to signal Augustus Ash, Marcus Slade and an unnamed police-man from Virginia City to stand down. Everything seemed fine. Which is what they did when Timothy Edwards Smith, "the stupid son of a bitch" Mort Spinnaker would later say, raised a firearm and took a wild shot in the direction of the officers present, striking the policeman in the chest. A volley of shots by the three men next to the officer killed Timothy Edwards Smith in return.

Mort Spinnaker would later say that his friend might not have lived anyway because of the infection he'd caught after being shot in the hip by the former reverend W. W. Ronin, but he felt no blame toward the man as God had no doubt used him as God intended.

He said all of this, according to Augustus Ash, from his prison cot in Carson City, where a Bible laid open most days and a serious effort was made by Mister Spinnaker to memorize its words.

# Chapter 64
# TABLE TOP

Ellie May pulled one of the chairs from the half-circle she had carefully made in their living room and placed it on top of a small wooden table she'd borrowed from the meat merchant next door. The effect wasn't exactly as she had pictured it — an elevated space from which to deliver whatever truths and insights people were hoping for. It put her on too high of a pedestal, she thought, as if she was speaking from a cloud or a pulpit, neither of which would make her approachable. And approachability, someone had said in one of their meetings, was key to her getting appointments with people who wanted "to delve more deeply" into the realm of the Spirit.

She pulled the chair table from the table and turned to her sister. "Alvira, I'm thinking this is too high up for folks to see. They'd hurt their necks, don't you think?"

Alvira smiled, but appeared preoccupied. Her conversation with her friend had her head swirling. "Alvira, are you okay?" her sister asked.

"I am. I had a talk with my friend Tony today," she said.

"Tony? I didn't know that you had a friend named Tony," Ellie said, putting the chair over by the doorway, where it wouldn't interfere with a display of materials from the Virginia City Spiritualist Society. "Tell me about Tony," she said, touching each stack of materials and contact cards then deciding to fan the latter stack so that it would be evident that they should be picked up and used by people attending the meeting. She looked up.

"You know Antonio. Toro Latigo."

"Of course, dear."

"I talked to him tonight at his wagon. He really likes me, Ellie. Did you know that?"

Ellie stopped fussing for a minute and considered her sister's words. She knew the day would come when Alvira would want to strike out on her own, assuming that she could, that is. She had made measured progress in the last couple of years. And if the times they spent together with men lent anything to consider, she had become more social as well. She'd even greet some men by name. And while they generally tried to keep Alvira's physical interaction with her overnight visitors to a minimum — she could get carried away, and too much woman was too much woman for any man, Ellie explained — she'd genuinely connected with a few of the men. It was touching, in fact.

"Tell me more," Ellie said, resuming her efforts to set-up the living room. "Give me a hand with this table? We'll put it out on the porch. I don't think we'll need it. I'll simply sit in one of the chairs instead."

Alvira took one end of the table. "You know how I've wanted to find my own man," she said. Ellie nodded. "And you've said that someday I might do just that, right?" Ellie smiled. Her mother and father would be proud that she'd come to a place where she was at least considering an independent life. She wondered if Alvira was at that point. "Well, I told Tony that I loved him tonight. And do you know what he said?"

"No, dear. I do not."

"He said he loved me, too."

She pulled a chair from the half-circle again and positioned it over by the closet she had fashioned with her sister. Alvira had yet to place inside of it the usual instruments and props they'd need for the meeting. She hesitated, turned toward her sister and kept her hands on the back of the chair so that she wouldn't forget what she was doing. "What do you suppose he means by that, dear?"

Alvira pulled a couple of boards from a pile beside the woodstove, and set them down on the floor. She grabbed a table cloth that her sister had set out to use for refreshments and, setting the chair up on the boards, about three inches off of the floor, spread it over the chair and boards instead. The effect was perfect.

"I think it means he wants to be with me, sis."

Ellie smiled, though other feelings stirred inside of her. If her sister wasn't careful, she'd end up pregnant. And a pregnant muse wasn't a helpful muse, to most men, anyway. More so, she'd hardly fit within the cabinet they used to provide "evidences" of the evening's activities. "You must be careful with men, you know."

"I know," Alvira said. "You've taught me these things, Ellie. I won't forget."

Ellie ran her hands across the chair they had set up for her to sit in. She'd be in a trance soon, listening to the spirits and talking with loved ones. The dark blue cloth was just right. And the chair sat at the same level as every other chair in the room — at least people would perceive it so. The slight lift would help focus attention on what she was doing. And the fact that it was higher would stir interest and influence as well. "I want for you the things that I want for myself," she said. "It's the golden rule, you know."

"To love others as you want to be loved."

Ellie May crossed the living room to make her point. Putting her hands on Alvira Fae's shoulders, she looked her in the eyes before moving one hand to her left eye to wipe away a tear. "Love, I know that life isn't what we thought it would be. But change is coming. And change is good. Promise me this. You'll do nothing about your feelings, or Mister Latigo's feelings, until we talk things out."

"Until we talk things out?" Ellie could see that she was confused and disappointed.

"I'm not saying it's not good, dear. It is what it is ..."

Alvira looked at her, still uncertain. "It's probably the most exciting thing to ever happen to you, isn't it?" Ellie asked. Alvira nodded. "Then it is what it is, sis. And we'll figure it out together!" Alvira smiled. "Help me with this cabinet?"

Alvira nodded, and with sudden enthusiasm began to pull things from the bedroom they would need for the evening: the trumpet, the chalk board, some silk and some small cymbals. "The spirits should celebrate with us tonight, Ellie!"

"I'm sure they will," Ellie said, as their first guest knocked on the front door. Ellie held her fingers to her lips. Alvira nodded vigorously. Life had spoken, and the sisters would make the best of it.

# Chapter 65

# BEHIND THE DOOR

Different people handle their feelings in different ways, his mother used to say when Ronin asked how an otherwise good marriage, to his own eyes anyway, could grow so stale that a mother and a father would choose to live in different homes in different states.

"It's a matter of one's constitution," Dorothy Ronin said. "Your father doesn't say much, except when he's truly happy, and I don't say much unless I'm really upset."

She must have seen the confusion in his eyes — he being the oldest, there were explanations to give to his siblings, and there was always the temptation to shame and blame — so one evening, while he was sitting by the fire helping the younger children with their lessons, she said, "It's just how it worked out, William. Good people don't always get along. And good people don't always get what they want, either." The words had stuck with him, during the war when he fought alongside of his father in a Confederate cavalry unit, and in the parish work that followed. It had given him a certain amount of confidence in life that no matter what happened, it was as it was. There were no guarantees.

He knew she wished his father well, working with what was left of the family farm in Obion County, Tennessee after the "War of Southern Independence," as his father called it, knowing the term said as much about his own personal beliefs as it did those of the confederate states. And maybe she even wondered what it would have been like to have followed him there, shutting down the house in Pennsylvania, bringing the kids with her. His dad likely wondered as well, had he remained in the Pennsylvania coal fields. But it was what it was, Ronin had concluded though it took him some time to think of things that way. Good people didn't always get along in life nor did they always get what they hoped for, either. Life did as life wanted to, and there was no better explanation than that.

He pulled his pants off and hung them over the headboard, next to his gun belt and hat. Had he gotten back to his room sooner he might have sent them to the desk for cleaning, but it was much too late now, having spent the last few hours with his friends.

Tomorrow, he'd get back on the Spiritualist controversy, as he had begun to think of it, not that he was against anyone practicing their religion in whatever way they wanted to. Still there was a job to do — Tom Kelly and Versal McBride had been clear about that. "One dead man wasn't our deal," they said, well McBride anyway, not that he had suggested such. And Kelly had almost been killed while guarding Mort Spinnaker, who surely couldn't have gotten away if he had tried, though his sliding down the stairs to see his friend — now the late Timothy Edwards Smith — had surprised everyone, including a sleeping Virginia City sheriff.

"I'm on it," Ronin had responded, though in reality Ronin wasn't at all sure what he was feeling about the woman on D Street who, while she wasn't of the same quality or character as Eilley Bowers or other better-known Washoe fortune tellers, was as good as the next person. I mean, how was it her fault? Or anyone else's for that matter that her fortune-telling — real or unreal, it really didn't matter. It was "entertainment," she'd explained — was taken so literally? Folks should be more careful when they're sitting for a séance. Hell, even if they're sitting in church, he figured. Discrimination, critical thinking, turning one's brain on and not off, were important actions. It took a certain amount of ignorance to believe something unseen, he figured, despite the Bible's pronouncement that "faith is the substance of things hoped for, the evidence of things not seen." In a perfect world maybe, but not on the Comstock, where misplaced hopes and dreams were regularly dashed by incompetence, criminality and general tomfoolery.

He sat down on the bed to remove his socks. *These have seen better days.* The decision to bring Jackson to Virginia City hadn't proved wise at all as it had limited his packing space, and he'd been so busy that he hadn't ridden back and forth from Carson City as he had intended. But the suit was nice. *It's holding up just fine.*

He laid back on his bed, naked. Pushing up on his pillows he reached for his journal and began tugging at the sheet beneath him until he got one foot underneath it. Then there was a knock at the door.

"Ronin?"

"Dusty? What do you want? I thought you were going to stay at the saloon for a while?"

"I'm headed back there. I just wanted to make sure you kept the door unlocked. I don't have my key."

"Doubt it, my friend, not in this town, not now anyways. What did you do with it? Hold on a second, I'll hand it to you." He looked about the room but didn't see the key sitting anyway.

"Um ..." his rarely speechless friend said. "Um ..." he said again. "I gave it to Squeek. I was thinking she might want to come up and see me at some point."

"You gave it to Squeek?" *Really?* He pulled the sheet up so that it covered his entire body and smiled.

"Don't judge me, Ronin."

"I'm not judging you." He laughed. "Look, I don't know what to say. Let me get the door. He began to get up when Dustsucker interrupted.

"Listen, don't get up, just leave the door unlocked. I'm going to head back to the Bucket of Blood and get my key back. I'm feeling stupid."

"Okay..."

"I mean I left it there without thinking."

"Of what?

"You know..."

"Yeah, I know." Ronin laid back on the pillow and thought for a moment. Life sure seemed to have its surprises. He'd never have guessed that he'd be killing Timothy Edwards Smith that evening. And he didn't much expect to be talking to his friend about bringing a girl home, or listening to him feel embarrassed and inadequate. "Tell you what, Dusty," he smiled. "I'm going to make a visit of my own tonight. You keep the room, my friend. It will be open all night and I wish you luck."

"Are you sure?" Dustsucker asked from behind the door.

"I'm sure."

"Well, take your time then. And I'll see you in the morning. I might be back in an hour or so. We'll see."

Ronin smiled, and laying back on the bed, cracked the journal next to him. Nothing was ever as it seemed. And more so, life had its surprises. What mattered most was enjoying each and every moment. When it's all said and done, he figured, there are too few.

# Chapter 66
# JOURNAL, FEBRUARY 1, 1876

Ronin licked at the tip of his pencil and then thought better of it. He was tired already. He didn't have time or energy to write. And if the hotel room was going to be Dustsucker's for the night — he couldn't imagine what for, given the tone of things at the Bucket of Blood — he'd want to keep his energy up and his focus sharp. If he wasn't careful, he'd be sleeping in a saloon, his head on a table or sprawled out on someone's floor. That was the best scenario. Worst, he'd end up in someone's bed, not that he was thinking about it, but then again he *was* thinking about it.

He sat on the edge of the mattress so that he wouldn't fall asleep, pulled his pants from the chair, laid them across his lap and decided to read from his diary instead.

Emma Nauman had made a gift of the leather-covered volume almost a year ago. He liked it so much that as soon as she gave to him, he began transcribing the pages of his previous journals so that everything he had written — from his entrance into Biffle's 19th Cavalry, his years in the church, his employment with the Pinkertons to the present day — sat in one volume. A lengthy crimson ribbon helped to separate the past from the present, and suggested that what he was writing — the thoughtful exploration of the events of his adult life — was just as important as any holy book. The present didn't just happen. It followed, he figured, from moments strewn intentionally and unintentionally throughout one's past.

He fanned the journal's pages, back to 1876, just prior to his leaving the Pinkertons' service and hung his head. He was emotionally exhausted. Each gunfight seemed to take something from him. And at each significant twist or turn in the road — his, someone else's, it didn't seem to matter — he found himself looking backward for clues to what might lay in front of him. It was a habit he learned in ministry, ancient pages lending contemporary truth or advice. Or perhaps it was the practice of every person who momentarily forgets what he or she is doing or why.

He flipped a few pages until he found an entry where he'd written about the outlaws, Jesse and Frank James. He grabbed his socks from the chair and began to dress himself.

*The remote offices are working fine, from what I can see. Pinkerton Detectives are only a spur-dig away from much of what is happening in the West that needs a lawman's attention. Banks, trains, strong boxes, it doesn't matter. The Pinkertons have offices everywhere so that wanted men and women can't hide, not for long anyway.*

*The notorious James gang has found the growing net of Pinkerton detective offices to be especially frustrating. But last month, the hunter became the hunted, that's the rumor anyway. "The old man" — who had everything to do with foiling an initial plot to kill Abraham Lincoln prior to his being sworn in, and whose removal from service in 1862 may have had something to do with John Wilkes Booth successfully killing Lincoln in 1865 — became the target himself of an assassination attempt.*

*In January, two members of the James family were unfortunately hurt by a Pinkerton-led assembly in search of the gang. The posse, believing they had cornered the younger brother inside of a small cabin near Kearney, Missouri, demanded that the bandit* surrender. Someone tossed an explosive through a window — or fired a bullet into a kerosene lantern, no one will ever know exactly what happened — and Jesse's mother lost an arm. An idiot step-brother was also killed. The resulting flare-up motivated the outlaw to travel to Chicago to kill the old man, though no real proof of his coming after him exists except for the bandit's boasting:

Still, the original incident has caused a public outcry. Sympathies about the agency (once positive) have plummeted in response. Similar issues face the Pinkertons back East, where the public regards the Pinkertons as the angry arm of wealthy industrialists, which may in fact be the truth.

Fact is, there's a certain amount of danger to what we do, and compromise sometimes happens, whether we want it to or not. The color of life is gray, it seems to me. And because it's gray, people get hurt. I feel more concerned about my safety now than ever.

Pinkerton's son, William, is no stranger to danger, though Allan Pinkerton's other son, Robert, is mostly office-bound. Levi and Hillary Farrington — from western Tennessee, though no acquaintance of mine — were arrested by Pinkertons a couple of years back in Illinois and Indiana. The arrests went poorly, particularly as it pertained to Hillary Farrington, who injured William during the course of his arrest by shooting him in the hip. Later, when he again struggled with the detectives, Farrington ended up falling over a paddleboat railing into its paddlewheel where he was, as William relates, "chopped to pieces." Levi Farrington and his accomplices were either shot to death or hung by the people of Tennessee — I don't remember which — giving credence to my earlier thought that that life is sometimes difficult, and more difficult for some than others. All of this has left me wondering if there isn't some better use of my time and training.

The other day, Kate Warne mentioned that there was the possibility of my being assigned to work with a team of men tracking a well-known Spiritualist. While I have no direct knowledge of the case — there is talk of the woman reading cards, gazing at stones, *hearing the voices of "departed loved ones" and marrying multiple people along the way — I'm wondering if it wouldn't be more interesting than keeping the bad guys out of the railroad's strong boxes. The latter has left me wanting more contact with people, so much so that I sometimes find myself distracted by the interests and background of the railroad's passengers than thinking about ways to protect the railroad's other treasure — its silver, gold and paper money.*

He put the book down and grabbed his left boot from beneath the bed. If he was to get moving, he ought to get busy. Otherwise, he'd be laying back in bed, remembering the good times and wondering what he was doing in Virginia City working for Versal McBride and a handful of careless geezers at the Washoe Club.

# Chapter 67

# AFTERGLOW

"Well, Mister Ronin. So we meet again!" Ellie May Livestock answered the door and smiled, then turned and continued to collapse the folding chairs she had taken from her shed and placed in her D Street home.

"Looks like you had a meeting, Ellie," he said, wondering if he'd used the right word. He wasn't as familiar with the Spiritualist movement as he thought he should be given his ecclesiastical background. Chasing two women out of town and putting a damper on similar meetings in Virginia City didn't really demand much more than he had. Still, he was addicted to knowing more than the next guy — for whatever reasons, he wasn't sure — and not knowing left him feeling kind of ignorant.

"I did," Ellie said, looking at him and smiling.

Ronin glanced around the room. A dozen or more chairs had been set in a semi-circle. Ellie's chair, at least the chair he took to be Ellie's chair — she had a flair for dramatic readings, he had been told — was covered by a dark blue table cloth. A crystalline ball sat next to the chair, the first one he had ever seen though he was no stranger to such practice, having seen peep stones, mirrors and other divination devices.

"May I?" he asked. Alvira climbed down from a stepstool where she was removing a similarly colored drape they had only hours before hung between the living room and bedroom. She shook her head no and frowned, picking the quartz stone up from the floor and taking it into their bedroom.

"Some people think the power is in the object," Ellie said, letting go of the stack of chairs and walking toward the entry-way between the two rooms where Ronin was standing. "I believe the power is in the person. I'm not one to believe in magic stones and ladders. Do you, Mister Ronin?"

"Life is what we make of it, ma'am. At least, it appears that way."

"You out climbing ladders, Mister Ronin?"

Ronin smiled. He hadn't figured the woman for Sunday School material and took note that she had repeated herself. "Not tonight, ma'am," he replied, recalling to mind the ancient story of Jacob, who while outwardly successful, wrestled all night long with an angel in hopes of securing something deeper or better than the otherwise rich life he was already living. "Thought I might catch you before I retired for the evening, ma'am. Do you drink, Miss Ellie?"

"As in a glass of wine, sir?"

"Exactly," he replied. He didn't know when he had last asked that of a lady, and hoped he hadn't suggested anything inappropriate.

"Love to," she said, without missing a beat. "Alvira Fae?"

"Yes, Ellie?" Ellie's sister appeared from the bedroom, wearing a gold tooth where her perfectly natural teeth had been a few moments before.

Ellie laughed. "Alvira, Mister Ronin knows that we are twins." Alvira wiggled the tooth for a moment and a gold cap came off in her hand. She smiled. "Sis," she continued, "Mister Ronin and I are going to get a glass of wine at ... where would that be, Mister Ronin?"

"The International?"

"Of course. That would be nice. May I bring you anything?"

Alvira shook her head, and then asked, "Do you want me to remain here, after I put things away?"

"Well where else would you be? Right, Mister Ronin?"

"Right." He felt his face flush, and wasn't sure at all what was being talked about. Somehow, the two of them being in the same room conjured up thoughts he wasn't at all comfortable with. Though he was no prude — not in his mind, anyway — he thought one man with two women was probably one woman too many, though the thought was apparently not shared by everyone.

"We'll be back in an hour or so, Alvira," he said, buttoning his coat around him. A single six-gun hung off to one side, angled through the side-vent of his suit jacket.

Ellie nodded to her sister before pulling a sweater off of a shelf near the front door and draping it around her shoulders. She looked back at Ronin to see if he was following. Ronin, transfixed by the fact that the two women looked so similar — even to the color of their eyes and hair — was staring at Alvira who was, in fact, staring back.

"Alvira?" Ellie asked. "Is there something I can help you with?"

Alvira shook her head, and turned her attention to the chairs that Ellie had leaned against a small bookcase. She frowned. "Are you okay?" Ellie asked.

"I'm fine," Alvira replied. "See you when you get back."

Alvira wasn't at all happy with Ellie's interest in the former preacher, who now lent his energy and guns, Tony had said, to persecute people who thought differently than him. It hadn't been that many days since she had helped Tony load and carry cartridges to a quiet spot on the mountain overlooking the city. They had paused among some rocks and shrubs a little ways from the top so as to fire the long rifle Anthony had brought to kill Ronin. Two shots and a shattered hotel window later, she discovered that Ellie was angry that Anthony had tried to kill him.

Alvira hadn't told her that she had been there. She had misunderstood Ellie's instructions, as had Toro, who had gotten into a shouting match a few nights before at the Bucket of Blood saloon over his standing on a table singing. The event had ended up scaring the two of them, especially when they watched Ronin run from the hotel's front entrance on C Street up the hill toward B Street, and look — she could swear he was looking right at her, the moonlight was so bright — up the mountain to the very spot where the two of them hid behind an old porch, frightened. She didn't like W. W. Ronin at all, and if she had her way, her sister wouldn't like him either.

She looked at the stack of chairs and wondered if she could get all eight of them into the shed in one trip. The meeting had gone pretty well tonight, she mused. Ellie had three appointments next week, and two of the women had already paid for their time. It had been her suggestion that they pay "up front," rather than pay later for the spiritual work Ellie would be doing. "Your commitment will speak volumes to your loved ones," Alvira had suggested from behind the curtain, pretending to be a spirit that knew such things. Two of the three women opened up their purses right away, counting out silver Carson City dollars. Ellie was pleased.

If there was one difference between her and her sister, it was this: Alvira wasn't afraid of getting what she wanted. And she wanted Ronin dead.

# Chapter 68

# OUT FOR A GLASS OF WINE

Ellie took Ronin's arm. They walked north along D Street, away from Saint Mary's toward the Silver Terrace Cemeteries at the end of E Street. Ronin had counted more than a dozen graveyards, though he heard there were as many as twenty or more etched into the deep ravines and steep hillsides of Virginia City by fraternal, civic and religious groups like the Knights of Pythias, the Pacific Coast Pioneers, the Masons and various churches. Nearly every plot was fenced or bordered, their wind-blown graves marked with wood, metal and, more recently, cut stone. As the night was chilly, Ellie pulled herself closer to Ronin than a single lady might normally. But then Ellie wasn't a lady, not in Ronin's mind.

Less than a half-dozen years prior, when he'd fallen in love with a similarly gifted woman practicing the divination arts, he'd made a promise to himself that if ever became involved with a woman again, it would be someone his mother would have approved of. Now certain that his parents had been as human as anyone — he'd proven to himself that he was as well — he wasn't sure it was a promise he needed to keep. Still, should he fall in love again, should he decide to take up with someone or even to marry, the woman he was in love with would be as taken with him as he with her. He didn't see how Ellie May Livestock could be that woman.

He was uncomfortable with her spiritual practice, not that he made a point of judging people. Seeking out the dead to discern secrets for those who are still living seemed at best to be silly and at worst to be dangerous and misleading. While the constabularies in Virginia City were reticent to prosecute the women for their obvious flimflam, and didn't believe that a jury would convict the twins for fraud, arguing that a seeress' services were free speech under the first amendment, Ronin felt otherwise. Fleecing an ignorant fella of his earnings, no matter how easy he had come by them, was as wrong as yelling "fire" in a crowded barn or church, and left the same kind of injuries.

He counted two dead: one Carson City poker player with a broken dream and an old man in a bed with what amounted to be a broken heart. He couldn't assess the losses of others who had sat with Ellie gazing into her crystal ball, or in a setting like last night, happy to pay God knows how much for services he figured were as fraudulent as any. Those that stayed over — and he'd almost been one — were at least getting something for their money.

The girls were cutting moral corners, and while he didn't keep account of that for people, there was sometimes a piper that needed to be paid. Occasionally, he was the one collecting the money.

They walked a few steps before Ellie turned and faced him. She pulled the shawl around her shoulders and buttoned it. Despite all of his mental machinations, she was an attractive woman. Her brown hair shone. Her green eyes spoke words he hadn't heard enough of in his life. He was happy to be there. "Ronin, thank you for coming by," she said. "I was hoping to see you."

"Pshaw," he said, looking down at his boots. On the one hand he loved the attention; on the other hand, he didn't know how he could.

"No, I'm serious, Ronin. I think in another time and place, we could've struck up a friendship, you and me."

He was surprised at her warmth and candor. He was certain she didn't appreciate the attention he and others had brought upon her spiritual practice, if you could call it that. It couldn't be easy, with Versal McBride, Tom Kelly and Augustus Ash bringing pressure to bear, though someone had argued at the Bucket of Blood the other night that "their persecution of the Spiritualist religion" was only making it more popular, if attendance at meetings was any way to judge. He didn't know.

"That's very kind of you to say, Ellie. But you don't know me."

"Of course I do, Ronin. May I call you William?" She was already in the habit. How could he deny her?

"You're the man every man wants to be. Cold, when pulling your hat down over your eyes simply won't do. Calculated, when decisions need to be made, especially the hard ones. Kind, especially to women, with whom I believe you've had a terribly confusing time. Loving, if you could find the right woman with whom to spend your life. I know you. And you know me," she said, pushing herself up against him. Her hips rocked forward as she lifted herself up onto her toes. Their knees touched. She kissed his cheek.

"Ma'am ..."

"Oh, stop with the ma'am. We know each other better than that."

"That's very kind, ma'am."

Ellie May smiled. There were certain men — clergymen, government men, Southern men, mama's men — that always kept their address formal, even when they were laying in-between your legs. Ronin was that kind of a man. "You from the South, William?"

Ronin smiled. He liked to think he kept a neutral accent. Occasionally, when upset or excited, he'd let go with a colloquialism that would give his Tennessee roots away. Most of the time he had concluded, the less people knew about him the better it was for everyone. Personal information, his in particular, was too distracting. "I am, ma'am. You?"

"Iowa City, actually."

"Huh," Ronin replied, remembering that Dustsucker was from an area outside of Council Bluffs known as the Eight Mile Prairie. He wondered how far apart they were. "Don't know much about Iowa. Spent a little time in Kansas, though."

"Yes," she said, "I remember. You were a preacher there, weren't you?"

"Episcopal priest, actually." He paused. "How is it you know so much about me, Ellie?"

"Well, that's my business, William. What I don't intuit from a person I often wonder about. And what I wonder about, I often ask about. And what I ask about, I sometimes know. Does that bother you, Mister Ronin?"

He thought for a moment and then nodded. "Nope. You just threw me a little bit."

"William," she cooed, "I wouldn't do that for anything."

"I'm sure," he smiled. He took her hand and turned right onto Union Street.

# Chapter 69

# UNION STREET

He was about to broach the topic of cold readings with Ellie — how some fortune tellers gained trust and information about their clients by engaging in high-probability guessing — when he noticed a woman on C Street who looked a lot like Ellie's sister. "Is that Alvira?" he asked, wondering how it was that the woman who had said she was staying home could appear so suddenly on the street in front of them. The quick change of mind indicated forethought and deception, he figured. She was too far away to tell.

Ellie looked north on C Street, and saw her sister and Toro Latigo in the shadows of a hotel talking. Their eyes met. "I'm not sure, William. I doubt it," she said, hoping to re-direct his attention. "Let's go inside. I'm cold."

"Afraid not, Ellie. If I'm not mistaken, that's Toro Latigo next to her, the short son of a bitch that I've been looking for while hoping to talk to the two of you."

"Latigo? I'm not sure I understand."

Ronin's attention was up the street where Latigo, who was wearing a hat similar to the one Dustucker had found on Mount Davidson a few days before, seemed to be arguing with Ellie's twin. Seeing the hat on his head and a whip looped over the revolver on his gun belt brought everything together. It was Latigo who had attempted to kill him, or perhaps kill them at the hotel by shooting through their window. And the presence of the Livestock girl suggested a motive for the man's malice. He looked at Ellie, frowning.

"What have the two of you done?" He pushed her into the side of the International Hotel as a rifle shot hit the boards beside him, kicking up dirt and stones. "Tell me!" he shouted, his eyes witnessing to a different side to his character than Ellie had seen before. "Fleecing old men for their money is one thing, but attempting to kill people?" She shrank in the face of the accusation and covered her face with her hands, crying. A second shot broke the glass, knocking down a hotel sign declaring "160 rooms on six floors, hot and cold running water, steam heat, gas lighting and a hotel elevator."

"I didn't intend for anyone to get hurt. Not like this," she sobbed, as a third shot split the window frame above her, sending splinters in all directions. It was a narrow miss.

"We can't stay here," he said, grabbing her hands. "We've got to move!" She resisted, pulling her hands free to hide her face, as if not seeing what was happening would keep it from happening. This wasn't at all what she had intended. It wasn't what she had hoped for when she and her sister had spoken to the disgusting little man who first demanded work at her D Street door. She was certain that she had clarified her intentions after the hotel shooting. What was Alvira doing downtown with Toro Latigo? And why were they shooting at them? She peeked between her fingers as a fourth shot rang out, and while watching Alvira point a finger in her direction, she crumpled to the street feeling as if she'd been punched in the stomach. Ellie May Livestock looked down. Blood moved from her middle and began to stain her dress.

"Ellie!" Ronin shouted, grabbing her. He lifted her up and over his left shoulder like a twisted bag of feed, and stumbling around the corner of the building, gained a clear view of the short little man who had tried to harm him twice before. The son of a bitch was grinning. Alvira was screaming. And Ellie May, the unintended consequence of Latigo's madness, was bleeding.

"No," he protested, looking at the blood-soaked cloth that had been, only moments before, an attractive woman's dress. "No!" he shouted, knowing that the person he was just coming to understand and appreciate was likely dying before him. He leaned closer to her and whispered, "Ellie."

"William," she breathed.

"Hang in there." And with that — the anguished, final uttering of his name — she died. Her eyes rolled back in her head and the light lent to her from the Giver of Lights above was suddenly gone.

He laid her down and began to wail.

There was a piece of Ronin that died in that moment. He felt it, the small sliver of life that Ellie and he had once shared — on the one hand small and never to amount to much, on the other hand as tall as any mountain or even the sky above. He stared in disbelief that this woman, who seemed a most curious mix of personal magic and ministry, loveliness and lust — was now folded before him, lifeless. Looking into her eyes, he felt the emptiness which was death pushing back, telling him that whatever moments he had hoped for, whatever possibilities he had ever once imagined or that she had ever hoped for or imagined, were now bleeding out on the sidewalk at Union and C Streets in Virginia City.

He looked up, his right hand still touching her, and glanced around the corner to see what he could see. There, in the middle of an amazed but unmoved Friday night pack of people, stood one short little man, laughing. And beside him, a sister, now very much alone, crying.

# Chapter 70

# REALIZATION

Toro Latigo looked at Alvira and wondered. He'd never had a girlfriend before, or a friend who was a girl. He was unsure what he was looking at with Alvira standing outside the densely-packed wagon in front of the Bucket of Blood saloon, crying. What he thought he'd see — a hugely happy woman hugging him, thanking him for doing what she had asked him to do and promising him a menu of heavenly rewards before sunup — he didn't see. Instead, he saw a woman acting like a baby, and it angered him.

"Why are you sobbing?" he agitated. "Stop it," he barked, hoping that the woman he'd most recently acquired — how, he wasn't quite sure — would act more like a man and make some sense. "I don't know why you're upset. I've done what you've asked!" he pleaded.

"You fool," Alvira said, looking down at him and putting her hands up to tell him to stop. "You shot my sister, you worm!" That's when the littlest man on the Comstock became instantly aware of what had happened. The goddamned gun had missed, and Alvira was blaming him.

It wasn't his fault, he figured. The bullets were as big as his head and the rifle practically as long as he was tall. He knew the gun was a handful as soon as he took it off the nearly dead bald man in Elko, who said he'd saved up "a fistful of time and money to hunt big horn sheep in the Ruby Mountains" along an old Shoshone Indian path. Latigo had overheard him speaking about the rifle at the Cottonwood Hotel, where Latigo's family in happier times used to stay when traveling through "The Crossroads." California-bound wagon trains frequented the tiny town as a welcome detour away from the barren not-at-all wooded shores of the Humboldt River. It was a fact the almost-dead man might have thought about, given that the safety of others might have protected him when Latigo borrowed the rifle to crack him over the head and leave him bleeding at the entrance of the Lamoile Canyon. The bald man in a store-bought coat and derby hat looked up at him just prior to taking his last breath and mumbled that it would be the death of him. *The death of him? I doubt it!* He'd stepped on the man's throat and couldn't make sense of anything the man said after that. He was dead — good and dead — and it didn't matter, he thought before taking the man's hat. Truth be told, the gun never fit him right, he argued with anyone who would listen. He hoped to trade it for a smaller Winchester or Marlin as long as it was something he could use and handle, and now the goddamned thing had cost him a good woman, or maybe anyway, and quite possibly allowed a very, very dangerous man to live. *Where was he?*

Toro Latigo — called "Anthony" by his parents and "Tony" by his friends, not that he had any except for the woman he was now standing beside — looked down C Street toward the swanky, six-story International Hotel where he'd last seen Ronin when he heard the clatter of a big man running toward him on the boards out front the saloon.

"You son of a bitch!" the large man yelled. He'd seen him before, at the Bucket of Blood with the marshal and McBride, the owner of the saloon. Three-hundred or maybe 350 pounds heavy, Latigo was suddenly happy that he still had the buffalo gun when he saw the deputy running his way, his tin badge flapping on a dirt-colored vest, covering a chest as broad and as strong as the front of his goddamned wagon. "Jesus," he muttered, as he chambered a round into his rifle, hoping he could fire it before the big man collided with him.

"No more killing!" Alvira yelled, knocking the barrel downward so that it pointed at his feet and discharged. A large caliber bullet careened off of a stone in the street and winged an unexpected and powerful path through the saloon's front door, hitting the bar where a young bartender was beginning to open a bottle of wine for a bosomy lady and her saddle tramp boyfriend from Carson City.

"Shit!" the bartender yelled as the bottle broke in his hands, spilling liquid and lovers all over the floor. McBride, who had just sat down at his usual table by his usual window in the north corner of the saloon, stood to see what was going on but couldn't see anything except a couple of people crouching on the floor and a newly fractured piece of wood missing from his front door. The New Jersey boy was crying. *Damn freak.*

"Should have hired a security guard," McBride said, looking around for someone with a gun. He was tired of the nightly nonsense that kept his saloon a one-bit bar instead of a two-bit tavern or public house, the difference inconsequential except for the bar's bottom line. He ran toward a back room where he was certain a shotgun lay, but intuitively knew that the time he wasted looking for a gun would be time he'd regret needing a gun, should the fracas outside come inside and begin to affect his welfare or business.

Dustsucker skidded into the back of the wagon like a shirt full of fleas, knocking the woman to the ground. Alvira, who'd never been under a man except to bring pleasure, didn't know if she should moan or scream, the hurt was so bad. And her baby — the little man she hoped to build a life with, the good-for-nothing who'd just shot her sister, who had taken her life without even knowing he had done so — was now cursing in an attempt to lever non-existent cartridges into a broken buffalo gun. He wasn't paying attention at all to where she was or what she was going through, goddamnit. "Excuse me, ma'am," Dustsucker said, placing a hand on her chest so as to push himself off of her and reach for the tiny little man he would just as soon crush as kill if he could get his hands on him.

Seeing no alternative, Alvira grabbed the deputy's privates, causing Dusty to scream and roll right onto his back so that he was looking up at Latigo while laying at his feet. Barely able to focus, but angry as hell, Dustsucker grabbed at the short man's ankles and finding meat — just a little bit of meat, it took some effort, but still — levitated the loser straight up into the air and launched him up and over his own feet into the street where W. W. Ronin was standing.

"Son of a bitch!" Ronin said, picking Latigo up by his shirt. The midget screamed. Ronin punched an iron-gloved hand into the little man's chest, cracking his sternum and driving the lower half of his fragile chest bone — "the xyphoid process," his bishop had called it when showing Ronin where and where not to hit — right up against the little man's liver. Ribs and cartilage fractured against Latigo's chest wall as he tumbled again into the air, skidding on his ass to a stop, his eyes crossed, his lips bleeding, holding his chest and side but sitting straight up underneath a wooden bench that he was too short to sit on but not too tall to sit beneath. Ronin strode angrily toward him, clenching his fists, when Dustsucker yelled out.

"Don't!" he said. He picked up his rifle and jogged toward the front of the saloon where McBride was waiting with Dustsucker's 10-guage shotgun. "We're not finished with him yet," Dustsucker said. McBride smiled.

"Bring him over here."

"I will not," Ronin hissed. "He's a dead man where he sits, and sitting is where he's going to die."

"Stop!" Alvira Fae Livestock yelled. And everyone — as if it had been choreographed as part of a military action or a Broadway dance or show — froze where they were and listened to the sister who was suddenly and unexpectedly beginning to feel very own voice.

"My sister, how is she?" she asked, quaking. Tears welled up in her eyes, and like the bubbles in a boiling pot of water, threatened to pop and explode.

Ronin looked over, at a woman he'd first seen pretending to be someone else, a gold tooth fixed to where an otherwise beautiful smile sometimes sat, and felt only shame. He had not protected her. And because of that, a beautiful woman, the late Ellie May Livestock — a woman who hadn't yet found her full stride in life, who he might have someday come to love — now laid dead. "Alvira, I'm so sorry."

# Chapter 71
# JOURNAL, MAY 13 1876

When he laid back down that night — Dustucker's plans having fizzled, Ellie's tragically even more so — Ronin remembered what it felt like to fall in love. He pushed a pillow into just the right position and turned the lamp up beside his bed so that he could read a bit before going to sleep.

It hadn't always happened in the springtime, he remembered. There were moments when love bloomed like sunny summer flowers, slowly and beautifully. And other times when it unexpectedly exploded like the color-drenched leaves of a sugar maple tree in autumn. Both kinds, the quick and the slow, pulled at his sometimes shriveled-up winter-like soul and convinced him that something somewhere — maybe not a gray-bearded God in heaven, or an equally unseen order to an otherwise chaotic universe — intended for him to be happy, to smile and to play.

Occasionally he believed these things, amidst the drama of solving someone else's problems in the middle of his own. But most of the time he just wondered if there wasn't some meaning behind it all. Bad men were as bad men did, but what of good men and women? How is it that they suffered at all? What kind of order in heaven would insist on such?

Having been raised in the church and then enduring its professional training in a Pennsylvania seminary, he'd come to think that the church's explanations of good and evil weren't good enough in the face of children dying or adults perishing before their time. That God cared, but didn't do what was need-ed? What kind of a God was that? Or that the Divine was im-potent to prevent the hurt and pain that good people suffered so that life allowed good and bad alike to choose freely? None of the explanations proffered by the professionally religious made him happy. Even the most heartfelt explanations sounded like crazy nonsense.

He pulled a small book from his saddle bag and opened it to where the red ribbon lay. He read the sentence that he'd underlined many times. "The first rule," Marcus Aurelius says, "is to keep an untroubled spirit. The second is to look things in the face and know them for what they are." If only he could know what he was looking at.

Ellie May Livestock was likely a good woman, amidst all of the hoopla and magic. And maybe he could testify to that, in her ministry to bring comfort and hope to people who had lost loved ones, even when her communications with the beyond weren't real. *They were never real.* There was her genuine effort to care for her sister, from the day they stepped out of the parental womb in Iowa to the world they were living by themselves in Virginia City. His intent was to simply to shoo her away, not see her convicted or God forbid, killed. Ellie May was not ready to die, and Alvira Fae was not ready to live alone.

There were good people and bad people who believed all kinds of things, he reminded himself, turning the pages of Aurelius' *Meditations.* Who was he to judge what was real and unreal, good or bad, too soon or not soon enough? They were simply feelings.

He flipped forward in the finely bound volume, just like a Bible he thought. "Accept the things to which fate binds you," he read aloud. "Love the people with whom fate brings you together. Do so with all your heart," he read to no one in particular, except to remind himself of what he knew to be true. And he'd done so. In fact, that was his calling: making things right. *That's what I do. That's what I've always done.*

He laid back in his bed and felt a cool September breeze blow across his body. The smell of sage was in the air. Yet despite the wind, he felt sad and wondered how to come to terms with everything. He couldn't bring Ellie May back. And he couldn't bring himself to believe that she could make her own way back. There just wasn't enough belief in him.

He put the Marcus Aurelius volume back in his saddle bag and lifted his journal from the nightstand. Maybe he wasn't in love with Ellie May Livestock, but she had stirred something within him, a projection of how he wanted to live his life perhaps, and with whom.

He turned to May 13, 1876, a Friday, and began to read the final entry recounting his involvement with Madame Bovary, the mystic with whom he'd fallen hopelessly in love. Her first name was "Emma," oddly enough. He began to read.

*It never occurred to me that the woman I was so infatuated with was not the woman I thought she was.*

*Madame Bovary turned out to be a fictional character in French literature, a first novel in fact. How embarrassing! And while I'll never read the book by Gustave Flaubert — feeling as if I've already lived it — I am impressed with the similarities between Bovary's life (the fictional character, I do not know the woman I was involved with) and my own. A doctor's wife, Emma Bovary found her charmed and privileged life to be empty. Striving to fill that emptiness, she succumbed to temptation.*

*I believe I did as well, having tried to fit everything that life is supposed to be into the singular dimension of a professional persona. Had I been told, or been reminded or somehow discovered the richness of what life could bring, it might have turned out differently. There is no greener pasture on the other side of the fence. There's only pasture. And it is what you make it to be.*

*According to the story as I understand it, Bovary came up empty. A series of affairs, extraordinary expenditures and debt brought her to her knees. And while I'll never understand how the woman I met was capable of such delusion and misdirection as to be married to so many men in so many places and still be involved with me — she no doubt was doing the best that she could do to fill her own emptiness, I can only guess — I got caught up in it. She succumbed to the one thing, as I did, that promised to make her real.*

*Diary, my friends tell me that a great many people thought Gustave Flaubert's novel to be obscene. The Pinkerton superintendent, who braced me with the news that I could no longer work as a Pinkerton given how compromised I had become, told me that the book wasn't obscene. It was instead quite real, perhaps too real. And that's what made it, and my escapade, so offensive.*

Ronin put his head back upon his pillow and wondered if Gustave Flaubert's novel took place in the springtime. And just as quickly, fell asleep.

# Chapter 72

# THE MARSHAL'S OFFICE

He wasn't a big fan of clocks. The ex-priest had, up until shopping for a suit at Koppel and Platt's place in Carson City, ignored them. But Ash had been adamant that they meet first thing this morning so as to swear out a warrant for Latigo's arrest and to discuss whether Alvira Fae Livestock should be included in it.

No one was sure how Toro Latigo had escaped everyone's notice the previous night. Dustsucker and Ronin had picked him up and put him in his wagon with the intent of taking him to the hospital to see what could be done with the man's broken body. Ronin was certain he'd fractured the little man's ribs and didn't know what else, not that he cared. So when the marshal and city police showed up to clear the pack of heartless lookie-loos wanting to know what had happened to Ellie May, who was lying dead on the boardwalk outside the International Hotel, and the little man who was near dead hidden inside a wagon tethered to a horse post nearby, everyone was surprised to see that the midget was missing.

"How the hell did he get out of here?" Ronin asked, aware that he had pushed his fist into the man's chest with such ferocity it was a miracle that the man was moving at all. "You laid him here, right?" he asked Dustsucker who was comparing notes with Tom Kelly, the Virginia City Sheriff.

"Sure as hell did. What are you saying?"

"I'm saying he's not here."

The two of them immediately scanned the crowd of people still standing outside on C Street and realized that both Alvira and Toro were missing.

"Goddamnit!" Augustus Ash said, pulling his slicker tight around his pajamas or long underwear. The evening was already an embarrassment to local law enforcement given that a woman had been murdered.

"Manslaughter," a local solicitor corrected, "criminally negligent or otherwise. Not murder."

"Go to hell," the three of them said simultaneously. Tom Kelly started to laugh until Marshal Ash caught his eye.

"Fuck off," Kelly said. The lawyer stepped back into the crowd. It was a couple of moments before the city's police had successfully cleared the street so that the lawmen could speak privately.

"What I want to know is how all of this happened?" Ash said, looking over at Ronin, who was beginning to tell his friend Dustsucker how he'd held Ellie May in his arms as she died.

"I don't have a hell of a lot to say," Ronin said. "It's late. I'm upset. And the last thing I need is some law dog misconstruing what I'm about to say."

"Fair enough," Ash replied, insisting that everyone meet in his office by 8 a.m. to swear out a warrant for the little man's arrest. "Murder, manslaughter, I don't give a shit. I want the man off the street. We'll talk about the dead lady's twin sister in the morning. That sound good?" Everyone sort of nodded, except for Ronin, who had to be pulled aside and banged up against a building when he started to mumbling something about "killing the son of a bitch."

"You don't get tired of those words?" Dustsucker said, relaxing his grip when Ronin eye-balled him to let him know he wasn't in the mood to be man-handled.

"It is what it is," he hissed, "and it's not like you weren't yelling the same words tonight when you stumbled into his sister. How was that, incidentally?"

Dustsucker blushed. "It was fine. I don't know when I've had my balls busted that way."

Ronin laughed. "I guess not." And with that the ex-minister turned man-hunter went to bed, and remained there until the rap on his door at 7:30 a.m.

"Good morning, Mister Ronin?"

He sat up, grabbing a gun from the table beside him. "Up. Thank you," he said, returning his gun to its holster and swinging his legs over the side of the bed.

The invention of the clock hadn't served anyone well, he thought, checking the gold-filled timepiece he'd brought along with him. *Churches, factories, schools and now a U.S. marshal. Where will it end?* Pulling his shirt and pants on, he shook some sand out of his boots and stood to put on his duster. *It used to be that man could sleep until he was rested. Now, everyone is in a hurry.*

He pushed himself out the front of the hotel on his way to the Odd Fellows building on B Street when Tom Kelly called to him.

"Ronin!"

"Tom, good morning."

"Sleep any?"

"Not much. All I could think of was that Alvira wasn't able to live alone. You?"

"Well, listen Ronin, that's what I want to talk about. I don't think there's a link to the anger and malice this guy has shown the two of you, except for Alvira. Could it be that the twins hired the little guy to hurt you?"

"That's funny, Tom. I mean, I spend a little bit of time on a saloon floor with General Tom Thumb here lashing at me with his whip and now everybody wants to make him into some hired-on killer. What's the chances of that?"

"Well, that's what I'm saying, Ronin. Ash told me about the opera singing thing ..."

"I don't think it was opera, Tom ..."

"Well, whatever. I'm thinking every time we run across this guy he's involved in some sort of mayhem. So I asked around a bit last night after you left, and do you know there isn't a regular guy in town who's ever treated him to a beer or sold him a piece of steak? More so, that damn wagon of his — all jiggered up to look like a funeral wagon — isn't anything like that inside. Did you look inside there?"

"I did."

"It looks like he's been living in it. He's not making caskets, or whatever the sign says."

"That's a good point."

"But he might be putting people in boxes, if you know what I mean. And the girls might have determined that it was time to put you in a box as well."

Ronin stopped in the middle of the street, parting his duster and resting his hands on his gun belt. A four-inch Colt .45 rested in a strong-side cut-down holster, angled slightly forward to allow for a quick draw. He'd got in the habit of pushing the gun right out of the back of the holster, tilting the barrel upward so that it rode right across the top of the holster when he fired. It was fast. A cross-draw holster held a 7.5-inch Colt in much the same position. Both were intended to be used by his right hand. "Tom, you're a good man. I liked you the first time I saw you." Kelly nodded. "I think you've stumbled on something. And while I'm not at all happy to think that Ellie might have decided to do me in before she was done in, it's a possibility — a real possibility."

"Well, I was thinking ..." Kelly started to add before Ronin cut him off.

"Tell Ash what you're thinking, and get two warrants just in case. I'm going back to my room to pick up my rifle. It sounds like we're going hunting and I want to be ready."

"Ronin?" Kelly continued.

"Yeah," Ronin responded, already a few steps away.

"Bring your horse. Time's a wasting — we don't want this guy to get away."

# Chapter 73
# ANTHONY AND ALVIRA

Alvira wasn't exactly ready to start singing children's rhymes — her life suddenly and horribly fractured by the death of her sister — but she was thinking that the broken man in the back of the well-worn teamsters wagon was the only possibility that she'd ever get to gain a normal life again.

When the lawmen turned away from Anthony, who was shoved into the back of his wagon like a green Iowa hay bale on its way to auction, she pulled her injured man friend out the front of the wagon and tossed him onto the nearest horse. It didn't take but a couple of minutes to find a dark place to put him down before returning to C Street to reclaim his wagon. Given how late it was, the lawmen and Ronin — the man they had hoped to kill — would likely wait until morning to figure out what just happened.

She parked Toro's wagon up by the cemeteries, its "We make caskets" sign hanging by one S-hook over the back flap. They would attract less attention there than anywhere else in town. Climbing into the back to see what she could do, she found her friend crumpled up in pain, cowering in one of the far corners biting his hand. Not having anything with her to treat his injuries and pain — no laudanum, no chloroform, no bandages — Alvira Fae put her hands on her little man's head and arms to soothe him.

"Baby, I'm so sorry, maybe you'll feel better by morning," she said. But the longer he laid there moaning — curled up like that, rocking himself from side to side when he chose to move at all — the more worried she became. "Sweetie, talk to me. I need to know that you're okay."

It wasn't as if Latigo didn't want to speak. He really did. He wanted to tell her that he felt sorry for what the gun had done, hurting her sister and all that. He wanted to know how she was doing, and whether he could have some of the money she had promised, given that he'd made two attempts to kill the crazy man who was bothering them so much. And he wanted to have sex, given that he had done, or almost done, what she had asked him to do. But he could barely breathe, the pain in his chest hurt so bad. It felt like he was having a heart attack, the center bone of his chest — the flat one between his lungs — felt like it had been kicked by mule or horse, especially along the edges where his ribs were connected. He curled up in a ball so that no one could touch him and accidently hurt him more. And keeping his breathing shallow — a little bit now, a little bit later, never a big breath like he usually breathed, just small ones now and then — there was the chance he'd maybe survive whatever curse the ex-priest had put on him. Nobody could hit that hard without someone's help. Maybe he was a *brujo*, a sorcerer.

"Baby, you're going to be okay," Alvira said, looking into his eyes. She was sure attractive. He didn't know if he had ever seen anyone as beautiful as her, except maybe her sister, but she was a complicated woman and now she was dead. There'd been a few women who had let him have his way over the years — in Humboldt Wells, in particular — but not many. And maybe he'd head back to Wells, now that the city had changed its name, not that it mattered. But none of those women had been as pretty as this one.

God forbid that he had killed her sister, not that she was the nicer of the two. The first time they'd met, Ellie May had yelled at him. Yelled at him, saying he should go back to whatever God-forsaken hole he had crawled out of! But then Alvira wasn't much different back then, either. She'd pointed an old Paterson revolver at him until he settled down and treated them with "some respect," they'd insisted. Funny two women would get the best of him like that. Respect was hard. Dying was more difficult. He looked up at Alvira, the sweeter of the two sisters, and wondered if they would have sex soon. But what if he was dying? He blinked both of his eyes. Maybe she'd understand what he was asking.

"See, I told you things would get better! You're able to move your eyes again," she said.

*What a dolt.* He pulled one hand out from between his legs where he had been holding himself, he was in such pain, and touched her hair. It was too difficult to smile, and he wasn't sure that he wanted to smile, not yet anyway.

"There you go, baby," she said in that little girl way that she'd sometimes talk. His mother used to talk to him like that, too. He liked that. It was a shame he had to kill her, but what was he going to do? Let her watch him kill his father and then testify against him? Or worse yet, drag him off to some doctor, hoping the doctor might fix his rage? The whole family had to die so that he could live. Someday he'd find his brother and do him in, too. That's just the way it was.

She sat there beside him, sharing an old blanket as she stroked his forehead. He'd probably feel fine in the morning. And meanwhile, Alvira Fae would protect him, that Paterson revolver on her lap. And if things got any worse — say if he started bleeding like that fellow in Lamoille, or he began to make no sense at all like that woman on Mount Davidson who went ape-shit just because he wanted to touch her — well then, maybe she could just shoot him. Maybe shooting him was what he needed. But then again, things couldn't get all that much worse. Perhaps instead they'd get better.

He looked up at his friend, his one and only friend he figured now that he was all broken up and unable to sing or dance or snap his whip or crack a joke, and he remembered why he was alive. Someday he'd "achieve great things," his mother had said, "like that midget in the circus," she'd often said when putting him to sleep at night. She hadn't meant anything bad by it. She only meant him good. And maybe that's what he'd do. He'd be good and he'd achieve something, he thought as he began to drift off to sleep. Or maybe he'd just get his ass out of bed and kill that son of a bitch that tried to hurt his woman. Maybe that's what he'd do.

# Chapter 74
# WARRANTS SWORN

Ronin grabbed his rifle from beside the bed and headed out the front door of the hotel.

Virginia City was civilized in 1880. Telephone lines, gas lamps, steam heat — it had all come together. And while mining was on the decline, causing some folks to move south toward Bodie, others to head north toward Montana, lots of Comstock folks were staying put, appreciating what they had built together, and hoping that tomorrow Virginia City would become an even stronger and better place.

Take the Virginia and Truckee Railroad Company, for example. In 1880, the V & T's capital stocks were worth $6 million. Four million dollars were spent on construction alone, and while the company was selling off unused rails for revenue it still reported over a $1 million that year in traffic receipts hauling passengers, freight, baggage and mail. No small piece of change, and with operating expenses nearly half of that, net earnings to the shareholders of the company were nearly a half-a-million dollars. Twenty-four engines, ten passenger coaches, four baggage, mail and express cars, seven box cars, 237 platform cars and 117 ore cars argued that the Comstock gold and silver rush was far from being over, at least in some people's minds. People still had hopes and dreams. So while population and mining numbers seemed to be declining, causing some people to leave town, others were sitting still where they were, waiting for what they believed to be as one Virginia City clergyman called it, "God's good future."

Which is why Ronin seized his Yellow Boy rifle from its leather scabbard laying on top of his bed at the International Hotel and headed out onto C Street, rather than attend a meeting called for at the marshal's office. Swearing out a warrant wasn't Ronin's way of dealing with danger. Some people might wait for that — marshals, sheriffs, people concerned about the orderly unfolding of progress and civilization — but waiting wasn't in Ronin's blood.

He pulled Jackson from the livery, paid the horse's board bills and rode up C Street like he knew where he was going. Turning his head from side to side, he was looking for either the mean-spirited and angry little man or Alvira, whom he now suspected of being Latigo's little woman. Someone will have seen something, he thought to himself, if even just a broken down freighter's wagon.

A few streets away, U.S. Marshal Augustus Ash couldn't wait any longer either. Turning toward Sheriff Tom Kelly, his sometimes deputy, and toward Slade, Ronin's friend, he asked if it wasn't time to take out the trash? "This city doesn't need this sort of thing," he said. "It's had its good times. And it's certainly gone through its bad times as well. But this doesn't need to be one of them," he said, waiving warrants for Anthony Latigo's, aka Toro Latigo, and Alvira Fae Livestock's arrests. Reporters from the *Territorial Enterprise* and the *Evening Chronicle* raised questions about an orderly arrest and trial, their hands in the air while their "lips were flapping," Ash would later say, but the marshal wouldn't tolerate the interruption. "Gentlemen," he said, "let's get moving. We've already lost one day."

"Part of a day," Slade said, always the stickler for lawful pursuit. But Ash had no patience for the Ormsby County deputy either. "Dustsucker," he took a deep breath, "you had hold of this man last night and you let him go. I'll not be tongue-lashed by a lawman who can't hold his own prisoner." Slade's eyebrows raised, but he kept silent. There were more important things at hand than addressing an ignorant marshal, but he'd have at it later when Kelly and Ash had their man and the matter was wrapped up. As for Alvira Fae Livestock? No one believed she had gone far, because her sister had yet been to be buried.

Versal McBride entered the room as the lawmen were picking up their rifles. He carried Slade's 10-guage shotgun and laid it across the marshal's desk. Slade picked it up. "My friends," he said, "this is not how we saw things unfolding. It is not what any of us intended. The Livestock women were a part of this town's business community, so I hope we'll show the requisite respect and kindness for this woman as her position deserves. But as for the little man..."

"Latigo," Dustsucker said, knowing that saying the man's name would argue for sanity in his pursuit and arrest.

"Latigo, yes. That was his name," McBride replied.

"*Is* his name, Mister McBride, not *was*," Dustsucker added.

"Indeed. Well, I don't care nearly as much about the painful little Mister Latigo as does Deputy Slade here, apparently. Bring him in. Shoot him down. I could give a shit. But order needs to be restored. And you men are the men to do it."

"Mister McBride," Kelly said, "order is restored. The chief of police has officers on nearly every street corner. There's very little chance that these two will get away, and even less chance that we'll see the kind of violence on the street again today as we saw last night."

"That's good, Tom. You all get going, you hear?" McBride sat down in the marshal's chair, behind a big oak desk in front of a rack of rifles and single and double-barrel shotguns. "And Augustus?"

"Yes, Versal?" Ash noted that the saloon owner was sitting in his chair but said nothing.

"Get that woman."

"Huh?" he said, surprised. "Nobody likes to kill a woman, Versal."

"'Some people need to die sooner than others,' your friend likes to say.'"

"No more women are going to die on my watch, Versal, no matter what you're suggesting."

"I'm just saying ..."

Dustsucker looked over at the two of them, a fierce feeling building inside of him. He wasn't a religious man. "Decently and in order," like the Presbyterians were accustomed to saying, wasn't a part of his vocabulary. But still, the law was as the law did. And if there wasn't any law, then a great many bad men would be doing worse things, and a certain number of otherwise good men would be doing bad things as well. "McBride," he said all pretensions to being a polite man now gone.

"Yes, Deputy Slade," McBride sighed.

"We've got our business to do. You've probably got yours to do, too. Isn't it about time you let us do ours?"

"Indeed," he said, looking at Marshal Ash. "Get it done."

# Chapter 75
# CEMETERY

When local prostitute Julia Bulette was found dead in her bed in 1867, a Comstock journalist wrote that her death by strangulation was "the most cruel, outrageous and revolting murder ever committed" in Virginia City.

Bulette was an otherwise common and unremarkable woman, except for the regular contributions she made to a local fire department that sometimes allowed her to accompany firemen on their fire calls. A popular "middle-rank" prostitute — which is to say she likely never saw the inside of the well-moneyed Washoe Club or visited the beds of rich men on A and B Streets — the trial and subsequent hanging of her assailant elevated her to a sort of sainthood among common folk.

Despite such, Bulette was buried on the *south* side of Six Mile Canyon, in an old and abandoned cemetery known as Mount Pleasant, which might have been a better place for Alvira Livestock to park the otherwise unexceptional wagon. But the little man who owned it, a former Latter-day Saint in good standing until he killed his parents in a short fit of rage. And he wasn't okay with the lesser places in life any more than he was comfortable not singing at the top of his little lungs in Nevada's friendlier drinking establishments. The creation of the new cemeteries on the *north* side of Six Mile Canyon, sometimes called "the Silver Terrace Cemeteries," inspired the abandonment of some of the older, more run down and idle patches of formally hallowed ground. Their appearance at the top of the hill in Virginia City put Latigo and Livestock in unexpected danger.

Julia Bulette's funeral was attended by eighteen carriages of friends, the Metropolitan Brass Band and sixty men from Virginia Engine Company No. 1. Toro Latigo's death, if Ronin had anything to do with it, would have a simple audience of one.

Jackson climbed E street at the bidding of its rider until the Silver Terrace Cemeteries came into view. Built into a barren hillside by citizens intent on creating an elevated park for the dead *and* the living, one could sit there amidst the colors — white and purple clover, yellow, green and orange locust trees — and gaze at the steeples and housetops in Virginia City, contemplating life's fullness. Despite their being built upon thousands of cubic yards of waste rock from the areas' mines, the cemeteries established a sort of equal ground between the "struggling present" and the "triumphant gone on." It was the former that Ronin was most interested in when he saw Latigo's wagon hidden behind a line of trees and fence.

He guided Jackson toward an iron fence and dismounted.

The former reverend had come to a kind of peace about these places. Burial grounds were a reminder of life's transience. Set outside a church building, they witnessed to the role of faith and order, to the importance of obeying the Ten Commandments and, if one was a Christian, to the hope present in Jesus' teachings. Set away from the church — as was the Lone Mountain Cemetery in Carson City and the gathered holy grounds of church, civic and fraternal groups in Virginia City — something more was being said. Mortality was universal. And faith — whether it was Methodist, Episcopalian, Roman Catholic, or even Chinese or Jew — was something to be wondered about as death visited everyone equally.

Ronin took the thumb strap off of the hammers of his hand guns and shifted his rifle to his right hand. It could come to him as well, he figured. *Not here. Not now.*

He knelt down by a granite gravestone and peered around a white picket fence — so much death, so many of them children, women dying in childbirth, men perishing in the mines or from disease — and he listened. An eagle floated silently overhead. An owl hooted, its plaintive sound echoing against the trees planted to his left and right.

A path appeared ahead, in the shape of a Masonic trowel, of all things. The working tool of the Master's Degree, the path reminded lodge members to spread the cement of affection and kindness while they still lived. Further on, the path split, leading uphill to the highest point of the cemetery where an Egyptian obelisk stood, commemorating the death of Captain Edward Farris Storey. Storey died during the second of the Pyramid Lake Wars, when famed Texas Ranger Colonel Jack Hays defeated Paiutes who had earlier raided the Williams Station and subsequently slaughtered a volunteer militia intent on punishing the Paiutes involved. Major William Ormsby died in the first war, he remembered, lending his name to Ormsby County and the Ormsby House. Storey did as well, when he was shot by an Indian. Storey County was his namesake.

*Left or right?* It didn't really matter. He picked left and began moving carefully along its path when he heard horses behind him.

"Ronin!" someone shouted.

*Jesus, seriously?* He turned around to find Dustsucker standing by Jackson at the cemetery gate, feeding him cheat grass with his right hand. *Really?* "Yeah?" he called out, figuring that any sense of surprise was now gone.

"It's just me."

*Great. Now you tell them how many of us there are.* "Where are the others?" he asked, motioning with his finger to speak more quietly.

"Right," Dustsucker whispered, tying his horse to the same tree. The two horses nuzzled each other. Hopefully that was all they would do. "We got two warrants," Dustsucker said, stretching out his hand to say hello. Ronin shook it. "And I mentioned that I thought Alvira wouldn't leave town until her sister was buried. Ash also thought that, so he headed over to the girls' house on D Street, and from there they were going to head over to the neighbor's house, when it occurred to me that if Alvira and Latigo are together in this thing ..."

"I think they are," Ronin said, keeping an eye on the cemetery behind him.

"... well, if they're together, they can't afford to stay in town. They need to get out of town. So I figured they'd either go to one of the furniture stores to see the casket or head up here to kind of say goodbye, hoping that other people would sort of take care of things. See the hill where she's going to be buried, that kind of thing."

"That was my thinking as well."

"Any idea what they've done with the body? Ellie wasn't a member of any church, as far as I know."

"Dusty, they don't keep dead bodies in churches."

"Why not?"

"Something about the Lord not staying in one, rising on the third day and all that. Trust me on this, okay?" Ronin said, smiling. Funny how his Iowa friend knew so little about religious things, or strange that he knew so much. Then it occurred to him that no mention had been made of the Spiritualist Society on B Street. "Dusty, any chance they may have gone to the Spiritualist Society?"

"To where?"

"You know, underneath the dentist's office?"

You mean that's where Ellie May is?

"I'm guessing."

"I don't know," Dustsucker said, pulling at his vest. "The wagon's here …"

"But Ellie May may be there …"

Dustsucker seemed torn by his friend's suggestion, his inference as well. He didn't need to say it. "How about I go check. But you don't get too far along up that path until I or the others get back?"

Ronin nodded. He didn't like the thought either, that an angry short man might be hiding behind a tree or tombstone hoping to make the next funeral held in Virginia City a two-some. "I'll be careful. Head back soon, and bring the others."

Dustsucker got back on his horse and galloped off. A dust cloud lingered with Ronin at the gate for a few minutes as the former Pinkerton thought over his options. The sun was high in the sky. It was noontime or thereabouts. There were no shadows, and the locust trees that set off separate sections of the cemetery were too small and too far apart to offer any concealment or cover. "Latigo!" he yelled out, expecting no response, when the stupid son of a bitch — who could have simply waited to shoot him as he ambled past a wooden or stone marker unawares and unprotected — shouted back.

# Chapter 76

# A FAIR FIGHT

"You broke my gun, you giant jackass," he yelled.

"Seriously?"

"Yeah, that fat friend of yours groped my girlfriend, too. What kind of deputy is that? What are you doing here?" *Latigo's voice sounded weak.*

Ronin knelt down and tried to fit up against a black locust tree. "What am I doing here? You know why I'm here. I'm here to take you in... or kill you. It doesn't matter to me."

Silence.

"On what charge?"

"You killed that woman, you stupid son of a bitch. I'm going to see you hang for it. Or shoot you in the head. Like I said, it doesn't much matter to me." He waited.

The awkward silence of the back and forth was broken suddenly by a woman's wail. Alvira Fae Livestock was crying again. The sobbing was heart-rending. Ronin took the opportunity to move forward, closer to where he believed the little man was hiding.

"Don't move," Latigo yelled, "I can see you."

"You don't have a rifle anymore. Remember?"

"You sure?"

Ronin wasn't sure of anything, other than the thought that he didn't want to die in a Virginia City cemetery.

The country had made significant strides in fixing its cemetery problem in the early 1800s. Prior to that time, the nation's burial grounds were considered overcrowded and unhealthy, and for the most part were located in particularly fast-growing towns and cities. Two-foot deep graves, bodies stacked on top of each other and rainy washouts had made the industry-wide problem a national problem.

A popular parody by Mark Twain called *Curious Dream: Containing a Moral* argued that the condition of some cemeteries had forced the dead to walk the streets at night, complaining. Twain's book, in which a deceased resident of Buffalo, New York, contributed to the national debate and caused significant improvements to be made. Virginia City made its fair share of them, reflecting a growing sense in Nevada's largest city that strangers couldn't find a permanent living place where a permanent resting place seemed so poor and unpalatable. A more garden-like setting was sought, and the Silver Terrace Cemeteries — Masonic, Odd Fellows, Sons of the Pacific Pioneers, Roman Catholic and so on — was the result.

Still, the conditions of the new burial grounds — marked by picket fences and well-graveled paths and stone walls, a $3,000 irrigation system, tanks, hoses and men to man them — didn't keep some from remembering Twains' words about the original Virginia City burial grounds. "The first 26 graves in the Virginia City cemetery," Clemens wrote, "were occupied by murdered men. So everybody said, so everybody believed, and so they will always say and believe." Ronin didn't want to be buried among them. He didn't need a big monument when he died. He didn't want a grassy hillside or path in which to hide his head. He didn't desire a huge stone as his final resting place or bed. What he wanted was simply not to be buried there, or to die there, either.

He rolled from behind a decorative orange tree into a plot that had numerous granite markers. "Latigo," he yelled. "Leave the woman where you are and come out with your hands up.

Leave your guns behind and we'll call it square, you and me. I won't shoot. We'll head back to the sheriff's office and I'll see that you get a fair trial."

"Really?" Latigo wheezed.

"Yeah, really."

Latigo waited. It seemed as if he and Alvira were talking. "Alvira's going to leave. Is that okay?"

"It's okay by me," Ronin said. "I can't swear to what the sheriff or marshal will want if you wait any longer." And with that, Toro Latigo stood up. About as tall as a taller grave stone, he walked onto the gravel path that marked the northern side of the trowel-shaped Masonic cemetery. "I'm here," he said. "Come and get me." He looked frail and in pain, leaning on a cotton-wood stick for support.

Ronin stood up as well and began walking toward the tiny man who had spread so much bad in Virginia City — and only God knew how much where else — and forgot about Alvira, who was readying a solution of her own to the problem that her man faced. When the thoughtful ex-priest got into range, she pulled back on the hammer of her giant Paterson revolver and pressed the trigger, pushing a .36 caliber ball into Ronin's side, spinning him into a tree, where he slid to the ground. He sat unmoving, surprised and wide-eyed.

"Who's the big man now?" Latigo sang, his small voice almost swallowed up by the Comstock winds. "Who's the foolish man now?" he crooned as if the operatic melody would someday become a popular refrain. "You're the foolish man, now!" he shouted, buzzing about like a tiny trumpet. "You're the big man, now!" his voice rang out, vibrato and all, his head wagging from side to side. A second shot rang out as Ronin grabbed for his long-gun, hoping to return fire. But darkness covered his eyes instead.

# Chapter 77

# WHERE ANGELS FEAR TO TREAD

Life and death are punctuated by the places in-between. Poured into a little child by a father and mother in love and sometimes not, the force that defines us as human beings is something more than that found in plants and animals of a significantly lesser order. Perhaps these also-living organisms don't keep time in the same way — ploddingly but not pensively considering the potential meaning of one event after another. But if they could, would these living, sometimes breathing, things be as complex or as sacred?

Ronin's head fell back against a locust tree, his eyes either closed or not, he wasn't sure. But consciousness continued as his heart pounded, proving he was alive and perhaps awake. His respirations challenged by the pain in his right chest, his judgment clouded, his sentience ebbing — all Ronin knew was that he'd been hurt somehow. A giant fist had balled up against his rib cage as he was pulling the longer of his two Colt revolvers into play against the little man who was now strangely dancing and singing before him. Yellow and orange-leafed locust trees now waved at him like a mother's goodbye. He felt a tear on his cheek and noticed that his right hand seemed useless, having dropped his firearm onto the stony path. He remembered watching as the Colt's dark wood stocks cracked on impact, the Colt's long, blue metal barrel clanging as if a church bell had been rung. They must have dried out in the Nevada sun, he thought before wondering if life — a force he had considered neutral since leaving the priesthood, devoid of any good or bad intent — had predetermined that they should break in that way.

"The days of our years are threescore and ten," he remembered the Psalmist saying, "and if by reason of strength they be fourscore, yet is their strength labor and sorrow."

Ronin's life, now streaming across the inside of his mind's eye, was not at all what he intended it to be, what he had hoped it to be, or his parents had desired it to be, believing that a man or woman's best breaths were breathed if he or she went into the Christian ministry. Neither parent preferred whether he prepared to be a Methodist circuit rider or an Episcopal priest, the worst paid and the best paid of religious professions. "As long as you aren't a Presbyterian," they said. "Too much order," they opined, "not enough ardor."

He'd grown up with his mother, in an argumentative household where smiles were rare, despite breakfasts and dinners together, Sunday go-to-meetings and attempts by the children to ameliorate or mediate the conflicts between his mother and his dad. His father left "to take care of the family farm," he'd said on his way out the door one night, his mother strangely happy that he'd finally fled to Obion County, Tennessee, where small farms proliferated along ancient river paths having hosted the Scots-Irish since Elisha Parker arrived there in 1819.

Davy Crockett was among those present when the county seat of Troy was laid out, the coon-skinned capped hero of every boy in America. Ronin had seen the hero's cabin and entertained the thought that he, too, might someday kill 103 bears — like the mighty congressman, Indian fighter and Alamo death star had — when visiting his dad during the summer months, wondering how it was that he ended up living with a Yankee mother instead of a Confederate father.

During the earlier months of the war, he'd witnessed the building of Camp Brown, a mile north of their farm in Union City, where thousands of Confederate soldiers readied to combat Union troops invading the officially neutral state of Kentucky. With neighbors choosing north and south despite northern incursions into the state, he and his dad had responded to Jacob Biffle's conscription of men to form a Tennessee cavalry. A 31-year old Wayne County captain, later colonel, Biffle led men who were proud to fight for the rights of southern gentlemen in the face of northern aggression. He was deeply disturbed over the issue of slavery — his father owned none, nor did many other farmers in the rural counties he'd come to regard as home — still, he'd chosen to ride with some of the finest Tennessee horsemen there ever were, including Confederate General Nathan Bedford Forest, Biffle's commander and friend.

Riding in Kentucky, Virginia, Alabama, Mississippi and Tennessee as part of a forage and wagon detail, he remembered a drive toward Union City — Trenton, Dyer Station, Rutherford, Kenton, Crockett, Troy Station and finally home — where Biffle, Forest and others painted a tree and wagon wheels black so as to demand the unconditional surrender of invading Union troops. War was hell — exploding ordinance, the sudden death of comrades and other combatants who would have been his friends in some other time and place, the capture of fearful Confederate and Union stragglers and setting them free.

The colors of war: blue, green, red, brown and black splashed across the face of his mind.

Despite his service as a young wagon driver and sometimes cook, his rifle skills were under constant demand by his corporals and higher-ups.

He tried moving, but was unable to. *Am I alive?*

After the war, when he returned home to Pennsylvania, he entered a Pittsburgh area seminary and while he didn't finish, the months of book learning under Culbert G. Rutenber — sitting in a chair on top of a table so as to be more easily seen while lecturing young seminary divines — made him smile and wish for the mission field again, where Episcopal young men and others hoped to churn a love of Jesus Christ from the milk of God's word. And still, when he arrived in Wichita, his first church with the likes of Dave Munger, an early justice of the peace, who despite being Ronin's good friend held stock in the Wichita Land and Town Company and wished him the best when he left his congregation to find his one true self, now sitting underneath a black locust tree in the Masonic section of Virginia City's prettiest park and cemetery. He tried to move. *Is this what death is?*

He spun the cylinder of the new pearl-handled Colt .45 his church had given him the night before — he sitting in a Wichita hotel room wondering what he had done now that he had no place to live, no people to call his own, no salary or promise of salary unless the Pinkertons picked him up, but he hadn't yet heard. The grips were too smooth and too feminine, he thought, too dandy, too flashy. He'd have to find something more durable if he was going to ride the rails and carriages the Pinkerton National Detective Agency were protecting.

He could tolerate the railroad if it got him west, which of course it did in time, after he'd killed a man in New Mexico while working for the company — the old man had passed on that, though it never felt right — and solved a murder in Idaho and followed a woman, a good looking woman at that, but married to a million men if any, he'd found out in Nevada, California, Oregon and elsewhere.

He followed her into his room, where she'd taken to sleeping because her life "wasn't safe at all," when in fact it was other people's lives that weren't safe with her proffering false prophecies via a crystal ball, cards and palmistry for money. He'd taken off his clothes. He'd laid with her. It was fun. He'd fallen hard — Emma Bovary or whatever her real name was — not that they told him anything given that he was "no longer allowed to be a Pinkerton Agent, or policeman or anything," they'd said in anger when they left him in Carson City to fend for himself. But he'd figured it out, and what he didn't figure out the Pinkerton superintendent told him. "It was all in the novel," he'd said, as if he should have read it instead of lingering so long in the biblical books of *Lamentations* and *Job*.

He met Marcus T. Slade — he never heard what the T stood for, not that it mattered, but still — an Ormsby County deputy who despite being a big man was a most humble and understanding man, having fished him off the floor during a saloon fight on Carson Street, the fancy kicks and punches the rural trapper had shown him — hell, had drilled into him just like the Right Reverend James O'Reilly had taught him. "Once you learn everything you think you need to know, something will come along to unsettle you. That's the way life is," the reverend had said, before setting on a train to Wichita, where he thought not just once but every day for three years that he wanted to be a Pinkerton man and not a clergyman.

The wind whipped at his hair and blew him over onto his side. He could tell it was dark out, though he wasn't sure if his eyes were open or closed, he couldn't see.

And then he met Emma, "another Emma," he said to himself when he first saw her at the doctor's office in Carson City. She was assisting the surgeon with his broken leg — God, how that hurt, a local son of a bitch had pushed him through a hole in the jail house floor. The doctor looked at him in the kindest way, smiling, like his mother who fried chicken like no other woman or man in Greensboro, Pennsylvania, where German glass blowers started an industry, never thinking that they'd die or that their efforts would live on in glass and stone-ware, in large part because of the Monongahela River, which brought their town an industrial and cultural significance they never really deserved. *God forbid any of us get what we deserve.*

This new Emma was beautiful, in a conservative sort of way. A schoolmarm, a missionary, but maybe conservative was what he needed given his lack of judgment in times more personal and religious, where he'd screwed up, which is why he was now laying on a path in a Masonic cemetery on the Comstock, of all places, *goddamnit.*

A white tunnel opened in his field of vision and a voice called to him, his mother's voice maybe, his father's too, though he couldn't be certain. A chorus of voices sang to him saying that it wasn't his time, that he needed to go back, that he couldn't come there yet. Another tear formed on his right cheek and dripped onto his ungloved hand.

"Ronin!" Dustsucker said, slapping him with the glove he'd torn from his right hand. He slapped him again. "Wake up!" he said. "Ronin!" his friend shouted. Dustsucker shook his shoulder. Ronin opened his eyes. And standing over him was his best friend, crying.

Angels fear to tread in these places, hovering above the whole of human life: the sacred and the profane. But sometimes they need to, so as to bring a person back, back to where they belong at least for the time being, the right now.

# Chapter 78

# A DAMN MUSKET BALL

Dustsucker continued to shake Ronin's shoulder as Tom Kelly grabbed a roll of gauze he had been intending to take to the Saint Mary Louise Hospital. "Put him over on his side so that we can stop the bleeding," Kelly said, pulling it from his saddlebag. He inspected the wound — small, red and sticky. "Could have hit the lung," he said, "might not have, though. I saw a lot of sucking wounds during the war. This doesn't seem to be one of those, lucky for him."

"Lucky for all of us," Dustsucker said. "I heard of a guy who walked a couple of miles to a field hospital during the war after his lung collapsed. Turned out he had a hernia, with a piece of his lung pushing through and some portion of his alimentary canal."

"His what?"

"His gut, mouth to stomach — it's how we get our food."

"Okay... So how do you know that word?"

"Food, my brother. If the word has to do with having something we eat, I'm on top of things."

"Okay ..."

"So the following day," Dustsucker continued as Kelly wrapped the gauze roll around Ronin's chest and back, pulling at it occasionally to make sure it was snug, "this guy has to leave the hospital because the enemy is approaching. A member of the 29th New York volunteers, I think, a Yankee. Anyway, he has to walk another mile and a half to keep from getting shot again. Can you believe it?"

"Did the guy live?" Kelly asked, tying a knot in the bandage and checking Ronin's color, which was pale, but not blue. The bleeding had stopped and no sounds were coming from his chest. It appeared as if Ronin's lungs were fine.

"He did. He passed the damn musket ball in his poo about five days later. His lung, stomach and so on eventually granulated in. Can you believe that?"

"I don't know what I believe anymore," Kelly said, "But people died of a lot less during the war than being gut shot."

"No kidding."

"Listen, Slade, I didn't get a good look at this wound, except that it's stopped bleeding. And given the amount of blood Ronin's lost — his shirt is soaked and the ground here is pretty dark — I doubt it's going to heal on its own. We need to get him out of here and over to the hospital." Dustsucker nodded. "What do you suppose happened?" he asked.

Dustsucker stood up and looked around. It was about 2 p.m. A few Paiutes were having an unplanned picnic on a Chinese grave where food offerings had been left. They scattered when Slade asked if anyone had seen anything. "We didn't do anything wrong," one of them said, picking up what the others had left behind.

"Everyone does something wrong," he'd replied, though it didn't get a rise out of any of them.

He looked up toward the monument. "I'm guessing he found what he was looking for, and the son of a bitch has gotten away."

"Latigo?"

"Exactly."

"Look, Slade," Kelly said. "Putting Ronin on a horse at this point could kill him, especially if that bullet is still in there. It could be pressing on his heart, his lungs, God knows what. I'm going to head back to town to get a carriage. You wait here. If he begins bleeding again or stirs and is in too much pain, put him on your horse and get to the nearest doctor. We'll have to take our chances, okay?"

Dustsucker nodded. "Listen," he said. You be careful, Tom. Latigo is still loose. And if he's got a friend, be it a man or a woman, you'll want to steer clear of the two of them. If they did this to Ronin, imagine what they might do to you."

Tom Kelly stood up, and remembering what had gotten him involved with the Livestock twins in the beginning — rich men, who should have known better when picking bed partners or people with whom to play cards — he nodded and turned to get on his horse. "Slade?" he said, pausing with one foot in the stirrup.

"Yeah?"

"Take good care of your friend, would you?"

"Of course, why?"

"Because I don't think we're done with these people. Whatever powers in heaven or hell they believe in, and whatever angels they're traveling with, if we're going to put an end to this nonsense we're going to need your friend. And besides that, there's a big check waiting for him at the Washoe Club."

Both men laughed. "Angels are all about us, my friend," Dustsucker said, "not that I believe in them. But something inside or outside this man is caring for him. And for that, I'm happy."

# Chapter 79

# THINKING RENO

Alvira was thinking Reno when she got into the wagon. She didn't know where else to go, and suspected that Carson City — the once rough and tumble frontier, now thought too toney by some — was perhaps too prominent a place for her man to retreat and repair.

Eilley Bowers was supposed to have a residence in Reno or so she had heard, her sister having often spoken about her talent and influence. But she didn't know the woman and didn't how to get hold of her except to go to Reno and ask around. Bowers was "a talented seeress," her sister had said, having foreseen the Comstock Lode before there was a Comstock Lode and the Great Fire as well, so it might be that she already knew of her sister's death. She didn't know, and up until this point didn't care, except for the question of whether she'd ever see her sister again in "the far beyond of it all," as her sister used to say.

Had Ellie May died or transitioned? Did she continue "growing," as she'd heard others suggest when she slipped the gold crown onto her front tooth so as to attend services at the Virginia City Spiritualist Society, people there smiling at her as if they knew they were twins but weren't saying? Should she be weeping, or should she "count it all joy, brothers and sisters?" She hated that phrase, whether it was in the Bible or not. "Only a nincompoop would believe that," she'd told her sister just a couple of weeks ago, when the old man died in their bed and they had to throw out all the covers because he bled and pooped and peed himself to death, or at least that's how it seemed.

She snapped the lines of Latigo's wagon — him sprawled all over a hair mattress, what there was of him breathing but barely alive after she picked him up off the gravel path where he'd fallen in the middle of a silly dance he was doing over the dead bounty hunter. She glanced at the rear of the wagon and saw that he was still sleeping. She didn't know what to feel, the son of a bitch, that's what they called him — the stupid man who shot her sister, even if it was "the gun's fault," as he had said. A giant ball rose in her throat but not from her stomach like other times, her face flushed hot as fire as tears flooded her eyes. She pulled up on the reins until the mules stopped.

Her parents had told them to be tough, she and Ellie May as they were heading out of Iowa City, their spalted maple headboard up against the pine dresser their father had made when he still hoped the girls would find suitable men with whom to settle down. They had in time of course, though their father wouldn't have considered any of them all that suitable or thought any of them all that settled. It wasn't their intent to bed so many men, her sister had said, their calling much more spiritual, religious even. But that's how it turned out, their having no other skills like laundry or cooking or sewing and such. Still, with all of that, nothing had prepared her for all of this.

She sat on the edge of what she guessed was an old prairie-style wagon or maybe a farm wagon — she didn't know, except that it was smaller than the prairie schooner they had borrowed passage in — a torn and weathered gray bonnet flapping around the fedora she had fashioned to her head with an old scarf, Tony's hat, not that he needed it right now, his entire body under the covers she had found in the back of his wagon. The blankets and quilts were well slept in and ready for the wash. Still, the wagon bed was nearly ten feet long and maybe four feet across. There was a lot of room inside, maybe enough space for them to live in comfortably for a time, until they could decide what they were going to do without her sister to take care of them, assuming she wasn't coming back and all. Wasn't there at least one man who had risen from the dead because of all his religious shenanigans? Not that she could remember.

The mules brayed, telling her that they were done standing still, their winnowing reminding her that food would be needed sooner or later, though the damned donkeys could eat grass, she imagined. *This would be a lot easier if Tony would just wake up.* She pulled at the reins to keep the creatures still.

How should she feel about Toro's accident with the gun? Would she see her sister again? Could her sister see her? It felt like she was around, like she hadn't left. She should have stopped by the hall underneath the dentist's office where her sister's friends sometimes met. They had laid her out there, "to pray" someone had said, though she couldn't imagine what they'd be praying about. She bit her lip. This wasn't time to cry, she counseled herself. Someone would be after them soon, if they weren't after them already.

She pulled the wagon back onto the Geiger Grade, taking care not to run over the edge and to watch for rocks and slides. A brisk wind blew, waking her man.

"Where are we going, sweetie?" he asked, pulling the blankets closer to his shoulders and peeking over the side. He recognized the road. Another dozen or so miles and they'd be in Reno, assuming they weren't challenged by highwaymen — he'd spent some time there, doing the very same thing — or stopped by policemen in pursuit.

"Reno, Tony," she said, hoping her lack of a smile didn't alarm or anger him. "I don't know where else to go. You need a doctor, I think."

"I don't need a doctor, Alvria Fae. I just need a place to rest, where I can be warm and safe."

"You lay down baby," she said. "I think I know where to find a place. There's a woman in Reno, if we're lucky. And while I've never met her," she began to cry, "my sister knew her, I think. Eilley Bowers?"

"As in the Bowers Mansion?"

"You've heard of her then?"

"Only the house, I think. I stopped there a few years back. It was owned by a man in Reno at the time, a hotel man. How do you know this Bowers woman?" He laid back down, listening, pushing a coat underneath his head as he was still too tired to sit up.

"She's a seeress, like my sister," she said, in-between the sobs and tears.

"Jesus," he whispered under his breath. "Baby, you still upset with me?"

Alvira Fae Livestock didn't know who she was upset with: her sister, her boyfriend, the man she just killed in the Virginia City graveyard or God himself, who allowed it all to happen. And she wasn't about to stop crying until she figured it out, goddamnit. "Tony, you can just shut the fuck up, right now!" she yelled, above the winds that were blowing, within and without, her heart broken and no sign coming that her life would ever be the same again.

"Yes, ma'am," he said, smiling. It was beginning to feel just like home.

# Chapter 80
# CIRCLING EAGLE

Emma took the soup off the stove and ladled a cupful into a small bowl made by one of the children at the mission. It was about 2 in the afternoon, she figured by the noise of little ones playing a traditional Washoe game outside her kitchen window. The older youth were on a picnic by the Carson River and wouldn't be back until just before nightfall.

She enjoyed the gentle rhythm of work and play that had become part of their life together at the American Gospel Mission just outside of Carson City. A new teacher at the mission was intent on introducing the children to working with clay. "Life is way too short to be taken so seriously," the young man had said at a recent meeting of the school's faculty and staff, whose ranks had struggled with the introduction of sewing, carpentry and other non-native arts and skills to the school's curriculum. "Put clay on a wheel and let your thoughts go where they might," he said, when describing the potential benefits of a series of pottery courses he was hoping to offer in the spring. "Sometimes you just need to play," he added, smiling.

Emma pulled the warm bowl of soup closer as she sat down in the kitchen, the window now closed, the area outside now quiet. "Don't you think that's the issue," she argued, "that the children are not focused enough to make something of themselves in the white man's world?"

The young Irishman nodded but did not agree. His habit was grating, despite his being a deeply interesting man. "If we must," he said, "we can draw analogies from the work in front of them. If the wheel is off center, for instance, the product is marred and not at all what we intended it to be, that sort of thing. But to be frank, I do not enjoy doing that, nor do I agree."

The method of drawing a spiritual truth from a temporal task or achievement was a proven one in American Indian schools. It fit an evolving point of view within the larger circles of American religion, that much of God's truth could be ascertained through that which could be seen, felt and heard by everyone. "The heavens declare the glory of God," the Bible said, "the firmament shows his handiwork." If words couldn't point to the obvious truths hidden within the tabernacle of human existence, what was their point? "You do not agree?" she asked, aware that other teachers at the table were wondering the same thing.

"Pottery is as life is, ma'am," he replied. "It is meant to be enjoyed, not used and abused by people who want to read something into it that isn't necessarily there."

Emma pushed at the soup's vegetables with her spoon, trying to remember which ones had been harvested by students at the school and which had been purchased in town, the teacher's words stirring thoughtfully within her. "Life is meant to be enjoyed," he said, as if the thought sprang from some inner rule or scripture. The man could be aggravating.

The young man's thinking was so different from her own. She stood up to take some coffee from the stove. Still, he was a welcome addition to the colorful quilt that made up the mission. "Red and yellow, black and white," she began to hum, before bursting forth with the words, "all the children of the world!" A familiar voice sounded in the front room.

"Miss Emma?" Happy Hands called, standing just inside the front door. "Mother?" he said. So much had changed between the two of them that Ronin's friend now felt comfortable entering her home and occasionally deferring in her direction.

"Happy Hands!" she answered. "Come and find me in the kitchen."

The Washoe medicine man laughed. "How is it that you are lost when you know where you are?" he yelled out.

"Silly man," Emma said, as she walked toward the living room, wiping her hands on a blue apron given to her by some of the children last Christmas after their return from the kidnappings in the Washoe Valley. "It is just a figure of speech."

"Perhaps," he replied, wondering.

They sat down in the living room, across from the large window that looked west toward the Sierra Nevada. The dust of an early September snow sprinkled the top of the mountains. The smell of sage was in the air.

"Have you heard from William?" Happy Hands asked.

"No, why do you ask?"

"I am uneasy," he continued. "When you saw him last, had he concluded his business in Virginia City?"

"No, he hadn't. In fact, we spoke about his just beginning to get involved with the twins, as he put it. I don't mind telling you that I was not at all comfortable."

"No, I imagine not," he said, looking at her eyes. There was an awkward and freshly chastened look about Emma that he hadn't seen before. *They had had words*. It was none of his business. "Emma, I'm heading to Virginia City this afternoon. A bear came to me last night in a dream and ..."

"Not more bears, Happy Hands," she said. "I don't know that I can bare it."

"I'm being serious, my Mother."

"Of course you are. I'm sorry."

"As I was saying, a bear came to me last night in a dream. It spoke to me."

"And?" she asked, leaning forward so that Happy Hands knew that she was listening. Much had changed between them over the last couple of months. When they were first introduced, they didn't much like each other. Later, when their minds had changed, their conversations were still stilted and careful. They were unable to share their personal lives or values, believing them to be so different that the other must be wrong. But in time, each had come to regard the other as "an adept," a skilled person within his or her own spiritual tradition. Perhaps they could learn from each other, enriching their own traditions and better understanding each other's ideals and perspectives.

"Mother, he repeated the message he had said to me before, 'Do not kill my children.'" Happy Hands was silent for a moment. It appeared as if he was in pain.

"Are you alright?" Emma asked.

"I do not understand it, my friend. But given that I dreamed it when Ronin and I were first visiting the Lake, I thought I would mention it to you."

Emma was quiet for a few moments. Happy Hands wondered if she was praying. An eagle appeared outside the front window, circling the corral. It hovered as if it were listening or watching.

"Happy Hands, Mister Ronin and I don't have the same sort of understanding that ..." She paused. "What I mean to say is I'm not sure that it's appropriate for me to constantly be caring about the comings and goings of our friend. Is that okay to say?"

Happy Hands looked at her and smiled. "The heart wants what it wants, my Mother. And you should not attempt to corral it." Emma glanced out the front window, where the eagle was now perching on a fence, looking at the house.

"Maybe so, Happy Hands. But I suspect that you may be asking me to go with you to Virginia City. And that I cannot do. I have duties here, and as I said, it is no longer appropriate."

Happy Hands grinned. "Then you will pray for us?" He didn't know whether prayer was helpful, but he knew it was the language of her soul.

"I always do."

"Then pray for your ..." Happy Hands stopped. "Pray for your friend. It may be that Ronin needs your prayers more than me."

# Chapter 81

# EMMA'S PRAYER

"Dear God in heaven."

It was evening when she started to pray. The children were in bed. Staff and teachers had either gone home or were working quietly in their classrooms or shops.

"It may be that you've chosen me to be with these people, these wonderful people," Emma said, thinking of the Washoe, Paiute and Shoshone children with whom she spent her life, "'red and yellow, black and white.' And it may be that you've chosen me to be with this man, this very conflicted man, strong yet weak, filled with peace and fight."

She adjusted her dress as she stared out the living room window, appreciating the evening's alpenglow. A blue and purple haze had descended upon the range of mountains she now knew as home. Nevada was a long way from West Virginia and Ohio. Her inner feelings felt distant as well. She tried to focus.

"Show me," she said, "your honest and humble servant, what I cannot see, or will not accept as true or real. Help me," she said, "to understand what it is that you ask of me so that I can sit before you and heal."

She took a step away from the window and picked up a small piece of pinyon pine lying beside the woodstove for the evening fire. She threw it in. The fire immediately crackled.

"I don't intend to be this way," she said, a confession she had made a thousand times if she had uttered it once, even as a child. It wasn't her choice to be headstrong or to be so guarded in her life. Her heart was just that way, in the same way that she had been born a woman and not a man, or on the east coast instead of the west. She had no choice to be other than what she was, none whatsoever.

"So determined that I grow grass where only rock used to be. I don't intend to be like this," she said, "the kind of person who ignores your possibilities because my mind is already so full of my own." She folded her hands and immediately began moving them, thumb over thumb over thumb over thumb again. It was a troubling habit.

Emma's mother used to say in exasperation that only a mule could be her equal. They were stinging words at the time, but in time she came to understand them. There was no reason for her husband to leave, save that he couldn't live up to her expectations. There was no reason she couldn't get the kind of attention she wanted from her friend, the former Reverend W. W. Ronin.

"I want instead to be the woman that you want me to be," she prayed, wondering if the evening's fire would be enough to keep her warm throughout the night. "I want to be the woman he wants me to be," she said, as she steadied herself by touching the arm of the well-worn rocking chair. The fire began to lick the sides of the soft, oily wood. Another piece would soon be needed.

"As embarrassing as this is to admit," she prayed, "I want to be the kind of person I'm supposed to be in 'this barren wasteland.' The phrase was her husband's, wherever he was and whatever he was doing. Pursing her lips, she tried to blow the tension from her body. It was almost dark out. She wondered if she should light the small lamp next to the chair in which she was sitting, a chair she relaxed in every evening.

"I want to be the kind of person that others want to be with," she prayed, bothered that her prayers had turned so personal. *I should be gazing at God and glimpsing at my own needs, not glimpsing at God and gazing at myself.* She wondered if Happy Hands had arrived yet and thought for a moment that he might have difficulty finding a place to stay, his being an Indian.

"I want to be the kind of person that Ronin wants to be with," she said, "whether that's right or wrong, I don't care, though I'll pretend," she said, touching the Bible beside her, "if you make me." She laughed, and folded her hands again, hoping to find the right frame of mind to finish her evening devotions.

"Help me be that kind of person, even more to be pleasing to you, dear God in heaven," she said as she closed her eyes, believing that nightfall had come and that it was time to put herself to bed. "Help my friend to be the kind of person you need him to be, today," *what's left of it,* "tonight and tomorrow. And bring us together again, if we've ever (truly) been together." She stood to take off her apron and folding it, put it over the back of a living room chair.

"But if there is a tomorrow for the two of us, let it be soon," she said aloud, hoping that no one could hear her, the honesty was so real and the pain so large that she was sure she had cried out in the light of the evening fire. "Lord Jesus, I ache in ways I should not, and if that isn't what you want me to do, or what I need to do, protect my friends and bring them home quickly."

Emma Nauman breathed a silent "amen" and began to undress, until she stood naked by her bedroom door. She folded everything into a neat pile of clothes, placing them at the bottom of her bed. And for the first time in her life — not that it mattered, but somehow she had been warned that it would — a proper missionary lady slipped naked between the covers, her warm skin upon the cool sheets and spread. And alone, in the middle of the night, without the proper bedclothes befitting a Christian lady, she began to dream, too.

# Chapter 82

# SAINT MARY LOUISE HOSPITAL

Ronin woke with a start and began to struggle. The son of a bitch was getting away. He was watching him as that woman — the sister with the gold tooth, Alvira Mae Livestock, as evil a woman as he was a good man — stood over him shaking her head from side to side, as if making difficult decision. She placed the heavy, long gray barrel of the Walker revolver against the side of his head. It would not be long now ... and then she didn't do anything. Maybe he was already dead. He didn't know and it didn't matter — most things don't matter.

He looked around the room — a simple bed, a cross on the wall, a Bible laid open on a cabinet next to him as if someone had been reading. At least it wasn't the cemetery, where wooden markers and engraved marble and granite stones would have argued that in fact he was dead, and would forever be.

Ronin remembered falling over on his side, his ribs aching as if a mule had kicked him there. He remembered his friend hovering over him, staring at him and calling his name, over and over again. Why wasn't he moving? Dustsucker had brought him here, but where was here? He glanced back at the white washed wall. It was a crucifix hanging there — the barely-robed body of Jesus nailed to an olive tree, not the plain Latin cross he'd used in the Episcopal Church. He was at the hospital owned by the Daughters of Charity. He was in Virginia City. And it was September.

Stars were twinkling in a clear fall sky outside his room at the Saint Mary Louise Hospital when his friend entered. "We were hoping you'd wake up," Dustsucker said.

"We?" His throat was dry. How long had it been since he'd spoken? *What day is it?*

"Well, Tom and I — Augustus, of course — and Happy Hands, who just arrived a few moments ago. Good to see him. Do you remember what happened?"

Ronin looked at Dustsucker. His eyes were sleepless and red. Perhaps he'd been crying. He hadn't been here that long. There were bandages tightly wrapped around his chest as if he had broken a rib. But a thick wad of cloth underneath them, snugly pulled up against his right side to form a pressure bandage, argued differently. "I had a thought that maybe I'd been kicked. But it appears that I've been shot."

"Shot is right, my friend, by the twin you felt a fair amount of affection for, if I remember right."

"You do not. Alvira Fae was always a little strange in my mind. She never had a chance," he joked, but it hurt to laugh.

"Something's wrong with that woman, to be sure."

"Well, yeah. I mean, given that she shot me!" Ronin remembered seeing the heavy Paterson revolver pointed his way. It was as if he could recall seeing the very bullet push its way toward him, clearing grave stones and trees until it punched him in the side like a skilled Irish boxer. "Did you get her?" he winced.

"Hell, Ronin, we barely got you. We didn't get her, but Ash is out looking."

He turned away from his friend and looked out the window. He began counting the days it would take him to be up and around, to be able to ride a horse again, to be able shoot. He'd kill that little man or see him sentenced to a circus.

"I can't believe I've been injured. Jesus Christ."

"Well, I don't think he had anything to do with it, reverend."

"Funny." Latigo and the last of the Livestock twins would be gone by the time he was off the mend to be sure. He counted the months. It would be Christmas. Then where would he be? Where would any of them be? "I'm not at all happy with this," he said as Happy Hands entered the room.

"My friend, it is time for you to get going. Can you move?"

"Hello to you, too, you big dumb Indian."

"I am sorry. Have I said the wrong thing?"

Dustsucker put his arms around the Indian's shoulders. "Our hero is having a bad day, Happy Hands. And he believes that the world is circling around him, he being the sun ..." Happy Hands looked confused. "It's a saying, Hands. I'm suggesting that Ronin here is pretty self-absorbed right now, get it?"

"Always did," the Indian responded before returning his gaze toward his friend, "just not funny. It is time for you to go, William, assuming you can move. I'll take you to Carson City, if you like. Will the doctor permit this?"

"Who cares what the doctor will permit. If I can move I'll determine my own destiny, thank you." Ronin pushed himself up on one elbow. The pain was extreme, but bearable. A cold wind blew through the window. "Where is it we're going?"

"To Miss Emma's ranch, of course, where the children are playing and Miss Emma herself is praying ..." Dustsucker and Ronin looked at each other. "... and the weather inside feels like springtime."

# Chapter 83
# A NIGHT TIME COACH

Happy Hands broke a promise to himself when he accompanied W. W. Ronin down the hill by coach toward Carson City. He'd been telling everyone that he would never again ride in the white man's conveyance, no matter how much of a hurry he was in. Having ridden to Glenbrook with Ronin and his friends a few months prior, enjoying the accompanying attention of two wonderful women who had never seen a tall Washoe man or at least one up close, he'd suffered countless months of derision and indignities after the fact by otherwise good and sensitive folks who had never heard of a Washoe man enjoying a white woman's affection.

The two women had subsequently passed into the night like most white women had in his life — the Washoe ones tended to hang around for a while, at least his wives did — but the reactions of his friends had given a whole new meaning to his name, "Happy," not that it was his real name and not that it mattered. It was simply bothersome.

To his surprise, he'd had little difficulty convincing Ronin to accompany him to the American Gospel Mission. Ronin had been there before and enjoyed the hospitality of its director, Emma Nauman, often addressed as "the Widow" or "the Missus" depending on one's perspective of what actually had happened to the poor woman's husband, Henry Nauman, who Happy Hands knew to have fled the capitol city, having become way too involved with the city's women, some of whom were well-known women of the night. But it wasn't his place to inform Emma, or to pass judgment on any man or woman who found themselves in that situation. Life was what life was, he'd come to believe in his own world and to observe in the white man's world as well. And magic — what he'd learned of it as a Washoe holy man and what he'd come to experience as a sometimes not-so-silent sojourner in the white man's culture — had only so much effect on how things ultimately turned out.

Happy Hands had learned to see the future at times, and had come to know the presence of certain spirits — some of them healing, some not so healing or helpful — and had decided that depending on a person's practice and intention — magic was a possible reality. But having seen what he'd seen and done what he'd done, he'd yet to change the mind of a woman or be able to help a man un-complicate his life once a woman determined "to help." That's exactly what Emma Nauman was doing by inviting the former reverend Ronin to stay at her mission again.

"The old men at the Washoe Club said they had a check for you, William, when you are able," Happy Hands said about half way down the hill to Carson City, after they had passed the turn off to Dayton and the Carson river mills. "Perhaps there will be two checks? I was unable to secure the other one you asked me to pick up."

"Really?" Ronin replied, smiling.

"Yes, something about a big Indian standing in their living room, one of the men remarked. I did not remain long in their house as even bigger men than me asked me to leave instantaneously," he stuttered.

"Instantaneously, you say?" Ronin laughed, though laughing hurt his side.

"Is that not the right word?"

"No, it is, I suspect." The laughter made him cough, which hurt even more. He wiped his lips as he was now spitting across the floor onto Happy Hands' seat.

The attempt to speak a second language — however difficult or stuttering — was something he respected, having failed to master anything other than English, and that at times to the confusion of his western friends who had never heard a Tennessee man speak. "I apologize for my friends, Hands," he said, noticing that Happy Hands was looking out the window, barely concealing his disappointment. "Nor do I mean to laugh. I'm sorry."

"They are not your friends, William. But your apology is accepted." The Indian picked up Ronin's feet and placed them in his lap as the ex-minister groaned. *It was a good deal easier being a preacher. Church folks could be cruel, but they hardly ever shot at you.* "You are very much in pain?"

"I am," Ronin answered. "The doctor said it'd be a good couple of months before the wound filled in, though I imagine I'll be able to get moving after a few weeks' sittin' and jawin' with people at the mission." Happy Hands smiled. "Did Miss Emma actually say she didn't mind me coming there for some recuperation?" Ronin looked at his friend, sheepishly. It was hard to conceal his excitement.

"You know how she feels, William. She would hear of no other place for you to convalesce than to stay there with the children."

"The children, of course," he said. The thought never crossed his mind. "Well, I guess staying with a single Protestant missionary beats staying with a half-dozen nuns, doesn't it?"

"And a female one at that," Happy Hands said, closing his eyes. His white friend was an amazingly curious man.

As a warrior, he'd seen him take on men twice his size and prevail, which of course was not a test of one's courage as even a foolish man would sometimes run at an angry mountain lion. As a priest, he'd seen little of the devotion and service he'd come to expect of the white man's religious workers, but he'd seen less of their cruelty. He could excuse one for the other, but it left him wondering. The Spirit could only take so much double-mindedness before it took a second mind of its own. As a man — and he constantly had to remind himself that Ronin was just a man, white men believed their heroes to be so much larger than real life — Ronin had been a good deal kinder than most. Like the white men who began fencing land and water in the Washoe Valley in the mid-1800s, or those who came when silver was discovered a few years later, though there were legends of priests having visited the area one hundred years before, speaking Spanish and seeking a way to the Pacific Ocean. The same men and the flood of women and men who followed them cut down their forests, raised cattle that ate their grasses and scared off the game by which they had subsisted for literally hundreds of years. A kind and understanding white man was still a rarity, even thirty years later. But still, this man — this curiously complex man — had a weakness for women, despite spending so little time with them.

"Ronin, what do you expect to come of this relationship with your friend Emma?"

"What do you mean?"

"I mean, is it honorable for you to keep her guessing?"

Ronin looked across the coach, leant to them by the livery at the request of the U.S. marshal. He'd come to appreciate the man, though he was very different than the men he had grown up with. The more he come to know Indians like Happy Hands — the Washoe and Shoshone men at the mission just south of town, or the Paiute men in Virginia City — he'd come to believe that men so different than him only wanted what he wanted: a suitable shelter, family and friends to call his own, meaningful work, food and a means of commerce or trade that allowed a man to get what he needed or wanted. Their languages were different, and their cultures — even the different tribes — were so different he didn't always understand. But the man inside the man was the same.

"Happy Hands, I don't know."

"Think about it, would you?" the red man said.

"I will."

And with that, the gentle rocking of the stage, and the rhythmic sounds of the horses' hooves, the white man fell asleep — a man who wasn't all that much whiter than the red man, who was really brown and not red, despite being seen that way by people who had little color to their skin, and sometimes even less to their souls. He slumbered until the sun came up on a corral just south of Carson City, where Emma Nauman was waiting.

# Chapter 84
# POGONIP

"My Mother," Happy Hands said as they stepped from the stage. An early frost coated trees and fencing, painting the corral at the American Gospel Mission shades of gray, lavender and blue. Except for the mission director, who was waiting anxiously by the main gate in a dark red housedress and coat, the scene was without significant spot or color and was almost silent.

"Pogonip," Ronin muttered, pulling a scarf up around his face as Happy Hands helped him off of the stage. He grabbed his right arm threw it over his deerskin-covered shoulder. The word was Shoshone — though some argued it was Paiute — and meant simply "cloud," though certain weather conditions made the icy fog a good deal more complex. It was the first September freeze. The humidity was nearly 100 percent as a cold, snowy mist covered the corral rails, the house and anything else of permanence or value.

"You'll be fine," Emma said, taking his left arm and pulling it firmly to her chest.

"White death," he said, as they walked toward the house.

"You're not going to die," Emma continued. "You've been shot and we're going to take care of you. That's all there is to it. You don't need to worry about the fog outside." They trudged a few hundred feet toward the door of the main residence before Emma pushed the door open with her right foot. "Let's put him next to the fire," she said.

Happy Hands propped him up in the old rocking chair by the living room stove and pushed a pillow behind his back to ease his pain and give him comfort. "How does that feel?" he asked, not expecting an answer. Ronin was fast asleep, hunched over like an old man whose head had fallen into his breakfast cereal.

"He's been up all night, Miss Emma. But the bleeding has stopped. You should let him sleep, though perhaps there is better place for him to rest than this chair." Emma knew the pine rocker to have an unusually soothing aspect, having slept there many evenings, wrapped in a blue wool comforter, waiting for her husband to come home. More recently, it had been an equally lonely place for meditation and prayer.

"I have every intention of doing that, Happy Hands. The Lord will give him rest, now that he is here." Happy Hands looked about the house, wondering if there was something special about it since he had last visited.

"I hope so," he said, "No one else has given him rest the last few days and nights."

Emma opened a living room chest in front of her davenport and pulled from it the bluest of wool blankets. It had come west with her from her husband's home in West Virginia. It had a certain magical appeal, though no Christian woman, let alone missionary, would ever have admitted that except to acknowledge the special influence that heirlooms have in the minds of those who love and remember. "My mother made this for us," Emma said, referring to her husband and a time when the only worry the young couple had was whether the neighbors were able to help them with a crop ready for harvest. "It is the color of heaven," she said, "and forgiveness," she added, though no church or book had ever officially recognized the color as meaning anything special at all.

"And of the sky, my Mother. It is an appropriate cover for our friend."

Emma smiled and motioned Happy Hands to follow her into the kitchen. She placed a kettle on the massive black stove and took a yellow cup from the shelves above the wash basin. "Will you stay for tea?" she asked, pointing toward the table and chairs.

"I will for a while, Miss Emma unless I am interrupting? It appears that your table is set for supper." Extra silverware was everywhere, Happy Hands noted, and plates, too. It brought to mind their sharing a dinner together at the Ormsby House several weeks back. It was not altogether a comfortable experience.

"Too many utensils?" she smiled.

"I'm sure there will be enough," Happy Hands laughed, thinking that white men and women had curious habits when feeding themselves. Where fingers and a knife would do for his kinfolk, Emma's friends insisted on setting several spoons, forks and knives adjacent to multiple plates, bowls and glasses.

"Would you join us?" she asked. "Tonight, around six p.m. Deputy Slade will be here, as will Marshal Ash and Versal McBride, I believe."

Happy Hands looked up. The last time he had sat at the table was after the events at Lake Tahoe. It had been a happy experience until he talked of Ronin's possible involvement with a couple of women in Virginia City. The trip had turned out exactly as he had foreseen it. "Am I welcome?" he asked.

"You are always welcome, my friend."

She poured the steaming hot liquid into his cup and was about to put the kettle back on the stove when Happy Hands raised his cup and said, "Then I will come. Here's to you and the friendships around this table, Miss Emma. I would live my life no other way."

They sat together, until the sun was up and the morning frost was gone.

# Chapter 85

# THE LORD'S SUPPER

"I'm so glad you're here!" Emma said, as she opened the front door of the house. A good deal heavier than it used to be, Ronin had reinforced the door during his stay at the mission the year prior recuperating from a broken leg. The door was unusual in more modern times, in that it now offered a firing port, more typical of frontier homes expecting an Indian attack.

"I visited family and friends while I was gone," Happy Hands said, offering his host his right hand. Emma squeezed it and then embraced the Washoe man with both arms.

"You're practically family, Happy Hands. Shaking hands is something you do with strangers."

"Ah," he said, before nodding to Dustsucker, who was sitting in the rocking chair Ronin had been in earlier that morning. The deputy nodded back.

"It's quite comfortable, you know. A man could sleep here, I imagine, the right man, anyway." Happy Hands smiled. It didn't take a Washoe medicine man to know that Deputy Marcus T. Slade wasn't that man. Ronin was. But then if Ronin didn't know that, then maybe Dustsucker would do.

"Is he up?" Happy Hands asked.

"I have no idea," Dustsucker said, frowning. If he wasn't in the living room, there was a good chance he was in the bedroom, and that wasn't a pleasing thought at all. Happy Hands sat down on the floor by the fire.

"Would you like something to drink?" Little Wolf said.

"My son!" Happy Hands jumped up. "I did not know you were coming!" The pleasure between the two — the tribal holy man who had raised the boy in borrowed homes in the Washoe Valley rather than see him raised by his mother, and a Washoe boy experienced beyond his years — was palpable, and brought a smile to Dustsucker's lips.

"He works here, Hands. You didn't know that?"

"I did not know that. When did you begin?" he said.

Little Wolf looked at the floor. He should have said something sooner. It was not right to embarrass his father this way. "It's too late in the year to be working at the lake, as you know. So Miss Emma, on her last trip to Glenbrook, mentioned to me that she might have a position. She has employed me here! She likes that I've worked in a restaurant before and promises that I will soon become 'the chief washer and bottle cook' for the whole mission."

Dustsucker laughed, as Happy Hands and Little Wolf looked at each other wondering what was funny. He put his bear-like arms around the two of them, patting them on their backs. "I'd have something to drink, Little Wolf, coffee perhaps?"

"Of course, deputy. I'll be right back." A father and his friend watched Little Wolf return to the kitchen to get coffee for Miss Emma's guests as Versal McBride tied his horse to the corral fence.

"McBride, you son of a bitch, I can't believe you rode down the hill!" The marshal was standing at the front door and was surprised to see the Virginia City businessman riding like a cowboy. He'd imagined him a carriage man. "Run out of money?"

"I took the train, Ash. As you were — nothing going on here."

"Nothing except language I won't have in my house," Emma said, coming up behind the marshal with a cup of tea. "Here's the beverage you asked for, Augustus. Good to see you, Mister McBride. I'm so glad you could come to my home."

"I am, too," McBride said, stepping onto the porch. "You've done a good work in the Carson Valley, ma'am. Why, all over northern Nevada for that matter. Any children from Virginia City, if I may ask?"

"I don't believe so, Versal, what with the Daughters of Charity school and others up that way. But I wouldn't be against it," she said, smiling.

"I imagine you wouldn't," he said, offering his hand to Dustsucker and to Tom Kelly, who was seated nearby.

"Gentlemen, it's time for supper," Emma said, wiping her hands on her apron. "If you'd take a seat around the large table in the kitchen — it's where I take all my meals. It's where the children eat as well."

W. W. Ronin stepped from Emma's bedroom. Little Wolf smiled when he saw him. "Mister Ronin."

"Son." He put his cane by the back door and sat down at the table as the others were coming in.

"There's our hero!" McBride said, extending his hand. Ronin looked up before taking it and shaking it.

"Happy to help, McBride. But a hero, I am not."

"Oh, I don't know about that. The men at the Washoe Club think so, Mister Ronin. I've brought a little something from them, incidentally. I'll give it to you after dinner."

"Thank you," he said, before sitting down.

"The women are gone ..." McBride continued. Ronin looked up. *A better phrase perhaps should come out of your mouth.* The Virginia City saloon owner caught the look in Ronin's eyes as he pulled out a seat facing the back door. "I'm sorry, Ronin. Perhaps I should have said, 'Have left town.'"

Ronin nodded.

"One of them left town," the marshal said. "The other was killed, of course." Ronin looked over at Augustus Ash, who he believed to be a more sensitive man. "Which is unfortunate, to be sure," Ash added, noting Ronin's displeasure. "And the matter is closed until I can speak with a Utah marshal."

"A Utah marshal?" Dustsucker exclaimed. "What am I missing?" Ronin's eyes were squinting, his left eyebrow lifted as he listened.

"It is believed that the two of them — Toro Latigo, now known to be in fact 'Antonio Latigo,' formerly of Salt Lake City, and Miss Alvira Fae Livestock, his accomplice — are headed toward more familiar territory, where we believe that Mister Latigo is also wanted for murder."

"And you know this how?" Ronin asked.

"A police officer in Reno heard them talking."

"Okay, and this is in Utah?" Ronin asked.

"Negative, Mister Ronin. It is in Wells, Nevada, formally Humboldt Wells, along the train line. Ever hear of it?"

"I know it," Ronin said.

"There's the possibility that they've holed up in Lamoille, though we don't have an exact address."

"Bad men don't keep exact addresses, marshal," Ronin said.

"I'm aware of that," Ash said. "Should I assume you want a piece of this, Mister Ronin?" Ash's tone was confrontational.

"Only what I am due, sir."

Emma interrupted, shooing Ash and Kelly to their seats. "Gentlemen, let's sit down. You all can talk sheriff's business later."

"This is marshal's business, ma'am. It's not Pinkerton business, though I've gained a considerable amount of respect for you, Mister Ronin. And it's not sheriff's business, Mister Slade. It's marshal's business."

Ronin picked up his fork and stood it on end. "You see, that's where you're wrong, marshal. It's my business, Mister Ash. And I'll see it through."

# AUTHOR'S NOTE

With a third offering in the Ronin series of Westerns, it occurs to me that certain thank yous are needed. This book, and the others that precede it, are not solitary efforts. They are, I hope, reasonable attempts at writing "historical fiction," and as such reflect a good amount of research, conversation and effort on the part of a good number of people.

When I first moved to Nevada, I wanted desperately to find a few Nevada-based Westerns, books that that I could enjoy and use as a jumping-off point for learning about my new home. Fresh from a small church in New Jersey to a little larger parish where I carried a significantly greater responsibility, I wanted to know about my new state, its people, its history, its hopes and dreams.

I credit the List family — Frank and Alice, their son Bob (a former governor) and his wife Polly — for stirring some of that initial passion. So too, Carson City historian Victor Goodwin, spoken about in one of my earlier books; Jack and Betty Blaikie, who first encouraged me to move to Nevada by mentioning Irving Stone's book, *Men to Match My Mountains;* Byron Waite, a friend and coworker at the First Presbyterian Church in Carson City, who introduced me to the rural beauty of Nevada's history and ghost towns; and Joel Ierien, the First Presbyterian Church's office manager and my good friend, who at one point encouraged us to make northern Nevada our permanent home by selling us her Gold Hill home. I still wish I had taken her up on that offer.

I didn't appreciate these people as much as I should have at the time. But their contribution lingers in these Two Bears Books publications featuring the early history of northern Nevada. "Real people. Real places. The way the West was *really* won."

I wanted this third book to tell some of the back story of my fictional character, the once-reverend W. W. Ronin. To that end, I've used actual family history in Obion County, Tennessee. My great-great-grandfather, William Washington Townsley, served as a private in Jacob Biffle's 13th Tennessee Cavalry, though there is no evidence he served as a cook in that unit or hated horses. The church Ronin served, Saint John's Episcopal Church in Wichita, Kansas, is real, as are the Presbyterian, Methodist, Episcopal and Roman Catholic Churches in Carson City and Virginia City. I have related some of their history in these three books and much appreciate the cooperation of staff and volunteers in these churches for having conversations with me or sending me their material.

Similarly, I've made efforts to put real detail to Eilley Bowers, "the Washoe Seeress," and to the mansion in Washoe Valley. I was the beneficiary of conversations with Tammy Buzick, the curator of Bowers Mansion and arguably the leading content expert for the late Mrs. Bowers. Buzick is the author of the mansion's tour book and hopes to see her book on Allison Oram Bowers, as she is more formally known, published in the near future. I recommend it to you.

I have written about the clubs, hotels, retail businesses, sheriffs and marshals as best as I've come to understand them. My appreciation again to the Silver State National Peace Officers Museum in Virginia City for their excellent exhibits. It is my hope that they and you will excuse a couple of changes I've made to dates in Virginia City Police Chief / Sheriff Tom Kelly's life, so that I could include him in the story.

An ongoing conversation about the historical sources I've used in the writing of these books can be found on my website, www.greggtownsley.com.

The Bucket of Blood saloon, the character of Versal McBride and others — for example, Dustsucker, Happy Hands, Emma Nauman and so on — are a matter of my own imagination. That being said, my children enjoyed many a sarsaparilla at the Bucket of Blood saloon in Virginia City while they were growing up. You can enjoy one there, too. Should you visit the saloon, say "hello" to Squeek. She performs regularly at the saloon and other venues in northern Nevada. Be gentle with her. She's probably not aware that she has a cameo in this book.

*The Pinkerton Years* features fewer than a dozen fictional journals by W. W. Ronin. These have been carefully researched. The Pinkerton National Detective Agency was America's first detective agency. The Pinkertons provided significant services to the federal government beginning with the Civil War and later to the nation's developing rail and mining businesses. One can't tell Western stories without noting that Pinkertons occasionally served as an unofficial police and security force throughout the rural west. While some consider the Pinkerton history to have been sullied by their involvement in 19th and 20th century labor disputes — to be sure, there was much abuse on all sides — there is much to appreciate. I hope I've contributed in some small way to that conversation.

Some additional thanks: to Stephanie Patterson, whose insights into the divination arts then and now were much appreciated, as well as her willingness to explore the cultural and gender equity dimensions of women involved in palm reading, crystal ball gazing, tarot and so on. For an extraordinary exposition of 19th century Spiritualism in America, I recommend *Revelations of a Spirit Medium,* by Harry Price and Eric

J. Dinwall (New York: E. P. Dutton & Company, 1922). The book was written in 1891 by a writer named Charles F. Pidgeon. The real authorship of the very valuable discussion of the Who, What, Where, Why and How of Spiritualism is still very much debated.

Deep thanks are due my writer wife, Nancy Lashbrook Townsley, without whose help and enthusiasm this book, or any of my others, would simply not have been written. Nancy is managing editor of two weekly Pamplin Media Group publications, the Forest Grove News-Times and the Hillsboro Tribune. Her writing can also be seen on her own blog, www.nancy-townsley.com and in various online magazines, including www.therivetermagazine.com and www.runnersworld.com.

This book is dedicated to my children. Rachel, my oldest, whose attention to family and faith is most instructive. You didn't learn it from me. My youngest son Josh, whose entrepreneurial interests and skills far surpass my own, including his commitment to a wonderful organization, Habitat for Humanity. Good on you! And to my late son, the one who still sits with me, walks with me and inspires me by his example and affection: Jared, you are very much missed.

# ABOUT THE AUTHOR

Gregg Edwards Townsley is a reflective, free-thinking ex-pastor, martial artist, writer and western fast draw enthusiast living in St. Helens, Oregon. No stranger to the places his characters inhabit — Reno, Carson City, Virginia City and Lake Tahoe — he raised his children in northern Nevada, from 1984 through 1993, while serving as pastor and head of staff of the First Presbyterian Church in Carson City. Gregg enjoys hearing from his readers, posting updates and background to his work on his website and blogging at www.greggtownsley.com. You can find him on Facebook: www.facebook.com/GreggEdwardsTownsley, or subscribe to his Twitter updates at http://twitter.com/greggtownsley. The author encourages your review of this book and his others at www.amazon.com.